For J.C. + Rodney

Bill Smith

1994

THE WARS WITHIN

A NOVEL

William French Smith III

TopWood Publishing

All characters, compounds and companies in this book are fictional, and any resemblance to persons living or otherwise is purely coincidental.

THE WARS WITHIN
A TopWood Publishing Book / published by arrangement with the author
TopWood Edition 1994

ISBN 0-9643593-0-2

PRINTED IN THE UNITED STATES OF AMERICA

PREVIEW

Dr. Steven Capterville has created revolutionary water formulations with his secret new technology. A mysterious Russian food, an unusual kefir, for thousands of years a staple in the diet of the long-living Abkhazian villagers, is taken to the West and is savagely stolen.

Ten senior partners of a top California law firm dedicate their careers to the protection of the priceless technology and the kefir ... and in the process, uncover illegal financial networks that threaten to blanket the world and monopolize global commerce.

While the doctor's astronaut brother, Jake, is in perilous orbit, the doctor's daughter, Corrie, is abducted from their family home. Had the Capterville expedition to Russia been responsible? Everyone sensed a connection, but there was no proof.

From inner circles in Washington D.C. to Moscow's White House to international finance meetings within the European Economic Community, evil struggles with justice for supreme control.

My profound thanks to Mary, my wife and editor, who has proofed more versions than she cares to remember, and to my mother, Marion, Master Editor and grammarian, who only subtly and infrequently suggested I might consider pursuing other, more substantive endeavors, and to Jerre Bannister, anointed guardian in the west of so much from the east, and to Lee Lorenzen whose inquisitive mind continues to reveal the many and elusive mysteries of water.

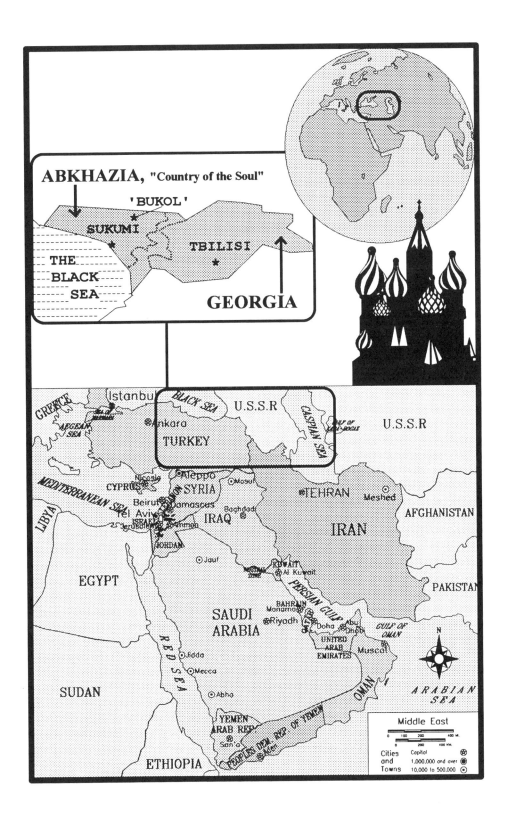

For the young at heart, of ancient age
Your active minds and playful ways

THE WARS WITHIN

CHAPTER 1

AUGUST, 1983
Abkhazia, an autonomous republic within Soviet Georgia

Members of the scientific research team, in awe of their surroundings, finally reached the altitude of nine thousand feet, high above the Black Sea. In another thousand feet they would arrive at their destination. The ancient village of Bukol was above them, waiting.

Dr. Steven Capterville, the expedition leader, inhaled the cool mountain air. He paused briefly on the narrow rocky trail observing the frightening beauty all about him. Clawing at distant cirrus clouds, jagged snow-capped peaks rose into the air for what seemed to be miles. Waterfalls cascaded for thousands of feet into unseen valleys far below, and the water sound was ever changing, a living symphony at once hissing quietly and then, a turn away, thundering with unimaginable power and mist.

From a distance the seven member group became an insignificant line ascending an alp in a vast series of valleys. Well in front of Dr. Capterville, their guide Tengiz could be seen keeping a steady pace. Near the rear of the line Dr. Megan Rankin, the team's botanist, could not help stopping regularly to collect rare flower samples, and then she and the others would run to catch up. In this way, the expedition inched up the mountain, caterpillar-like, expanding and contracting.

Amid deep, difficult breathing came inevitable, audible thoughts.

"I feel like we're in a land that time forgot."

"It's so ... different ... in this country. I've climbed mountains before but I've never felt a place so ... different."

"This path was made by goats, for goats. One bad step and it's good bye."

"I do believe I preferred the warm coastal beaches of Sukumi down ... well, down there somewhere."

"I thought I was in good shape but this fellow is somethin' else."

"Yea, he never stops."

Their guide, Tengiz, was a wiry, elfish man with a long thin nose, a conical fur hat and boundless energy. He had set a forceful pace ever since joining them at the five thousand foot trail head. He spoke with the fluid, almost song-like Abkhazian tongue of the Iberian-Caucasian language group. He spoke no English. And he was a documented 144 years of age.

"Steven, when we get to Bukol I have a few questions for ol' Tengiz here. The guy's amazing."

"I'm sure Professor Kitovani will be happy to translate for you, Jake. Just try not to offend anyone this time."

"Yes, brother dear."

Steven and Jake Capterville were brothers, both brilliant, good natured, good looking and unmarried. They were very close, their parents had seen to that, but they were different as night and day. Steven, at 37, was a year older.

Dr. Steven Capterville, the conservative, model leader of this expedition, possessed doctorates in both bio-chemistry and bio-physics. He was the creator and inventor of the

Cluster Conversion Process, a process capable of imprinting vitamins, minerals and drugs into water, thereby eliminating potential side effects of the compounds. And he had a theory, which he would divulge to no one, about how and why people like Tengiz are able to live and remain active for so many years.

Jake Capterville, restless and adventurous, held a degree in astro-physics and was intent upon doing that which he had always wanted to do ... go to Mars. In May he had been selected to begin what was planned to be ten years of training for the first manned space mission to the red planet. Beginning in the Fall, thirty-five eligible astronauts would enter the program. Ten years later, with precise, once in a lifetime planetary alignment, three astronauts would go. Jake intended to be one of those three. In the meanwhile he was on this expedition, at his own expense, mainly because of his interest in his brother's work, and because he was curious, like the rest of the world, about the long-living energetic villagers in these mountains, the Caucasus mountains of the Soviet Union's Abkhazia.

Theoretical discussions between Steven, Jake and their colleagues had been endless. How long can a person live? Why do some people outlive others? Could Steven's latest technological advances provide answers concerning the nature of the aging process? Was there something in the diet of the Abkhazians that was responsible for their longevity?

Steven Capterville's interest in the mountain people was peaked in 1973 by an article in National Geographic Magazine written by Dr. Gordon Teague, Chief of Medical Services at Boston's Massachusetts General Hospital and Jackson Professor of Clinical Medicine at Harvard Medical School. Dr. Teague, supported by the National Geographic

Society, journeyed to the little village of Tutol, not far from the team's present position, to study the hearty long-living people. Diet and exercise was found to be important, but there was little in exercise or habit to distinguish the Tutol villagers from other peoples who did not share the same longevity and health.

At Professor Kitovani's insistence, Steven determined to venture higher into the mountains for possible answers. Now, at nine thousand feet above sea level, and one thousand feet below Bukol, he prayed he had made the right decision and that he would not let down all those who had supported him. It was difficult enough to maintain funding for his company's medical research, but to convince the University of California at San Bernardino and several private groups to back a far flung adventure into another country had taken years of effort. Now his reputation and future research was on the line.

UCSB and those contributing to the expedition grant had insisted upon the inclusion of several of the team's members. Megan Rankin, at thirty years of age, was a faculty member at UCSB. As a botanist with a remarkable background in bio-chemistry and nutrition, the university and Dr. Capterville considered her an essential member of the expedition that would seek to determine practical means to extend the quality and length of human life.

Critical to their efforts would be Dr. Khotsiya Kitovani, a long-time colleague of Dr. Capterville who had received the Nobel Prize for his work in Structural Biology and Cellular Signal Transduction. As head of the Tbilisi Gerontological Center he had made a study of the Abkhazian culture for many years. A tall man and very fit, his leathery, tanned face and large rough hands told of much outdoor work. A Georgian by birth he had come from the University of Tbilisi,

Georgia, less than 200 miles away. Most importantly, he was the only member of the expedition who spoke fluent Abkhazian and superior English.

Dr. Markhti Tarba, also a Georgian from Tbilisi, was a world renown geologist. He had two professional passions; the classification of Antarctic strata, and the study of Burgess shale high in the Canadian Rockies. The Burgess formation, in which he was considered an expert, he believed to be the only exposed formation in the world containing first evidence of life at the creation of the earth. Small of stature with large thick eye glasses, quiet and introspective, he was inwardly excited about discovering a correlation between the long-living mountain people and the electrical properties of the stone and thermal cirques in which they lived. He spoke Georgian and flawless English, and had a limited ear for Abkhazian.

Marlin Moss, a computer specialist who Dr. Capterville found rather provoking and unpleasant, was a last minute addition to the trip. RAM Pharmaceuticals, Inc., the expedition's largest contributor, had insisted upon his presence, presumably to accumulate and tally the team's data. Exactly how that was to be accomplished at ten thousand feet above sea level with no electricity or computer access had escaped Dr. Capterville, but he had not wanted to rock the boat of his greatest benefactor.

So this was the intellectual core of young Steven Capterville's research expedition that found itself winding upward through towering mountains overlooking the Black Sea to the west, and the Caspian Sea to the east. To the south lay Turkey, Syria, Iraq and Iran. Far to the north, Moscow.

Steven Capterville was elated. He had assembled a well qualified and decidedly colorful team; a bright female botanist from Southern California with long blond hair, an Abkhazian-speaking Nobel Laureate, an introspective bespectacled geologist, a rude out-of-place computer wiz and, of course, his Indiana Jones astronaut brother, Jake.

As Dr. Capterville put one cold foot in front of the other, along an uncharacteristically flat and boulder-strewn portion of the trail, he noticed a strange and lovely purple flower. Bright gold pistil and stamens in the center of the flower reached out like the fingers of a hand. The flower was perched atop a thin spiny stem which, in turn, grew out of spirals of heart-shaped leaves. The plant was rooted in a bed of wet, cracked shale.

The doctor's first thought was that Megan Rankin would not be able to pass it without stopping. Steven had only recently met the energetic botanist at brief organizational meetings, but he had already come to delight in her contagious enthusiasm, and he knew nothing could prevent her from examining the unusual plant.

"Tengiz, in twenty yards, stop ... stop." Realizing Tengiz understood 'go' and 'stop', but little else in English, Steven pointed ahead and repeated the command. In a minute the group had come to a welcome halt. Steven looked back. Sure enough, Megan Rankin was already on her knees busy with her specimen kit, eyes aglow with the same excitement he had noticed many times.

Steven rolled the pack off his shoulders, rested against a boulder and leaned his head all the way back until his eyes saw nothing but mountain tops and sky. He slowly shut his eyes, sighed, and thought back to ... Los Angeles ... then the flight to Rome ... and on to Tbilisi, Georgia, and then ... the overloaded aircraft had lifted itself off the Tbilisi runway with only a few yards to spare. The Russian made TU-154, with full cargo and a crew of six, had flown them and ninety other passengers from the Georgian capital to Sukumi, the capital of Abkhazia.

They had landed heavily at the Sukumi Airport just south of the city. Steven remembered that this is where he had first laid eyes on Marlin Moss. Curiously, Mr. Moss had just landed separately in a Georgian Air Force fighter jet. When asked about this unusual circumstance, Mr. Moss had retorted sarcastically that he was really a communist in disguise, and he had said so with such abuse that no one dared question him further.

His head still laid back against the rock, Steven made a mental note to investigate Mr. Moss.

After walking through the colorful tile-domed Sukumi terminal building, the group had boarded an antiquated green tour bus, reserved just for them, that propelled itself forward by blasting black smoke out its back side.

Though they were only passing through, what they saw of Sukumi, they loved. It was a seaside paradise looking west over the Black Sea, a favorite resort of eastern Europeans. Toward the mountains, away from the pristine beaches, the sweet smell of tangerine groves mingled with eucalyptus. Even at the modern beach front hotels there lingered an old-time friendliness, an unmistakable archaic hospitality honed over thousands of years.

The old green bus, which came to have many nick-names, miraculously pulled them through beautiful green foothills up to the five thousand foot trail-head ... and to the waiting arms of their guide, the youthful Tengiz.

"Vasta, vasta!" Tengiz was tugging at Steven's sleeve, motioning to Steven with his hands and tapping the corroded Elgin watch on his sun-spotted wrist. It was time to move on. This was no time for day dreaming. They would follow the only trail, the one clinging to the right side of the canyon, and they must reach Bukol before dark.

"Yes, of course, Tengiz," Steven acknowledged, "lead on."

Dr. Capterville shouldered his pack, turned to Dr. Kitovani who was immediately above him and asked in a low voice, "Kit, have you heard music? Any singing? I think I heard people singing ... just a minute ago ... far away."

"I heard no singing, Steven. I can barely hear myself think with all these waterfalls."

"But you've taken this trail over the years, Kit. Surely ...."

"There is much you must experience for yourself in these valleys," Dr. Kitovani said obliquely. "We should be moving, Steven. We still have a long way to go to reach the Wall of Water. Bukol is not far above that."

Steven swung around and took off at a brisk pace. "Tell the others there will be no more stopping," he ordered. "Samples can be taken on the way back."

Tengiz was well up the trail, waving them on.

"144 years old!" Steven thought to himself, "and he's out-hiking all of us!"

Inside almost vertical canyon walls, three-thirty in the afternoon looked more like evening. Marbled rock browns, oranges and greens had already turned to muted silver-gray. And the steep canyon walls, as the group ascended, had come perceptibly, tactually, closer together.

"Dr. Tarba, I feel I could almost touch the other side," Megan said to the peculiar geologist.

Trudging directly behind her, Dr. Markhti Tarba was having difficulty watching his step while mentally logging formations and strata that only fellows of his profession could

8

fully appreciate. Several feet away, he had seen Dr. Rankin's lips move but he could not hear her words above the mounting roar of water that was racing down the canyon at them. His glasses were collecting mist and he was constantly wiping them. With much indignation and effort he squinted, over and over, attempting to clarify the precious lithic world around him.

"The Wall of Water is beyond this granite palisade," he yelled to her. She did not hear him.

The path now was solid rock, with tall steps hand-cut by someone long ago. Only three feet wide in places, the left edge of the trail dropped straight down hundreds of feet to a river that could be heard, but rarely seen through clouds of mist and spray. Odd ferns, lichen and mosses seemed thriving on the wet cliff walls. A tiny blue throated bird darted about the crags oblivious to the presence of people.

The stone steps, uncomfortably high for human legs, arched upward to the right around the cliff face so that those in the rear lost sight of those advancing in front. As each member of the team turned the corner of the precipice, they joined the others in a shallow stone grotto, and they beheld a sight so startling that it became difficult for any of them to move. For support they each placed an arm or a hand against the recessed rock wall. They stood in awe of one of the great, and little known, wonders of the world ... a wall of water that crested five hundred feet above them and fell in an even silver sheet at least that far below them. It spanned the entire canyon, wall to wall, with no possible passage beyond it. Sheer cliff walls ascended vertically for thousands of feet on either side of the fall which fell with a thunder into an inaccessible black lake far below them. Each, in turn, had a priceless expression. Each, in turn, spoke a telling comment, but not one was heard over the din of the falls.

At once wakened from thoughtful wonder, Steven was being struck on his arm. It was his brother Jake, who was excitedly pointing up the trail. Neither could believe his eyes. There was no more trail. The grotto, only eight feet high, was but fifteen yards long. At its far end, the rock wall curved smoothly to the side of the slippery perpendicular cliff. There was no way around. A frayed and moldy hemp rope supported by wooden posts ran the length of the grotto, the only barrier between them and the rocky pool below.

Steven composed himself and took stock of his company. Marlin Moss stood erect, his long arms folded across his chest. He was looking across the canyon, but seemed to be staring beyond the falls with the same lack of expression the others had come to expect. Megan Rankin had torn her attention from the falls and was beginning to eye the grotto plant life. Dr. Tarba was sitting on his haunches with an incredulous expression on his face, still staring at the Wall of Water, his cupped hands shielding the spray from his eyeglass lenses.

"Steve, Steve!" Jake screamed, "Where is Tengiz? ... and where is Dr. ...?"

Tengiz and Dr. Kitovani had disappeared.

Steven grabbed his brother's arm and hollered at him over the rumble of the water, "Jake, keep the others here. Don't let anybody leave the grotto. I have a hunch."

Leaving his pack behind, Steven ran to the other end of the grotto. Jake turned quickly to check on the others. If anyone but Steven had told him to stay put, he would have paid no attention. Jake was always the one to jump into the breach first. Jake always needed to see what was on the other side of a door. He loved an unsolvable puzzle ... and here, on the side of a perilous Russian alp with people disappearing before his eyes, was a classic mystery worthy of his attention.

"Wait a minute!" he thought, spinning around.

Steven too had vanished.

Jake motioned to the others. "Follow me," he waved, and he set off for the end of the grotto.

There was no sign of Steven, Tengiz or Dr. Kitovani. Jake examined the stone floor. No traces. He studied the wall. Nothing. Finally, he moved his hands across the cold, marbled wall, feeling with his finger tips, and he discovered the answer.

"Well, I'll be ...."

What appeared to be one wall was really two, the one nearest him four feet in front of the other, but both stone slabs were blended identically in color and texture and appeared, even up close, to be one.

"An optical illusion in stone," Jake said slowly, still feeling the edge of the wall in front. "Hey, Dr. Tarba, you're gonna love this!"

Dr. Tarba couldn't hear him.

"I'll get Steve for this if it's the last thing I do," Jake grumbled. "OK, everybody, follow me," he yelled. "Stay close!"

The stone walls remained about four feet apart up to shoulder height, but converged and closed into solid rock some twenty feet above. They walked carefully in a straight line for thirty or more feet, feeling their way in dim light. The passage abruptly emptied into a medium sized, boulder-strewn cavern. At the far left corner of the cavern was a ten foot, almost oval, opening that once again looked out upon the falls. Sound and mist and light flooded through the opening into the stone room, but much to their relief, it was quieter. At the far end of the opening was the beginning of a natural tunnel that appeared to climb upward toward the falls.

Standing and talking around a large boulder in the middle of the cavern stood Steven, Tengiz and Dr. Kitovani. Even Tengiz had a grin on his face.

Jake headed straight for his brother. "And how long have you known about this little surprise?"

"I swear I knew nothing about it, Jake. I discovered it like you just did."

"Right! You weren't in too big a hurry to get back to the rest of us, were you? And what's with the big smile?"

"Well, let's just say that I'm following Dr. Kit's advice."

"And what, may I ask, is that?"

Steven looked at Dr. Kitovani and winked. "Kit says there is much we must experience for ourselves in these valleys. And I know how much you like experiencing things for yourself."

Jake gave his brother an unpleasant look.

"Besides," Steven continued, "it didn't take you long to disregard my commands. I gave you thirty seconds to forget what I said, but it only took you ten."

"All right you two," Dr. Kitovani interrupted, "we must continue on."

Once again, Tengiz was motioning them onward. With the quickness of a cat he disappeared into the darkened tunnel.

Swinging his pack over his right arm, Dr. Kitovani said to Steven, "Get your people together. Have them clip on to the climbing rope at intervals as we discussed. We will remain on the trail, but it can get slippery. Bukol is just above us now, but the going is very steep. And remember," Dr. Kitovani had recited more than once the three cardinal rules of mountain climbing, "respect the mountain for it is dangerous, check your equipment and know your route."

"Know your route! That's a laugh," Steven said.

"That's why you have Tengiz and me."

"Any more surprises ahead?" Steven asked wryly.

"That depends on what you consider a surprise, Steven. The first time up this canyon is full of the unexpected, no matter what you are told at the beginning."

"We've known each other for years, Kit. I had no idea you became so worldly outside of your office."

"After a few days with these mountain people you will have different perspectives yourself," Dr. Kitovani said flatly.

"I see ...."

"Steven, let's be off!" Dr. Kitovani said cheerfully, "Follow me, you're in for a real treat just around the corner."

"What corner? All I see is a cave."

"Come on, man, you're wasting time." Dr. Kitovani disappeared into the tunnel. From out of the darkness, Steven and the others heard his voice echoing, "Take it easy until you get used to the rope, and no matter what you see, keep moving! We're behind schedule!"

The expedition was once again on the move, Dr. Kitovani's last words ringing in their ears, *"... no matter what you see, keep moving!"* All tethered together, Steven led the way into the tunnel. Marlin Moss took up his usual position at the rear of the line, behind, and watching, everyone else.

While the floor of the rising passage was relatively even, the tunnel was clearly not man made. It was possibly the result of flowing water or, more likely, the product of one or more earthquakes that are endemic in the region. The rock above them and on either side was jagged and broken, forcing them to weave from side to side in order to advance. Like a snake through rocks the roped group moved steadily upward.

13

"Where do you think Tengiz is?" Megan asked in the dark.

Jake responded, "Dr. Tarba, what's the elevation of the highest peak in these parts?"

"13,274 feet right here ... to the east ... 25,550 feet."

"Our guide, Tengiz, could be there by now," Jake said in jest.

Dr. Tarba chuckled quietly, "The way he moves, he could be back by now."

Just as the light from the cavern behind them began to dissipate, a faint pewter light began to grow in the tunnel ahead. The passage had taken the team into the cliff to the right, away from the falls, and then slowly had curved, in an awkward upward circle, back around to the left, so that eventually they were hiking back in the direction from which they had come.

"Boy, am I lost," Megan said.

Even Marlin Moss, known for his economy of words, blurted out, "Where the hell are we?"

"Quiet, everyone," Steven said, "we're about to find out."

The light grew brighter as the opening approached.

"According to my calculations we have to be behind the waterfall," Dr. Tarba said.

"Impossible," Marlin Moss grumbled, "besides, there's no sound of water. It's quiet out there. We must be coming out on the other side of the mountain."

"That cannot be," Dr. Tarba said sharply, "I know my directions."

Each team member was forced to bend when emerging from the passage. As they stood, each in turn was speechless. Each was wide-eyed, even Marlin Moss. None could follow Dr. Kitovani's advice ... to keep moving.

The passage emptied into the recesses of another grotto, this one, four hundred feet high, hundreds of feet deep. The floor was perfectly flat stone, forming a semi-circle, and they stood against the curving inside wall, looking out. They beheld a symmetrical arch, a rainbow hollowed into a vertical cliff. They were standing in half of an enormous vine-strewn dome. And Dr. Tarba had been right. They *were* behind the falls. The translucent wall of water fell just a few inches outside the grotto in an even, plumb sheet blanketing the entire arched opening.

But most remarkable of all, there was no loud water sound, no roar, no thunder, no spray, no mist. With the exception of a hushed hiss, all was quiet. Even the plop of water droplets, collecting and dripping from overhead ferns, could be heard in the still vacuum of the grotto.

This was the first time since Marlin Moss had joined the team at the Sukumi airport that any of them had seen him interested in much of anything. He was still reserved, but now there was a radiance to his usually stoic face.

"Sound that emanates from within the dome ... is audible," he spoke, as if to some imaginary entity, "but sound orchestrated outside ... cannot be heard within. Fascinating. An acoustical feat worth exploring ... yes ... yes, indeed."

"Steve," Megan whispered up close, "I think he's talking to his computer!"

"I have a lot of questions for Mr. Moss, and for RAM Pharmaceuticals," was all Steven said. What he noticed foremost was that Megan Rankin had called him Steve. It was the first time she had ever addressed him as anything but 'doctor' ... and nobody but Jake ever called him Steve, not even his parents.

Diminutive against the backdrop of the falls, Tengiz and Dr. Kitovani waived to the others from the far side of the grotto with much animation and concern. There was no doubt as to the urgency of the team's departure.

15

"This is unbelievable geology!" Dr. Tarba expounded. "Why have I not heard of it before?"

"My Heavens," said Megan, "I could spend a lifetime studying just this ceiling."

"Well, Steve, look what you've got us into now," Jake said with admiration. "Dr. Kit was right, this is a real treat. Look at the falls, Steve ... all the way across." Jake swept his hand in front of them. "It's like looking out a gigantic window."

Steven was amazed at the sight. "It's incredible!" he managed, "the water is so clear and so thin you can see the outline of the canyon cliffs beyond it."

Jake's eyes were glazed, "This could keep an artist busy for years."

"Hundreds of artists, Jake, hundreds ...."

Steven's voice trailed off. He was feeling responsible for his group, and its specific mission. He, above all others in this strange and wonderful land, must not lose his focus. The weight of leadership displaced artistic expression. "Dr. Kitovani said to keep moving," he said firmly to the others. "Stay roped, we're headed into another tunnel."

Inside the waterfall at the far end of the grotto, opposite the side of the valley that had enabled their ascent, was another passage that looked to have been made by man or, perhaps, artfully enlarged. It was only twenty feet long and opened into a very steep cone-shaped canyon. As each member of the expedition left the passage, they balanced, arms out-stretched, over a small stone bridge that crossed a tiny splashing creek. Lining both sides of the creek were hundreds of the same purple flower, the one with the golden center they had seen below. Along the black cliff wall from which they had just emerged, ran long, thick vines of climbing roses, some of the vines fifty feet long with dozens of tightly packed roses, all the same shape and color ... pale yellow petals with dark orange centers.

Megan Rankin had already unhooked her rope and was busy studying the roses.

"Well, Dr. Rankin," Steven smiled, "have you discovered something new and exciting?"

"Exciting, yes," Megan said without turning. "New? Definitely not."

"Really?" Steven asked.

"This is an ancient rose, a wild rose. It was first painted and described in literature thousands of years ago in China."

Megan picked one and spun it slowly in her fingers. "See ... five simple petals, not like the full modern roses we've created by grafting. This is great-grandpa in the rose kingdom."

"Really?" Steven repeated.

"What is surprising is that a climbing rose could survive up here, in such a cold climate."

Steven pondered that, then turned to assemble his group. "There is a lot up here that is ... surprising," he said expressively.

Dr. Kitovani was calling to them, "Dr. Capterville, please!"

"We're coming, Kit."

Steven surveyed their surroundings. To their immediate left, and folding in front of them, rose a vertical cliff. The other side of this cliff was the cliff face supporting the Wall of Water, the one that they had seen on their way up the main valley. The expedition was now behind it.

"Listen," Jake said, "you can hear the roar of the falls again, from over the mountain."

"Yes," Megan said, "but, goodness! Look at that!"

To the right was a steep talus slope that funneled up the canyon. Irregular boulders rested heavily in fields of crumbled, decomposed granite, and occasional scrub pines and weathered junipers sent roots into broken rock. A worn trail with many switch-backs could be seen zig-zagging all the way to the top.

Markhti Tarba looked upward and groaned. He pointed at the upper trail, "Dr. Kitovani, are we hiking up that today?"

"Yes, Dr. Tarba, we must. But take heart. It is not nearly as bad as it looks ... and Bukol is at the top." Looking back at the others, Dr. Kitovani said, "Keep attached to the rope!"

Shifting his pack, Steven shouted, "Let's go!"

With every switch-back, especially after passing the midpoint of the talus slope, the view became more and more spectacular. They were looking down upon the west flank of the Caucasus mountain range. In places, they could see the Black Sea, deep blue, far below them to the west. To their right as they climbed, a pure white, ribbon-thin waterfall fell uninterrupted into a dark forbidding valley .

Tengiz, now comfortable that his followers were within reach of Bukol and that his duties had been discharged honorably, had returned to the group and was speaking with Dr. Kitovani.

"Tengiz wants me to tell you," Dr. Kitovani pronounced, "that the wind will blow the waterfall today."

Steven looked across the deep valley. The water was falling in a thin straight line. "It seems calm enough to me."

"Tengiz says this waterfall is named Bridalveil Fall. He says to watch when the wind blows the white water. It looks like a white lace veil."

As they watched the long ribbon fall, a gust of wind hit the water and spread it far to the right.

"Look at that," Steven pointed, "it really does look like a veil."

Tengiz was looking at Megan, then the fall, then back at Megan, and was motioning and speaking in his flowing native tongue.

"Tengiz says," Dr. Kitovani repeated with a smile, "that any woman ... let's see, how to translate this ... any woman who looks upon the falls when the wind is blowing the veil, is sure to be married soon to the one with whom she travels."

"Heavens!" Megan mumbled. Her deep ranch tan could not contain the blush on her beautiful face. Unconsciously she pulled the brim of her hat lower.

Tengiz broke into an enormous smile and his dark knowledgeable eyes seemed to pierce her, and to soothe her at the same time.

"Tell Mr. Tengiz," Megan said with masked composure, "that I love his story, it is very romantic, but considering the caliber of my present company, I am quite sure his story can never come to pass."

They all roared with laughter. Dr. Kitovani translated for Tengiz as the sound of humor echoed through the canyons. Then when he understood what she had said, Tengiz began to laugh louder than any of them. He looked back at Megan with those eyes of his, and shook his finger at her as if to say, "You will see!" and then he was off up the mountain.

"I hear voices, Kit, lots of voices," Steven was saying as they made the final turn on the trail.

"You should, Steven. The whole village knows we're coming. Look up here."

Against a dusking sky Steven could see above him the silhouettes of milling people. As the team crested the ridge, they were, one by one, greeted with the most remarkable hospitality and warmth. Before they could even discard their packs and equipment, still roped together, they were handed glasses of dark red wine and small plates filled with unrecognizable foods. There were young people, old people, children ... dancing, welcoming and celebrating the arrival of their guests ... there were chickens and pigs and black and white cows.

"How'd they get a cow up here?" Steven wondered.

Among the translating, untethering and dropping of packs Steven scanned, just for a moment, the village of Bukol. In the fading light he beheld a small stream-filled valley, smaller than he had expected, that was ringed with soaring, majestic mountains. Toward the base of each mountain, away from the stone houses and assorted buildings that made up the village, the land was terraced with rows of crops he could not identify in the dark. At the center of the village stood a tall church steeple capped with a sharpened spire that joined the surrounding peaks in pointing to Heaven.

"Steven, have you tasted this wine?" Jake asked, putting his arm around Steven's neck. "It's fabulous. I have a theory ... *this* must be the answer to extra long life."

"Jake, you promised ...."

"OK, OK. But we'd better get back, Kitovani wants you. We've been invited to dinner, and we're advised to hit the sack early."

"I can handle that," Steven said, "that pack has reshaped my shoulders."

The two brothers stood quietly together, away from the others, as dusk turned to dark and village windows glowed gold with the fires within.

"I wish Elliot could see this," Steven said suddenly.

"You mean *the* Elliot, Elliot Jaynes? What in the world made you think of him now?"

20

"I'm concerned about him, Jake. He would absolutely love this place, but he's so wrapped up in his law practice he never has time for anything else."

"Don't all lawyers go through that?"

"It's still not healthy ... doesn't seem to me to even fit his personality. When I asked him to join the expedition, he wouldn't even consider it. Something about a corporate takeover and a hearing in Delaware."

"Elliot knows what he's doing. He'll work through it," Jake said incisively. "Maybe it was just bad timing."

Jake and Steven could hear excited villagers escorting the team members toward the village.

"Oh, by the way, Steve ... can I give you some brotherly advice?"

"What?"

"Try not to be too bloody obvious, will you?"

"About what?"

"You're staring holes through Megan Rankin."

"That's preposterous!"

"Come on, Steve ... you're talking to Jake."

There was a long silence. Jake studied the starlit sky. Unblinking, with an orange tinge, the planet Mars shined distinctly in the upper right quadrant. Jake instinctively knew the Penny Nebula, though not visible to the human eye, was in his line of vision far beyond and slightly below Mars. Cita's Rings, also not visible, would be just to the left. Thoughts of training and his future mission began flooding back to him ... but Steven finally spoke.

"Well ..." Steven took his baseball cap off and wiped his forehead with his arm, "has it been that noticeable?"

Jake laughed, "No, only to me I think ... just a warning, though. She's terrific, and I don't want to see you blow it.

Besides, you're the commander of this outfit. You have to be careful. You have many roles."

"Good grief," Steven moaned. "Are you, are you sure I haven't ...?"

"Naw, don't worry about it. Nobody's noticed a thing. But you've got good taste, I'll say that for you. If I wasn't committed to another planet for the next few years, I might be after her myself."

"Over my dead body ... anyway, Jake, thanks for the advice."

"That's what younger brothers are for! Now about that dinner, I'm starved."

Two miles high in the sky the Capterville brothers walked in silence into the alpine village of Bukol. Just before entering the home of their mountain hosts, Steven stopped with his hand on the thick wooden door.

"Jake, down below the falls, in the canyon below the Wall of Water, I mean ... did you hear singing? Like a choir?"

"You know, I thought I did, several times, but then I figured it was all of those waterfalls."

CHAPTER 2

Steven awoke the next morning at first light to the sound of chirping birds. Jake was sound asleep, buried under handmade quilts on a cot across the room. Lying on his back, covered with blankets up to his nose, Steven marveled at the hand-cut and fitted rock walls. Hewn wooden beams ran the length of the ceiling. A four paned window in a hardwood frame was mitered perfectly into the rock wall above him. Upon the sill rested three silver frames holding vintage photographs of people ... very old people.

Quiet voices and a fire crackling in the next room coaxed Steven out of bed. Looking out the window across a field of low manicured tea shrubs, he viewed, on either side of a babbling stream, rows of apple trees loaded with bright red apples. The rock-filled, chilly stream meandered in esses through the apple trees.

Then he noticed Megan. She was standing by the stream under an apple tree brushing her cascading blond hair. It was the first time he had seen her with her hair down. Even in frayed jeans, a worn khaki shirt and a faded green parka, he thought her beautiful and exciting. She was gesturing to another woman who Steven recognized from the night before as the daughter of his hosts, Tarkil and Khfaf Lasuria. Megan would be staying with their daughter, Shirali Lasuria, for the three nights they remained in Bukol.

With effort, Steven drew his thoughts back inside the room. He said to himself, "Thanks for the warning, little brother."

Steven shaved using the wash basin at the end of the room and dressed quickly. Pushing open the door, he entered the main room of the house.

Khfaf Lasuria sat in an old wooden chair, morning sunlight bathing the sleeves of her blue print dress. She was staring out her favorite window, sipping vodka from a small crystal glass. She wore handmade blue leather shoes over black woolen stockings. She had wrapped a white silk scarf around her forehead and tied it in the back. Her right arm outstretched, the palm of her hand rested lightly upon an intricately carved cane.

As Steven watched unnoticed, she delicately placed her glass on the window sill, took a puff of a cigarette and continued to gaze across the valley that had been her home for many, many years. Her children, to no avail, were always asking her not to smoke cigarettes. But who was to match habits with Khfaf Lasuria? She was 173 years old, still active and exceedingly alert.

Khfaf's daughter, Shirali, had returned from the stream and was busy at the end of the room that served as their kitchen. Another four paned window above the sink framed snow capped peaks to the east.

A long, scarred wooden table was centered in the room, running from the kitchen at one end, to the massive rock fireplace at the other end. The fireplace and supporting rock formed the entire wall at that end of the house. The fireplace opening, and the log mantle above, were enormous. Picture frames of all shapes and sizes adorned the mantle. A sturdy iron grate held flaming logs, and suspended at the tip of the flames was a large black cauldron. Hissing steam escaped periodically from under its battered black lid.

Tarkil Lasuria and Dr. Khotsiya Kitovani sat at the heavy table near the fire. They were deep in conversation and had not noticed Steven.

Shirali had just finished placing clean tea cups in the cabinet over the sink when she saw Steven standing at the door. She cheerfully expressed 'good morning' and other words of welcome in her native tongue.

Khfaf put her cigarette out, raised her glass and smiled at Steven. She began speaking to him.

Dr. Kitovani leapt up from the table and said enthusiastically, "Well, good morning, Steven! Mrs. Lasuria wants to know if you'd like a nip of vodka to start the day."

Steven looked confused. "Perhaps you could thank her," he said haltingly, "and tell her I'm a tea and coffee man, myself."

"All right, but you are passing up a very old tradition. Many of Khfaf's relatives ... it goes back generations ... are fishermen on the Caspian Sea to the east of here. They rise early, before dawn, and prepare their boats to catch the great sturgeon fish, and the prized caviar inside. Before they weigh anchor they always drink an ounce or two of vodka. They claim it fights seasickness."

"Interesting," Steven said.

"Mrs. Lasuria has a glass every morning to honor them, and wish them good fishing. There are few of the big fish left nowadays."

"In that case, Kit, please tell her I'd be honored to have a sip ... but not too much. We have work to do. Tell her I hope her family catches the greatest of the fish. And tell her I doubt that I will get seasick up here."

Dr. Kitovani translated, and Tarkil and Khfaf Lasuria broke into wide smiles and began to laugh. Shirali smiled warmly, raised her eyebrows in thought, and went back to her work.

"They like you, Steven. You should be pleased. They are very important people in this part of the world."

"How so?" Steven asked.

"Well, there are some things ...."

"I know, I know, there are some things I'll have to experience for myself ... right?"

"That would be best, yes," Dr. Kitovani said. "Mr. Lasuria has a few things he would like to say to you. Come, bring your vodka and join us at the table by the fire."

With the exception of a soft white scarf fitted around his neck and crossed behind him down his back, Tarkil Lasuria was dressed all in black. He wore high black leather boots, black free-fitting pants and a long sleeved black shirt. Below the white scarf and just under his black lapels was a puffed red ascot. He had a large but handsome nose, tall ears and brown leathery skin. A thick gray-white mustache, well cut, graced his experienced face.

They were a study in contrast, he and Steven. Steven sat across the table, bigger physically, but smaller of features. Steven was considered handsome by western standards, but lighter of skin, complexion and eye color. Steven's hair was light brown, Tarkil's eyebrows, jet black.

Steven greeted them warmly, but he had an odd look on his face. "Please tell Mr. Lasuria that it was a pleasure to meet him last night, and I thank him for his hospitality."

"I will do so," Dr. Kitovani said, "but ... is there anything wrong, Steven?"

"No, Kit, I was just thinking, in the U.S. when I fill out applications or file for permits I check the box titled 'Caucasian'. Yet here I am sitting across the table from a true man of the Caucasus, and I look nothing like him. Who's the Caucasian, I wonder?"

"You are not so different as you may think, Steven."

"Oh?"

"It is said your race, his and yours, began here," Dr. Kitovani said wisely, "but events and time have made many changes."

Dr. Kitovani repeated their discussion for Tarkil who without expression said simply, "I am Abkhazian."

Silently and gracefully, Shirali placed before them a large blue plate filled with bread, cheeses and fruit. In the center of the blue plate stood a round white pot of golden honey, and a wooden spoon with a long curved handle.

A while later she brought three blue glasses filled half way with sour milk. From a matching pitcher, she poured cold water into each glass until it was full. Steven tasted it.

"This is interesting."

"I know," said Dr. Kitovani, "it is delicious, and bad tasting all at once."

"You could be more tactful, Kit," Steven said, "but not more accurate. I like it."

"It is a homemade kefir. They make it daily, in goat's milk."

"Why the water?"

"It is served many different ways, with and without water, with different tastes to accompany different foods. They even make a special salad dressing out of it."

Steven had a bite of the warm bread with melting honey. He took another sip of the kefir.

"Strange, wonderful in a way. The more I have, the more I like it."

"Get used to it, my friend. You are in Abkhazia now."
To Steven's surprise, Dr. Kitovani suddenly raised his glass,
thumped his fist on the table and bellowed, "To Abkhazia!"

All three repeated, "To Abkhazia!"

"You must also get used to toasting, Steven. These
people love a good toast, and believe me, they will toast to
anything and everything ... you will see."

Dr. Kitovani and Tarkil began speaking with one another
in Abkhazian. After some discussion, Dr. Kitovani turned to
Steven and said, "First, Mr. Lasuria would like you to call
him Tarkil, but no one else in your party, including myself, is
to do so. I will explain this to the others. Steven, this is a
great honor and, to be honest, I do not understand why he is
doing so. It will mean for you a silent standing or rank
throughout the mountains."

At the other end of the room, Shirali and Khfaf glanced at
one another. Shirali raised her eyebrows once again and kept
to her work.

"Secondly," Dr. Kitovani continued, "he says that any of
us may feel free to ask questions of anyone in the village. He
has heard of our qualifications and he knows we want to
discover how his people are able to live so long."

"Thank him for me, please. I have been concerned about
how the villagers would respond to us."

"He has sensed your concern. That is one reason he likes
you."

"But, Kit, what does he mean about knowing of our
qualifications? Just what does he know?"

"I have told Mr. Lasuria what time has allowed, but it is
clear he already knows far more than he has learned from me.
Lastly, he says that we are to let him know of any supplies or
provisions we will need. If he has them or can acquire them,

they are ours. Oh, and Tengiz has expressed interest in serving as our guide should we wish to explore."

"This is overwhelming," Steven said sincerely. "Please extend my profound thanks, and let Mr. Lasuria know we will do our best not to interfere with the work of his people."

"Mr. Lasuria says, you are welcome, but he wants me to convey that these are not *his* people. He is just one of many villagers willing to help. Nevertheless, Steven, only you are to address him as Tarkil."

The bedroom door opened and a sleepy Jake strolled out, stretching his arms into the air, "What's all the commotion about?" Spotting the men at the end of the table, he opened his arms wide and said loudly, "Tarkil, my good man, I trust you slept well."

Steven buried his head in his arms, Tarkil Lasuria smiled a thin smile and Dr. Kitovani quickly said, "Ahh ... Jake, may I speak to you for a moment."

The balance of the day was given mostly to interviews and discussions with the older people of Bukol. It was not always easy to validate the ages the old ones enjoyed to profess. Documents showing dates of birth were considered the best evidence, but passports, family letters and even carvings on door posts and walls proved valuable. One stone house had an interior wooden support beam covered with notches for height, accompanied by the name of the individual and a date. Ages at marriage were relevant, as were the ages of children, grandchildren, great-grandchildren, etc.. Often, memories of events proved to be important. A man who associated a marriage or a birth with the Russian Revolution, the Russo-Turkish War or even a great snow or flood was helpful in validating other dates and facts.

Marlin Moss was expected to accumulate all of this data and to use his experience with computer software programs to find correlations and validate dates and trends, with the ultimate goal of finding one or more factors that assure long life. But Mr. Moss had no practical way of accomplishing this without transcribing the notes of the others or interviewing them. And that sort of thing was below Mr. Moss.

Markhti Tarba spent little time in the village. He and Tengiz could be seen darting off into a crevasse here, or onto a ledge there. He was like a child in a candy store and he readily admitted it. When the collection of rock samples in his back pack became too burdensome, he was forced to return to the village, gleefully recording his findings and, where appropriate, relaying to Dr. Capterville his theories of how the resonant properties of a particular strata might affect human longevity.

Late in the afternoon, Steven remarked to Megan, as they sat with a woman who they had determined to be between 130 to 135 years of age, "If there is any possibility at all that the rock in these mountains has something to do with advanced age, Markhti Tarba will be the one to find it."

"He seems to think the mountain stone has changed the lake and stream water somehow," Megan said. "It might help explain the differences in plant life."

"And animal life," Steven said quickly. "There are many examples around the world of so-called 'healing' spas and pools. The Roman baths, Lourdes in France, Kiyumizu in Japan."

"That water is different?" Megan asked.

"There are many kinds of water, Megan. Those waters have been subjected to tremendous pressures and electromagnetic fields within the earth. By the time it comes out of the ground, the electrical properties of the water have been changed considerably."

"Electrical! This is all so exciting," Megan said. "No wonder Dr. Tarba is busy collecting all those samples."

"He was the perfect choice for this trip," Steven said with pride.

Steven then thought to himself, "I wish I could say the same about Mr. Moss. I must remember to ask him why he is really here ... to keep an eye on me and RAM Pharmaceutical's investment, I'll wager."

"Dr. Tarba is right," Megan said, "this place is no movie Shangri-La. This is an industrious community, with each person hard at work from the day he is born until the day he dies. And, have you noticed, they are all happy and seem to be doing exactly what they want. The old ones play a key role in the community. They are revered, and sought constantly for their advice. And they are so active in their labors ...."

"Just getting around this country means labor," Steven interrupted.

"I just wish we had more time to spend here," Megan said as she gazed at the surrounding mountains. "There is so much to see and do."

They had been told to listen for the Lasuria dinner bell which would signal the end of their work for the day. The old brass bell was now ringing and echoing through the valley in the inviting key of 'C'.

"I feel like I'm back in camp," Steven sighed.

That evening, as the sky once again darkened, the expedition members and the Lasuria family, with assorted relatives, gathered around the long wooden table for dinner. The old table had been transformed, covered with white

31

tablecloths and buried in plates of food and bundles of hot homemade bread sticks. There were pitchers of wine, vases with roses, sauces and red pepper spices, and vegetables and cheeses piled everywhere. Large plates of chicken, goat's meat and beef were within reach of everyone.

Tarkil Lasuria was seated at the head of the table with his back to the fire. To his right sat his young grand-nephew Khimbei Ladariya. To his left, his grand-niece and Khimbei's sister, Vasha-Tamava Ladariya. Steven was seated next to Khimbei, and Dr. Kitovani was seated on the other side of Steven so he could translate. Jake was already in heavy discussion with Vasha-Tamava, though neither understood a word the other was saying.

Markhti Tarba sat on the other side of Jake with a small collection of rocks he planned to show everyone should the opportunity present itself. To Steven's delight, Marlin Moss was wedged in between two wizened little ladies who kept poking his arms in an effort to determine how any one man could grow to be so big. Megan was seated with Shirali and Khfaf who were squeezed together at the far end of the table. All in all, there were twenty-one people at the table.

Tarkil rose from his chair, raised a tumbler of Georgian brandy, and proceeded to give a rambling and spirited toast in which he welcomed everyone. After praising Steven and his companions he put the tumbler to his lips and swallowed half of his brandy. Without a pause he carried on about his precious Khimbei and Vasha-Tamava whom he loved dearly, whereupon he drank the rest of his brandy and sat down to loud applause.

The evening progressed magnificently with everyone, even Marlin Moss giving a toast. With Dr. Kitovani translating, as he must with each toast, Mr. Moss, surprisingly, brought tears to everyone's eyes with his description of the grotto hidden behind the Wall of Water. Those from Bukol who could not understand his words, but who were not hearing anything they did not already know, were nevertheless genuinely moved by the passion with which he spoke. Steven was amazed.

Dr. Kitovani was busy all evening helping with words and phrases, in English, Abkhazian and Georgian, but it was remarkable how easily everyone conversed with one another. Though the Georgian and Abkhazian languages are as different as Chinese and English, fast friendships developed during the course of the evening.

After dinner, pipes were lit and glasses were continually re-filled. Long tales from Abkhazian legend were faithfully re-told, with each important story accompanied by expressive hand movement.

Eventually, after many heartfelt *good nights* and *wonderful to meet you's*, most of the guests had left. With all the dishes washed and put away, Megan was talking and gesturing in the kitchen with Khfaf and Shirali. Jake had gone for one of his walks under the stars. Dr. Tarba and his little pile of rocks had repaired for the evening, presumably to become better acquainted.

At the end of the table by the fire, wine glasses before them, sat Tarkil, Steven, Dr. Kitovani and Khimbei and Vasha-Tamava Ladariya. All five were sitting up straight with their arms on the table, in serious discussion. It looked more like a business meeting or a strategy session than an after dinner conversation. Tarkil was frowning. Khimbei was doing most of the talking. Periodically, Vasha-Tamava would jump in to validate what Khimbei had said. Dr. Kitovani was quietly translating for Steven as best he could.

The discussion was about the · Abkhazian culture, its people and Abkhazia's place in history. Khimbei was very opinionated and chauvinistic, almost war-like, and was attempting, respectfully, to convince his great-uncle that the Abkhazian people and their culture were in grave danger of extinction should they not arm themselves and strengthen themselves politically within the Soviet Union.

"I have no love of the Russians," Khimbei was saying, "but, mark my words, one day we will be overrun by the Georgians. Tbilisi will attack, make no mistake."

"What makes you so certain, Khimbei?" Tarkil asked calmly. Tarkil respected his young relative's opinion. In fact, of all the people born in Bukol during Tarkil's lifetime, Khimbei was probably his favorite. Khimbei was headstrong, combative and full of ideas that he did not hesitate to share with others.

"Because they hate us," Khimbei said with emotion. "Vasha-Tamava and I have just come from Tbilisi. There is a strong undercurrent. Since we speak their language and know their customs, we can blend in. And you should hear how they speak of us. It is disgusting."

Quietly, Khfaf pulled a chair up for herself between the two men. It was a time tested tactic of hers. Discussion would never turn to argument in her house. As she poured more wine with a grace reserved for the old and the respected, Tarkil and Khimbei fell silent, thinking. Khfaf rose slowly and left the table. After a while, Khimbei took a deep breath and prepared to speak. Tarkil raised his hand as if to say 'not now', and Khimbei knowingly lowered his eyes in respect. Tarkil knew, and Khimbei should have known, that Khfaf would be returning to her chair. She had made herself a part of the after dinner talk, and it should not continue without her. Tarkil respected her opinion, and though she voiced it rarely on matters of politics and war, it was important to him that she understand the facts that were being presented.

Khfaf eventually returned to her chair and set a tray on the table. Lifting it carefully from the tray, she placed an oval white dish before them. It was filled with chocolates, arranged in a spiral pattern that all who knew her had come to recognize. Then she presented each one of them with a small white cup into which she poured, from a round teapot, a thickened white kefir.

Pained by his mistake, Khimbei would not be the first of them to speak. Tarkil was sipping his wine, deep in thought. Steven had remained politely quiet, and terribly curious. Dr. Kitovani took the opportunity to explain the conversation to Steven in English.

Dr. Kitovani spoke quietly and rapidly, "Politically, Abkhazia is an autonomous republic within the Georgian Soviet Socialist Republic. In past centuries Abkhazia has been ruled, in turn, by the Roman, Byzantine and Ottoman empires. When she fell under Russian domination in the 1860's many were forced to flee into what is now Turkey and, consequently, they lost their native language. Most of Abkhazian literature is held in the provincial archives, in the library in Sukumi, but little of it is published or copied. Much is passed down in song."

"And Khimbei is obviously upset ... about what?" Steven asked.

"Abkhazia has less than 100,000 people, and it's the size of, say, Puerto Rico. Unprotected, it would not be difficult for a larger power to swallow her up and, in the process, erase her entire language and culture. All that is unpublished or passed down in song could disappear overnight. Khimbei wants to prepare for what he fears is going to happen."

"I see," Steven said. "What does Khimbei think is going to happen?"

"He believes the Georgian army will eventually control the railroad between Tbilisi and Sukumi, and command the seaports on the coast."

"What do you think, Kit? You're Georgian. You live in Tbilisi."

"I don't think it will happen. Khimbei is right that there are some Georgians who hate Abkhazians, but there are many Georgians and other peoples who live in this country. Bigotry, unfortunately, is not unique to Georgia ... and it does not mean there will be civil war. There are too many other factors to consider."

Khfaf was chewing on a chocolate and watching Steven and Dr. Kitovani intently.

"And what is Tarkil's opinion?" Steven asked.

"He is accumulating information and is saying little. He has said, though, that Georgia will do nothing without direction from Moscow. I believe he is concerned, but he does not share the same sense of urgency that Khimbei is expressing."

The conversation continued for another half an hour. Megan, Shirali and Vasha-Tamava eventually said good night and then Khimbei, paying his respects, left for his family home across the village. Steven thanked the Lasurias one last time, and shut the bedroom door. Jake was sound asleep under his quilts.

Tarkil Lasuria sat alone before his fire. He was thinking back in time, sifting history and the deeds of many, calling upon all his knowledge, all his instincts. Firelight lit his leathered face. No smile would be possible tonight, and he fought to keep a smile, even a small one, in his heart.

Khfaf blew out the last candle in the house, crossed the large room and kissed her husband on the cheek. "Khimbei was in rare form tonight," she said sweetly.

Tarkil looked up at her. His eyes were full of great respect and much love. Once again, her few spoken words had said far more. He squeezed her hand gently and said, "You alone can always find a way to cheer me, Khfaf."

She asked him softly, "What is troubling you, dear one?"

Tarkil remained quiet for a moment, staring at the last of a long, eventful fire. From behind him, Khfaf wrapped her arms around his neck. She knew his thoughts.

Tarkil said quietly, so only they could hear, "Khimbei is right, Khfaf. He is right in everything he says. Some day his country will need him."

CHAPTER 3

The next morning Dr. Capterville was collecting water samples from streams and pools in the valley. He and colleagues had years before demonstrated that different types of water have different resonant properties, and emit varying degrees of energy. Therefore, Dr. Capterville theorized, it is possible that the water in these mountains may contain an energy field that is beneficial for the people in Bukol.

He was particularly interested in testing the water in the thermal pool he had just reached. Tengiz had directed him to it and had just left to find Dr. Tarba. This particular water percolated up through the rock from deep within the earth, and he was hoping to find unusual and medically exciting properties created by the tremendous pressure and electromagnetic fields within the earth's crust.

He had finished capping his last sample when he heard someone calling to him. It was Markhti Tarba on a ledge far above.

"Wait there!" Dr. Tarba was calling out, "wait there!"

A few minutes later Dr. Tarba came huffing and puffing through the rocks surrounding the pool.

"Steven, I've been trying to find you for an hour. Have you seen them yet? Did anyone tell you they were coming?"

"Calm down, Markhti. Tell me what you're talking about."

"The caravan! People! Horses! I spotted them this morning when I was way up ... there!" Dr. Tarba pointed straight up above them.

"Horses?" Steven asked.

"Yes, several. I counted fifteen people ... and two dogs. When I first saw them they were coming into the valley from another canyon ... way north."

"So," Steven thought, "there is another route into the valley! How many? Could this village be one of many, linked together like Swiss ski resorts?"

By the time Steven and Dr. Tarba reached the village the pack train had already arrived and there was considerable activity in the square by the church. The people were, indeed, from a village across the mountains and they were busy bartering goods and exchanging information. They had not been due to arrive for two weeks but they had come early because one of their children had become seriously ill.

Steven was right. It turned out that there were a number of villages linked together by trails and passages known only to the people of the mountains. And it became apparent that when a person fell ill, that person always headed for Bukol.

In a crowd of animated people Megan rushed up to Steven, "I'm glad I found you," she said. "They have asked that you take a look at a sick little boy."

"But I am not a physician."

"They know that, but Mr. Lasuria, himself, has asked that you see him."

"Where is the boy?"

"He's in the church with his parents, and Khfaf ... come, I'll take you."

The little boy was sitting on a bench just inside the door, with his parents on either side of him. His eyes grew wide when he saw Steven and Megan. He had been told of the strange people with a different voice from another land. He smiled at them.

"Well now," Steven said to him, "what seems to be the matter?"

Dr. Kitovani was not present, but the mother knew by sound that Steven was there to help. Khfaf squeezed her hand, telling her it was all right. She lifted the boy's shirt. Just below his rib cage, on his left side, protruded a tumor the size of an orange. Steven felt it and carefully explored around it. He could see the boy had become quite thin and he asked in sign language if he had been eating. He had eaten nothing solid for twenty-four hours.

Steven could not let his anguish show. There was nothing he could do for the boy. He expected that even modern surgical techniques could do little for him. He looked at Khfaf, trying his best to keep his feelings hidden.

"Dr. Kitovani ... must translate," he said simply.

Khfaf nodded that she understood. She reached into her sack-like purse. She lifted out and unrolled what appeared to be cheese cloth smeared with a white thick paste. She covered the tumor with it and tied it lightly around the boy's chest with a series of strings. She was still speaking with the parents when Steven and Megan left the church.

"All the training I've had and I can do nothing," Steven said sadly.

"Some day you will, Steven. From what Markhti and Khotsiya have said, your work is very important. Maybe your water is the answer. Maybe some day you will be able to help millions of little children."

"Thanks, Megan."

Just then, Marlin Moss approached them.

"So, Doctor," Moss asked sarcastically, "have you reconciled your Cluster Conversion Process with the long life of these people yet?"

Steven was shocked but did not allow his face to express it. CCP was his patent-pending process that only appeared in his patent applications, which the United States government had placed in a classified status, and in his most recent scientific paper ... that had not, as yet, been published.

"You are well informed, Mr. Moss. Since you are being so direct, allow me to do the same. What in the world are you doing on this expedition?"

"I just told you. I'm interested in how your Conversion Process will extend life."

"Yet your interest does nothing to further this mission, does it?" Steven said coolly.

"Let us not forget that the correlation of your data will be critical."

"To whom?" Steven asked pointedly.

"To you, of course."

"I think not. What you really mean is that you're looking out for the interests of RAM Pharmaceuticals."

"You could say that also," Moss said with a grin.

"And if in addition to long life you could uncover the key to the Conversion Process your employer would not be disappointed?"

Moss grinned. He said nothing.

"You may as well pack your bags, Mr. Moss, you'll get nothing from me, or this expedition. And I intend to speak with your employer on my return. Good bye, Mr. Moss."

It was mid-afternoon. Jake was out climbing the mountains with Tengiz and Jake's new-found friend, Markhti Tarba. The two shared many common interests, it turned out, and over-abundant enthusiasms to match their interests. Steven and Megan were alone at the Lasuria's long wooden table. Steven was storing his water samples in a protective

41

case, and Megan was busy writing descriptions and sorting camera film shot during the morning. The front door opened, flooding the room with light. Shirali Lasuria and Khotsiya Kitovani entered.

"I hear you needed me this afternoon," Dr. Kitovani said.

"To be honest, Kit, I'm glad you weren't there. We were able to leave gracefully without upsetting the parents. There is nothing I could have done for the boy."

"That is not why you were asked to be there."

"What?"

"You will see. But that's not why we're here. Shirali has invited you and Megan to join us. She wishes to show you a place that is very special to her. It's a ways up the mountain so we should leave now if we are to go."

"The last time I heard that line," Megan said, "we climbed five thousand feet."

Dr. Kitovani smiled politely, "The place is secret, but the path is easy.

"But Kit," Steven said, "we leave Bukol in the morning. There is so much left to do."

"Trust me, Steven. Get your coat. We will not be back until after dark. Shirali asks that you mention this to no one."

The sun was still touching the tallest peaks when the four of them arrived at the lake. Dr. Kitovani had been correct. The walk was easy, but twisting, and difficult to follow without the experience of having been there. The trail wound up the side of a mountain, opposite Steven's position in the valley earlier in the day.

One by one they had squeezed between two huge slabs of rock. It was only then that they had seen the lake, which was more like a large pool, a high mountain cirque with enormous boulders dropping out of sight yards below in the crystal clear water. Climbing to the sky on all sides, the flanks of the mountains formed the small but very deep lake. The surface of the lake was absolutely calm, like a sheet of glass.

Shirali put her finger to her lips to encourage them to remain quiet, but Megan could not contain herself.

"I've never ..." Megan whispered, "I swear I'm in another world ... you can even *feel* something different."

Shirali motioned them forward. She took them around, over and under boulders and rock shelves until they emerged onto a flat stone outcropping that hung over the lake like a large diving board. They all sat down, perched only five feet above the water.

"Shirali wants me to tell you that this is her favorite place," Dr. Kitovani said softly. "She asks that you remain quiet and still until the sun has left the peaks. She encourages you to look and listen in silence."

"But why the sun ...?" Steven started to ask.

Dr. Kitovani just looked at him.

Megan was so mystified and bewildered she was not aware she was speaking her thoughts aloud, "There could be a huge prehistoric bird soaring in this sky ... a dinosaur might come crashing through those rocks ...."

"Hush, Megan!" Dr. Kitovani whispered, "If you stay quiet and perfectly still, you may get to see your dinosaur."

No one said another word. All was perfectly quiet. Looking up they could see the top of the world, looking below, clear glass that gradually became deep green-blue. Surrounding the pool, immense boulders and stone slabs reached downward into the frigid water. How far, they could not guess.

Minutes of wonder passed. Shirali's sunlight crept up the tips of the snow covered peaks. A pebble broke loose high above the group. It clacked and cracked with clear, precise sounds as it fell to the lake. There was a final strike, still far above them, then seconds later the pebble crashed with all its might into the placid lake. Concentric liquid circles moved steadily outward, searching, reaching. Impatient boulders, waiting so long, caught the rings and hurled them back across the lake in patterns impossible to draw. Then stillness was ordered. Boulders assumed their positions. Energy was spent. The surface was once again glass.

More minutes passed. Steven and Megan were in a trance, detached by their physical surroundings. Suddenly, Shirali tapped Dr. Kitovani on his knee. She pointed across the pool to the right.

Dr. Kitovani nudged Steven, then Megan, and put his finger to his lips signaling quiet. He pointed across the pool.

What they saw first appeared to be a sharp knife blade, tip straight up, slicing through the water. It was weaving slowly, methodically, following the shoreline and coming toward them.

Steven almost asked, "What is it?" but caught himself in time. Megan's eyes were as big as saucers. With the dorsal fin some twenty feet from them, it came into full view.

"Heavens!" Megan uttered.

"There is your dinosaur, Megan," Dr. Kitovani said with fascination. He could not take his eyes off the creature. None of them could.

"It's incredible!" Steven said, "it must weigh a ton!"

"Three thousand pounds," Dr. Kitovani concluded, "maybe a bit less."

"It looks something like a huge shark," Steven said excitedly, "but slower ... and its whole body is covered with armor plates! Its entire head is protected by plates, like a dinosaur."

The giant fish cruised mechanically, directly below them, its protective plates sliding over one another as its body ponderously waved from side to side, propelling itself forward with a sharp sickle shaped tail.

"Heavens!" Megan repeated, "Kit! What is it?"

"It is the great Beluga, Megan. It is a sturgeon."

"It looks like a dinosaur!"

"I know, Megan, they've been swimming the seas since the time of the dinosaurs. Its ancestors first appeared in the Jurassic Period."

"Incredible."

"They have no bone, only cartilage," Dr. Kitovani continued proudly. "And they have no teeth. They feed by sucking food into their mouths."

"Beluga caviar!" Steven exclaimed.

"A thousand dollars a pound, last I checked," Dr. Kitovani said. "It is measured by the ounce, like gold."

"How did a three thousand pound sturgeon get way up here?" Steven asked. It was Steven's nature to always find out why things got to be where they got to be.

"I do not know, Steven. I believe Shirali knows the secret of the majestic fish, but no one has told me."

"Why don't you ask her."

"This is her place. She will tell us when she wishes."

Steven persisted, "But where could it have come from, Kit?"

"Perhaps from the Caspian Sea just to the east of here. Ninety percent of the world's black caviar comes from there."

"But, Kit, we're at ten thousand feet."

"Steven, I do not have the answer you seek," Dr. Kitovani said patiently. "It is well known that sturgeons have migrated a thousand miles from the southern reaches of the Caspian Sea up the Volga River to spawning grounds north of Moscow. A thousand miles, Steven! An incredible journey."

Steven thought it best to ask no more, but Dr. Kitovani continued, as if thinking out loud, "Man has built dams on the Volga, Terek and Kuma rivers, the three major rivers flowing to the Caspian. The sturgeons are now unable to reach their ancient spawning grounds ... but the Beluga can live for a hundred years ... and the headwaters of the Kuma River are not far from here ... hmm ... I wonder?"

The giant sturgeon passed them, lowered its position in the water and with one last elegant wave of its tail, disappeared below the surface.

The last ripple of the Beluga's presence made its way across the lake. There was no more sunlight upon the peaks, and the brighter stars were appearing in the sky.

"This water," Steven moaned, "I wish I had been ready to take samples. Who knows what we might find? The properties of the surrounding rock alone ...."

Dr. Kitovani placed a hand on Steven's arm to get his attention. Then he unzipped the large pocket on the left side of his safari jacket and lifted out three glass vials the size of cigar containers.

"I hope you will forgive me, doctor, but I took these from your sample case before we left. I could not tell you where we were going and I expected you would be wanting them."

"Kit, you are priceless."

Suddenly Steven froze. He listened. "There it is again!" he said. "Those voices, people singing."

Steven rubbed his ears, concentrating ... listening. "I think maybe I'll need a long rest when I get home."

Dr. Kitovani smiled, "Your ears do not deceive you, Steven."

The beautiful sound increased slightly, no musical instruments, just people singing, singing wonderfully, far away.

"I knew it!" Steven said, "the same voices I've heard before ... so did Jake, down below the falls. Meg, have you heard any mountain singing?"

Megan was flustered. Steven had called her 'Meg' for the first time. Only her immediate family had ever called her Meg, and he had said it so naturally. She liked it.

"Umm ... every day," she said, "but mostly in the early evening. Except down in the lower canyon. They were singing all the time when we were down there."

"But ... why didn't you say something?"

"Why didn't you ask?" she answered cheerfully.

Shirali was standing against a boulder to one side of the stone shelf, trying not to laugh.

"Kit, who are they?" Steven asked.

Dr. Kitovani remained silent for a while. The voices were becoming stronger. He recognized the ballad of war and triumph being sung, and he knew it to be just beginning.

Gazing at the sky and listening to the singing in the dark, Shirali's smile melted away. She was overwhelmed by intense emotions that only one of her culture and background could fully understand. She had heard this song a hundred times, yet her eyes once again became full and overflowed.

Dr. Kitovani finally answered, "It is the voice of Abkhazia, Steven. It is the history of Abkhazia, her legends, her culture ... in song. They are the Nartaa Long-Living Men's Choir, a choir of elders voicing experience found nowhere else in the world. They can be heard throughout the mountains most of the year."

Another song began, this time loud and clear as the night, falling down upon their lake as if it were being sung in front of them upon a stage. Steven and Megan leaned back against a smooth curving rock and looked up, listening. They needed no interpreter. The song began in low oboe tones with war and grief, then messages of wisdom and understanding, and finally, victory and joy.

Shirali was sobbing. And it was not only the music that brought her so much joy. She was truly happy that people from the west, people she knew she could trust, were beginning to understand her family, her people and her life. She was happy, very happy. She knew the future for her would be meaningful. She knew her painful decision to leave Bukol had been correct.

"We'd best be getting back," Dr. Kitovani said energetically.

***

Early the next morning, Steven quietly left the Lasuria house and headed for the stream that ran through the apple trees. He wanted to be alone on this last morning in Bukol, to see the sunlight bathe the mountain tops and run down the cliffs until it warmed the trees. He wanted to listen to the stream, to drink of the water he believed in. Before he left for civilizations below, he wanted to absorb as much as he could of the wonderful land he wished he could call his home.

Reaching the stream he wandered among trees laden with dark red apples, and ... there was Shirali, talking with Megan, who was combing her hair.

Megan saw him first and said, "Steven! Shirali has the most wonderful news. Come and listen!"

"Meg, what are you ...?

"Steven, Shirali is coming to America ... some day. Isn't it exciting?"

"Well, yes, of course."

When Steven was within reach, Shirali took his hand firmly. She did the same with Megan who was on her other side. She brought them together and placed their hands tightly between hers. She looked upon Steven's face in a loving but penetrating way, and then did the same with Megan. In English, with flawless diction but with a hint of her lilting Abkhazian tongue, Shirali said, "There comes a time when pretending must stop, and life must go forward."

"Shirali!" Steven exclaimed, "you speak English!"

With their hands still pressed between hers, Shirali said, "There is always more to learn, and many to care for, but you must be patient, especially you, Steven."

"But ...?"

With a thoughtfulness and severity that surprised them, Shirali said slowly, "There is much good in the world, but there is also evil ... evil that you will not always be able to see. It is through faith that you will succeed. You must have faith."

"Faith in what?" Megan asked quickly.

"Faith is the substance of things hoped for, the evidence of things not seen."

Megan tried to absorb the meaning of what she had said, and then asked, "But faith in what?"

"That is something you will have to discover together."

That was all she said. She let go of their hands and she disappeared into the apple trees. They did not see her again ... for a long, long time.

At the crest of the switch back trail, still early in the morning, the entire village, man, woman, child and several

49

goats had gathered to bid their new friends farewell, long life and safe journey.

Jake was there, still rubbing his eyes and stretching his arms wide. His backpack, prepared by Khfaf the night before, was slung across one shoulder. Even half asleep, he was intent upon helping his brother discover the secret of long life. He had decided the answer was exercise, Abkhazian coffee, vodka and the sour milk kefir. So he had gotten out of bed, stretched vigorously, and had asked Khfaf to fill him a large mug with ample and equal amounts of each. The mug was now almost empty and Jake was almost ready to depart.

Tengiz, at his own request, would again take the lead. Tarkil Lasuria had arranged for several villagers to help carry their samples and supplies to the lower trail head where, hopefully, the old green bus would be waiting for them. The bulk of the weight was courtesy of Markhti Tarba who had accumulated a good portion of the mountain range for his studies.

"Markhti," Steven asked, "are you sure you have enough?"

"For now," Dr. Tarba mumbled, organizing his sample boxes. "But I can't wait to come back ... I have heard of a magnificent pool on the other side of the valley with incredible magnetic boulders, and mountains that stretch to the sky! And the music! They say the rocks can sing! Dr. Capterville, are you certain we must leave today?"

"Yes, Markhti, we must," Steven insisted, "and where is Mr. Moss? Tengiz says we must be off."

Dr. Kitovani put his hand on Steven's shoulder, "Steven, Tengiz has said that Mr. Moss left by himself yesterday afternoon. He was seen speaking with you, then he packed his things and left down the trail without saying a word to anyone."

"Very well," Steven said, "then I suppose we are ready."

Just then the earth shook. It was very brief, a second or two and no more.

"What was that?" a startled Megan Rankin asked.

"Only an earthquake," Dr. Kitovani said easily, "a small one. They are common in the mountains."

"Only!" Megan said, "... goodness!"

Steven was watching the villagers who were all talking and waving as if nothing had happened.

"Where is Tarkil?" Steven asked. "We must say good-bye to our host."

Looking through the crowd Steven saw Khfaf Lasuria coming toward him. With respect, the villagers parted and encouraged her to pass. Holding her hand and walking beside her was the little boy from the church. Steven bent down to his knees to talk with the boy, but before Steven could speak, Khfaf raised the little boy's shirt and peeled away the cheesecloth bandage. The tumor had vanished. There was some skin discoloration and he was still thin ... but the tumor was gone. The little boy was smiling, he was laughing, and he threw his arms around Dr. Capterville and squeezed as hard as he could.

"This is the first time since I've been a doctor that I've felt like a doctor," Steven thought, "and I have done nothing."

Khfaf came close to Steven and stared into his eyes. She put her open hands on either side of his face and squeezed gently with discerning fingertips. She looked at him. She said something soothing he could not understand, and she walked back through her people. Steven never saw her again.

"We must be going, Steven," Dr. Kitovani was saying.

"But where is Tarkil?" Steven asked again, "I will not leave without seeing him."

"He is right behind you," Dr. Kitovani said. "Mr. Lasuria has asked me to tell you that you are his friend and he is sorry to see you leave. He says to tell you that you are welcome any ...."

While Dr. Kitovani was still translating, Tarkil Lasuria and Dr. Steven Capterville embraced. Not fully expressed until now, an unbreakable bond between centuries, racial contrasts and cultures had been formed. Whatever it was that allowed instant friendship had worked doubly fast with Tarkil Lasuria and Steven Capterville. They were genuinely fond of one another. They had become blood brothers in an uncertain world.

Steven removed the precious watch from his left wrist. He handed it to Tarkil and said, "My great-grandfather gave this to me. I would like you to have it."

Dr. Kitovani translated for Tarkil as Steven took his first steps down the mountain.

"Steven!" Dr. Kitovani called down, "Mr. Lasuria says it is beautiful but, with all due respect, a timepiece is not needed in the mountains. He does not wish to know the time."

Steven was well down the trail and shouted back, "Tell him, I know that. The darned thing hasn't worked for years."

The roaring laughter of Tarkil Lasuria, it was later told in song, could be heard echoing forever through the valleys of his cherished land ... Abkhazia, country of the soul.

CHAPTER 4

The same month - August, 1983
London

The opulent office in London's financial district was divided into three distinct conversational clusters, but the expensive mahogany and green leather furniture was arranged in such a way that the library blended spatially with the sitting area, and both, in turn, focused forcefully on Mr. Otterstein's massive marble topped desk. Four heavy wing back chairs formed a semi-circle around the inlaid front panel of the desk. The entire room was decorated impeccably with rare lamps and expensive esoteric objects from around the world.

But the interior designer responsible for the elegant room would never have envisioned such a depressingly low level of light. At mid-morning the office was dark. Three ceiling lights above the library's three bookcases had been turned to their lowest setting. The only other light entering the room filtered through the leaded glass window directly behind the desk.

It was here, before the beveled window, that Lucius Otterstein stood, a short trim man made even smaller by his surroundings. He wore a hand tailored dark gray suit. His thinning graying hair he had combed from one side of his head to the other. He stood motionless, in thought, staring out the window at the falling rain, waiting for his last associate to arrive. A few inches from his pallid face, silver rain drops were running down the sides of diamond shaped lead strips, collecting, and then dripping with monotonous taps on the sill below. All else was oppressively quiet.

Two of the four wing back chairs were occupied. The figures sat in silence several feet below an undisturbed blanket of gray cigar smoke that was eerily lit from above by the three library lights. The door to the office opened and very quietly a tall man crossed the room and seated himself next to the others.

Lucius Otterstein continued to stare out the window, twisting with his small fingers an ever-present, smoldering cigar. Slowly he turned, disturbing ever so slightly the smoke layered just above his head.

"Marlin, you are late," he demanded, smoke releasing from his nostrils.

Marlin Moss did not respond.

"Marlin, our software, can it be completed and loaded without notice ... within our ten year plan?"

"Without question," Marlin Moss replied, "but the others must be ready."

A sturdy, severe woman with close cropped black hair fidgeted in her chair, noticeably disturbed by Moss's comment.

"Edith, I can see you have confidence in your readiness," Lucius said.

Edith Wolman said nothing. She knew the others respected her financial prowess.

Lucius persisted, "Marlin does not question your abilities, I am sure, but what of those you must ... trust?"

"I trust no one," she said with no emotion.

"All right then, those with whom you will have to work closely. You cannot be expected to achieve your goals, our goals, without help."

"What are you getting at, Lucius? I know you. Something's on your mind."

"I am concerned about Mr. Bulow the banker."

"He has been reliable ... but I will watch him."

Looking toward the ceiling, Lucius blew a cloud of smoke upward. His eyes lowered and riveted on the third chair, "Giancarlo, your infiltration of the terrorist groups has begun?"

"Yes," Giancarlo Panatta answered, "we are becoming well positioned."

"Excellent!" Lucius barked.

Giancarlo Panatta relaxed, his athletic Roman frame sinking with confidence into the brass-nailed leather chair.

Lucius lay his spent but burning cigar in a large crystal ashtray and lifted a fresh one from the antique humidor on his desk. He turned his back to his guests and once again looked out the window. The rain had stopped but drops were still tapping on the outside sill.

Without turning, Lucius said, "Marlin, Mr. Weaver at RAM Pharmaceuticals tells me you were disappointed in your trip."

"I learned nothing," Marlin Moss responded.

"But you must have come up with something," Lucius prodded.

"They're up to something ... I just couldn't find out what."

"Who are 'they'?" Lucius asked, turning around.

"That Capterville fellow, and his girlfriend. They kept whispering about some kefir, a goat milk culture the old people gave us."

"I see," Lucius puffed.

"Capterville was taking water samples and a geologist, that Tarba fellow, was going nuts collecting bags of rocks and passing information to Capterville."

"What about the Cluster Process?" Lucius asked raising his eyebrows.

"He was on to me. I got nothing new."

"Too bad."

Edith Wolman and Giancarlo Panatta both shifted in their chairs.

"Well, it's not like I had a cover," Moss said defensively. "I was told to leave at once. There was no time to prepare. You all know that."

"No one blames you, Marlin. You had no notice," Lucius Otterstein said. "But this is precisely the kind of blunder we must avoid in the future ... if we are to accomplish our objectives."

Lucius thought for a long while, twisting his new cigar. The others remained motionless and silent.

"Tell me, Marlin, this ... kefir, you called it ... do you think it might have something to do with Dr. Capterville's water solutions?"

"No, I don't think so, but they're up to something for sure."

"Very well. We will monitor the situation closely without drawing attention to ourselves. Giancarlo, any future intelligence gathering will be your responsibility. Marlin is to concentrate on his computer networking. Edith, you know your responsibilities. Without your financial positioning we cannot move forward. We will meet at our scheduled time next week. That will be all for today."

The three rose and departed swiftly, creating swirls in the thick layer of smoke. Lucius followed them and made certain his office door was locked. He went quietly to the library and pulled a hidden lever on the side of the far bookcase. The bookcase swung open like a door. From the long high-back library couch two human figures stood, faced one another, nodded, then silently passed into the dark beyond the bookcase. Lucius Otterstein shut the bookcase, listening for the low click that assured its closure. He walked back to his desk and pressed his intercom.

"Yes, sir?"

"Get me Mr. Weaver at RAM Pharmaceuticals."

He tapped the top end of his gold pen impatiently upon his marbled desk. Lucius Otterstein wanted answers.

CHAPTER 5

Ten years later - August, 1993
Sukumi, Abkhazia

Commander Khimbei Ladariya was carrying a fully loaded Kalashnikov assault rifle, his finger resting against the trigger guard. The barrel was still warm. Many Georgians and many Abkhazians had died this morning. He and his sister, Vasha-Tamava, walked cautiously through the Sukumi Airport terminal building, their boots crushing shards of glass and plaster. The beautiful tile and plaster dome was now riddled with bullet holes and cracked by the shock of exploding grenades. They were the only living people at the airport.

"Vasha, bring the car around. We must check the library downtown."

Outside, the airfield was pockmarked with craters. Pile upon pile of Russian made bombs surrounded the terminal building waiting for someone to explode them. The remains of a Georgian transport plane, still full of Georgian troops, billowed with clouds of black smoke in the center of the runway. Commander Ladariya's men had hit the slow moving craft with a heat seeking missile just as it was touching down.

The airport was empty. Except for those in hiding and a handful of Abkhazian troops, Sukumi was empty. The Georgians, at least temporarily, were in retreat. Three separate Abkhazian companies, following Commander Ladariya's orders, were forcing them back into Georgia to the east.

Weary of days and nights of fighting, weary of the horrible sounds of war, Khimbei lowered himself into one of the terminal's few remaining benches. Even in fatigue he must think, he must plan, he must lead. It was to him that Abkhazia now looked for her salvation. He had studied his country's history. At his great-uncle's urging he had learned the languages, customs and political processes of the peoples around him. Now he must apply all that he had learned. Now he must be wise.

"Why must so many innocents die?" he asked himself rhetorically. "Perhaps, perhaps it will help to think back ... one more time."

Commander Khimbei Ladariya rested his head against the back of the bench and looked up at the battered ceiling. Far to the east he could hear the muted sounds of gunfire.

"We trace our roots two thousand years," he thought back, "even under Soviet rule, Abkhazia and Georgia were separate republics ... then Stalin came, Joseph Stalin ... 1931 ... he abolished the Abkhazian Soviet Republic and made us an autonomous region within Georgia, and subjected us to direct administrative control from Tbilisi. They banned our language and moved Georgians into our country to assimilate us, but we fought back, we regained legal status for our language ... why must we always fight for what is ours? ... we built a university, a television station and forced a majority in Abkhazia's Parliament."

There was a volley of gunshots and artillery explosions in the distance, then quiet. Khimbei sighed, and forced himself to think.

"When the Soviet Union fell apart in 1991 ... yes, Tarkil, you were right after all ... Tbilisi abolished the Georgian constitution that gave us our rights. And last summer when we revived our own 1925 Abkhazian constitution, the Georgian army poured into our land with tanks and troops and began the slaughter of our people."

Vasha-Tamava pulled up to the main door in a Russian made compact car. She left the engine running and came to Khimbei. She could tell he was thinking. The brother she adored possessed the same creased frown she was used to seeing on their great-uncle Tarkil when he was deep in thought.

"What are your thoughts, Khimbei?"

"The Red Army has given us help this time, but I wonder about the future. The new Georgian president used to be the Foreign Minister in Moscow. He has fought for Georgian independence, but now ...."

"He will fight even harder," Vasha-Tamava interrupted.

"Yes, but we have defeated him this time, Vasha, we have beaten him badly, with an army one-sixth the size of his."

"Thanks to you," Vasha-Tamava said proudly.

"His forces remain much larger than ours, and he knows we have been supported by Russian equipment and supplies."

"So we have beaten him, Khimbei."

"But he has been humiliated politically. In such a position he is likely to turn to Moscow where he is very well connected. He will probably try to enroll Georgia in the Commonwealth of Independent States."

"And ... we lose the support of Russia, our strongest ally."

"Yes, Vasha, the Commonwealth of Independent States now counts eleven former Soviet republics but it is dominated by Russia. It will make it much harder for us to keep the support we have now if Georgia is admitted."

"But Russia still needs us, Khimbei! They need our sea ports. And you have brought together our mountain tribesmen, the Afghan veterans and the Cossacks. Think back, Khimbei, when no one would listen to you. You are the reason we have come this far. You will find a way."

Khimbei put his hand on his sister's cheek. "Ah, Vasha, you have always been my greatest strength. I pray to God you are right."

"We know the mountains, Khimbei!" Vasha-Tamava said defiantly. "The mountain people will not die!"

Their small compact car had been the only moving vehicle on the roads from the airport to central Sukumi. What they had seen had sickened them. Once a land of beauty and architectural subtlety, it was now an idle war zone, houses and buildings bombed, burned and looted. Dead human bodies were missing fingers, taken as tokens by opposite sides in a bloody war of ethnic cleansing.

Vasha-Tamava Ladariya and her brother Khimbei now walked in horror through the ashes of the roofless and burned central library. Chapters of priceless manuscripts, books and records, the written and pictorial history of Abkhazia lay smoldering on the ground.

"The worst I have feared has come to pass," Khimbei said in a low angry voice.

They stood together in the center of the great main room. The intricate vaulted ceiling, once the pride of the city, a symbol of centuries of knowledge, was collapsed in ruins below their feet. Minutes passed. Neither of them could speak. Their sorrow, their grief, was too great.

Then, in the quiet, they heard footsteps.

"Get down, Vasha!" Khimbei whispered.

"Whoever it is ... is coming in through the back," Vasha whispered back.

The footsteps became louder, and closer, crushing fallen rock. Silently, Khimbei lowered the barrel of his rifle and moved his finger from the trigger guard. Vasha readied the ever-present knife at her side, then firmly gripped her pistol in both hands.

The footsteps stopped. Whoever it was, was listening. Then a voice called out.

"Commander Ladariya! ... Khimbei! ... I watched you drive up." The words echoed through the remains of the library.

Khimbei sighed with relief.

"Thank God," Vasha-Tamava exclaimed, "it's Tengiz."

Khimbei called back, "We are over here, Colonel!"

The three relatives came together and embraced.

"How much were you able to save from the library before the attack?" Khimbei asked quickly.

Colonel Tengiz Lasuria looked down, pushing glass and black ash with his boot, "Not enough, Commander, but more than we expected. At your command we have been moving the unpublished materials to the mountains for weeks ... but they struck without warning. They hit the building with incendiaries, the dome collapsed and everything started to burn."

"The pigs!" Vasha-Tamava spit.

"It was the first thing they did," the Colonel continued, "before your first company could engage ... there was confusion, a U.N. team, the Red Cross, the fire department all came ... but their soldiers blocked the way. They would let no one pass. They just laughed, and watched the building burn."

Colonel Tengiz Lasuria, wiry, tough, respected and experienced, second in command to his grand-nephew Khimbei, appeared exhausted and unusually emotional.

"They want to make certain there is no trace of our culture left," Khimbei said angrily. "That is why they have destroyed our archives. They want us absorbed into their

62

own civilization. They want our grandchildren to be Georgian babies."

"They arrested the head of the U.N. team," Tengiz sighed, "and the Red Cross chief. Then they started shooting. Everyone scattered. While they were shooting we got the last of the Sagas out the back ...."

"Then you saved *all* the Nart Sagas?" Khimbei asked in astonishment.

"They are safe for now."

"But that is incredible, Tengiz!" Vasha-Tamava said with delight. "Our heroic legends, the matriarch, the ninety-nine sons ... you have saved our history, Tengiz!" She threw her arms around him and kissed him.

"It was made possible by the foresight of your brother. Had it not been for him ...."

"And with the Choir," Vasha-Tamava said excitedly, "the rest of our legends will survive."

Tengiz glanced at Khimbei uncomfortably. The glee on Vasha-Tamava's face vanished.

"What is wrong, Tengiz?"

Tengiz sighed, "Several of the Nartaa Choir have already been hunted down and killed. At least twenty of their relatives have died."

Suppressing a scream, Vasha-Tamava picked up a large object and hurled it furiously against the far wall.

"That is sad, very sad," Khimbei said. "The rest of the choir members must go to the mountains where we can defend them."

"Most are already there," Tengiz replied. "We have ample provisions, and remain mobile. We can move our camps at will."

"Excellent."

There was quiet for a time. Commander Ladariya broke the silence.

"Tell me, Colonel, how is your brother, Tarkil. He and Khfaf are well, I trust?"

"Yes," Tengiz answered, "and he has a message for you. He says to never give up, and that he and Khfaf are thinking of you always. He always knew you would serve your country well ... he is very sorry that it had to be so soon and under such circumstances."

"We will never give up!" Vasha-Tamava confirmed.

"You two have always been his favorites, you know. He loves you very much."

"And what of our great-aunt, Khfaf?" Khimbei asked.

"She tends her goats, grows her kefir and somehow heals all who need her."

"She still smokes?" Vasha-Tamava asked.

"Of course," Tengiz answered, "and she has her morning vodka, and in her quiet way she makes certain Tarkil's decisions are wise."

"Has she forgiven Shirali for leaving?" Vasha-Tamava wanted to know.

"She and Tarkil still fight like a couple of old roosters about Shirali leaving Bukol. In all their decades, they disagree about nothing. But Shirali! Ahh! It never ends."

"At least she is safe in the west."

There was another time of quiet and thought, then Tengiz spoke.

"I am afraid I have further bad news."

"What is it, Colonel?"

"At headquarters, this morning ... a coded message from our contact in Moscow. Georgia is going into the C.I.S.. There will be no more assistance, officially, at least."

"Damn!"

"Moscow has pledged troops to keep the rail lines open between Tbilisi and Sukumi. Officially, they will not assume a combat role unless the trains are attacked."

"I need to inspect our front lines immediately," Commander Ladariya said with force. "We must determine where to consolidate and when. Colonel, take your men and secure the low passes."

"Yes, sir."

"Vasha, we leave for the front."

Tengiz moved off to the rear of the library building, swiftly and quietly as a cat.

Khimbei called after him, "Tengiz, my friend, be cautious! If anything happens to me, you are in charge!"

Turning to his sister, he said, "Vasha, there is no time to lose."

Vasha-Tamava's small sturdy body slid easily into the passenger's seat. Her round dark eyes, set in a round expressive face, flashed with anticipation, with anger, with suppressed fear.

Khimbei was thinking fast, and moving fast. He folded his tall strong frame into the small car and started the engine. He stared straight ahead for a moment, his angular profile prominent behind the wheel.

"It's hard to believe ..." Khimbei said, clutching the steering wheel with one hand, and shifting into gear with the other.

"What, Khimbei?"

"That Tengiz, with all that he does, is almost as old as his brother."

The little car raced out of Sukumi to the northeast. The long valley leading to their high family home was directly in front of them, and on either side of the road as they sped by, fields of tangerines hung rotting on withered branches.

They veered to the right, directly to the east, in search of their forces. The orders Commander Ladariya had given were to push to the east without exposing their flanks. They must not over extend themselves. The enemy must not be allowed to cut them off from behind.

There was a distant blast. A round from the cannon of a Russian tank exploded just in front of them. Both Khimbei and Vasha-Tamava were thrown from the speeding car as it flipped in the air, landed upside down and screeched horribly to a flaming stop in the middle of the road. Khimbei flew to the left side of the road, landed in soft grass and mud, and crawled on his stomach behind a burned out bus. Vasha-Tamava was thrown into a ditch on the right side of the road.

Khimbei called to her. There was no answer.

Another blast could be heard, then a fast whine as a shell passed over them and exploded behind them.

"Khimbei!" Vasha-Tamava called to him, "My arm is broken."

"Stay down!" he yelled.

Enemy troops were running across the field at them, in front of the grinding metal treads of the tank. Bullets began piercing the bus making circular holes with sharp warped edges.

"Stay down!" Khimbei yelled.

A round struck the bus above his head, ricocheted, and fell harmlessly into his lap. He picked it up, turning it in his fingers. It was still hot, a graceful miniature sculpture, an instrument of death.

"Mined in Abkhazia by Georgians, to kill Abkhazians ... Oh, no! ... No! ... Vasha, go back!"

Vasha-Tamava was running as fast as she could across the road to her brother. Shots rang out. The enemy was near. She leaped behind the bus and rolled in pain into the ditch beside her brother. She was holding her arm and grimacing.

"You never have followed my orders, little one."

"Tarkil said to never give up!" she winced.

The tank had stopped. The firing had stopped. The enemy soldiers, only twenty yards away were surrounding the bus. Commander Ladariya could hear talking, orders shouted.

Lying next to her brother, Vasha-Tamava stared into his eyes with that piercing family look, "What are you orders now, Commander?"

A shot rang out. The bullet went through Vasha-Tamava's heart and slammed her against the ground. Khimbei pulled her into his arms and pressed her head against his chest. Squeezing her as hard as he could, he rocked back and forth moaning unintelligible words, words from his soul, words between himself, his sister and God.

He heard voices close by. He heard the laughter of the enemy. He heard footsteps. "Vasha! Vasha!" he cried. From the corner of his eye he could see a rifle barrel rise to him.

The ground began to shake, lightly at first. There was no more laughter from the enemy. Then the main jolt hit. The earthquake split apart the earth underneath the bus and the shock threw Khimbei and the body of Vasha-Tamava thirty feet away. A series of parallel fissures opened across the field. The tank disappeared into the earth. Soldiers ran for their lives screaming. One of the world's greatest earthquakes wrenched the land and shook the Caucasus Mountain Range as though it were a string of beads ... and then suddenly, it let go.

Lying on the still earth Khimbei held his sister's hand. Before he lost consciousness, Commander Ladariya looked up to the mountains, into the valley that was home. Clouds of dust and debris rose thousands of feet into the air. The valley had taken a different shape.

"Vasha, my love, I will never give up."

He squeezed her hand one last time ... and there was darkness.

CHAPTER 6

Tarkil and Khfaf sat alone at the far end of the scarred wooden table that had been the centerpiece of the Lasuria family home since before memory. Nighttime firelight once again lit the room and danced across their leathered timeless faces ... faces creased with the unbearable horror that had just befallen them.

Unable to contain the wrenching emotions within her, Khfaf Lasuria screamed to the world, "It is gone! Our family is gone! Everyone is gone!"

Quietly she collapsed into her husband's arms. She groaned into his chest, "It is gone, Tarkil, it is gone."

Outside, brilliant sparkling stars pressed down upon the chill, still mountain air that belied the violence wrought upon this once peaceful Abkhazian village. The earthquake had not rumbled, nor rolled nor given any warning. It was the sudden sharp thunderous crack of Russian alps fighting for position. In an instant the tiny village of Bukol had disappeared. No barking dogs, no crying babies, no shouts for help. The village had vanished.

The only evidence of human life at ten thousand feet was a dozen well-tended tea shrubs, a few apple trees and the Lasuria's small three room stone house that was now perched on a ledge, atop a sheer thousand foot granite wall.

Tarkil Lasuria, in his one hundred seventy three years of life, had survived wars, plagues and all manner of human discord. Yet this, to him, was the most intolerable.

He was torn inside, but he knew it was his turn to be strong. He adored Khfaf who was ten years his senior, and in their one hundred fifty three years of marriage, despite his position, rank and honors, it had always been Khfaf who had been the strongest and most decisive in times of true crisis.

But this time God or something had taken from her almost everything that was of importance to her. Their relatives, save those below, had died this night. Their friends from decades of living had been crushed in the dark. A way of life had been destroyed and their ancestral village for centuries, was gone forever.

Tarkil mustered his strength and spoke with authority and resolve, "Khfaf, my love, we must persist and look to God for our strength. We must remember the lessons of the prophets and try to ...."

"Do not talk of a God who would ..." but she forced herself to stop. She knew in her heart he was right. She knew in her heart she would regret her words.

With an even, soothing voice, Tarkil continued, "One daughter is alive and well in America. Our great-grandchildren, and our great-great-grandchildren and our great-great-great-grandchildren are alive and well down below."

With that, Tarkil fell silent. He knew instinctively not to speak, not to touch her, not to move. No matter the circumstances or how grave the pain, these few words had always brought her cheer.

After what seemed like hours, Khfaf turned to him and looked into his eyes with an emptiness he had never seen before. He guessed what she was thinking.

"There is war below," she said.

"But there is hope."

He stared at her with his piercing eyes for the longest time, and at last he found the slightest smile, undetectable by anyone but him. He wrapped his arms around her and held her tightly.

"It is gone," Khfaf had cried, and Tarkil knew quite well what she meant. She spoke not only of her family, her friends, her village. She was deeply troubled at the loss of something she knew in her innermost thoughts was to have an influence that went far beyond her little world.

At dawn Tarkil and Khfaf Lasuria pushed open the heavy wooden door of their house and stepped into a world much changed. All the familiar shapes of centuries past ... the landscape, even mountains, had shifted as though weight was of no concern. Birds chirped and butterflies floated through the air claiming no change, and precious warmth from the morning sun poured into the new alpine valley.

Tarkil quietly set up a small table and two chairs in the sunshine a few feet from the house. He waited for Khfaf to finish making their tea. Khfaf was always singing as she sipped her vodka and made the morning tea. Today, Khfaf had determined, would be no exception.

They sat without talking for the longest time, sipping tea and trying to understand. Tarkil looked down upon the old watch that had been a part of his wrist for the past ten years. He rubbed it lightly, as he always did, with the long right sleeve of his black silk shirt.

"I wonder how my young Steven is getting along?" It was a question he asked himself every day with a great deal of feeling. It was a question, he knew, that all elders ask themselves every day, and a question the young ones only fully understand when they too become old.

Tarkil had a sip of tea, then set the cup down on its saucer. His thoughts went to his brother, Tengiz. "Ah, Tengiz! Perhaps back then we should have told Steven who you really are ... but no, we needed caution with the others. I pray for you, my brother ... take good care of our Vasha, and our Khimbei."

Tarkil looked over the cliff, down toward the sea, toward war. In his thoughts he said to Tengiz, "At least you have a watch that works, my brother ... I expect you are needing it these days."

When Tarkil looked up, he noticed Khfaf gazing across their new valley. Tarkil had circled the house and found it untouched, an island in a sea of transformation. Not ten feet from Tarkil's chair was the edge of the cliff. Behind the house, where once lay fields of apples and tea, stood the base of an immense vertical mountain wall. A series of three majestic waterfalls, not present just hours before, cascaded from above and fell past them down into the valley.

Tarkil took another sip, placed his cup down with a rattle and asked, "Do you think we could grow it back in the small amount of milk we have here?"

"You know the little ones will not reproduce without the presence of the parent group," Khfaf replied.

"But, Khfaf, might we not find a lost parent somewhere in all of ... this?" As he spoke his eyes surveyed the destruction about him and he knew it to be impossible.

"Tarkil, my love, you are always the optimist. We have no goats left, thus we have no milk for growing. And as energetic as we both are, there is no way we can possibly get down from here."

"Hmm ..." Tarkil watched her closely, not wanting to press his thoughts too quickly. He could sense her emotion.

Khfaf looked upward, past the blue of the sky, "God gave the kefir to our village thousands of years ago and now it is gone. We have had special health, long life, our children, our ... oh, God ... now everything is gone."

"Not quite," Tarkil barked with a touch of fierceness.

Her eyes went to him, "What do you mean, Tarkil?"

"I speak of Shirali," Tarkil stated firmly.

"Oh dear, I had forgotten," moaned Khfaf.

"I think not, my love."

Tarkil debated the wisdom of raising the one issue the two of them had disagreed so vehemently about for most of their marriage. He decided that now it might help.

"If Shirali had not taken the kefir with her," Tarkil insisted, "all the parent samples would be dead ... down there." Tarkil pointed with his bony finger over the edge of the cliff.

"Perhaps you are right, Tarkil. It appears you have been right all these many years. I feel so foolish ... have I been that selfish?"

"You, above everyone, are not selfish, my love. You have been generous, but protective. We in the village have had a great responsibility in protecting the kefir. You know that."

"Then ...."

"Yes, Khfaf?"

"Has Shirali not allowed the secrets to pass to the west?"

"Hmm ...."

"Don't *hmm* at me Tarkil Lasuria. It is just common sense that this, this catastrophe, is all the product of evil."

Tarkil did not speak.

"Yet you are about to tell me that all of this is in God's great plan and that our precious, blessed kefir is in His hands. You have always said it had an importance beyond us, and that Shirali be encouraged in her mission."

"It is not important, dear Khfaf, that I am right or wrong. But we must face events. Except for the small jug of goat milk inside, it seems the only person on earth with the knowledge and the parent is our own Shirali."

The two of them sat alone, perched on a ledge of rock in the sky, gazing at one another with the kind of love that is only fashioned by decades, centuries, of pain and joy.

"Tarkil, what will happen with the kefir? What will become of us? What will the world come to?"

Tarkil's one hundred seventy three years answered Khfaf, "God will do what He will, with us and with the world ... but every day is a blessed gift, Khfaf, when I am with you."

"Oh, dear ...."

"God tells us that He is to be first, but in your case, Khfaf, He and I have words."

The ground shuddered briefly. Water continued to fall.

"I love you," they both said at once.

CHAPTER 7

The gavel thundered to the bench with a report that startled everyone in the courtroom. Even veteran Sheriff Thorne, his hand reaching for his standard issue pistol, came clear out of his seat.

Los Angeles Superior Court Judge Eve Richardson, known by trial lawyers throughout the California Bar Association as a thorough, calm and eminently fair jurist, was for the first time in her career positively furious. For courtroom spectators, the placid expression on her small hawk-like face may have concealed her feelings, but her fury had been expected by the attorneys readying for argument.

"Will counsel approach the bench?" she barked.

Her eyes were darting back and forth as she tracked the lawyers approaching her. The lawyers in this case she knew to be exceptionally intelligent, well versed not only in trial skills but also in business law. Yet she knew from their pleadings that something was amiss. She suspected that something was intentionally being omitted, that something was being concealed from her.

"Well ...?" She stopped and waited.

The lawyers looked at one another.

"Will one of you please explain to me the real importance of this case?"

An awkward silence ensued. Judge Richardson donned her eyeglasses. She took a deep breath and sighed.

"Gentlemen, this court has no intention of wasting its time attempting to determine what is truly at issue here. My file in this case is already three inches high and I don't even ...."

"Excuse me, Your Honor."

75

Marcus Baranoff, lead counsel for the defense and a senior partner with the New York firm of Manning, Cush and Baranoff sensed an opportunity to strike.

"If you believe our verified Answer to be vague and uncertain, it is because the Complaint was absurdly so." Mr. Baranoff stared at the Judge. "Yet Your Honor has elected not to grant our Motion to Dismiss."

Judge Richardson slid her glasses down so they were resting on the end of her nose. She returned Marcus Baranoff's stare. "My frustration, Mr. Baranoff, lies in my belief that there are important justiciable issues somewhere within the fog that is shrouding this case. The Plaintiff, Pacific Rim Incorporated, alleges it invented and that your client, RAM Pharmaceuticals, Inc., stole from it the product in question. That seems a rather simple contention on its face. Yet the documentation presented by both of you confuses the facts considerably."

Judge Richardson took her eyes off Mr. Baranoff and leafed through the pleadings. There was an awkward silence in the courtroom. Finally, she closed the case file and carefully set it aside.

"Now then, Mr. Jaynes ..." the Judge's look bored into Mr. Elliot Jaynes, who had steeled himself for this uncomfortable moment.

"Mr. Jaynes, Mr. Baranoff has an excellent point with respect to the construction of your pleadings. I believe I have been more than patient. Is there any reason I should not now grant his Motion?"

"Your Honor, I could not complain if you did so, but I would ask the Court's patience, and request that you not do so ... we need additional time and we ask for a Continuance. We have new information concerning the patent process in question, which I believe will allow us to clarify our position.

76

As you know, the patent for this product is still pending and this has made the presentation of our case more difficult than it ordinarily would have been." With that said, Elliot Jaynes abruptly stopped speaking and looked respectfully at the judge.

Judge Richardson, Marcus Baranoff and Elliot Jaynes, himself, all knew that he had not given the judge a satisfactory answer. He said no more, and faced the judge with complete composure.

Baranoff stood nonchalant before the bench with the grin of a Cheshire cat. A dismissal would mean his client RAM Pharmaceuticals, Inc. would have the unfettered right to market a lead product he knew full well had been developed by Pacific Rim Incorporated. But that is not what elated him. He was confident the judge would *not* dismiss the case. A Continuance for his client, in a perverse way, meant time ... and time for his client at this juncture was more precious than money.

Mr. Baranoff had not misread his judge. Judge Richardson had become intrigued with the personalities in the case and with the facts ... and with what she perceived to be an important lack thereof.

She asked herself, "Why would a brilliant, experienced business lawyer like Elliot Jaynes risk his client's position by preparing a weak case and then, of all things, admit it to the Court? And why had Mr. Baranoff and his three associates, representing the largest pharmaceutical concern in the world, not been even more forceful in pressing their position. On statutory grounds alone they could have dispatched with the case."

Both lawyers, while so different, she believed to be of high integrity. Each of them, she supposed, deemed it paramount in the representation of his client not to reveal certain facts or

77

raise particular issues until the time that was considered most effective.

"Both lawyers," she thought, "seem to want this case to drag on, when a fast decision would be of great benefit to the winner. Why? Are they jockeying for position, for some advantage?"

Judge Richardson was sharp as a tack, very quick in her thought processes, and extremely intuitive. She was correct about one thing. Opposing counsel had not determined what the other was up to. They were approaching the end of the game, and both were still holding back critical cards.

Judge Eve Richardson studied the demeanor of each lawyer and wondered if there might be a high stakes prize concealed behind the limited facts that had been presented to her. This is the thought that had upset her professionally, and she was truly upset ... yet, personally, she was fascinated. She was obliged to apply the laws of evidence fairly, but as a judge she had wide discretion and power in controlling the course of a trial. Should she dismiss, or should she hear the case?

"Thank you, gentlemen. Please take your seats."

Elliot Jaynes strode back to the plaintiff's table. The table was devoid of paperwork. He had counted on the judge to continue the case. He sat down next to his client, Dr. Steven Capterville, president of Pacific Rim, who was rummaging through his briefcase in search of something completely unrelated to the legal matters at hand. Elliot Jaynes wondered how a Nobel Laureate in physics and biochemistry, so meticulous in his formulations, so conscious of the slightest bacterial count, could work out of a briefcase that resembled the back of a refuse truck.

Marcus Baranoff, a short stocky man, paced purposefully to his associates who had amassed the Defendant's table with briefs, books and reference periodicals in preparation for absolutely anything.

After surveying her courtroom and glancing briefly at each lawyer, Judge Richardson spoke quietly but firmly, "Mr. Baranoff, your Motion for Dismissal is denied. Mr. Jaynes, how long will it take you to amend your Complaint?"

"I can have it ready within forty eight hours, Your Honor."

The Judge perused her calendar, adjusted her eye glasses and then looked up. She gazed first at Mr. Baranoff and then at Mr. Jaynes, searching one last time for an expression or movement that might tell her something.

"I should like all pleadings filed within three weeks, the hearing set for five weeks from today."

Her eyes were flashing.

"That should be ample time for both sides and the Court to, shall we say, understand one another. And, gentlemen, by the time we meet again I shall expect all of the facts to be presented, and I do mean all of the facts."

CHAPTER 8

"Mommy ... has Uncle Jake landed on Mars yet?"

"We don't know for sure, Corrie."

"I wish I could go to Mars. I'd like to be there with Uncle Jake right now."

"You'd like to be with Uncle Jake no matter where he is."

"Yea, but Mars would be the best."

"Maybe someday you will, Corrie. Honey, put these dishes in the cupboard. We have a lot to do today ... did you feed the dogs?"

"Yep. Topper didn't eat much, though."

There always seemed to be a lot to do around the old ranch house, but to the Capterville family it was worth the work. The turn of the century Victorian home had been built by Megan Capterville's grandfather, Joshua Rankin. The land, which used to lay miles from its nearest neighbor, had covered three hundred relatively flat acres, planted almost entirely in orange trees. But now the County of Los Angeles had grown to it and around it. Only twenty seven acres of the original farm remained, but to the Captervilles those twenty seven acres represented a special way of life removed from the busy congestion of the city.

"Will Daddy be home early today, Mommy? He promised he would try."

"I hope so, Corrie. He had an appointment in court with Mr. Jaynes and didn't know how long it would take."

Megan Capterville had other pressing matters on her mind and did not want to be reminded of their legal problems.

"Daddy doesn't like going to court, I can tell."

"No, he doesn't, dear, he surely doesn't. But he feels he must, to protect us ...."

Megan hesitated. The telephone was ringing.

"Honey, go get the Critters will you? ... Hello, yes, this is she."

"Mrs. Capterville, this is Captain Siever at Houston Mission Control."

"Oh yes, Captain, thank you for calling."

The Captain's voice had an odd sound to it. "I wanted to brief you on the latest ...."

Megan interrupted, "Steven and I have appreciated your constant attention. You must have your hands full, keeping the families updated all these weeks, in addition to all your other duties, I mean."

"Well, Mrs. Cap .... "

"Please call me Meg, Captain, we feel like you're part of the family."

"Very well, Meg, but I'm afraid I have some rather disturbing news ... although I hasten to point out that nothing is confirmed and, in fact, there is very little we can make of the data we are receiving."

Megan took a deep breath. There were no facts or events in her life that told her to expect this, yet she had. And it came on top of her concern for her husband, Steven, and her worries about her little Corrie.

"What has happened, Captain?"

"We have lost voice contact with Little Freedom."

Megan felt a bit of relief. She had expected much worse. She was by no means trained in the ways of space travel but this did not sound critical.

"But is that so important, Captain? Haven't they been in deep sleep for quite some time anyway?"

Captain Robert E. Siever continued calmly, "This is true, of course, and there is still quite a bit we do not know about the effects of our new propulsion system in deep space. As you are aware, the system has shortened the flight from months to weeks. It is possible that this has in some way altered transmission or reception, and we are working on that. Although, we must remember that the Voyager probes functioned well at much greater distances with less sophisticated equipment. However ... I am afraid this is not our greatest concern at the moment."

"What is it, Captain?"

"We have no trace of the vital signs for two of the three astronauts. We don't know whether it's part of the communication problem or whether they have died in flight."

"Dear heavens!"

"And we cannot determine whose vital signs we are receiving. I am sorry to have to report this to you, but you will remember that given the perilous nature of the mission we agreed to pass along all information honestly and directly."

"Yes, Captain."

Megan felt a tugging at her leg. It was her eight year old Corrie. Corrie was looking up at her with an expression one would expect from someone much older, someone with the experience and wisdom that comes with time. The look in Corrie's eyes startled her mother.

"Can I help, Mommy?"

"Could you hold a moment, Captain?"

"Corrie, it seems your Uncle Jake may be in some kind of trouble. Oh, dear ... your father should know. He'll be so upset. Maybe I should call him ... but, no, he'll be home soon."

"Mommy?" Corrie was tugging on her mother's arm.

"Yes, dear?"

"Uncle Jake is all right. I just know it. Trust me, Mommy."

There was something about Corrie's words and the way she had said them that brought a smile to Megan's face. She melted. It was the one thing she needed to hear, and from just the person she needed to hear it. Corrie was for the most part an inexperienced fun-loving kid, but at times she had a gift of wisdom and insight far beyond her years. Steven and Megan had repeatedly found themselves surprised and sometimes shocked at the maturity and spirituality of Corrie's comments. Whatever it was, Megan felt without a doubt that Jake was alive and well.

"Thank you, Corrie, that helps a lot. Remember to wash out the Critters, will you, dear? And put them in a cool spot. The summer days are getting warm. Oh, and put Woody and Topper out ... OK?"

"OK."

Releasing her moist hand from the telephone she said, "Excuse me, Captain, but your news was a bit of a jolt."

"I understand. I really have nothing else to report. I wish I had something more positive to pass along."

"Will you let us know of any further news? I'll inform my husband of your call."

"Yes, of course. Good bye, Mrs. Capterville."

Megan poured herself a glass of cool water and then poured herself into a comfortable wicker chair on the outdoor back porch. She loved her garden. It always helped her to put the events of her life into proper perspective. The daffodils and iris were beginning to fade but the roses, daisies and petunias, in full bloom, colorfully edged her bright green lawn. The smell of orange blossoms was heavy in the air.

In the shade of a healthy apple tree, a bed of unusual purple flowers had made its home. The bright gold centers seemed to reach up to the apples, encouraging them to grow.

"My little piece of Abkhazia," she thought.

She took a drink of the cool water and tried to relax.

"Now let me see, Steven is in court right now, probably under stress and quite uncomfortable, trying to do what he thinks is best ... and his brother Jake is scheduled to be in orbit around the planet Mars, and he could be dead, but Corrie says he is fine, and Corrie is always right about that sort of thing ... and the horrible earthquake this morning in Russia, and the terrible war within Georgia and Abkhazia. Oh, I hope everyone's all right. Shirali's in Africa on her mission, and due back soon. She's always helping people, just like her mother, Khfaf. I miss her so. So does Corrie. Hmm, Shirali ... maybe that's how Corrie's become so ... spiritual."

Megan poured some water on her fingertips and blotted the cool water on her forehead. She rested her head against the back of the chair, and thought. She had arrived at what was troubling her the most. Her daughter. Corrie.

"Corrie ... if I could only understand what is happening to her, what is bothering her. She keeps insisting that someone is watching, someone is just outside the window, just around the corner or behind the big oak out front ... and she insists with the same determination, with the same conviction that she believes her Uncle Jake is alive. Yet no one is ever there ... and I would know ... I've lived here all my life ... I know every sound."

The old screen door squeaked slightly as Corrie walked across the wooden porch and crawled into her mother's lap.

"I put the Critters away, Mommy."

"Thank you, Corrie." Megan gave Corrie a big hug.

"Mommy?"

"Yes, dear?"

"Tell me again about your trip ... when you and Daddy met, and about Tarkil and the purple flower and the neat waterfalls."

Megan squeezed Corrie again, "Not now, Honey, we have too much to do."

"Please?"

"Well, all right, but just for a minute. What do you want to hear about?"

"Shirali, tell me a story about Shirali."

"OK ... well, you know Shirali could speak English the whole time, and none of us knew it."

"Yea, that was neat."

"The people in Bukol have to be very cautious about who they trust. For a long time they've had important things to keep secret. And they wouldn't want a person like Marlin Moss to find out about them."

"Yea, Mr. Moss ... what a creep."

"Now, dear, don't talk like that. And please don't say 'yea'. The word is 'yes'.

"OK."

"One morning, the last morning we were there, I went down to the stream under the apple trees ...."

"And that's one of the apple trees over there," Corrie said pointing into the garden.

"Yes, Corrie, from one of the seeds we brought back. Anyway, I always went to the same spot because I knew your father could see me from his window. I was madly in love with him, but I wasn't about to let him know that."

"That's smart, isn't it, Mommy?"

"It turned out to be, dear."

"He even stopped all the scientists just so you could see a flower," Corrie added.

"Yes, it was very sweet. That's when I first knew your father was interested in me."

"That's neat."

"So the last morning, Shirali came down to the stream. She was showing me how to wash the Critters, save the milk and refill the sack with milk and Critters for the next day ... just the way you do now."

"It was made out of goat skin," Corrie said with pride.

"Yes dear, and all of a sudden Shirali started speaking in English ...."

"That's because she trusted you, Mommy. What did she say?"

"First she told me that I would be marrying your father."

"Wow!"

Corrie crinkled her cute little nose and twirled the end of her ponytail with her fingertips, the same way she always did when she was thinking hard. "Shirali knows things like that," she said.

"Yes, dear ... I guess she does, doesn't she?" Megan was again surprised by her daughter. She wondered if all eight year olds were this perceptive. She didn't recall being nearly as mature at that age.

"What happened then, Mommy?"

"Then Shirali said she would be coming to America, and wanted to see us."

"To bring us the Critters, I'll bet," Corrie said, "Shirali is very wise. She loves God very much."

Megan raised her eyebrows, and gazed down at her remarkable young daughter. "What did you say, dear?"

Corrie was still making loops with the end of her ponytail.

"You have to have faith, Mommy."

86

It was not the first time Megan Rankin Capterville had heard this.

"In what, Corrie?"

Corrie looked up at her mother with her wide brown eyes. Though sweet and young, they had a penetration to them that Megan had not seen for many years.

"In God, of course ... Oh, Mommy, you're being silly. You're teasing me."

"Yes ... yes, of course, dear."

"Then what happened, Mommy? Tell me the rest of the story."

"Then we started down the mountain and ... goodness!"

"What, Mommy, what?"

"I hadn't thought of it until now, but there was an earthquake ... even back then ... a small one."

"Wow!" Corrie said, "what was it like?"

"We were standing right on the edge of the canyon, getting ready to leave, so it was pretty scary. But it didn't seem to bother anybody else. Dr. Kitovani said it was because they were so used to them."

"Gee. What else, Mommy?"

Megan shifted in her chair. She was preoccupied. There was much to do, and much to understand, and now she had something else to bring to the top of her list ... faith in God ... which, it appeared, she had paid less attention to than her eight year old daughter.

"That's enough for now, honey."

"Just one ...."

"No, dear, we've got to get our chores done."

"Oh, OK."

Mother and daughter sat quietly in each others arms for another minute, looking out at plants and flowers collected from all over the world. Abkhazian apples, beginning to turn

87

red in the summer sun, hung weightlessly over hundreds of purple petals. Long vines of strange and wonderful yellow roses ran for yards along the back-yard fence. There was peace and comfort in summer, and a great deal of thinking, in the Capterville back yard.

At once, both springer spaniels began barking out front.

"I wonder who it could be?" Megan asked, "I didn't hear anyone drive up. And what an odd bark. They don't sound like that if there's an animal in the yard."

Corrie frowned.

"Woody hardly ever barks," Megan said with concern, "even at strangers."

Corrie moved restlessly in their chair. With both hands, she tightened her grip around her mother's wrist.

The dogs continued to bark.

"We'd better see who's there, Corrie. Maybe it's the mail truck. Your father was expecting something today."

"No, Mommy."

"What's the matter, dear?"

"Mommy?"

"Yes, Corrie?"

"I didn't tell you today. There was something outside the window again. I couldn't see ... but there were two of them this time."

CHAPTER 9

Dr. Steven Capterville and attorney Elliot Jaynes, both dressed in dark business suits and carrying briefcases, pushed open the heavy glass doors at the east end of the downtown courthouse building, marched down the worn stone steps and walked five blocks to the underground parking garage below Elliot's office. They were now locked in rush hour traffic on the San Bernardino freeway headed east.

"Corrie's going to be upset with me, Elliot. I promised her I'd be home early."

"I wouldn't want Corrie upset with me," Elliot said with a smile. "Those big brown eyes ... her looks could knock over an elephant."

Steven Capterville and Elliot Jaynes, both natives of Southern California, had been friends since childhood school days. They gazed through the thick orange-brown smog that had become an inescapable part of Los Angeles life. A faint, pencil thin outline of Mount Wilson was drawn high in the haze to their left. Both sides of the freeway were completely stopped.

"This looks more like the Dodger Stadium parking lot," grumbled Steven.

"Yea. Ever wonder who named these things freeways? Had a lot of foresight, didn't he?"

"Remember when we were kids, Elliot, and you could see the mountains every day?"

Elliot was half listening, and half thinking about something else.

Looking ahead at a child making faces in a back window, Steven continued, "I remember my grandparents describing the day they first came into Los Angeles on the Santa Fe railroad. They stepped off the train and looked through the crystal clear air up to the snow capped mountains. It was a land of unbound opportunity, only then you could bound and breath at the same time. Elliot! ... hello! ... you haven't heard a word I've said."

Elliot was peering through the haze, deep in thought. He finally said, "We have a day like that once in a while. But your technology, Steven ... the water based fuel additive could be cleaning up this air right now."

"It could, if anybody would listen to us."

They both looked forward as the traffic began to move slowly. A large flat-bed diesel truck signaled itself in front of them as black smoke belched out its stack.

"You've heard it all before, Elliot. Major oil companies have thrown me out the door. Test data disappears. The Department of Agriculture refuses to even look at data. The American medical establishment has considered me a crackpot for years. I guess I've been laughed at by the best of 'em."

"Or the worst of 'em. Are you angry?"

"No," Steven said honestly, "I've had to realize these things take time."

"It's got to be frustrating, though."

"Creating something worthwhile is one thing. But in order to achieve acceptance, creation is not enough. Proof that it works is not enough. There are other factors to contend with."

"Indeed," Elliot said, well aware of the war Steven had been forced to fight alone.

"Money, power and politics await the altruistic," Steven offered.

"Catchy phrase, but you forgot thievery and deceit."

"I included those in 'politics'."

Elliot grinned. The line of cars in front was moving at a fairly steady five miles an hour.

"I used to feel sorry for myself," Steven reflected, "but Corrie broke me of that. She called my bad moods *pity parties* and she'd give me one of her looks of disgust. You can't stay moody very long with an eight year old doing that to you."

"Like I said, I don't want her upset with me ... say, I forgot to ask you, what's the latest on Jake?"

"As of this morning, all systems were go," Steven answered, "they're set to enter orbit sometime tomorrow."

"The guy's amazing. I feel sorry for the Martians, the place'll never be the same."

Steven laughed, "You can say that again."

"He's still giving me a bad time about not going with you on that Abkhazia trip ... ten years, and he still zings me."

"He wouldn't be after you if he didn't consider you part of the family, Elliot. You should feel honored. Jake doesn't tear up just anybody."

"Have you heard from anyone in Georgia?" Elliot asked.

"We got a letter from Dr. Kitovani last month. It's tragic, the civil war. It's hard to believe there is so much fighting in such a wonderful place."

"Wars are always fought in beautiful places," Elliot said.

"I called Dr. Kitovani in Tbilisi after I got his letter. He said we wouldn't believe the changes. Life is very painful for everyone. I never would have imagined Kit and Khimbei on the opposite sides of a war. And now, the earthquake ... we don't know what's happened."

The traffic was loosening up. Steven gazed out the side window, remembering the unique beauty of Abkhazia and Georgia. He tried to imagine what it might be like now.

What of the villagers in Bukol? What of the surrounding mountain villages? What of Sukumi? What of the kefir? What of Khfaf sitting in the sunlight by her window sipping vodka from her small crystal glass? And what of Tarkil? Just the thought of his friend Tarkil could bring tears to Steven's eyes, in a way Steven had yet to comprehend. The bond between the two men, though they were worlds and languages apart, had with time become stronger in the mind of each.

Steven pictured Tarkil sitting in his favorite chair by the fire. "I hope you are taking good care of the watch, my friend."

There was a long silence. Elliot pressed lightly on the Mercedes' accelerator and the car floated into the fast lane.

Elliot Jaynes was a striking man, handsome, with chiseled features and jet black hair that he combed straight back. He wore wire rimmed glasses that, for him, added years of experience to a face already etched with four decades of concentration and study. Elliot took his eyes from the road momentarily. He glanced at Steven. Steven was still far away, re-living the mountain passes of Abkhazia.

"Steven, I understand your frustration ...."

"What?"

"Not having acceptance of your theories ... and your processes."

Steven just listened, sorry to be back in Los Angeles.

"The international scientific community is just beginning to embrace your ideas and your new forms of water, but you remain in a very difficult position. You've had just enough exposure to gain you a lot of unwanted attention ... without the resources and political clout of a large company to back you up. RAM Pharmaceuticals for example."

"And RAM goes back at least ten years," Steven said, still thinking of Abkhazia. "Let us not forget our good friend, Mr. Moss."

"Exactly. And RAM, in your case, has more than money to work with."

Steven looked at Elliot with interest. Elliot's profession forced him to pay attention to detail, but he also had an uncanny way of viewing the entire picture. He was able to understand individual facts in context, within a larger meaning, and he was not afraid to make decisions based upon that understanding.

"What are you getting at, Elliot?"

"Since you have not been able to spend decades, and hundreds of millions of dollars convincing the F.D.A. your products are safe, RAM Pharmaceuticals and others like them are able to create the presumption that your work is not serious and that your waters don't work."

Steven frowned.

"You are a victim of the fraud that has preceded you."

"I suppose."

"Haven't you said your waters, your solutions, strengthen the body's immune system."

"Yes, the ones that are designed for that purpose."

"And they're helping people with cancer, AIDS, arthritis and different viruses and diseases."

"Yes, and I've told you, they're completely harmless," Steven said, "all the solutions are non-toxic."

"Precisely. And we've just described the magic cure-alls that quacks and charlatans have been defrauding people with for thousands of years."

"Thanks a lot."

"You know what I'm saying, Steven ... that's why we've got an FDA. Somebody needs to protect the public from quacks like you."

"I never thought you were a fan of the Food and Drug Administration," Steven said.

"I'm not, but that's not the point. The point is this. Who's going to believe that Dr. Capterville from California can cure disease with water?"

"But there's a difference," Steven insisted, "I can prove it."

"I know, Steven, I know. But here in the America we both love dearly, you can't tell the public what your waters can do ... at least not yet. Even though you're professional, you have the results and you're right, you'd be making medical claims, and by so doing, it makes it easier for companies like RAM to see to it that their competition ... you ... are shut down."

"I do have the proof," Steven said.

"But not enough for the federal government. The system dictates that you spend two hundred million dollars to license one of your solutions as a drug, when it really is not a drug in the first place."

"Of that, I am aware."

"Who were those patients you told me about?" Elliot asked, "Helen and ...?"

"She had acute rheumatoid arthritis," Steven said, "she couldn't even walk without the help of her walker, and now she's·moving about with no pain at all. And John Tison ... stage one diabetic, and his insulin requirements dropped fifty percent in ninety days."

"How?" Elliot asked, knowing the answer.

"They drank a harmless water solution."

"That's all?"

"Well, yes and no. A patient's existing medication is always a concern. With the supervision of their personal physician, we start them on the appropriate water and as we increase the amount of the water consumed each day, we reduce the amount of their prescription medication. Eventually, the patient finds little or no need for the former medication, and the side effects usually disappear right away. But the answer to your question is, yes, only the water. We recommend a healthy diet and proper exercise, but no drugs. The effects of the water solution, in most cases, make the drug unnecessary."

Elliot's thick black eyebrows were raised above the wire rims. "So, after ten years and two hundred million, you'll legally be able to tell Helen and John that it was your water that did it."

"They already know that. So do hundreds of others."

"Of course they do. All you need is a few million people like them."

"How about if we listen to the news?" Steven suggested. "You know they're going to tell us the traffic was caused by a three car slammer and a jackknifed big rig, and it's bound to be thick on the flip side 'cause of gawker blockers."

Elliot laughed, "Do you think your grandfather would have understood freeway talk?"

"I would like to think not."

Steven reached for the radio, but Elliot stopped him.

"One more question?"

"Sure."

"I've got to be ready for Baranoff and the judge next time. Baranoff doesn't seem to think he's got much to lose for his client and, after today, Judge Richardson is going to be hot on this case."

"Fire away," Steven said.

"Your present products are not really the issue, are they?"

"No, Elliot, they're the tip of the iceberg. It's the technology ... the process by which the products are made that is so important. There are an infinite number of applications in industry, agriculture and medicine once the Cluster Conversion Process is understood."

Elliot thought for a few minutes. The traffic began to loosen yet again.

"Your company, Pacific Rim Incorporated," Elliot finally said, "is in good shape, at least legally. And your patent lawyers have done quite a job with the international strategy ... very impressive work."

"I was unaware lawyers complimented one another," Steven said dryly.

Elliot said with a grin, "The good ones do ... when it's warranted."

"Then I suppose I'll have to regard you with a new respect."

Elliot smiled. "Only if it's warranted."

"So, are you finished? Can we listen to the news?"

Elliot was not finished.

"What did you mean when you said it was impossible to reverse engineer your products?"

"You're not going to give me any rest this trip, are you?"

"Just preparing your case. Besides, we seem to have an abundance of time."

"It is not possible to reverse engineer the products in order to discover how they are made. In other words, it is not possible to reconstruct from the end products the processes that make manufacturing possible."

"I see, and how was Dr. Capterville able to achieve this breakthrough?"

Steven smiled at his life-long friend, tempted to take advantage of an opportunity to regale him with endless and impressive scientific knowledge.

"I made a mistake in the lab," Steven said flatly.

Elliot grinned back at Steven, "And here I thought I was in for a long scientific treatise."

"I figured I'd best tell the truth to my lawyer."

"Good thing."

"Why's that?"

"Meg already told me," Elliot said, picking up the pace of the conversation, "so what is to prevent someone else from making the same mistake in the lab."

"Oh, it's always possible, but highly improbable. It was actually a series of mistakes ...."

"Jake says that's how you got Meg," Elliot interrupted.

"Very funny."

"Sorry, but someone's got to fill in for him while he's gone."

"Anyway, to answer your question counselor, science has simply not progressed far enough to even begin duplication of the process. There are too many variables."

"May I be blunt?" Elliot asked.

"That's a rhetorical question, isn't it?"

"If the bad guys put a gun to your head what's to prevent you from telling them all your secrets?"

"They could give me truth serum and I would not be able to tell them enough. The process is far too complex for any one person, including me, to complete all the necessary steps without access to several data bases ... coded information centers we have established at different locations."

"Interesting," Elliot said.

"Our Board of Directors controls the various codes, which we change frequently, and different combinations of board members at Pacific Rim control individual computer access codes. We have a backup scientist for each stage of the process, in case anything happens to me, but no one individual knows the entire process."

Steven stopped. He glared at Elliot and said, "Of course, you'd know all this if you'd agreed to join the board when I asked you to."

"OK, OK, but I've been ...."

"To busy servicing your high paying clients. That's what Jake would say."

"Jake *has* said that," Elliot said uncomfortably, "and he's right. You both are, and I apologize. But it hasn't been about money. I've really wanted to build something ... just like you want recognition for what you're doing."

"Apology accepted."

The traffic was moving slowly but steadily. Elliot tried to change lanes but an elderly lady with thick oval glasses refused to let him move over.

"How about your patent firm?" Elliot asked, "how much do they know?"

"I'm the only one who understands the whole process. As long as the company keeps the technology, the processes, in a pending status there is no requirement to divulge everything we have. And I certainly have not revealed everything to a bunch of patent lawyers I hardly know."

"Naturally," Elliot mused.

"Which reminds me, Elliot, I'd appreciate it if we could keep the key patent work in your firm's safe. I'd feel better."

"Just say when."

"When I die, all patents and manufacturing secrets remain in trust with a Board of Trustees that will protect the processes pursuant to a Declaration of Trust. In this way Pacific Rim can assure buyers of continued production."

"I can see I've missed out on a lot," Elliot grumbled. "Who has drafted this trust for you and given you all this advice?"

Steven leaned back against the headrest and closed his eyes. A tired smile came to his face. "Actually, Elliot, I was hoping you could start on it tomorrow."

Neither Elliot nor Steven spoke for some twenty minutes ... approximately three miles. Steven was half asleep. Elliot was busy thinking.

Finally, Elliot thought out loud, "So who stands to lose financially, and lose big?"

"What are you talking about?" Steven asked without opening his eyes.

"When your products move into the marketplace, beyond the limited distribution you have now, I mean ... who's going to lose?"

"If I can't listen to the news, at least let me sleep."

Elliot answered his own question, "Chemical companies and drug manufacturers ... but it's much more than that, isn't it Steven?"

Steven kept his eyes closed.

"Face it, Steven, you're a good guy trying to help people. You've developed something that can change life on earth, and you're becoming a serious threat to a financial and political system whose participants, individually and collectively, have a tremendous financial interest in the status quo."

"Very eloquent, Elliot."

"Three different multinational companies have tried to steal your technology, someone rammed your car, your briefcase has been stolen, and we have had to sue RAM Pharmaceuticals because they are claiming one of your products to be theirs ... which is a real joke since they have no way of knowing how to make it."

"What do you think they're really up to?" Steven asked.

"I can't be certain just yet, but I have some ideas. We need time, Steven. The clinical data from the new studies will strengthen our position. And, most of all, I need time to investigate RAM Pharmaceuticals. I can feel in my bones they're up to no good, in ways that go far beyond stealing something from you.

"The nature of our suit allows us to discover facts we may never have uncovered otherwise. It also serves as a diversion. If they think your greatest concern in life is protecting a water product, it may help divert their attention from your more important work, my investigation of them, and of course the kefir."

"What's the next move?" Steven asked.

"We need time to learn RAM's true motives. Stealing a product they know they can't manufacture, and winning a judgment that allows them to do so, just doesn't add up. They're after something more important. I can't be sure but I think Judge Richardson has realized that we're on the right side. She knows something's up and she's curious."

"She's not the only one," Steven said.

Elliot's analytical mind was in high gear, and he sounded an aggression reserved for his worthiest opponents, "By the time this is all over, I predict we'll advance the laws of riparian rights to the sub molecular level."

"Water laws for atoms, an intriguing concept," Steven said with interest. "The sub-molecular lawyer, a new breed."

"It's folks like you that keep us lawyers on our toes, Steven. You changed the shape of water, we didn't."

The traffic had finally broken up and the slate blue Mercedes was moving silently through the dusk at seventy miles per hour.

"Let's get together in a day or two, Steven. I promise to have interesting news about RAM Pharmaceuticals."

"Good, Elliot, now how about the news?"

"OK, OK."

Steven turned on one of the two Southern California all-news radio stations and they listened.

A Los Angeles jury was concluding deliberations in a racially sensitive case. Prominent citizens were pleading for reason. There must be no riot! The people of a city just north of Los Angeles had united. Posters had been printed and police sketches were televised ... the little girl that had been kidnapped two weeks ago must be found. The shuttle space walk to repair the earth orbiting telescope had been a tremendous success.

"Thank God for a bit of good news," Steven said.

The excited newscaster continued. Another country had developed a nuclear weapon. The Russian president was fighting with Russia's Parliament. Independent Georgia was no longer independent. She had joined the Commonwealth of Independent States.

There was no mention of Abkhazia because few in the west had ever heard of Abkhazia. But the meaning was clear to Steven, and he felt sad. "Tarkil, my friend, I know you knew long ago. Khimbei was right all along. That is why you listened quietly that night and did not argue with him."

"Steven," Elliot asked, "doesn't that mean Abkhazia is in grave danger?"

But the newscaster continued urgently, "We interrupt this broadcast to bring you a bulletin from Houston. Go ahead, Houston ...."

The reporter in Houston could be heard through heavy static, "Captain Siever, over here, please!"

The reporter's voice faded out briefly so that it could not be heard at all. Then it came in clearly, "N.A.S.A. has lost all radio contact with the Mars ship, Little Freedom. It appears two of the astronauts have died in flight. Families have been notified ... Captain Siever, excuse me, Captain ... can you give us any more details?"

Steven and Elliot were shocked. Elliot said the only thing he could think to say.

"Oh, Steven ... I'm so sorry."

CHAPTER 10

"Sure you don't want me to drive you up to the house, Steven?"

"No thanks, Elliot. After today I can use the exercise. Give me a call when you're ready."

"You got it. And, Steven ... really sorry about Little Freedom. But you know Jake, he'll be back. He probably shut off communication himself just to get attention. It'd be just like him."

"I wouldn't put it past him," Steven said. Steven smiled, but there was an obvious concern in his voice.

"I'll give you a call tomorrow," Elliot said as Steven shut the car door.

Elliot waved as he drove off.

The driveway to the Capterville home was a winding quarter mile lined with orange trees and an occasional palm. Steven walked briskly, almost running. *How are Meg and Corrie? How is Jake? What will the latest water analysis prove? How can the kefir be mass produced? How can a new laboratory be financed? Don't be upset, Corrie, the traffic was terrible. Meg, I know I should have called. Captain Siever must have telephoned. What exactly did he say? I know Jake is OK ....*

It was dark when he came within sight of the house.

Red, blue, piercing yellow lights were flashing from police cars, reflecting off his home and surrounding trees. The yard was lit like an eerie scene from a science fiction film. Men in dark uniforms were moving strobe-like through doors and windows and around the grounds. Corrie's bicycle lay on the driveway below the front porch. Voices of dispatchers blared over police radios.

Megan, tears streaming down her face, was gesturing to a police officer and two FBI agents. When she saw Steven she ran to him and threw her arms around him.

"What has happened, Meg? Where is Corrie? Why the police?"

"Someone has taken Corrie ... Oh, Steven, it's all my fault, I wouldn't listen to her."

"What do you mean someone's taken her?"

"She's been kidnapped, Steven, she's gone."

Steven felt like he'd been hit by a truck. Corrie gone? Impossible! An unbearable emotion welled inside him. His very being, his family, had been violated. Nothing worse in the world could possibly have happened to him.

"But, how ...?"

Megan was frantic, "Remember how she kept saying someone was watching?"

"But, we always checked, there was never anybody there."

"Oh dear, Steven, it's all my fault, I should have listened to her."

"Meg ...." Steven couldn't think. He couldn't speak. A deep, searing anger consumed him. He would find his Corrie ... and he would kill, and he would kill again until there was nothing left. He was squeezing Megan in his arms. He tried to calm himself. Over her shoulder, he saw officers moving through his house.

"The house, Meg ... the house?"

Megan cried, "they have ruined the house, smashed everything, not just to steal things, but terribly mean, like they hated us or something. And our little Corrie! Oh, I pray she has not been harmed ... Oh, Steven!"

Steven's initial shock became anger.

"We'll find Corrie, Meg. Show me what's happened ...."

"Dr. Capterville, my name is Lieutenant Greaves. Do you know why Satan worshipers would be in your house? This place is a mess ...."

The ordinarily kind Steven Capterville held up his arm demanding silence. He stepped threateningly between Megan and the Lieutenant and growled in the Lieutenants face, "Hold your tongue!"

In an instant, guns were drawn and trained on Steven.

The Lieutenant backed away, "It's OK, Sergeant, have your men put their weapons away. It was my fault. It was all my fault!"

Megan was crying, her hands folded over her face. Every muscle in Steven's body was tightened.

"Forgive me, doctor. I was out of line ... it's just that we like to move as quickly as we can."

"Where is my daughter?" Steven barked.

"We're doing our best to find out, doctor."

Steven was trying to calm himself, but he was seething inside. Someone had touched his little Corrie.

"You have no idea where she could be?"

"No, doctor, not yet. There are a few things that are puzzling. A breaking and entering during the day with people home ...."

"During the day?" Steven interrupted, "When did this happen, Meg? I should have called."

"Just an hour ago, Steven, it was still light."

Lieutenant Greaves looked uncomfortable. He didn't want to offend again. He began, "And the inside of the house ... ahh ... perhaps we should discuss this at a later time."

Megan snapped, "There is nothing you cannot say in front of me, Lieutenant." This kind of consideration no matter how tactful had always irritated Megan Capterville.

"Very well then, the last time I saw the likes of your house was in a raid we made on one of those devil-worship cults. You know, the pentagrams, the ritual implements, the altar, the blood from the sacrifices ...."

"The what?" Steven shouted.

"Perhaps I should come back ...."

"No," Steven strengthened, "Tell us what you know about ... about sacrifices, and what it could possibly have to do with our daughter."

"The blood, excuse me, the red, wiped across your walls, is not blood. It's ketchup. But the diagrams, the evidence of their behavior, and the stench, the incredibly horrible smell, is familiar to me. They may have ..."

"They?" asked Steven.

"Well, Mrs. Capterville said she was out back, at the most, for twenty minutes. Everything in the house has been opened or torn apart and, of course, your daughter is missing. It would have been difficult for one person to accomplish all this in that amount of time. And Mrs. Capterville has said she heard a car."

Megan composed herself and dotted her tears with a handkerchief. "Yes, Steven, that's right. I asked Corrie to finish cleaning up the kitchen, and I went out back with the dogs, to get some things out of the tool shed. I wanted to plant the flat of petunias. I had to get my mind off ... Jake ... oh, Steven, have you heard?"

"On the radio," Steven said with defeat.

"I tried to get through to you at the courthouse ... can all this be happening to us? I just finished talking with that Captain Siever about Jake, and I had to get some air ... and Corrie said she heard two of them this time ... oh, dear."

"And you believe you heard a car?" asked Lieutenant Greaves.

106

"Yes, when I was out back, I know I heard a car or truck, but I thought it was the mail or the UPS delivery you were expecting, Steven."

"And you did not hear your daughter calling you? You heard no noise at all from the house?" pressed Greaves.

"No, which is very strange, because it's always so peaceful out here. And, Steven, your spare briefcase, your samples and all the papers that were on your desk ... have been taken."

Lieutenant Greaves turned to Steven.

"Do you know any reason why someone would want to do this, doctor?"

Steven thought to himself that because of his work, because of the technology, and the kefir, there were many possible reasons. But to the Lieutenant he replied, "No, but I will certainly be thinking about it."

"I understand. Also, we found footprints and crushed flowers outside the kitchen window," the Lieutenant continued, "and we are studying the tire tracks.

"I know I need not say the obvious, Dr. and Mrs. Capterville, but you realize both your daughter and your papers were taken for a reason. I shall do my best to determine that reason, but I expect I shall have little success without your help."

"Yes, of course, Lieutenant."

Greaves studied each of them. His years on the force had made him an excellent judge of character. He knew the Captervilles were good people. But he also knew he would get from them only the information they felt absolutely necessary for his investigation. These were terribly private people, deeply hurt. They now found themselves involved with something so evil and so far-reaching that it, whatever it was, had invaded their privacy and threatened their very existence.

"It would be best for you and for our investigation if you were both to stay in a hotel tonight."

"Yes, I suppose that would be best," replied Steven, "but I would like to have a look inside."

"There is no need," Megan said.   She knew what concerned him.   "Besides, Steven, I don't want you to go in there tonight."

"We'll be done with our work here by mid-morning," said Lieutenant Greaves, "so you can return any time you like. You are nice folks, I just wish there was more I could do right now.   You have my number, and I will call just as soon as I hear anything."

"Thank you, Lieutenant."

The Lieutenant's unmarked car moved slowly down the driveway.   Several investigators remained in and around the house.   The lights had been turned off on the remaining police cars, and except for dim light from within the house, the front yard was dark.   Steven and Megan Capterville stood in their driveway looking not at their home, but at each other.

"Meg, where is the kefir?"

"It's gone, Steven.   They stole it."

"Oh, no," Steven moaned, "Then why would they risk taking Corrie ... if they got what they wanted?"

"I don't know," Megan answered.   She was beginning to sob again.

Steven felt terrible despair.   He wrapped an arm around Megan and looked toward their house.   He asked himself, "Why is all this happening to us?   My daughter has been kidnapped, my brother could be dead, I am in court with the largest pharmaceutical company in the world, my house has been invaded, my formulas stolen ... and I must now face the ridicule of having been irresponsible enough to lose the one

God given substance that could have changed the world. This is a horrible, horrible nightmare."

Megan Capterville stood with her arms folded, tears streaming down her face. She was shaking. But she was born of tough country stock and she would recover. She would recover now. "Get a hold of yourself, Meg! This is no way to get Corrie back." With Steven's arm still around her she straightened and wiped away the tears.

"Steven?"

Steven squeezed her to him.

"You remember ... what Shirali told us?"

"Shirali has told us a lot."

"I mean, a long time ago ... in Bukol. She said there is much evil in the world, and we would not always be able to see it."

"I remember," Steven sighed.

"She said we must have faith, remember?"

"Yes."

"And I asked her 'faith in what?', and she said we would have to find that out for ourselves."

"Didn't she give some definition or something?"

"Yes," Megan said. "I wrote it down in Bukol and memorized it."

"You never told me that."

"I never really thought about it until I was talking with Corrie today. Corrie has faith in God. So does Shirali. I felt embarrassed."

"Why, Meg? We believe in God."

"I know, but not like them."

"What do you mean?"

"It's hard to explain. I guess ... we believe it, but we don't do anything about it."

"I still don't know what you're getting at, Meg. What are we supposed to do?"

"I don't know, Steven. Corrie said something today that made me think. She said having faith in God was harder than believing in Him."

"Corrie said that?"

"Then I started thinking about what Shirali said. She said that faith is the substance of things hoped for, the evidence of things not seen."

"I didn't understand her the first time she said it."

"Me neither, so I asked Corrie."

"What did she say?" Steven asked.

"She giggled. She thought I was teasing her ... like I should already know. That was the second time I felt embarrassed. But I asked her again, and you know what she said?"

"What?"

She crinkled her nose, you know how she does, and she said, "Miracle on Thirty-Fourth Street!"

"What?"

"That's what *I* said. She said, 'Come on, Mommy, you know, you've seen it, the Christmas movie. Faith is believing things when common sense tells you not to! Jesus said so too."

"No kidding," Steven said, "Corrie said that?"

Steven and Megan Capterville turned away from the house and looked up to the star filled sky. Jake would be there. They thought that, perhaps, someone else might be there, someone they needed to get to know better. Megan put her arm around Steven's waist.

"Steven, do you believe in angels?"

"The ones we put on our Christmas tree?"

"I'm serious."

"Well, I guess so ... but I've never seen one."

"Corrie says you don't have to see them. She says they're around us all the time, protecting us."

"Ours must be on vacation."

"That's not funny, Steven."

"Maybe, but ...."

"Corrie says you have to believe they're there before they can help you."

Steven said nothing. Even as Megan was talking of angels, feelings of hate, remorse and retribution were welling up inside him.

"Steven?"

"Yes?"

"Do you believe in the devil ... and hell?"

"I don't think so, but tonight could change my mind."

"Shirali believes there is a lot going on that we can't actually see." Megan looked at their house, "People may have done this to us, Steven, but Shirali would say there is more ...."

"More?"

"Like evil beings in a spiritual world, making people do things like this."

"Evil spirits? Come on, Meg."

"Steven?"

Steven was staring at the sky.

"We can't fight these things alone, Steven ... we'll go crazy."

"Shirali was right about one thing," Steven said, "there is a lot of evil in this world."

"I think we need to have faith, Steven, faith that God will fight the battle for us, faith that He will fight the wars within our world, and the wars within His ... faith that Corrie is safe."

"That will not be easy, Meg. I'm ready to kill somebody."

"Corrie said it wouldn't be easy."

The Capterville's left for town in the old family pickup truck. They wound down the orange-scented driveway speaking infrequently. But they were both of one mind. Whatever it took, they would find their Corrie.

As they approached the main road Megan said, "You know what Corrie would say to us right now, Steven? I can hear her just as if she were here."

"What?"

"She'd say the same thing she said about her Uncle Jake. She'd say, 'Hey guys, don't worry about me, I'm just fine.' And you know Corrie is always right when it comes to things like that."

"You're right, Meg, and somehow, I feel sorry for whoever, or whatever, has Corrie."

"Whatever? Steven, what do you mean?"

"I don't know, Meg. I can't explain it. Maybe it's like Shirali said. We won't always be able to see it."

As the tail lights of the pickup turned on to the main road *it* watched from the topmost gable of the Capterville rooftop.

With an evil hiss of immense satisfaction *it* basked in the terrible success *it* had achieved, and *it* intended to make certain that credit and praise were given, where credit and praise were due. But the mission was not yet complete, and there could be no mistakes.

Unable to be seen or heard by human senses *it* readied to move into the night. *It* contemplated *its* priorities.

"The girl, yes, the girl must be secured."

Emitting a repulsive smell *it* spun around violently and snarled, "Yes, the girl, and we shall have our answers. After all the lost time, we shall finally have control."

In an instant, *it* was gone.

CHAPTER 11

The canister-like spaceship was in its pre-programmed orbit around the planet Mars, well inside the orbits of Mars' two elliptical rocklike moons. But it was tumbling awkwardly, out of control. Commander Jake Capterville, still not fully recovered from the effects of deep sleep was frantically trying to correct the ship manually.

"Blast it, Orville, I need more power on this side ... I've asked you twice. You're going to kill us!" Jake screamed.

"Jim!" Jake hollered, "give me our position, bearings will help ... as far as I can tell we're in a perfect orbit, how could this have happened ... this deep sleep stuff is for the birds and NASA's going to hear about it."

Commander Capterville was manually firing jets as he felt necessary. He had practiced manual corrections, they all had, many times before at the Cape but there was something very different about it this time. They could all perish in a matter of minutes.

"Confound it, Orville, more power! ... wait, there, I think I've got it coming around, yes ... a bit more on this ...."

The ship came gradually into its correct attitude.

"Jim, see if you can restore communications. I'm going to check this software ... find out what happened to ALPO."

Jake had no passion for computers but this system and program he knew backward and forward. It was the Automatic Orbiting and Landing Program that was designed to allow them to orbit, land on the planet, and return to the command ship without having to touch a single manual control. The technicians had nicknamed it ALPO.

"Orville, three times! ... three times I ordered you to give me more power. Why ...?"

Jake turned from his controls and for the first time since waking in the tumbling craft, he was able to look behind him. Jake froze at the terrifying sight. Colonel Jim Thurmond and Dr. Orville Bittain stared past him, wide-eyed. They were dead. Still in their space suits, they floated next to one another in standing positions, anchored to the floor by magnetic boots.

Jake's first thoughts ... "What had happened? A meteor? Radiation? Electrical failure? Why am *I* alive?"

Then thoughts, remembrances of years spent with Orville and Jim began to flood into his mind. His close friends, his comrades in life and in flight, were dead. But he checked his emotions, he cut off all familiar thoughts. He had to, or he and their mission would die.

Jake marked the time on his watch and compared it with the reading on the ship's computer. They were the same. He had a little over thirty minutes to decide. Was he to attempt the descent to Mars by himself? NASA, he was certain, would not allow it, but then he had not spoken with anyone from the planet earth for almost four weeks.

He made his decision.

"If ALPO is clean in twenty minutes, I go," he spoke decisively.

He called up the **ALL SYSTEMS** menu; two areas to format, and what appeared to be three lengthy mathematical recalculations due to an imperfect approach.

"Blast!" he exclaimed. With total concentration he attacked the first math problem.

In fourteen minutes he was done with all three. Formatting was relatively simple.

"The techs at Houston central will howl when they hear I solved this with an ALPO tutorial."

Climbing into the cramped Lander he settled into the seat that had been designed for his body. He was positioned as though he was resting in an extended lounge chair, a chair containing much of the computer hardware vital for navigation. He was surrounded by switches, digitals, gauges and levers, all present solely for manual override. All were within arms reach. Even the engineers acknowledged that need for their use meant the mission was likely doomed. But if there was failure in the automated systems and there was a chance for manual control ....

Jake slipped his hands into the data control gloves at the end of each arm rest. The familiar neon blue and orange screen appeared before his face. All flight instrumentation and systems data were consolidated here. He would monitor his descent and ascent, and if all went well he would need to touch nothing, he would need to take no action whatsoever.

The Lander had five mechanical landing legs, loaded with pneumatic shock absorbers, high tension carbide springs and computerized altitude sensors calibrated to Martian gravity. For good reason, the earth-bound mission specialists had named them Crab Legs. Even **SYSTEM ACCESS** on the Lander monitor read **CLS**, for Crab Legs System. Jake moved his left index finger within the left data glove and hit **CLS Test**, then **ENTER**. He felt a low vibration, and looking out his port window, then starboard, he watched the legs unfold and lock in landing position. Still in test mode, the computer automatically searched for **CLS** errors. A **SYSTEM REVIEW COMPLETE** light signaled accurate altitude sensing, then full system clearance. The legs then retracted and locked behind their shields. All systems were 'go'.

Jake was painfully conscious of his two friends, still floating in their same positions just a few feet away in Little Freedom. But now that they were not alive, his primary obligation was to the mission. His two comrades would insist upon it.

"Until we meet again, my friends ... in four hours."

The experiments conducted by the unmanned Viking Lander in 1976 found no evidence of life on Mars. But they had not proven conclusively that there was not life on Mars. As the only human visitor to the planet, Jake would be able to conduct testing first hand. In addition, he had far more sophisticated equipment he could employ.

He shut the hatch to the Lander and secured it. A countdown began in large black numbers on the monitor. It was all automatic now. There was no turning back. In two minutes, forty-eight seconds the Lander would release.

MARS (marz) n. The fourth planet from the sun, having a sidereal period of revolution about the sun of 687 days at a mean distance of 141.6 million miles, a mean radius of approximately 2,090 miles, and a mass approximately 0.15 that of Earth.

As a little boy Jake Capterville had memorized the dictionary definition of the planet on which he was about to land, and the view from the Lander window was even more spectacular than he had dreamed as a child. He looked upon massive craters, volcanoes and sunken canyons, all painted in reds, off-whites and burnt umber browns ... an oceanless colored sphere set against the jet black backdrop of space.

The earth, which was temporarily in his field of vision, appeared as a pinpoint of light, less bright than many of the stars in the sky. For an instant he thought of that summer night at ten thousand feet, on one of the earth's majestic mountains, when he had looked up to the planet Mars with longing.

"That was a long time ago," he thought, "Corrie had not even been born."

Jake focused on the small unblinking dot of light that was home. Little Corrie would be there, gazing at the sky each night wondering about her Uncle Jake.

"Think of the stories I'll be able to tell her," he thought.

There were fast unlocking sounds followed by ignition.

"Pray for me Corrie. Here we go!"

Jake Capterville, one hundred ninety seven million miles from earth, was on his way to the surface of the red planet Mars.

CHAPTER 12

Steven and Elliot pulled into the empty parking lot at the same time. They parked next to one another and shook hands on a grassy knoll that overlooked the city. Steven had insisted on talking outdoors. He had asked Elliot to meet him on Mount Hollywood, in the parking lot of the Griffith Observatory and Planetarium.

"Thanks for meeting me on short notice, Elliot."

"No problem, Steven. I wanted to talk to you anyway."

"There's someone I want you to meet," Steven said excitedly. "She should be here any moment."

"Any word on Corrie, Steven?"

"No, Elliot, nothing. The pain is something you can't imagine. Meg is distraught. She's meeting with Lieutenant Greaves right now. But there's no trace of Corrie. No ransom, nothing."

"Well, if there's anything I can do ...."

"You are doing plenty, Elliot. You said you had some news?"

"Yes, and I think you'll find it most interesting. I haven't got it all connected yet, but I've come up with enough information to raise the eyebrows of any stockholder in RAM Pharmaceuticals. And it's all from public records, their annual reports, etc.."

Steven was hoping for any bit of good news, "Anything helpful for us?"

"Not yet, but I'm convinced there will be if we follow the trail. Listen to this. RAM had a total income last year of close to one billion dollars, yet their reported net income was only one hundred and five million."

"So?" Steven asked.

"In their adjustments to gross income I calculated total annual payments of one hundred seventy six million dollars to a company called Preferred Financial, Inc.. PFI is a relatively obscure firm whose sole business appears to be the preparation and filing of payroll tax returns for large, multinational companies who do not want the headache of doing it themselves. On a quarterly basis a company like RAM transfers money to PFI who, in turn, pays the State, the IRS, and even foreign governments on behalf of its client."

"Rather specialized business," Steven commented.

Elliot continued like a detective who was hot on a trail. "PFI makes its money in two ways, at least that we know of now. It charges nominal fees, but it makes most of its profit on 'float', the interest it earns on its client's money between the time it receives funds, and the time it actually pays the tax. As far as I can determine, this is perfectly legitimate."

They walked slowly on the grass in front of their cars. Steven stopped, put one foot on a concrete bench, gazed over west Los Angeles and listened intently.

"We're not talking small change, Steven. Like to guess how much money is passing through PFI each year ... from RAM and its other clients?"

"How much?"

"The company is private so I don't have access to all that I would like, but the number so far is in excess of *twelve billion dollars.*

Steven whistled.

"That's with a *'B'*, Steven."

"If the company is private, how do you know ...?"

"I knew you'd ask. I had Alice run a legal action computer search. It turns out the IRS filed suit against RAM

Pharmaceuticals two months ago for one hundred twenty-five million dollars in back taxes."

"It's nice to know I'm in such good company," Steven said sarcastically.

"In answering the complaint," Elliot continued, "RAM admitted to the total amount, but maintained it had paid the amount in full. Two weeks later the suit was dismissed with prejudice, meaning that any further action is effectively barred."

"I think I see ...."

"I don't think you do, at least not yet. Under normal circumstances RAM would have filed a cross-complaint against PFI alleging PFI's liability and its obligation for paying the tax. The fact that RAM did not do so, got me thinking about the relationship between RAM and PFI. RAM's annual report lists eighty three million dollars paid in payroll taxes, yet it paid PFI one hundred seventy six million. So what happened to the other ninety three million?"

For the first time in days Steven's mind was not consumed with thoughts of Corrie.

"Is it possible," Steven asked, "that PFI's other clients are doing the same thing?"

"I still can't be certain that RAM is doing anything illegal. But we're getting very close. If you read the fine print on a subsequent page in their Financial Section, they carry the ninety three million as an expense item called 'Financial Services'.

"This is getting interesting."

"In reviewing their schedules which were intentionally, I believe, attached as a separately bound supplement, we find that the ninety three million was paid to PFI.

"No kidding."

"And listen to this, Steven. In verified pleadings before the Tax Court less than two months ago PFI stated that with the exception of payroll work, it had no dealings in financial services. Nor does it have the licensing to do so.

"Well now!" Steven said, "Sounds to me like we've finally got some leverage."

"It would be most interesting to find out if PFI has carried the ninety three million on its books and if not, where it has gone. Also, I'd like to know which entity finally paid the IRS."

"Should we confront RAM? ... make them confess what they've done?"

"Not yet."

"Why not?"

"Several reasons, Steven. First, the two of us could wind up on our backs in a dark alley staring at the stars."

"I've thought of that."

"Also, there is much more to this than I originally thought. I think we are very close to something very big and, at this point, RAM is not aware of how much we know."

"I see."

"Lastly, and this is a real long shot, Steven ... could there be a connection between RAM's finances and your Corrie?"

Steven's face went blank as he considered this. Then a wide grin spread across his face. He was jubilant. It may be a long shot, but it was something.

"Whatever you need, Elliot, just ask, absolutely anything. And you know," Steven's eyes were sparkling, "there could be a connection ... I mean, Meg and I have been asking how all this could happen at once."

"Well, don't get your hopes too high."

"OK, so what's the next step?"

"I need you to dig up some information for us."

"Anything," Steven said eagerly.

"Analyze the ingredients in the top ten, best selling products that RAM is marketing. Take a look at their gross sales and see if you can back into RAM's bottom line cost for each item. We'll subtract those figures from retail sales and see what the profit margins are. I'm guessing you're going to come up with numbers that every RAM stockholder will be interested in."

"I already know some of the ingredient figures," Steven said with excitement. "It won't take long to nail down the rest."

"Good. I'll bet you a steak dinner at the old Brown Derby that RAM or PFI or both are illegally transferring large blocks of money."

"But where ... and why?" Steven wondered.

"Good questions, that need answers. I intend to start with Prime National Bank."

"Why?"

"Prime Bank is RAM's lead lender, which means they must have a healthy depository relationship ... and perhaps more."

The two men were distracted by the sound of an engine. A faded and very old blue Ford station wagon pulled into the parking lot and parked next to Elliot's Mercedes.

"Oh, good," Steven exclaimed, "Elliot, here she is, at last."

Out of the station wagon stepped a stately, trim and eminently striking woman who appeared to be in her late forties. She gave Steven a warm, long hug and then extended her hand to Elliot. Elliot gently took her hand in his. Without knowing precisely why, he felt true respect was due her.

With unusual emotion Steven said, "I should like you to meet a dear friend. Elliot, this is Shirali Lasuria."

"So you are ... Miss Lasuria. I ... I am delighted to meet you."

With only a hint of accent, Shirali replied, "Steven tells me you are a trusted friend and a brilliant legal mind."

"I said no such thing," Steven said playfully, "at least not the last part."

"Oh, yes you did Steven." Shirali gave Steven one of her looks. "That is one reason Elliot is to know."

"Know what?" Elliot asked, absolutely fascinated by the woman.

"About the kefir," Shirali said, "You will become one of only a few people on earth to learn about it."

"Must I, Miss Lasuria? Steven has seen to it that I have a very full plate at the moment."

Shirali looked into Elliot's eyes. She was intrigued. This man has a keen wit, she thought. And a kind face.

"You may not be able to help him unless you do know," she said. "I believe Corrie has been abducted because somebody, someone powerful wants the kefir."

"Then why, Miss Lasuria ...?"

"Please call me Shirali."

"But the thieves stole the kefir from Steven's house, Shirali. They already have it. Why would they be interested in a little girl?"

"Because, Elliot, they do not know how to grow it or care for it. Within a few days, without care, it will perish."

"But Shirali," Steven interrupted, "Corrie doesn't know how to grow the kefir. Meg showed Corrie how to wash it since we couldn't be home all the time. We've been careful not to tell Corrie what it is. She thinks it's just another one of my experiments. She nick-named them the 'Critters' because they move around so much. It's something she plays with."

"But *they* don't know that, do they, Steven?"

Steven's face went blank.

"Meg said Corrie kept hearing something outside the windows."

"Oh, no," Steven groaned. "Shirali, you're right."

"And what was she doing from time to time but washing the kefir ... her Critters?"

"Oh, no," Steven moaned again, "how could I have been so stupid?"

A wave of guilt washed over Steven Capterville. "Shirali, how would anyone know we even had the kefir in the first place, let alone that it has to be cared for?"

Shirali answered quietly, almost sadly, with a voice of long experience, "It is difficult to keep a miracle a secret, Steven."

"I feel so inept. I should have paid attention!" Steven cried.

"It is not for you to feel inept, Steven. Sometimes God allows us to be painfully placed, so that He can work wonders elsewhere."

There was silence for a minute or two. Steven stood a little taller. He took a deep breath and put his hand on Elliot's shoulder.

"Elliot, Shirali has a remarkable story to tell. She has just returned from her mission in Africa. She is resuming her teaching."

"What do you teach, Shirali?"

Shirali once again studied Elliot's face. Looking directly into his eyes she said, "The Bible, Elliot. I teach the Bible to children."

Elliot did not know what to say. It was obvious her answer had surprised him. He had expected a profession the world would give more weight to.

Steven continued, "Shirali is one of the few people ever to leave her ancestral village in Abkhazia, Elliot, and she is the only one, as far as we know, to have left with a portion of the parent kefir."

"What is this kefir you keep talking about?" Elliot asked, "and you think someone kidnapped Corrie because they believe Corrie can grow it?"

"A kefir, *this* kefir, is a very complex living culture," Steven answered. "It is a combination of micro-organisms, bacteria and yeasts, growing in a nutrient medium which, in this case, is goat milk..

"Sounds delicious," Elliot quipped.

"You've heard of the kefir milk drinks you can buy at the market?"

"Sure."

"They're good for you because they contain friendly bacteria, but you'll find only two or three beneficial strains. Lactobacillus acidophilus is a good example. Great for the digestion."

"OK."

Steven paused and looked around the parking lot to make certain they were alone. "But in this kefir from Bukol ... our laboratory analysis showed an unbelievably complex family of twenty-eight micro-organisms. Twenty-eight, Elliot, all competing with one another."

"Competing?"

"Right. They all grow at a different rate, and at any given point in time they have a different medicinal activity. The Abkhazian villagers grow it in a goatskin sack, in goat milk, hanging from a tree in the mountains. They have the equivalent of a drugstore in a tree. They found over centuries of use how long they should grow it before consuming it for a particular ailment ... eighteen hours for the flu, twenty hours for headaches, twenty-four for general health maintenance, and so on."

"I think I'm beginning to understand."

"Think about it, Elliot, a God-given totally natural cure for disease!"

"I see ...."

"Ten years ago I was called to a church in Bukol to see a little boy. He had a tumor on his side the size of an orange. There was nothing I or any physician could have done for him. Shirali's mother treated him with a compress soaked in the kefir and by the time we left the tumor was gone. I saw it with my own eyes."

Shirali was looking down at the leather valise she had placed on the grass next to her. She seemed uncomfortable. "Steven, perhaps we should ...."

"Yes, of course, Shirali, you're quite right. Elliot, Shirali has brought the ancient Abkhazian texts with her today, and we ask that you lock them in your firm's vault at the bank, to be placed along side my patent work."

Shirali handed Elliot the worn leather case.

"The English translations are in the case also" Steven continued, "along with appropriate instructions ... and both of our Wills."

Steven returned to his truck and lifted a thick manila envelope from the seat. He handed it to Elliot and said, "Here are the balance of the patent papers, and a drawing of the most critical stage in the Cluster Conversion Process. Don't take your eyes off them until they're in the vault."

Creases frequently appeared on Elliot Jaynes' forehead when he was concentrating or worried. They were there now. "I see why you wanted to meet here, Steven. These documents are of tremendous importance. And the kefir, the 'parents' you mentioned ... there is some kind of connection with your technology, isn't there?"

Shirali was becoming agitated. She sounded extremely urgent, "There is much that can be said about the kefir and the technology, Elliot, but under the circumstances ...."

"I agree completely," Elliot said, "these papers should be under lock and key as we speak. I shall have them banked immediately. Perhaps ... we could arrange to meet again ... so I can get to the bank." For reasons Elliot could not explain, he was drawn to this woman. He truly did not want to leave.

"Thank you, Elliot," Shirali said sweetly, "it was a pleasure to finally meet you. Steven and Meg were right about you."

Shirali gave Steven a kiss on the cheek and said, "Tell Meg she is in my prayers, Corrie too ... and, Steven, please be patient. Remember to let God do his work. You do yours, but let Him do His ... OK?"

"I promise I'll try, Shirali."

"Good. Hi to Meg," and Shirali was off to her car.

"Steven, what did she mean about letting God do his work?"

"I've been trying to understand that woman for ten years, Elliot, and I still don't get it. Meg says it's my scientific training, the way I look at things."

Elliot smiled, "Maybe you should join one of Shirali's classes."

"Maybe."

The smile left Elliot's face and the creases returned to his forehead. "It is possible that science and law won't find Corrie, Steven ... maybe that's what she's getting at."

"Meg seems to think so. She keeps saying we need to have faith."

"Well," Elliot asked, "don't you?" His forehead was still full of creases.

"You probably won't understand this, Elliot, but I really don't know what to do, to have faith, I mean. It's hard for me to believe in things when I can't see them or touch them."

"I understand that better than you may think, Steven."

Elliot and Steven watched Shirali's station wagon make the final turn out of the hills. She stopped at a stop light, looked up to them and waived.

"Steven, she's incredible, a remarkable woman. I already feel like I've known her for years. If she were ten years younger ...."

"If she were ten years younger, Elliot, she'd be one hundred and three years old."

CHAPTER 13

The small, damp room was pitch black dark. Corrie Capterville lay curled up on a cold metal table in the center of the room, unable to see a thing. She was trying her best to ignore the painful burns on her arms and legs. Corrie knew the two men would be back.

There would be a blinding light when the door swung open, and then darkness, and another blinding light as a match was struck, and then the pungent smell of cigarette smoke mingled with the horrible body odor of the two approaching men. Then the pain, and the smoke from her burning skin.

"Why are they doing this to me?" she cried to herself. *"What have I done to them? Why are they asking all those strange questions? Where is Mommy? And Daddy? Where am I? Ohh, the burning, it hurts so much."*

"Maybe, if I think back," Corrie reasoned, "I can figure it out ... oooh! ... it's so cold in here. I remember putting the Critters away, and going back to the kitchen.

"Two big hands grabbed me, and the other man pulled me by the hair and wrapped tape across my mouth ... and then my eyes ... it hurt.

"One man picked me up and the other said, 'Good! Throw'er in the truck, and let's start trashin' the place ... and keep yer eyes open, stupid.'

"Then the man that was carrying me said, `Yea, yea, and be quick about it, Slavic, the ol' lady's not too far off.'

"He threw me in the truck and I hit my head hard ... that's all I remember ... until this place.

"What can they want with me? And all those questions about kefirs and cultures. What are cultures, anyway? I thought they were countries. Ohh, I feel so alone. I hope Uncle Jake doesn't feel this alone. Oh, God, please ...."

Then Corrie became warm inside. She had remembered about God, her other Daddy, the one person who knew all the answers when all else failed. She had His love and His power. All she needed to do was use it. He had promised her!

"Faith! That's it. Shirali says you have to have it when things look the worst. OK, I'm ready. Corrie, you're a dummy. You should have thought of this before."

All of a sudden it didn't matter why she was here. She was here for a reason, and if God didn't want her here, the doors would open wide and she'd walk out ... just like Paul and Silas, she thought.

She heard a familiar noise, and then the sound of those metal locks. Fear and terror came upon her once again, but this time she trusted that God would help her.

"OK, God, you promised!"

Corrie clenched her fists in the dark.

"They may be bigger and stronger and smellier, but this time we'll take control, nasty cigarettes or not."

She steadied herself, sat up on the edge of the table and got ready for the blinding light. The door swung open with a crash and light poured into the small room. The same two huge figures moved into the room but this time the door remained open.

"What d'ya think the Six want with this silly kid, Slavic?"

"I don't ask questions, Bob, that's why I'm still alive. You'd be smart t'do the same, or the Committee o' Six'll have yer head."

Slavic approached Corrie who was still rubbing her eyes from the light, "Turn around, kid."

Corrie wouldn't move. Slavic grabbed her with his huge hands, spun her around like a small top and held her fast. Bob taped her mouth and eyes.

"Let's go kid."

Slavic took her roughly by the wrist and dragged her out of the room. Corrie could not see a thing. The air was cold and very still. She tried to listen as best she could, but it was not easy because she was being dragged and pulled at a very fast pace. She could hear the heavy breathing of the two big men, and the constant stomping of their huge boots. It sounded to Corrie like she was in a long, long passageway. It seemed twenty minutes, at least, that they had been moving through the passage. But then the sound changed. Large doors creaked open. She could hear them. Yes, they were definitely doors. Big doors.

"We're in a big room," Corrie thought, "the sound is much different."

The man called Slavic growled at Corrie in a low voice, "Stand still, kid." Then he ripped the strips of tape off Corrie's face.

Corrie rubbed at the pain with her hands. As her eyes began to adjust she saw she was in a large wood-paneled hall. There were no windows. Gray cigar smoke hung in thick layers throughout the room. Corrie rubbed her eyes one more time. She looked around the dark hall, then she looked up ... in front of her, some distance off, at a raised table sat three men and a woman. They were facing her, looking down at her. She could see them, but not clearly because of the haze, and the strange orange light filtering through the layers of smoke.

The woman, seated second from the left, feigned friendship but to Corrie she sounded evil.

"Corrie dear, if you will just tell us what we want to know we will let you go home to your parents."

"How do you know my name is Corrie? Who are you?"

The woman, who had a large round face with short, perfectly trimmed black hair would have no patience with a child who spoke back to her. She made no further pretense at friendship.

"That is of no concern to you, Corrie. Now, tell us what you know of the kefir, and tell us quickly."

"I've never heard of a kefir," Corrie said. "I don't even know what one is. Go ahead and burn me, but I still don't know what one is."

"Well then," the woman said angrily, "we will see how you like ...."

The woman was interrupted by the man seated next to her. It was apparent to the man that this manner of questioning would not be productive.

He said, "Perhaps, Ms. Wolman, our little Corrie really *doesn't* know about the kefir."

Looking down at Corrie he said, "Corrie, I would like to help you, but you need to help us if you want to go back to your mother and father. What can you tell me about your father's experiments?"

"Nothing," Corrie said abruptly. Corrie was resolute. These people were mean, and she had already decided that God was going to handle this. He had promised.

"Where his laboratories are for instance?" the man persisted, his voice growing deeper.

"Mister, I may be small but I'm not stupid."

Corrie knew this was not the most tactful thing to say, but she knew her Uncle Jake would love it. She could see him laughing as she told him. "Boy, am I going to have some stories for Uncle Jake," she thought.

Ms. Wolman leaned over to the man and said, "Lucius, they were right, let's move on."

Lucius Otterstein looked directly at the two men behind Corrie and ordered them, "You were correct to begin with, gentlemen. Take her away, and do whatever it takes. Start with injections and report back to us."

"Yessir, Mister Otterstein, sir," Slavic said nervously.

Corrie was taped once again and led out of the hall. As the enormous steel doors were closing behind her, Corrie heard Mr. Otterstein say, "Summon that banker from Prime Bank, what's his name, Edith? ... yes, that's it, Bulow ... Karl Bulow."

The doors slammed with a thunder, and Corrie was once again in the dark.

CHAPTER 14

The tiny Lander containing Jake Capterville, following its pre-set trajectory, glided over the Tharsis Mountains and over the giant volcano, Olympus Mons, a seventy-one thousand foot reminder of Mars' violent geologic past.

The landing site close to a gigantic canyon had been selected primarily for climatological reasons. At this particular position in the orbits of both planets, summer in the northern hemisphere on earth was also summer at the Grand Canyon on Mars.

The landing had been so smooth Commander Capterville was unable to tell exactly when he had touched down.

"My compliments to the Crab Legs guys," he had exclaimed.

He was standing close to his craft, having taken only a few steps through small chipped rocks and red dust.

He checked his watch. He had five hours of oxygen which he prayed he would not need because in exactly three hours the Lander would blast off with him, or without him, and due to Little Freedom's orbit, there was no possibility of leaving sooner.

"Sudden Martian sand storms come up with unpredictable fury," he thought correctly, "and if one blows through in the next three hours I'll be spending the rest of my brief life right here, one planet out from where I should be."

The first step by man on the earth's singular moon had been an event celebrated by all of humanity. Apollo 11 had taken eight years and 25 billion dollars to complete. The efforts of 300,000 technicians, a Cold War and a murdered president's dream had hung in the balance as the Eagle lunar module landed manually on the moon.   All earthlings watched, and rejoiced.

Jake's first step, however, on this rocky, reddish-brown landscape had been taken in solitude.   There were no cheers at home for the first human footprints on Mars.

Jake was forced, once again, to suppress a blend of emotions that neither he nor anyone else had ever experienced ... sadness, fear, obligation, the excitement at what might happen, the terror of what might happen, and the incredible beauty of this foreign, cold world.

"I'm on Mars!" kept racing through his mind, but the tremendous responsibility he willingly shouldered brought him back to earth.

"I must concentrate," he told himself, "there is much to do. I've got to find protected homes for the LDCUs."

Jake double-checked his watch.   He took a temperature reading off the sleeve of his suit.

"What I thought, twenty degrees Fahrenheit, a warm summer day."

He deployed the miniature solar panels that would power the experiments. They would also power the communication of the results to the earth for years to come.

"Once I disperse the Life Detection Communication Units, earth will be able to monitor this planet ... at least as much of it as I can cover in the next two hours and nineteen minutes."

Jake was now involved, 'locked on' as Orville and Jim used to say. He secured the master LDCU, and the seismic and atmospheric experiments in a rocky crevasse to protect them against the Martian storms.

In fifty minutes all base camp equipment was functioning and all power sources had been tested.

"There," Jake said into his dead microphone, "If earth cannot hear me, at least in ... let's see ... about three hours,

NASA should start receiving this data. At least they'll know somebody up here is alive and kicking."

And then he had an idea, "Seismic is a constant signal. If I short the signal in Morse Code I could send a message ... but no, they'd just figure it's interference, and I only have an hour and a half to place the other nine LDCUs. I'll just send 'JAKE' and they'll know I'm here. No, no, even better ...!" and Commander Capterville tapped out in code,

C..O..R..R..I..E

"She'll like that," he beamed as he secured his Martian camp. "The boys at Mission Control will go nuts, probably think they're hearing from Martians. But Siever will straighten 'em out sooner or later."

Jake could not comprehend it, but for the first time in a long while he actually felt at home. He couldn't explain it, but here on the fourth planet from the sun, he was at home. He had forgone marriage, a normal social life and many other interests, to come ... here. Now that he was here, now that communication had been established, he felt none of the panic or stress predicted by well meaning earthlings. To the contrary, he felt a surge of strength. He felt power and peace and love pouring into his body. He believed ... he felt it, and it was unmistakable ... somebody somewhere had taken an important stand.

"So, OK, let's see how much of this iceberg we can cover in, hmm, one hour and ten minutes."

He picked up his container of LDCUs and slung it over his left shoulder. The sun, the same small star that was sending life giving light to planet earth, illuminated in oranges and blues the irregular pock-marked valley that lay beckoning before him. Phobos and Deimos, Mars' battered moons, hung warlike in the red sky above him.

"Looks like Steven and I both got what we dreamed about," he reflected as he started up the valley.

"I actually made it to Mars. And, Steven, you've changed the shape of water ... and medicine, for all time."

Jake was no longer able to see earth in the windy Martian sky but he looked up anyway through his rounded face mask. He waved.

After a while he shook his fist toward the earth and hollered into space, "Steven, you've got it too darned easy! I'll bet you're sittin' on the back porch at the ranch right now, drinkin' orange juice, everyone tellin' you how all-fire smart you are ... Meg and Corrie waitin' on you hand and foot."

Jake took several more steps into the stunning valley, stopped, and looked up. "Oh, and Steven, call Captain Siever. Tell him to brush up on his Morse Code."

The enchanting sculptured valley was at once strikingly beautiful, yet also poisonous to human life. Jake checked his air supply, the integrity of his suit and the time. He looked up one last time.

"Pray for me, Corrie, the winds are coming up."

Fine red dust was blowing in gusts across the Martian landscape.

CHAPTER 15

Shirali Lasuria and Elliot Jaynes were sitting across the table from one another in a torn and very worn vinyl booth. The nondescript and not so famous Downtown Villager Coffee Shop was as old as Los Angeles itself. Still in its street corner location in one of the city's oldest office buildings it was known by locals for its tumble-down interior, and its fantastic food.

"Sorry to bring you down here at six in the morning, Shirali, but I thought the four of us could beat the traffic and have some privacy here. I have a hearing at nine and the courthouse is just around the corner."

"This is just fine, Elliot. You know I'd do anything in the world for Steven and Meg," Shirali said earnestly.

"Shirali, it's been on my mind since we met ... can you, well, there's more about the kefir, isn't there?"

"I hope you speak more clearly at your hearing, Elliot," Shirali said teasing him.

"I seem to be able to speak quite well to anyone other than you."

"While we wait for Dr. and Mrs. Capterville, I shall be happy to tell you of the kefir. The names we have for it in Russian, Persian and several other languages you could not pronounce. But in each instance the translation is the same. It means 'Life, given by God'."

Elliot's brow furrowed. He said nothing, watching Shirali intently.

With the grace of her mother, Khfaf, Shirali sipped her tea. She eventually continued, "Much of what I am going to tell you I cannot personally verify. However, it has been common knowledge in my village ... written, spoken and sung for thousands of years."

"Sung?"

"Much of our history has been passed from generation to generation in song, Elliot. We have wonderful choirs in the mountains."

"So Steven has said."

"Throughout the Bible, Moslem texts and other religious writings there are many references to something that is best translated in English as 'sour milk'."

Shirali took pride in speaking her second language properly and she spoke with almost perfect diction. She continued, "The kefir is grown in milk and is quite sour to the taste. In the mountains we use goat milk, but it can be grown in any fresh milk."

"And this sour milk, this kefir, is a medicine?" Elliot asked.

"Steven didn't believe me at first."

"I can see why."

"Steven always needs proof of things ... his precious clinical data."

"Steven is trained to analyze and understand. There's nothing wrong with that," Elliot said.

Shirali smiled and stirred her tea. "Steven was humoring me when he finally asked the university to study the kefir."

"What happened?"

"Just what I told Steven to expect. They all got terribly excited ... woke Steven up in the middle of the night."

"What did they find?"

"Millions of little creatures they couldn't identify or explain. They tried to grow it in their laboratories, but the little ones all died within hours. It sure got Steven's attention."

"Why did they die, Shirali?"

Shirali raised her eyebrows and smiled sweetly. She reached across the table and took Elliot's right hand in hers. "You have strong hands," she said.

"You didn't answer my question." Elliot pressed.

"Steven will give you any number of technical biological answers," Shirali said.

"None of which are completely satisfactory, I presume."

"You are correct."

"Then, why?"

Shirali was still holding Elliot's hand. "It is my belief that God would not allow His gift to grow while in their hands. Do you believe that, Elliot?"

Once again, Elliot Jaynes was speechless.

Shirali continued quietly. "Think of the ancient kings, the prophets of centuries past. Many of them lived to advanced ages, and in most cases passed valuable information and secrets from one generation to the next. Abraham, for instance, died at one hundred seventy five years of age, his son Isaac at one hundred eighty, his son Jacob over one hundred thirty, and so on."

"And the kefir was responsible?" Elliot asked.

"God was responsible for it, Elliot, but we believe the kefir to be a wonderful blessing from Him. It has been handed down family to family in our village for generations."

Elliot thought a while, then said, "Steven's expedition never did produce a scientific explanation ... for long life, I mean?"

"No, and we in the village knew it would not. There are many other villages in the region, and around the world that have similar diets and exercise. But nowhere are people as active, healthy and long lived as in my village of Bukol."

"And Steven did not make the connection ... with the kefir?"

"No, but that is not surprising. To those from the west, the kefir appeared as one of many unfamiliar foods. This is why my mother, Khfaf, showed Steven the little boy."

Elliot thought for a minute as he drank his coffee. "You'd think, with Steven's smarts, he'd have figured it out on the spot."

Shirali squeezed Elliot's hand and then let it go. She had another sip of tea and put her cup down with a rattle. She looked him in the eyes and said, "God allows His people to see things in stages, Elliot, in His time ... and His time is not always the time we would prefer."

"Now I know why Steven gets so frustrated," Elliot mumbled.

"What's that, Elliot?"

"Oh, nothing, Shirali, nothing. Tell me more about the kefir."

"In Bukol, for generations, no one was allowed to take the kefir from the village. If someone married and moved outside the village he or she was not taught the ways of the kefir or permitted to grow it. This was understood from birth."

Elliot did not want to offend his fascinating new friend. He chose his words carefully, "Isn't that rather ...?"

"Selfish?" Shirali finished his question.

"Yes."

"That is what I thought, and my beloved father agreed with me. We believed the kefir should be made available to everyone. My mother disagreed entirely, however, and she and my father, Tarkil, argued horribly about it for many, many years."

Shirali paused for a moment, then said, "And I hope they still are."

"You hope they still are?" Elliot asked.

"My mother is a wonderful, loving and principled woman and she is not at all selfish. She, like the rest of the village, simply believes that God commanded that the kefir remain in Bukol."

"But you received the kefir, didn't you?"

"Since I was not married, and because I had committed my life to God's work, I was, at my father's insistence, ultimately permitted to take a parent sample with me."

"Why does your mother, and the village, believe God commanded the kefir remain in Bukol?" Elliot asked.

"Partly because it had been there so long. If God wanted it somewhere else, the thinking goes, He certainly would have moved it long ago ... and everyone felt such a responsibility for its care."

"I see."

"But it is more than that, Elliot, and I confess I do not understand all of its history. Father says that historical records in our archives in Sukumi show that six centuries after Christ, Mohammed came to our village and received the kefir. I am told that reference is made to this in the Koran."

"Interesting," Elliot said.

"Through the centuries there have been many times when the kefir was stolen or destroyed. But somehow it always returned to Bukol. I expect these events over time encouraged our isolation and the protectionist sentiment within my people."

Elliot said kindly, "Don't feel you have to continue, with the story I mean, Shirali ... if this is upsetting to you."

"No, Elliot. It is as I have said, I am not certain you can help Steven unless you understand what we are dealing with."

"When you talk of the kefir you mention the 'parent'. What is that?"

"Steven's studies have proven the kefir to be extremely complex, and like many of the complicated things God has created it grows quite naturally and simply. But if it is not in the right hands, and those hands do not have the knowledge of its care, the kefir or its holder, or both, will perish."

"And this could be why Corrie was taken," Elliot surmised.

"Yes, Elliot. The parent lives indefinitely, constantly producing offspring which have the medicinal qualities Steven has spoken of. But the children do not become, nor do they create, new parents."

"Then how does a new parent come to life?" Elliot asked.

"From an existing parent. My mother knows how to do it. I know how to do it. No one else."

"Fascinating!" Elliot said. "Rather makes one question the theory of evolution, does it not?"

"All life evolves, Elliot, but only after God creates it. All the species Charles Darwin studied did not crawl out of a swamp. They adapted to their surroundings after God created them. I know this, because ...."

"Because you were there!" Elliot blurted out. Then, turning red, he said "Oh, I'm ... sorry, Shirali, I, oh gosh, it's just that Steven has told me of your age and I ...."

For an instant Shirali was surprised, and then she laughed merrily. She reached across the table and once again took his hand into hers. The firm, experienced skin on her beautiful face arranged itself into a picture of joy. For the first time in a long, long while her smile became that of her mother, Khfaf.

"If this man were only a hundred years older," she thought to herself.

"Elliot," she said, "you are wonderful. We shall be great friends."

"I am so ... embarrassed," he muttered, "Steven will kill me."

Shirali just smiled.

Elliot sipped his coffee with his one free hand. "Shirali, you said you *hoped* your parents were still arguing. What did you mean?"

The joy left Shirali's face. She became unsettled. She released Elliot's hand and drew a handkerchief from within her woven purse. She blotted the tears that came to the sides of her eyes. She said, "I am sorry, Elliot."

Elliot watched her carefully. He had no idea what to say or do.

Shirali finally explained, "What Corrie calls the Critters was actually the parent kefir. The bottle that was stolen from Steven's house was the only kefir left on earth."

"What?"

"That's right, Elliot." Shirali began to cry softly.

"But what about Bukol, your parents, the kefir there?" asked Elliot.

"The earthquake destroyed Bukol. It disappeared with everyone, Elliot, in one night. Bukol is gone. The kefir is gone."

Elliot finally understood. Shirali hoped her parents were still arguing ... because she hoped they were still alive.

CHAPTER 16

"Look what we have here," Megan said to Steven as they approached the coffee shop booth, "They've only met twice and they're already holding hands. Isn't that sweet?"

Megan and Steven slid into the booth. Steven said, "Romance so soon, Elliot? You don't give a girl a chance, do you?"

"Very funny," Elliot said, retrieving his hand. Unconsciously he began twisting a spoon in his fingers. "Shirali has been telling me of Bukol. It all sounds like something out of an incredible novel. I'm beginning to understand the difficulty and the anguish in the decisions she has made."

"It has not been easy for her," Megan said.

"Shirali," Elliot asked, "you and your father came to believe that you should be the one to take the kefir from the village ... to help others?"

"Yes. The simple answer is that I wanted to help people, more than just the people in my village. Steven can tell you that in the years I have been growing the kefir, it has cured many people of disease. But the more difficult answer, Elliot, is that my father and I believed I was supposed to take it with me."

Elliot regarded Shirali with immense respect. He said sensitively, "Under the circumstances, it appears you and your father were right."

A waitress arrived to take their order, and then left.

"And the idea," Elliot pursued, "is to make the kefir available to everyone in the world?"

"That is correct," answered Shirali.

146

"But the kefir, the part that is consumed ... doesn't it grow in goat milk?"

Shirali smiled at Steven and Megan. All three knew where this was leading. Shirali winked at Steven and said, "I believe you're next, my friend."

Steven smiled and took a deep breath.

Elliot noticed, but was not about to be distracted. "How could you possibly ship raw goat milk all over the world?"

"It cannot be done," Shirali replied, "at least not now. With a tremendous amount of money and effort it will be possible. But to process, refrigerate and ship the kefir to millions of people will require money that we don't have."

Elliot thought a bit, still twisting the spoon in his fingers. The creases in his forehead dissolved, he looked up and his eyes became wide and bright. He smacked the palm of his hand on the table with a startling *crack!*

"I should have known it, Capterville! The kefir is going to the world with the help of your technology."

Elliot hit the table again, "By golly," he said with his eyes flashing, "I should have figured! But how, Steven, how?"

Steven put his arm around Megan and carefully viewed the room. One of the two waitresses, wearing a bleached pink uniform, was cleaning the old fashioned soda fountain counter getting ready for the breakfast rush. The other waitress was taking an order from an older couple seated across the room. Save the cook, who was out of sight in the kitchen banging the instruments of his art, there was no one else in the coffee shop.

"It's OK," Megan said, pinching Steven's arm, "complete the story for Elliot. I agree with Shirali, he must know everything."

"Know what?" Elliot asked, becoming impatient.

"Well," Steven began in a low voice, "since it is not at this point feasible to manufacture the kefir itself, we have developed a process using cluster technology ...."

"I remember," Elliot interrupted, "you invented it."

"No, no, Elliot, I did not invent it. Cluster technology is the product of a tremendous body of research by many, many people."

"I am afraid I still don't understand," Elliot confessed. "What is it you have done? I thought you said your products are the tip of the iceberg and it's the technology that's important."

"I have created a process called Cluster Conversion Process. We have employed principles and theories from microcluster technology in creating new manufacturing processes."

Megan began to fidget uncomfortably. She believed that Elliot would never be able to help find Corrie if he did not fully comprehend Steven's discovery.

"Elliot," Megan said, "a 'cluster' is just that, a cluster, like a bunch of grapes ... only Steven works with the atoms, with the molecules, that make up water. The patent papers he has filed cover a process that groups molecules of water together in microscopic clusters."

Shirali studied Megan carefully, and she was touched. She was impressed by this woman whose only child had been stolen. She recognized the strength and the support Megan had provided her husband in a time of true crisis, and she was reminded of her parents ... and of the resemblance between her mother and Megan.

Megan continued excitedly, "See the water in your glass, Elliot? It's full of free-floating water molecules ... H_2O. But Steven's water is different. If you could see it up close, it would look like millions of bunches of grapes, forming and reforming into interesting patterns. Only it's still pure water."

"So that's what you meant, Steven, when you said you had altered the molecular structure of water?" Elliot asked.

"That's right."

"Then why don't you bring Megan with you to all of our meetings?" Elliot said cheerfully, "that way we won't waste so much time."

The four of them laughed and ordered more coffee, tea and toast as the room began to fill with people.

Elliot asked, "Your water is *clustered*, isn't that the right word, Steven?"

"That's right, Elliot. Over the last ten years or so we've found that the water in the cells of the human body is not the same as the water in your glass. It is highly clustered ... lots of bunches of grapes as Meg would say. We have known for a long time that the body functions by using chemicals, but we have now proven that the billions of cells in the body communicate with one another by sending and receiving electrical impulses. The cells are actually singing to one another. And the transmitters and receivers, in the case of living systems, are the water clusters within the cells."

"Fascinating! So what does your water do?" Elliot asked.

"In altering the structure of water, we are changing the frequency emitted by the water. We are changing the songs that the water sings. We are using our waters to send messages to the body."

"You mean this water right here is sending out an electrical signal?" asked Elliot.

"Yes," continued Steven patiently, "although tap water like this is so full of minerals and other elements, any beneficial signals are effectively blocked."

"So," Elliot pursued, "the water in each individual cell of the human body is special, because it's clustered, and because it's clustered it's able to communicate with all the other cells, presumably to keep the body healthy and growing and so on. Am I close?"

Elliot's enthusiasm was infecting the others and Megan was delighted. She said, "You're right on target, Elliot. The human body, when it's healthy, is in tune. It's very much like a symphony orchestra with all the instruments, or cells, playing together. When we get sick, it means that one or more of the sections in the orchestra are out of tune."

"Meg's quite right," Steven said. "As a matter of fact our studies have shown that well before we notice the symptoms of an illness, the frequencies in our cells have already gone out of tune. So if we can keep our cells in tune and communicating, singing properly, if you will, we stand a good chance of remaining healthy."

"And your water, your solutions, communicate with the body in the same way?" Elliot guessed.

"Excellent, Elliot. Because our solutions are clustered they react with the body not chemically, but electronically. We are actually working with the laws of physics, yet on a level that is completely safe to living systems. We are using our water solutions to send healing signals directly to the cells of the body, without toxic side effects."

"No kidding!" Elliot said.

"It is called cellular signal transduction, Elliot. The National Institutes of Health has just established a new Department of Structural Biology to study protein folding and the effects of cellular impulse transmission, and," Steven grinned, "last week they finally agreed to begin testing of two of our solutions."

"Congratulations! Now I know why your briefcase gets stolen so much."

Megan frowned.

Steven stirred his coffee, "The wars within us, Elliot, are far different than previously thought."

"Isn't that the truth," Shirali said with a smile.

"You're familiar," Steven continued, "with the PS-51 solution, the one that RAM Pharmaceuticals claims is theirs?"

"Of course," Elliot said, anxious to fully understand the product he had been representing in court.

"It would be impossible for them to manufacture the same product," Steven continued, "because they don't have the technology to do it. They're using the same ingredients, the same compounds, but the real effectiveness of the product, as we make it, is in its electrical conductivity. Our PS-51 solution sends the benefits of the ingredients directly to the cells of the body ... and it does so in seconds."

"In seconds?" Elliot asked with surprise.

"That's right," Steven said, "when you put a few drops of the water into your mouth, it will register electronically on the bottom of your foot in two seconds. But do the same thing with RAM's phony solution and it won't register a thing. At best they have a very dilute mineral solution, and I'm sure they know it."

"I knew it was a phony," Elliot said, "but now I know why. This helps ... helps a lot."

"To further answer your question," Elliot, "our waters help regulate the body's communication system. They help our cells sing in tune. They help keep everything tuned and healthy and in some cases give a real boost to the immune system."

"In some cases?" Elliot thought out loud.

"PS-51 is just one of thousands of potential products and applications. It's the Cluster Conversion Process, CCP, that made the manufacture of PS-51 possible. It's the Cluster Process that's so important. And that is why the patent work has been so carefully crafted."

"You can design different solutions and waters to do different things?"

Shirali had been intently watching both men. She broke in, "Of course, Elliot. Why do you think I am here?"

"I think I'm lost again," Elliot confessed.

Shirali continued, "Steven has managed to change the shape of water, but that is only one of the wonderful discoveries God has given to him."

Elliot still looked perplexed.

"Steven has also come up with a way to ... oh, how would you say it, Steven ... to imprint things directly into water."

Meg jumped in, "So that you have the good qualities of a vitamin, or mineral, or drug captured in the water. And when you drink the water it can't hurt you, because it's only water.

Elliot was more curious than ever. "How in the world do you do that?"

The four of them had been so caught up in their conversation they had not noticed the now noisy coffee shop was completely full, with several people waiting outside. The waitresses were rushing from table to table, and the top of the cook's white hat could be seen bobbing to and fro in the kitchen. They ordered more coffee and tea, and Steven began speaking ... so quietly that Elliot was leaning over the table to hear.

"We take a molecule of, let's say, vitamin C, and we collapse water molecules all around it, forming a cluster. The cluster is now vibrating not only with its own frequencies, but

152

also with the frequency of vitamin C. Then in our process we wash out the vitamin C."

"Incredible!" Elliot said.

"The result is pure clusters of water that are vibrating with the frequency of the vitamin, yet without containing the vitamin itself. And there are billions of these vitamin C clusters in each drop of water."

Elliot was entranced. He was in new-found awe of the knowledge he knew his unpretentious friend must have. Then, finally, he made the connection.

"Wait a minute! This is what you've done with the kefir!" he shouted louder than he intended, "and this is how it's to go to the world ... in, of all things ... water!"

Shirali smiled. "God frequently uses simple things to confound the wise, Elliot."

"I wouldn't exactly call this simple, Shirali, but I think I understand what you mean."

Then Elliot looked directly at Shirali. His eyes were flashing. Very slowly, emphasizing each word, he said, "I believe you will find in the Book of Ezekiel that water is said to be the symbol of the cleansing power of God."

"Why, Elliot, I had no idea you knew of such matters," said a surprised Shirali.

"One should never judge a book by its cover," he said good-naturedly. "And speaking of judges, I'd better be off. Thank you, all of you, for making me understand. I have some ideas concerning our friends at RAM, but how all this might lead us to Corrie ... I'm afraid we'll just have to keep digging."

Megan looked visibly upset. She had hoped the conversation would open Elliot's eyes to something ... anything.

At the center of the table Shirali cupped both of her hands around Megan's. She looked at Megan with a face that spoke more than words.

"Thanks Shirali," Megan said.

"Steven," Elliot said, "your work is even more remarkable than I had guessed."

"Thanks, Elliot."

"I suppose I'll have to regard you with a new respect."

"Only if it's warranted," Steven grinned.

"OK, you two!" Megan said. "Let's get going. There is much to do."

"Right," Steven said, "we'd best be off."

"I agree," said Shirali, "it is time."

The group walked among the tables toward the busy front door. Steven paid the bill at the antiquated NCR cash register that remained eternally fixed to the end of the yellowed counter. The old machine, host to thousands, still rang and clattered a welcome reminder of days gone by and, without fanfare, suggested caution in moving too swiftly from one's past.

The four friends moved outside together onto a busy downtown sidewalk, said their good-byes and departed.

Inside, at the next booth, a gaunt intense looking man with thick round eyeglasses remained seated with his back to the booth where Steven and the others had been talking. He was hunched over, thinking, with a thin, perverse smile shaping his thick lips.

Just inside the coffee shop door, waiting for a table, stood four elderly ladies. They were glaring at the man.

"Just look at him," one of them said, "all of us waiting in line, and he sits there by himself in a booth for six."

"And all he's ordered is coffee," said another, "we should talk to the manager. He's such a mean looking man."

The man abruptly pushed his coffee away from him, spilling some of it on the table. He rose slowly, adjusting his eye glasses, and stood next to the table for the longest time.

"I think there's something wrong with him," one of the ladies whispered.

Finally, the man reached into his pocket, left a meager tip, crossed the room with a mechanical, calculated walk and paid his bill. He pushed past the four ladies and flung the coffee shop door aside.

Karl Bulow glanced briefly at his gold Cartier watch and became part of a crowded Los Angeles morning.

CHAPTER 17

Commander Capterville had already placed and energized six of his ten Life Detection and Communication Units. His video recorder had exposed hundreds of feet of film. The winds which he feared would become a full Martian storm had subsided, and the sharp angle of the sun created dramatic and colorful definitions in the landscape.

To keep himself company and to provide narration for the video, Jake continued speaking excitedly for his absent audience. "I've covered close to a quarter of a mile, and I have forty-one minutes left."

He clenched his fist and reminded himself to make the most of this precious time.

"Before lift off," he said while panning the valley, "I must record the view from the summit across the valley and place the last Unit there. But first I've got to get rock samples from the arch formation in this wall. Markhti Tarba would give his right arm for a chunk of this."

Jake had followed the western rim, or at least what he thought of as the western rim of the valley, so he could examine and take samples from a variety of geologic structures. He had just noticed the unusual arching shape. It was outlined in the sun-bathed face of the jagged cliff that rose before him.

"Why do I feel I've been here before?" he asked himself.

After describing the surroundings in some detail for those whom he hoped would some day become his audience, he leaned against the sheer cliff face with his left hand and struck the weathered stone firmly with the sampling pick in his right hand. With a crash not audible to Jake or to his audience, he fell headlong through falling rock into the dark.

"Blast!" he hollered as sensors automatically lit emergency lights on his suit. Even before he was back on his feet he was instinctively checking every square inch of his all-purpose suit.

"One tear in the wrong spot, and I'm Martian history," he grumbled, brushing off dust and dirt.

"This is just great," he thought, without speaking into his recorder. "Two hundred million miles from home and I have to fall into the side of a mountain." He felt like he'd fallen down his basement staircase back home.

Jake completed his equipment check. "No leaks, thank you very much, but LDCUs Eight and Nine smashed to bits. Now ... where in this world am I?"

Jake switched on the powerful spotlight sewn into the left elbow of his suit and slowly turned in place viewing his surroundings. He was in a spectacular cavern, about the size and shape of a motion picture theater. It was rectangular, almost symmetrical.

"Magnificent, absolutely magnificent," he recorded. "This place could have been made by someone ... someone wonderfully artistic. It reminds me of the grotto, the one behind the waterfall on earth. But no, this place, this is not the same. It is different from anything I've ever experienced."

After studying the cavern more closely he said, "It could just as easily have been nature at work."

"If Corrie were here," Jake thought, "she'd look up at me with those big brown eyes and say 'God did it, Uncle Jake!'"

Unaware that he was speaking aloud, Jake said, "I expect you're right, Corrie. There's something mighty unusual about this place."

157

He proceeded very carefully, one step at a time, circling the floor of the unique stone room, filming and explaining all the while.

"Ah, yes," he said, "this will be a perfect place to set Unit Seven ... Steven will be pleased ... took me months to convince Control to put Steven's water in one of these Life Detectors."

He activated Unit Seven, stood up and moved his lights randomly about the cavern.

"One thing for sure," he said aloud, "there was water here at one time, and a lot of it. The stalactites and stalagmites are huge, and look, a whole row of them against that wall, floor to ceiling, fifty feet high, like Greek columns all colored in purple and dark greens. The walls behind ... glossy orange with thin vertical streaks of yellow."

Jake checked his watch.

"Twenty-seven minutes," he recorded, "and I'll need all of that to cross the valley and get back to the ship. I'd best be off," he said, and he smiled at the phrase. Steven used it so frequently because Steven was so frequently late.

He turned to climb the rocks and rubble he had fallen in with. He noticed for the first time that the arched entry, which was now back-lit by the Martian morning, was a perfect semi-circle.

"How curious," he thought, "the people from Bukol must have already been here!"

But he was pressed for time.

"Move it, Jake," he scolded himself, "NASA says the last Unit, number Ten, on the far ridge, is the most critical."

Jake shined his light downward to take his first step and placed his left foot on a perfectly flat rock.

"And what, is ... this?" he stuttered, while his heart leapt to his throat. Only one small corner was exposed, but there was no doubt.

"This is a solid stone stair cut with precision, definitely man made ... no, no, of course not ... but milled by someone, someone smaller. This is a half or a third the size of a human step. Let's see ... I'll move this ...."

He pushed away more of the debris, revealing a perfectly cut and polished stairway that rose to the crescent door. He was stunned.

"So there *is* life on Mars ... or was."

Standing, shaking with excitement, at the foot of the steps he filmed the staircase. He debated, "Unit Ten can wait ... but, no, I must go. Steven's Unit Seven is activated. Twenty-three minutes left."

Jake turned off his suit lights so he could take a final effect photograph of the arching entry. He secured his equipment and glanced down at the stairs preparing to leave. On the floor, several inches to the right of the first stone step, his eyes fixed upon several sparkling particles. They were the size of grains of sand, only they were twinkling ... sparkling oddly in the low gray light.

All of Jake's life he had taken action first, and then asked questions. Being on another planet had not changed that. He instinctively bent over and pinched several of the glowing grains between the gloved fingers of his right hand. Standing erect and still, he gently dropped them into the palm of his left hand. He watched, transfixed, attempting to comprehend what he was seeing.

"This is not sand, or glass," Jake said in halting speech, "and this is not reflected light. These are crystals of some kind, or at least they appear to be, and they are ... Wow! ...

159

emitting their own light. They're somehow generating their own power!"

Keeping his left hand steady Jake trained his right elbow light on the palm of his left hand and turned it on. Before his eyes the sparkling crystals instantly transformed into a tiny visible cloud that hovered an inch above his hand.

"From solid to gas, in the presence of ... light?" Jake wondered.

He turned off his light and the gaseous little cloud reorganized into glittering crystals in the palm of his hand ... and there were more of them.

"This is absolutely, oh, no ... time's running out ... I have to go."

Jake tossed the sparkling crystals into the air and turned to leave. But when the crystals touched the floor, the room lit up with a light so bright Jake was forced to cover his mask. From the fifth small step he spun around. He tried his best to see. Hands shading his face, he overlooked a carpet of pure light. Contact by the falling crystals had in a fraction of a second lighted all the other crystals in the room. The beautiful colored hall, for the first time in how many millennia, was once again aglow in radiant animated splendor.

Jake was amazed.

"A coherent wave," he thought. "One oscillating crystal hit the floor and created a coherent wave, and millions of them, whoever or whatever they are, amplified the signal instantly and created this, this light, which ...."

The floor beneath him began to rumble and vibrate. The wall directly opposite the entrance was moving. Jake was trying desperately to keep his bearings, keep his senses. Too much was happening too fast, and he was out of time.

He recorded, "Look! The wall behind me, no, not the wall, it's a semi-circle like the entrance, two round panels are

160

separating from the middle, opening. It's another entrance, it's black, completely dark inside."

The vibration stopped. Jake looked at his watch.

"Nineteen minutes."

Jake never completely understood why he did what he now chose to do. He again pinched a few of the glowing grains between his fingers, walked with purpose to the newly opened door and with a snap of his wrist flipped the crystals into the dark. Another black realm came alive with brilliant light. With a firm grip on the left side of the entrance Jake leaned forward, his head and shoulders straining into the ....

"This is indescribable! It's another world!"

His mind was racing, "Another world!" he repeated trying to invent words that would be adequate.

"There is nothing with which we are familiar."

He knew he must go or he would perish, yet before he left he took a long, memorizing look.

"As far as the eye can see," Jake said in a strange halting voice, "geometric patterns, hexagonal, with energy transfers everywhere ... three dimensional, or four ... constantly changing ... lattices, a matrix ... it seems solid, yet always moving, a liquid crystalline array ... power, light, from point to point ... sending, receiving ... communication!"

Jake's eyes could stand the light no longer. Shielding his face he turned away. Then the light suddenly went out, and Jake could see nothing.

"It all came instantly to life, if that's the right word, with the touch of an object the size of a grain of sand. I've got to ask Steven about this, lots of similarities ...."

Jake Capterville was at this moment farther from earth, farther from the sun and farther across the solar system than anyone from earth had ever been. He pegged his chances for survival as slim, but believed his efforts worth the risk. Had

161

he even the slightest inkling of the truth in the events he had set in motion, his belief in his efforts would have been confirmed. He could not now be expected to understand, but he knew deep down that someone he loved dearly would, in due time, impart to him the truth of this experience. For now, in this present darkness in a cavern on the planet Mars, live or die, Jake would take action.

Jake bolted up the stairs four at a time and flew through the crescent opening. He ran across the valley floor and with LDCU Ten strapped to his back he began the scramble up the eastern ridge. He climbed upward anxiously through truck-size rusted boulders, across slides of fine yellow sand and finally, almost to the top, scrambled on all fours up a steep rock slab. His legs were moving as fast as they would carry him. He lunged, farther, upward, and gasped in terror with the one step that was too far. His momentum sent him over the edge, and only his intuition held him by his fingers to the lip of the cliff.

"If I can pull myself up far enough, maybe I can ... there," and he got one leg over the ledge, then the other, and was able to roll back over the top.

Before looking over the ledge or even standing, Commander Capterville swiftly deployed Unit Ten.

"There, mission accomplished," Jake proclaimed proudly. And with that, he rolled over on his side and pulled himself to the edge. Looking down, what he saw could not be measured in meters or even miles. The distance was so great he was barely able to see the base of the canyon. The far eastern rim, which he knew to be there, was beyond his field of vision. He knew from detailed Mariner and Viking mapping that the Great Canyon of Mars was longer than his America was wide.

The programmed landing site had been one half an earth mile to the west of the Great Canyon, but perhaps because of the imperfect entry to orbit the Lander had come to rest where it did.

"Mission Control is going to hear about this," he grumbled.

"Eleven minutes! Move it, Jake." Jake Capterville ran, and ran, awkwardly, as fast as he could move his encumbered feet in the weightlessness of his freezing, hot-colored world.

Two minutes, eighteen seconds. He opened the hatch to the Lander and climbed in. The blue monitor was flashing a bright orange *ERROR ... ERROR ... ERROR.* On the keyboard Jake hit **ALT, FILE, LIFE** ... blinking orange light ... Jake typed, **HELP**, and on the blue screen in orange letters appeared ... **WEIGHT OVER MAXIMUM** ....

"Dang it all!" he said, knowing what he must do. The rock samples, so precious and telling to people on earth, could mean his death.

Jake dropped two containers ... blinking orange light. Jake dropped all four containers ... orange lights.

"Blast it all! What else?"

Thirty seconds.

"I've stripped the ship ...."

Twenty seconds.

"Oh, yea! All right, the A/V goes," and Jake ripped all the audio-visual systems out of his suit. All records of his having been there, all cameras and tapes, he dropped, and they fell those several feet to the Martian plain beneath his ship. Though small and light, they made the difference.

Jake latched the Lander hatch, typed, **HELP** ... green light ... two seconds, one ... the landing craft shuddered briefly and with a spray of dust and rock it lifted off the reddish

163

landscape with ease, leaving the long Martian morning for the blackness of space.

Jake looked upward. He said earnestly, "Thanks! None too soon."

At two thousand feet Commander Jake Capterville looked below him. Less than a mile from his landing site, to the west, a brown ominous mass filled half his field of vision.

By three thousand feet he was praying that the same program that erred in setting the landing, was about to redeem itself by completing a flawless docking with the mother ship.

By four thousand feet the summer storm at the Great Canyon, violent even by Martian standards, had already erased all visible evidence of the one brief visit from planet earth.

CHAPTER 18

Oppressive heat and summer tourism swelled the crowded terminals and air traffic controls at Rome's International Airport. The several aircraft above, forced into elongated holding patterns, were pleading for permission to land. On the ground the crew of a polished silver and unmarked 747 jet finished its pre-flight checks and awaited instructions.

A side door in the security area of the Global Airways terminal opened onto the tarmac, and a tall lean man dressed in an expensive business suit walked unhurried with a briefcase in the direction of the jet.

From the other side of the terminal a black Rolls Royce Silver Spur III limousine advanced slowly toward him and stopped under the left wing of the aircraft. The chauffeur, in black suit and cap, sprang out of the car, ran to the passenger side, composed himself militarily and opened the door. Out stepped a heavy set woman with a round stern face and close-cropped black hair. She was followed by a tanned and fit-looking man whose handsome face was distinguished by a large Roman nose.

They unemotionally received the tall man who without hesitation handed the briefcase to the woman and departed. Deep in conversation, the man and woman climbed the transportable steel stairs and disappeared into the plane. The side door of the aircraft was promptly secured behind them.

The captain, receiving immediate clearance from the tower, taxied the giant craft into position and, with permission, turned onto the runway in front of sixteen waiting passenger jets. Without braking, the powerful engines roared and pulsed at full throttle and within seconds the 747, with a

165

passenger list of two, banked sharply north-by-northwest heading for its first stop in Paris.

"Are they all there, Edith?" the man asked. He was not looking not at her but at the Capitoline Hill disappearing in the distance, five thousand feet below.

Dr. Edith Wolman, holding doctorates in finance, political science and mathematics from three different universities did not answer for several minutes. When she did it was in her usual abrupt manner. "There is only one this time."

"Only one?"

"Only one, Giancarlo, but it will suffice." She sounded quite pleased.

"But is it worth the trouble? For just one?" Giancarlo asked. Giancarlo Panatta acknowledged he may not be as bright as Dr. Wolman. He knew his limits and he was extremely pragmatic. Any intellectual shortcomings he may possess were more than balanced by the awful influence he wielded within his dark world. Giancarlo Panatta was, without notoriety, terribly, terribly powerful.

"It is worth the trouble," Edith Wolman responded with satisfaction, "when it's an eighteen billion dollar United States treasury note."

"Eighteen billion in one note?" Panatta asked.

"That's correct. It was a partial borrowing from Japanese interests. The U.S. is famous for borrowing to cover its debt."

"And the interest rate?" Panatta pursued.

Edith Wolman broke into one of her rare smiles looking like the wicked cat that had swallowed a fat canary. "Seven and one half percent."

"What? That's impossible in this market. We must have paid a premium."

166

"We paid slightly more than sixteen billion, more than a ten percent discount," Dr. Wolman said. The tone of her voice indicated there was more to come.

"Unbelievable! That's fantastic," he said.

"Cash talks, Giancarlo."

"And, as usual, the principal and the interest are fully guaranteed," Panatta volunteered. His years of association with her brilliant financial mind told him she would accept no less.

"By the full faith and credit of the United States government," Edith Wolman said almost maliciously.

"And ... there is more ...?" Panatta asked, knowing her extraordinary skills in negotiation.

"You are quite right, Giancarlo."

Edith liked this simple man whom she knew to be her academic inferior. "He would make a fine husband," she thought to herself, "if I chose to make time for such things."

Edith's life was forever in paradox. A bit of her yearned for motherhood and family obligation, but her drive for ultimate control always relegated such thoughts to practical insignificance. The critical decisions in her life were always governed by her compulsive and unquenchable thirst for power.

Her thoughts returned to the financial and political calculations at hand. Giancarlo Panatta was not a potential parent, he was one of six partners ... at least for the time being. He was a well orchestrated pawn who could be moved to any position that served her purposes.

She explained, "In addition to the note, our sixteen billion bought us almost two billion in American real estate equity ... existing office buildings, shopping centers and the like in major U.S. cities."

"How in the world did you manage that?" asked Panatta.

167

"Our sixteen billion was simultaneously re-loaned to a consortium of American real estate and oil and gas portfolios. As a condition of the transaction, I demanded, and received, twelve percent of their equity. In all cases we are in second position in the form of a second trust deed or mortgage ... based on current appraisals. On sale or refinance if our twelve percent equity exceeds our mortgage, and I believe it already does, we are paid that amount also."

"And the interest rate?" Panatta asked, trying to follow her.

"Thirteen percent."

"Saints alive! Edith, how ...?"

"And," Edith continued, "the recorded notes and deeds of trust provide that the properties cannot be refinanced without our permission. Here, take a look at these," and Edith handed Panatta fifty pages of property summaries.

"You are telling me that we, the Committee, effectively control all of these assets and we don't even own them?" Panatta asked sounding even more respectful.

"Well, I suppose an owner could attempt a transfer but no title insurance company would insure the title for the new buyer. So yes, Giancarlo, we have acquired control over more than two billion U.S. dollars worth of American real estate, three and a half billion if you choose to believe the new appraisals that are being prepared."

"And," Giancarlo said respectfully, "we own an eighteen billion dollar U.S. treasury note bearing seven and one half percent interest ...."

"For a time," mused Edith.

"For a time? You would sell an asset like that? Why?"

"You will see very soon, Giancarlo, very soon," Edith said. Her mind was penetrating other matters.

Edith Wolman stared out the window. The French countryside was passing far below. Under her breath she said, "Today's accumulation will serve us well. Soon we shall be ready."

Suddenly, with a piercing look, she turned to Panatta. "Is everything prepared for the G-7 flight?" she asked.

With a malevolence she had not heard from him before, Panatta growled in a low voice, "Do not question my preparations, Doctor Wolman. You do your work, and I'll do mine. Be assured, you will not be disappointed. And I trust I, and the others, will not be disappointed in you. You are very creative in what you do. Just be certain you do not become too creative."

With no hint of expression Doctor Wolman ignored the warning.

Shamefully unappreciative of their lavish surroundings the two dissolute partners fell into icy silence. The giant jet, recently converted for world wide communications and state of the art business capabilities was also opulent beyond belief. The upcoming flight from Paris to Los Angeles would be little different than an evening in Manhattan's most luxurious penthouse.

***

It was a quarter to three in the afternoon as the silver jumbo jet prepared for its approach to Paris. Dr. Edith Wolman and Giancarlo Panatta, the lone passengers on board, said nothing further to one another until they passed through the heavy brass doors of Prime Bank Paris and walked, without appointment, past a security guard and a secretary into the office of the president of the bank.

"Good afternoon, Karl," Edith said, fully intending to startle the man. "You remember Mr. Panatta, I presume."

Karl Bulow had been mired in quarterly reports, preparing himself for the evening Board of Directors' meeting, and he was genuinely shocked. He detested interruptions almost as much as he detested Edith Wolman. He was, indeed, terrified of her.

"Yes ... yes, of course. How are you Mr. Panatta," Bulow mumbled.

Panatta said nothing.

"Here, Karl," Ms. Wolman said, sliding the treasury note documents to him across his sacred desk. "Please make us an offer on this note." The tone of her voice let him know she required an answer before leaving.

"But Doctor Wolman, I have a directors' meeting presently and I really ...."

"I know that," snapped Wolman, "it will be the perfect time for you to have this approved."

"But ...."

Wolman and Panatta stood at the front of Karl Bulow's desk towering over him. Having no choice, he finally collapsed into his antique swivel chair and said, "Very well, let's have a look."

The banker studied the papers intently. Behind thick Coke bottle glasses, his eyes opened wider and wider. He looked up slowly to find his guests calmly sitting in two of the five Renaissance chairs that surrounded his ornate desk. The last thing he wanted now was a negotiation with Edith Wolman. He rose from his chair to assert his authority.

Pressing the tips of his fingers against the edge of his desk to steady himself, Mr. Bulow said, "I can assure approval for

170

seventeen and a quarter billion, cash, U.S. dollars ... not a penny more. We shall have to participate the purchase with others, of course, but I can promise the seventeen now."

"... and a quarter," Edith sneered.

"Yes," Mr. Bulow sighed.

Panatta was watching Dr. Wolman wondering what she would say next. Bulow braced himself for anything.

Dr. Wolman stood up abruptly and said, "That will be just fine, Karl. Please have the paperwork completed and approved this evening. I shall need the monies transferred by the day after tomorrow to the usual accounts."

President Karl Bulow said the only thing he could say, the only words that were permitted of him. "Very well, Doctor Wolman, very well."

To the relief of Mr. Bulow his two uninvited guests left their chairs and walked to the door. Holding her arm, Panatta leaned over and whispered to Edith, "You just made us a five billion dollar profit ... in a matter of hours."

Edith Wolman made no attempt to lower her voice. "More than that, Giancarlo. The value of the U.S. dollar will rise by at least twenty-two percent in the next four months."

Knowing Mr. Bulow was listening intently she spun around. Bulow was leaning over his desk, nervous fingers fidgeting with a blue silk tie.

Arrogantly she said, "This transaction will be a feather in your cap, Karl. But if I were you I should move my private accounts from yen and marks into U.S. currency."

Karl Bulow was stunned.

Trying to maintain his composure and the counterfeit expression on his face, Bulow was thinking as rapidly as he could, "I can understand her knowledge of currency fluctuations. As the new Chairwoman of the International Monetary and Markets Fund she's got finance ministers and

171

central bankers of the world's largest industrial democracies reporting to her regularly. But ... how? ... how does she know my personal accounts are invested in Japanese and German currency?"

Bulow straightened. He attempted to organize himself. He swallowed the little pride he still possessed. "Ahh, yes Doctor, I believe that is very good advice. Thank you."

The two once again started for the door, but Dr. Wolman turned and looked menacingly at Bulow. She asked quietly, "Have you any news from your Los Angeles vacation?"

"I have, indeed," he replied.

"Do you believe we are pursuing the proper means ... with the doctor?" she asked.

"Absolutely, yes."

"Good, good ..." she said unpleasantly.

"But there is more," Bulow said. "There are others, particularly one, that much can be learned from. In Los Angeles, in a coffee shop, I overheard ...."

"Excellent, Karl, but not here. Save it for your testimony before us."

Looking at neither man, Doctor Wolman terminated the meeting with, "Let us go, Giancarlo."

In a slow motion that he intended to savor forever, Karl Bulow watched Panatta open the door for the revered Edith Wolman. Sadistically, he wanted to record her next expression in his memory for all time.

Panatta was following Dr. Wolman out the door and was about to shut it when Karl Bulow said imperiously, "Oh, excuse me, Edith, but there is one more bit of information I believe you will find important. It seems the girl ... what's her name? Corrie, yes, that's it ... Corrie Capterville. It appears she has escaped."

CHAPTER 19

Corrie Capterville was peeking between two of the weathered granite boulders that towered like primeval monuments at the edge of the searing desert that lay before her. Not far away, a tiny town, a ghostly remnant of another century's mining boom, sat toy-like on the vast baking earth. Given motion by the high desert winds, yellow tumbleweeds had wedged themselves against fences with a prickly insistence. The land was quiet. A small bird called to its mate.

"There are people here," Corrie thought, "I saw a man. And there's the mail box."

The mail box! Less than a hundred yards away ... maybe the only link to her world, her family and, possibly, her life.

"Should I run for it now or should I wait for dark?" she asked herself. "Dark would be better, they won't see me. But what if they pick up the mail? It'll be an extra day. Uncle Jake would go for it, I know he would. But wait, Daddy says to always go over all the facts."

Corrie huddled beneath the immense stone shapes, seeking shade. She crossed her burned and bruised legs and looked at the soles of her filthy shoes. They were coming apart.

"Mommy won't like this a bit," she said.

She took a deep breath, and then another, and tried to relax.

"OK, let's start from the beginning. That's always best."

With the back of her hand she wiped the perspiration from her forehead. She closed her eyes, and felt herself falling, falling back in time ... to ....

"Oh yes, the passageway, and the door to the big room with those horrible people ... it just closed. I must remember those names, Otterstein, Wolman and, and ... oh dear ... yes, that's the name, Bulow. Whew!

"The long passageway back, I don't know how far we went but far, very far, and the pain on my arm from Slavic dragging me. Ouch! And so wet and clammy cold. Yuk.

"Then the fight started. What was it about? Slavic and Bob. All that horrible talk, and hitting and grabbing. Slavic dropped me. I pulled off the tape and just ran and ran and ran, back in the direction of the big door. Rock walls, it was a tunnel, all dark except ... a few orange lights on old hanging wires.

"Then I saw it. Another tunnel, a smaller one. Off to the left I went, don't know where, just running and running. I heard Bob.

"*'Where's the kid, you fool?'*

"They were coming after me.

"*'I'll go down here, you check the main tunnel ... what 'n idiot you are.'*

"I could hear Bob's big feet coming after me, and then I saw another tunnel, almost missed it, another tunnel, even smaller, to the right. I ran.

"Bob stopped. I heard him.

"*'Hey, Slavic! Come 'ere. Think I found the kid's footprint.'*

"Oh, dear. I ran, but it was all dark, no lights. Slavic found Bob. Oh, no. I tried to hear what they said.

"*'Bob, you check the small tunnel. I'll follow this one. She can't get away, or we're dead meat.'*

"More footsteps, closer now. I must run faster, but then ... BLAM! ... I smashed into the end of the tunnel in the dark, solid rock, Oooh, did it hurt, still does.

174

"Footsteps! Closer. I crept back along the wall, feeling ... ahh, here. I rolled up into a tight little ball and held my breath.

"STOMP, STOMP, STOMP, he's running, heavy breathing, his pant leg hits my arm, he goes past in the dark and then ... CRASH! ....

"*'Damn!'* he shouts.

He turns, swinging his arms, feeling for me, the air moved my hair, went across my face.

"STOMP, STOMP, STOMP, he went past me again.

"*'Hey, Slavic, the li'l brat ain't 'n 'ere.'*

"*'She ain't in this one neither. No prints outside 'n the dirt. Must be back 'n the main tunnel. Let's go.'*

"I listened for them to leave. Was it a trap? No. They were still talking, off in the distance. I got up, quiet. Be quiet, Corrie!

"So, there must be an outside! *'Prints outside 'n the dirt,'* Slavic had said. Back down the second tunnel. Out I went, turned right this time at the end of the small tunnel. I ran and ran, then, brighter, brighter, very bright, SUNSHINE! SQUIRRELS! PINE TREES! CHIRPING BIRDS!

"Be careful, can't leave footprints Corrie. Slavic's clever.

"I started down the mountain, ohh, so beautiful, a mountain forest, butterflies, pinecones and lots and lots of ... sunshine. Down and down and down, all morning, no people.

"The pine trees disappeared, lots of oak trees, then just bushes. A little white bridge! Great for a picnic. It's getting hot. Keep going lower and lower, then, WOW! ... a small town, or something, a ways off, down below, and ... OH, YEA! ... a big road, concrete.

"Be careful, Corrie. Bob and Slavic could be watching.

"Crawled up to the road, staying behind the bushes. A white road sign, full of bullet holes, it said **'STATE HIGHWAY 173'** and that's all ... DARN!

"Then I spotted it, yellow and dirty, but it was sharpened, with a good eraser. I found a piece of paper under some brush.

"Wrote this note to Mommy and Daddy. Made sure I included the names, the **'173'**, good descriptions ... and that I love them. Even explained, for the post office, so they'll send it. Address in big letters.

"THERE! Now if they catch me, Mommy and Daddy will know where to look."

Corrie once again wiped her forehead with the back of her hand. It was hot, real hot. Uncle Jake would call this a 'lizard day', and Corrie knew why.

"So here I am, sitting under a hot rock ... what should I do?"

Corrie could have waited for dark. She could have waited for the postman. But Corrie was a Capterville. She'd run now, and ask questions later. She was off running as fast as her little aching legs would carry her, straight for the mailbox.

"I made it!" she gasped, out of breath and leaning against the red, white and blue box.

On her tiptoes, she pulled the handle back. The handle was burning hot, but she had to hold it in place until she could drop the letter with her other hand.

"There!" she sighed, "now it's ...."

A large powerful hand slammed down on top of hers. She felt a sharp pain in the back of her neck and the last thing she saw was her dusty roadside letter being crumpled inside a great, hairy fist.

Corrie Capterville was once again in the dark.

CHAPTER 20

In the pounding heart of London's financial district, Edith Wolman removed herself from her limousine, ignored the driver, and ran ponderously up the broad stone steps. She hesitated briefly before the massive brass and glass doors, gazing up at the Romanesque letters cut deeply into dark gray marble.

Inside, people of all responsibilities were perfectly dressed and conservatively busy. The walls were paneled in deep red mahogany and the decor was decidedly old world British. Edith crossed the floor of the vaulted main room and headed for the office of the senior partner. With rude indifference she acknowledged his secretary and without stopping, opened his door and entered.

The immense office was piled high with reports, periodicals and financial data, and his massive desk was buried under pounds of paper. Even the floor of the elegant library was layered with financial reports from around the world. The plain paper fax machine behind him was hissing out sheets of quotes from a Hong Kong trading office.

Lucius Otterstein's left thumb and index finger were hooked through his left suspender while securely pinching a smoldering Cuban cigar. His right hand held to his ear one of three telephones. The other two were on hold, impatiently blinking.

Edith said with a smile, "Really, Lucius, you should get this place cleaned up. All your people would quit if they could see this mess!"

"Edith, my love, come in. Please sit down, I'll be with you in a minute."

"And, where do you suggest I do that?" Edith asked, teasing him.

"Do what, Edith?"

"Sit, Lucius, sit. Where do you expect me to sit. I see no chairs, do you?"

"Ahh, all right ... yes, will you hold please ... Edith, be a sweetheart, just toss those papers, the Ross files there, on the floor." Lifting the phone back to his ear, he listened briefly, then said, "Yes, very well, call me at 8 AM. I'll have a decision for you then."

"Heavens, Lucius, I've made an important discovery. I think I've found one of your chairs."

More than any person alive Edith respected this genius of a man. Lucius Otterstein was respected world-wide as a shrewd trader and securities dealer. There were no desired honors in his profession that had not been bestowed upon him. He was about to celebrate his sixty-fifth birthday but his lifestyle was that of a man forty years his junior.

He hung up the telephone, placed the cigar in a large crystal ashtray, and came around his desk. He bent over, took Edith's hands into his and looked into her face.

"Edith, my darling Edith, how are you? I thought you were on your way to Los Angeles with Giancarlo."

"I was, but ...."

"He wouldn't be a bad catch, you know."

Edith refused to acknowledge his comment. She moved uncomfortably in the chair.

"Very well," Lucius said, "that's the last we shall speak of that. But tell me, why have your plans changed?"

"The G-7 talks were moved up by the heads of state. It became necessary for Giancarlo to go directly to Geneva ... to finish preparations," Edith said.

"I see," he said, watching her carefully, "you do not sound as though you approve ...."

"Oh, I approve, Lucius. I approve of any means whatsoever that will accomplish our objectives."

"But ...?" Lucius prodded.

Edith spoke quietly, staring at the floor. "It's just that terrorism is so unpredictable, so messy, compared with the rest of our plans."

"But," Lucius said kindly, "Panatta's role is absolutely critical if we are to implement the entire plan."

Placing his fingers gently below her chin Lucius tilted her head so she was looking into his eyes.

"You are a rarity, Edith Wolman, one of a kind, and you deserve to be in a position of control in the affairs of men. The Six will accomplish that for you, but give Panatta his due. He may surprise even you some day. And besides, if he should fail there is nothing that can be traced back to us, any of us, including him. He tells me his people are using explosive components having the signature of well known terrorist groups, so any investigations would lead elsewhere. My advice to you, Edith, is that you concentrate on the financial matters for which you are so well equipped."

Lucius finished his advice and, as always, could read nothing in Edith's face.

As though he had never spoken, Edith Wolman pronounced coldly, "I must know every detail of your securities strategy if I am to be completely effective. Shall we begin with PORTFOLIO 30?"

Thinking far ahead, Lucius Otterstein rubbed a small piece of tobacco back and forth between the palms of his hands.

"As you know, all thirty companies have been painstakingly selected and groomed over the past nine years. Let's sit over here, Edith ... you can review the list as we speak."

"Have there been many changes?" Edith asked as she perused the impressive list.

"Very few. We have replaced two in order to go with stronger competitors. The U.S. government awarded large contracts to the competition, information networking in one case, space to surface laser technology in the other."

"I'd have expected you to know these things before they happened, Lucius."

"Perhaps. But it's impossible to make all political judgments correctly, even for us. That's why I insisted upon a ten year schedule. And we are now ready," Lucius said pridefully.

"Did you take my recommendation for Neelai Data Systems?" Edith asked.

"No," Lucius said flatly.

Uncharacteristically, Edith pleaded, "But, Lucius, Taiwan will very soon be admitted to the General Agreement on Tariffs and Trade, and Neelai is so undervalued."

"True, and I took into consideration your valuable position with GATT. Your placement within the organization that administers the world's trading system was a real coup. Our influence upon GATT membership will be important in the years to come. Neelai is an excellent company, a candidate for future acquisition. But for now, we have most of her capabilities covered in our portfolio."

"And the thirty corporations, they are accountable to us?" Edith asked with interest.

"Of course. In each instance we have placed a controlling director or officer, or both."

"But that ... is not ... enough," Edith said slowly as she thought aloud. Edith Wolman had long ago trained herself to speak only when she had thoroughly analyzed the matters at hand. But with Lucius she always seemed to be a little off guard, always stretched to her intellectual limits.

"No it is not enough," Lucius said, "in and of itself. But through our subsidiaries we have acquired voting control through our stock positions. The combination shall prove most effective."

"And no one company, no officer, knows of our dealings with the others?" Edith asked for confirmation.

"Of course not. Only the six of us."

Edith studied the impressive list of highly rated corporations.

"So the four groupings have not changed."

"Aerospace, computer science, pharmaceuticals and banking. That's it. See ... here ..." Lucius said pointing to the top of the rumpled sheet, "They are arranged into the four categories. Of the nine aerospace companies, three are former defense contractors with sizable government guarantees."

"Which company do you consider the most valuable ... for our purposes?"

Lucius looked at Edith curiously. "An interesting question, my dear. You are always surprising me."

"It would be typical for you to have a favorite ... but, thank you, Lucius."

"When the U.S. completes its banking industry reforms our holding companies will control the world's most powerful

181

network of banks, insurance companies and securities firms ... critical to our strategy, I'm sure you will agree. However, everything considered, I believe RAM Pharmaceuticals has the greatest potential. Given its structure, its products, the people we have placed, its control over other entities and the relationships we have developed ...."

"*You* developed, Lucius."

"RAM is set to become our flagship, Edith, especially if we can obtain the water technology and the kefir."

"We shall, Lucius, we shall," Edith said with vicious determination.

"Once the new technology is united with RAM's financial position, her distribution networks and manufacturing capabilities, we shall control a concern that will have the lead in industry, agriculture, medicine and most modern forms of communication."

Lucius Otterstein's eyes had become glazed. The thought of limitless applications, the leverage, the bargaining power ... and the attendant political prestige and influence.

"Edith," Lucius asked, "what of Dr. Capterville's kefir specimen? The one we got with the girl. I understand from Marlin that our scientists have been unable to reproduce it."

"That is true," Edith said, "but we'll be able to very soon."

"Oh, and speaking of Marlin, he is expected here shortly. Something seemed to be concerning him about our cash transfer systems."

"There is nothing wrong with our systems," Edith said protectively.

"Yes, yes, I know Edith but give him a good hearing anyway. Few have been in criminal enforcement as long as he, and fewer still have been a double agent ... twice ... for both sides."

182

"You are right, of course, Lucius. It is a time for extreme caution. But it's difficult, after all the effort ...."

Changing the subject Lucius said, "That nasty little banker, Bulow. I've never felt good about him. He called this morning. Said the girl had escaped. He seems to know more and more of our affairs."

"He is not correct," Edith stated firmly. "The girl has not escaped. She is in her cell at this moment. As for Mr. Bulow, you are quite right. He is beginning to know too much. I have discussed this with Marlin and Giancarlo. We shall do no further business with Bulow or any of his associates. Should he become troublesome, even once, Giancarlo will handle it."

Edith gave Lucius an odd look and remarked, "Well, Lucius, don't you think it's about time you told me?"

"Why, what do you mean, Edith?"

"You tell *me*, you old fox. I know you've been up to something for some time. There's some kind of twist to your planning. I can sense it."

Lucius laughed a deep, smoke filled laugh and finally said, "Well, a fellow must keep his options open, mustn't he? Besides, Edith ...."

The door opened and a tall dapper Marlin Moss entered the room.

"Ah! Marlin, you've saved me," Lucius said, still chuckling. "Edith was excoriating me mercilessly. She was about to roast me like a stuffed pig for not divulging all my secrets."

"I can relate to that," Moss said dryly.

Lucius Otterstein's demeanor changed in a matter of seconds. He became excessively focused and intense. Lines drawn by years of negotiation and pressure formed on his forehead and beneath his eyes. This was the Lucius that Edith Wolman loved. When immersed in the complexity of competition there was nothing that could distract him.

"I am glad," he began, "that you both are here. And I am sorry that Giancarlo could not be with us. We have bound ourselves together, the six of us, with a pact of explicit trust, and it is imperative that we all remain cognizant of the overall plan. It is, of course, impossible for one individual to track all of the details, which is why this arrangement works so well. Now that we are ready to begin making the moves for which we have so carefully prepared, it is prudent that we stay in close contact."

Lucius drew an engraved silver lighter from his trouser pocket in anticipation of a fresh cigar.

He continued, "Contrary to what Edith has just expressed, I have not been secretive. However, she is quite right about some new ... 'twists', I believe you called them, Edith."

"I knew it," she declared.

"I should like my prescience to receive complete credit for recent windfalls," Lucius said, squeezing his well spent cigar, "but, alas, the simple truth is that recent market events over which I had absolutely no control have placed us in a position that is even more advantageous than before."

"How's that?" Marlin asked admiring the electricity, the excitement in the man.

Lucius waded through papers and carefully lifted another cigar from the antique rosewood humidor behind his desk. Ceremoniously, he clipped and then lit the cigar while twisting it round and round between his fingers. He stared through his cross-hatched leaded window into a late English summer.

"As you know," Lucius said to his intent audience, "we have invaluable relationships with securities houses in all major cities, especially in New York, Tokyo, Hong Kong and here in London. As the market, particularly on the Japanese exchange, took its beating some of the securities firms began covering the losses for their most valued customers."

"Why?" Marlin asked.

"To keep their business, Marlin. They felt retention of their biggest clients through paybacks would, in the long run, generate profits that would dwarf the amount of such payments."

"And they're paying cash," stated Edith.

"Yes," Lucius continued, "But they disguise it in a variety of subtle ways. The cash transfusions, for example, are often accomplished by the securities company purchasing customer bonds at above-market prices."

"Clever," Edith said, "but doesn't that leave them rather exposed?"

"Not under normal circumstances," Lucius said, inhaling white smoke. "Many issues are held by institutional investors in interlocking share holdings that are not openly traded. So who's to complain?"

"Somebody must have."

"What nobody counted on was the press getting involved," Lucius grinned.

To Edith's relief, the cigar went out. Otterstein's office was now as gray as London in deep winter. Her relief, however, was short lived. Deep in thought, Lucius stood and methodically re-lit his cigar.

"Several securities houses world-wide used their subsidiaries to loan nine hundred million dollars to a company called Saka Industries. Whether they were aware of it or not, Saka was discovered to be owned by organized crime interests. Mercilessly pursuing their leads, the Fourth Estate revealed billions more in customer paybacks."

"Very ... very interesting," mused Edith.

"But how does this help us, Lucius?" Marlin asked.

"The companies that decided to cover customer losses are losing their reputations. They are busy defending themselves in court, as well as from charges of favoritism brought by the Securities Dealers' Associations. Ironically, they are defending themselves by asserting that the money was really entertainment and business expense. So, enter the taxing authorities, and a lot more trouble."

"How stupid," Edith stated.

"To complete the answer to your question, Marlin, Battengill and all the firms with whom we do business around the world, scrupulously avoided the practice of customer reimbursement. Consequently, the industry and the public are looking to us for guidance and counsel. And that is precisely what we shall give them starting tomorrow. PORTFOLIO 30, through a mix of houses, will be promoted around the globe."

"Incredible, Lucius," Marlin said. "Brilliant!"

"We have seen to it that no one has recommended any of our stocks for over six months, and all the while we have been steadily increasing our positions. By design, price/earnings ratios and other indicators have remained absurdly low."

"And tomorrow?" Marlin asked.

"Tomorrow, if our histories are repeated, we should see a twenty percent increase in our equity over night, and that as you know will represent billions."

Lucius blew an extra thick cloud of smoke toward the ceiling. Turning to Edith, he smiled like a proud father. "And we have you, my dear Edith, to thank for our ability to move with such alacrity. Your cash trades have been ingenious. They have provided us with the additional monies necessary to gain voting control. We shall now ramp these stocks and prepare ourselves for the next phase."

"Bravo!" Marlin said slapping his knee.

"As we speak, our lawyers are making a formal apology to Dr. Capterville on behalf of RAM Pharmaceuticals. The case will be settled. Our instigation of the Capterville suit has served its purpose in helping to hold the share price down ... a nice touch we have Marlin to thank for."

Lucius paused, taking a long draw on his now soggy cigar. "Edith, Marlin, think of it! When we have the technology ... and the kefir ... we will increase our profits and our control beyond comprehension."

"It is our utmost priority, Lucius," Edith volunteered.

"Good," Lucius said with encouragement. "Now then, Marlin, you had some concerns."

Marlin Moss shifted his tall frame within the green wing-back leather chair. He adjusted his gray silk suit coat and crossed his arms.

"I, also, have the highest regard for Doctor Wolman's abilities. And I do not mean to suggest that she has made a single error. But I urge extreme caution with any further sizable transfers. I am not concerned with the securities trades, especially after what I have heard today, but I am quite anxious about the appearance of large cash transfers."

Her stomach turning furiously Edith asked, "And why is that, Mr. Moss?"

"Easy, Edith," Lucius said, "remember Marlin is one of us."

"You will remember," Marlin recounted calmly, "that after my less reputable days, I worked for a number of years at the U.S. Treasury Department. Given my experience with the wrong sort of people, I wound up heading the Financial Crimes Enforcement Division."

Edith was listening intently. She quietly said, "So? You know we are aware of this."

"Most of our information and leads at Treasury," Marlin went on, "came from the IRS and the U.S. Customs Service."

"Sounds logical," Lucius said as he watched the two of them joust.

"But what you don't know is that the IRS and Customs' computers are now interfaced with an underground high-tech information highway that has specifically designed software programs that track world money flows."

"Good Grief!" Lucius snorted, gray-brown smoke rolling out his nostrils. He knew very well what Marlin Moss was about to say.

"The system," Marlin went on, "was devised to track laundered drug money. Yearly drug money transfers vastly exceed the combined revenues of GM, Ford, Exxon and Royal Dutch, so they're hot on it."

"Well, I appreciate your concern, Marlin, but I can assure you we are clean," Edith insisted. "Over a trillion dollars a day is transferred electronically among the world's banks, and our transactions are indistinguishable."

"I have no reason to doubt you, Edith. My purpose is not to denigrate your achievements," Marlin said, "it is simply to pass on what I know, so we can achieve our ultimate goals."

"Perhaps," Lucius interrupted, "you should explain to Edith how you know so much about this new computer network."

"Because, Edith ..." Marlin paused for effect, "I wrote the computer software programs for the government, and I carefully omitted searches in the very specialized areas that I knew would be helpful to you."

There was a reflective break in the discussion. Save the humming of the fax, the gray room was silent. Slowly, stygian smiles crept across their faces. The three confidants looked perceptively, intuitively from one to the other and, at once, they broke into conceited and forbidding laughter.

The Committee of Six, run by four, silently approved by two, had arrived. Their goals and their plans, chess moves ahead of everyone else, were fashioned for their own selfish successes and philosophies. If there was to be a new world order, they would be it.

Marlin Moss excused himself and left the room.

Edith picked up her valise and, saying good-bye, kissed Lucius on the cheek. She stepped carefully, negotiating the stacks of reference books and obsolete communications littering the floor.

As she departed, Lucius said evenly, "When Mr. Bulow called this morning, he asked me to exchange all of his accounts ... to U.S. currency, and cash equivalents. I found that curious."

Edith Wolman smiled politely. She left the room and shut the door quietly behind her. She was sick inside.

Lucius reclined in the swivel chair behind his formidable desk. He rested his cigar in the ashtray and picked up the telephone.

The two figures in the darkened library silently vanished, and Lucius Otterstein did not bother to look up when he heard the bookcase door close, and click as it locked shut.

CHAPTER 21

Corrie's eyes opened to blackness.

"I wonder if I'm blind," she moaned, "oooh, my head."

She recognized the feel of the cold hard table upon which she lay.

"Oh, no, I'm right back where I started. The mail box ... heck! I almost made it."

Slowly, Corrie sat up on the table she knew too well. She stretched her arms. Every muscle in her body was full of pain.

Then once again, footsteps, heavy footsteps. They were back!

The door flew open and hit the back wall with a crash. Light, blinding light flooded in, and the same two imposing figures entered the room.

But this time something was different. The two huge men possessed even greater strength, greater authority. Something horribly powerful was with them and Corrie sensed it immediately.

While most human beings would surrender to such overwhelming intimidation, Corrie would not. For the first time in all the black days and nights, she actually felt better. She felt stronger. She felt that somehow she could take actions that would make a difference. Now, when matters appeared most bleak, when she was in the greatest pain, when the forces aligned against her were at their strongest, she knew she could finally take control of the situation in which she found herself.

"Now we're playing ball in my park," she said under her breath, "... one of Uncle Jake's favorite sayings."

She remembered what Uncle Jake always told her whenever things seemed to go wrong, "We've got home field advantage now, baby, so swing away!" He'd lean back and laugh that famous Uncle Jake laugh that never failed to cheer her. Then she'd ask her Dad, "Daddy, is Uncle Jake fooling me?" And Steven would always answer, "Of course not, darlin', I taught him everything he knows." And then all three of them would laugh.

"So, bring 'em on," Corrie yelled into the little room, "we're in my ballpark now!"

Slavic stood behind her, ready to grip her with his powerful hands. Bob lit the match ... and as he moved it to the cigarette that was pressed between his large lips, Corrie saw in his face an evil, an ugliness she had not seen before.

Driven by something he could not understand Bob delighted in what he was about to do. The syringe he held in his hand was full of the drug that would make his young prisoner tell all. Smoke billowed from his orange, wrinkled face. All around him black, elusive shadows crawled and crossed from wall to wall.

Then Corrie saw *it*, just beyond Slavic and Bob. *It* was in the corner opposite the door, in all *its* heinous splendor, terrifying, evil and vicious. *It* was in full regalia, spewing a horrible yellowed stench. Acting exceedingly important, unable to be seen, *it* manipulated the two physically powerful men by whispering suggestions to them at appropriately deceitful times.

"Their conditioning is complete," the creature hissed with practiced conceit, "and they have been most useful."

Amid *its* intense concentration and manipulation *it* happened to glance from *its* two controlled subjects. *It* saw Corrie. Corrie was calmly watching *it*.

191

In that instant *it* knew *it* had made a fatal mistake, a mistake commonly made by those who commit themselves to evil. *It* had relied, albeit for just a brief moment, upon *its* perception of the physical. This horrific messenger from Satan, in examining the beaten and burned little girl had seen only that ... a weakened, helpless girl. *It* now found itself fully exposed, looking up defenseless at what *it* knew to be far more powerful than just a little girl. By legal stricture, committed thousands of years before, the strength and authority of Corrie's almighty living God was at her command.

Corrie viewed the wretched pawn of darkness with a special clarity that is bestowed only upon those who will have complete faith. The now pitiful creature cowered in the corner of the room that had been Corrie's prison.

Corrie studied the two giant men who had caused her so much anguish. Their decisions and actions were not entirely their own. They had allowed themselves to be deceived.

Slavic prepared to grab her. Bob grasped the dripping needle with his long dirty fingers. The glowing cigarette, pressed between his yellow lips, moved with him to her face.

Corrie fixed her eyes upon the demon and spoke the words she knew she must, but the forceful sound, the message, flowed through her, not from her.

"I COMMAND YOU BACK TO HELL IN THE NAME OF MY JESUS AND YOU ARE NEVER TO COME BACK!"

Corrie was a kid whose Father stood behind her. She was firm and without fear.

The creature cringed.

The two men froze.

Outstretching her arm, Corrie pointed straight at the demon. Her resolve was grounded in law.

192

She said ... she demanded, in a low and composed voice that sent terror through the evil being, "YOU ARE TO LEAVE NOW!"

It shuddered, and shrunk further into *its* tenebrous stench. *It* was contractually bound to obey the words she spoke, yet *it* hissed pathetically, not wanting to leave ... not wanting to concede defeat.

"NOW!" little Corrie shouted, and *it* disappeared.

CHAPTER 22

Late Fall in the Los Angeles basin brought cooler though still congested days. There had been no word of Corrie.

Steven Capterville sat alone at the head of the long table in the law firm's conference room waiting anxiously for Elliot Jaynes. They had not spoken for over two weeks but Elliot had left an urgent message with Steven's answering service.

"Get down here quick!" was all he'd said.

"It must be something important," Steven thought, "Elliot does not get excited easily."

Steven was bursting to hear the news. He and Megan had lived their lives day by day with nothing new to go on, and just the fact that Elliot had called meant there might be something.

"Steven!" Elliot burst into the room, and without saying hello, said, "Look at this!"

He pressed to the table before Steven a smudged and creased postcard. Steven took it in his hands and looked closely. It read:

> Cory
>
> RAMS
> Little White Bridge, yellow n Black
> The Big Six
> Bat Hill
> the Indian Chief
> Doc ~~~~~~

"See, the line after **'Doc'** trails off," said Elliot excitedly.

"But what could it mean?" Steven asked, "I've got to call Meg. What can you make of this? And why did ...?"

"Calm down, Steven, we don't want you to break anything," Elliot smiled. He was seeing some life in his friend for the first time in many weeks.

"It appears," Elliot said, "whoever wrote this was in quite a rush ... didn't have time to finish the last line. And look, it's postmarked three days ago in Apple Valley, just over the mountains in the high desert."

"Elliot! ... Corrie is ..." and Steven began sobbing, "... she's alive!"

Elliot pressed on, "It also confirms our original suspicion that there is a connection between Corrie's disappearance and RAM Pharmaceuticals. I must confess I was totally stumped until I saw this. But that's not the best part. The card was mailed to this address, but with your names, you and Meg. Turn the card over."

"That's ... it's Corrie's handwriting! Our names, anyway," Steven cried.

"Precisely what I was hoping to hear," Elliot sighed.

"Whoever sent this," Steven said, "wrote out your firm's address but taped in our names in Corrie's handwriting. How odd."

"Someone," Elliot said, "is trying to let us know Corrie's OK and give us some leads. Or, and we must consider this, Steven, it could be some kind of trap."

"It makes no sense that this would be a trap," Steven said instinctively.

"That's the conclusion I came to," Elliot said, "although not so quickly as you. The criminal mind can be terribly devious. The good guys don't have a monopoly on smarts."

195

"But this is not the kind of thing a criminal would do, Elliot. Corrie's handwriting, the urgent printing," Steven reasoned.

"Just the time to be wary. As I've said before, I believe we are dealing with something or someone very powerful and very clever. But in this instance I agree with you. This ... well, it simply makes no sense unless someone was trying to help Corrie."

"I agree," Steven said enthusiastically.

"If something was to be to be demanded of you for Corrie's return ... ransom, technology, whatever, they would have made the demand long ago."

"All these weeks, I would have welcomed a ransom note," Steven said.

"I know you would," Elliot said. It was a joy for Elliot to see the emotion and the pain, locked within Steven for so long, were beginning to dissolve.

"But let's concentrate on what we have here," Elliot said. "Assuming someone is trying to help us we've got to run down all the clues."

Seated at the table Steven's eyes devoured the little card. Standing behind Steven, with his arms resting on the back of the chair, Elliot looked over Steven's shoulder. Together they wondered about the card, and at this curious turn of events.

"Elliot, got any idea what **'The Indian Chief'** means? Or **'Doc'**?" Steven asked, completely puzzled. "And what's this about a bridge?"

"No ... but, wait a minute! I think I've got something. This **'Bat Hill'** ...."

"What in the heck is a Bat Hill?" pondered Steven.

"My gosh, that's got to be it!"

"What, Elliot, what?"

"I've been researching and analyzing everything I can get my hands on concerning RAM Pharmaceuticals. The supplier cost figures you came up with verify that RAM is making a far greater profit than is being reported to its stockholders. And we know that money is being illegally funneled through Preferred Financial, Inc., and possibly other entities.

"But none of it, Steven, without knowing more, can lead us to Corrie. That's what's been so frustrating. We have to think of Corrie first. It would be too dangerous to reveal what we know without being certain Corrie is safe."

"I agree," Steven said.

"And I might as well tell you, Steven, I don't think the people at RAM Pharmaceuticals know anything about your Corrie."

"Really?"

"I could be way off base, but in all the contact I had with their lawyers and with everything we have uncovered ... it, well, Corrie just doesn't fit into the RAM corporate picture."

"Interesting," Steven mused.

"But RAM, of course, *is* involved somehow."

"You aren't making any sense, Elliot."

"I think somebody is manipulating RAM to achieve some sort of advantage."

"And this **'Bat Hill'** tells you something?" Steven asked.

Elliot was turning a gold pen in his fingers. "Yes, at least I think so. I've been watching RAM's stock pricing every day for months and the week we settled with them, in fact, I think it was the very day, RAM stock jumped from seventy-nine dollars a share to one hundred two. It was one hundred five at the start of trading this morning."

"Interesting." Steven was trying to imagine a possible connection.

"And I doubt the settlement of our suit, small by RAM standards, could have been the sole reason for such an advance."

"What do you make of it, Elliot?"

"I haven't been able to sort it all out yet, but this postcard shines new light on the whole picture." Elliot held the card up so they both could see it. "Would you agree that whoever wrote this and mailed it was in a big hurry ... the uneven words, **'Doc'** trailing off like this ...?"

"Yes, yes," Steven said, "but you haven't answered my question. What about **'Bat Hill'**?"

"Yet he or she made the time to attach some of Corrie's handwriting ... a definite attempt to let us know she's alive."

"I wonder why they didn't just bring her back?" Steven puzzled.

"Don't know, but it seems Corrie has befriended someone," Elliot said.

Tears flooded Steven's eyes. He said, "There's never been anybody better at that. Gosh, I wish Meg were home. She doesn't even know yet."

"And, Steven, look at this block handwriting. It's childlike. That's what started me thinking. This, right here, is not **'Bat Hill'**. It's a contraction for what a child has heard ... Battengill."

"What?" Steven said. He was completely in the dark.

"Battengill Securities, Ltd. is an international brokerage firm," Elliot said.

"Yes ... yes, of course."

"But Steven, it is Battengill that has been promoting RAM stock all over the world," Elliot said excitedly, "and someone is trying to tell us there is a connection between Corrie, **'Bat Hill'**, and RAM ... or maybe just telling us what they've overheard, trying to help Corrie ... from Apple Valley."

Steven was ecstatic. He jumped out of his chair and started pacing around the long table. Finally he stopped in front of the plate glass window and gazed out over the city.

Elliot looked up to the ceiling, clenched his fists, raised his arms and shouted, "Steven! It's finally something! Something to follow that could lead us to Corrie."

From Elliot's conference room window on the forty-fourth floor Steven overlooked a strikingly clear Los Angeles. He could see distant Catalina Island resting in the blue Pacific Ocean, West Los Angeles, people busy bee-like in the cellular windows of several neighboring sky-scrapers, Dodger Stadium and ... mountains!

Steven picked up his coat and his beaten briefcase. He shook Elliot's hand so hard it was painful.

"Thank you, Elliot, thank you. Keep at it, will you? Meg will be so excited!"

Steven grabbed the postcard, threw open the conference room door and ran at full speed down the hall.

"Steven, where are you going?" Elliot shouted as the elevator doors closed.

"Apple Valley, of course."

CHAPTER 23

In the midst of loading top security customs exempt baggage, a handler unzipped a nondescript suitcase, activated the bomb's detonator and set the intricate timing device. Placing the suitcase on the transport cart, he and his partner finished loading the last of five carts. The pair quickly disappeared into Hanger 19, stripped off their mock Air Force uniforms and, without event, drove out the front gate of Langley Air Force Base in a late model Dodge van.

As the tractor-truck pulled the rolling baggage carts to the gray Air Force 727, Dr. Steven Capterville took his seat toward the tail of the aircraft and was greeted by his host.

"Thank you for taking the time to come across country on such short notice, Dr. Capterville."

"I'm still wondering why I'm here, Major."

Steven stowed his briefcase under the seat in front of him, put one foot on it and made himself comfortable.

Without attempting to sound important the Major said, "My name is Jerome Barnes, Army, not Air Force. Please call me Jerry. As I believe I mentioned, I am the assistant to the President's Chief of Staff."

"You must be a busy fellow," Steven said.

"My office is near the White House and I spend most of my time there when we're not traveling."

"Sounds impressive, Major."

"I will not pretend to be involved in policy, doctor, but I do have the ear of the Chief, especially on matters such as yours," the Major said.

"And what are my matters, Jerry?"

"Allow me to explain, doctor. I am the former Director of Combat Surgical Research and Chief of Staff for Resource Management of the U.S. Army Medical Research & Development Command."

"I see," Steven said, watching the Major closely.

"I also directed the Army's Biological Warfare Section III. Our job was not to develop biological and chemical weapons. It was to create effective defenses against them."

"That seems constructive."

"I have read of your breakthroughs in cluster technology with great interest," Major Barnes said earnestly.

"And just how did an Army major become interested in an area as remote as water clustering?" Steven asked. Steven recognized the need for extreme caution. They could be interested in his work for any number of reasons and he wondered if he was about to be volunteered ... or worse.

"My background is biochemistry, William and Mary College," the Major said. "I do frequent computer searches at the university just to keep my hand in. I certainly don't have your depth of knowledge, not even close, but I have been following Dr. Freiling and Dr. Rhodes in England and, of course, your brilliant work."

"Really," Steven said with interest. Whatever it was they wanted of him he was becoming convinced the young Major was an honest man.

"I heard about your daughter, sir, and I want to help. Whoever did such a thing should be shot," the Major said bluntly. "I've told the Chief, and he agrees. Has there been any word from her?"

"We received information leading us to the high desert northeast of Los Angeles ... a place called Apple Valley," Steven replied. He began to think back. Thoughts of his precious Corrie filled his mind. "After several days searching, the most I came up with was an antique soda fountain jerk in the middle of nowhere who imagined he saw a cute little girl playing hide-and-seek by herself in some boulders."

"Well, if there is any way I can help ...."

"I thank you for your concern, Major, but before we shoot anybody we need to find out where Corrie is." The longing gaze that had come to accompany Steven's recurring thoughts of Corrie abruptly left his face. He must focus on the present. He was on an Air Force jet and was still unaware of its destination.

"You didn't bring me out here just to discuss my daughter, did you?"

"No," the Major answered truthfully, "but as I said, I would like to offer you, or the Chief and I would, all the assistance at our disposal."

"That is very kind," Steven said. "How much of this does the Chief of Staff know?"

"You can ask him yourself, sir. He's about to board."

"Is that so?" Steven asked with interest.

"Doctor, we have so little time, especially when it comes to your ... Corrie, isn't that her name?"

"Yes."

"So let me be brief," Major Barnes said. "First, we are very concerned about the implications of your technology. I know you are developing products that can help to save mankind from disease and pollution and much more, but I'm sure you've also considered that what can be used for good can also be used for evil?"

"Of course, that's why I've taken the precautions I have," Steven said defensively.

"How so?" the Major asked.

"Our products are made in a variety of laboratories and no single person or lab is aware of all the necessary steps," Steven said.

"That's helpful, yes, definitely prudent," the Major said.

"But most importantly," Steven continued, "it is impossible to reverse engineer the technology."

"What do you mean?" the Major asked.

"I made the discovery largely by mistake, as so many scientific breakthroughs are made. It was one in a million, or trillion, or, if you happen to believe as I do, well ... Corrie would tell you 'God did it.' The most brilliant scientists in the world can analyze our products for years to come but they'll never recreate the process. It is often that I wonder why I was chosen to receive this information. It's a responsibility that has seen my daughter stolen and made a shambles of my life."

Steven fought the wave of emotion that always accompanied this topic. Major Barnes sensed the tension. "Doctor Capterville, I believe we will find your little girl. I asked you here so you could explain all of this to the Chief. He is very interested in the applications your technology will have in industry and agriculture."

"And warfare?" Steven asked pointedly.

"No, no, it's not like that," the Major said with sincerity. "Is it not true you have a solution that can be sprayed on different alloys of metal, like steel, during the manufacturing process that will prevent rusting and corrosion?"

"Yes, that's true."

"And is it not true you have developed water formulations that will eliminate bacteria in food processing?" the Major pressed on.

"Yes, we have several studies underway and the results have been most interesting."

"But none in the U.S., I'd venture to guess."

"That also is true," Steven replied, "too expensive ... and time consuming."

"We would like to help you in both respects," Major Barnes said, "no strings attached. I also understand that in Canada and Japan you've been successful in eliminating the need for antibiotics in the feeding of poultry, simply by the inclusion of your water in the drinking lines."

"Yes, the solution was specifically designed for that purpose," Steven said, delighted to finally have another advocate.

"But it's still non-toxic pure water, right doctor?" Barnes pursued.

"Standard testing will reveal only water," Steven answered.

"But," Major Barnes said, sounding more and more enthusiastic, "sophisticated testing will reveal much higher electrical conductivity, different pH readings, and a dramatic reduction in surface tension, is that not correct doctor?"

"Excellent, Jerry, excellent," Steven said. He leaned forward in his seat. "You have done your homework well."

"It's not homework to me," the Major said energetically. He too leaned forward in his seat. "I'm fascinated with your work, what I know of it. And I think I've convinced the Chief. But you need to speak with him yourself. He's already told me he will advocate your cause and I thought this flight would be the perfect opportunity for you to speak with him alone. Doctor, believe me, we can provide to you all the money and clearances you will need to follow through."

Two black Lincoln Continentals, officially dressed with fluttering American flags, stopped next to the aircraft. They were surrounded by seven attentive Secret Service vehicles.

Steven was looking out the aircraft window. "This is quite a ceremony."

"Security has to be tight this trip," said Barnes.

They watched the Secret Service agents, severe expressions to a man, spring from their cars.

"The Chief of Staff certainly does rate," Steven said.

"He does, of course," the Major said, "but especially so when he's traveling with the Chairman of the Federal Reserve Board and the U.S. Deputy Under-Secretary of State.

"They'll be accompanied by their staff, the Secret Service and about twenty members of the press. Let's go up front, I want you to meet them before the press board. You can speak with them privately after takeoff."

Major Barnes led Steven past several alert agents to the front of the plane. Without notice he was standing face to face with the Chief of Staff, confidential advisor to the President of the United States.

"It's a pleasure to meet you, Chief," Steven said.

"Dr. Capterville, hello ... calling me Chief already, I see. You must have been speaking with Major Barnes," the Chief said with a grin.

"Indeed," said Steven, also smiling.

"Well, doctor," the Chief looked approvingly at the Major, "you have been in good hands. I look forward to discussing your theories and water products, and in particular speaking about their applications. I hear from Major Barnes that you are about to revolutionize life on our planet."

"That will take some doing," Steven said.

Turning to the Chairman of the Federal Reserve Board, Major Barnes said, "Excuse me Mr. Chairman, I would like to introduce you to Dr. Capterville from California. I know you will enjoy speaking with him. He has come up with some rather remarkable ideas that may be beneficial to you in the upcoming talks."

"How do you do, doctor."

"Mr. Chairman."

"*Capterville!*" the Chairman said with emphasis, "... certainly is becoming a household name. Is there news of your brother."

"None yet," Steven answered.

"It seems he has the whole world captivated."

"He'd done that before he left for Mars," the Chief interjected.

"I can't argue with that," Steven said.

The Chairman continued, "I've heard about your predicament ... your business struggles, and if you don't mind my bringing it up, this awful situation with your child ...."

"Excuse me, Mr. Chairman," interrupted Major Barnes, "but we're about to be overtaken by a group of reporters. Perhaps you could all talk privately after take-off."

Major Barnes and Steven Capterville, sandwiched between a dozen zestful members of the press, forced their way back to their seats. Over the intercom a flight attendant insisted helpfully that everyone fasten their seat belts in preparation for take-off.

"Excuse me, Major," Steven said, "but I think I'll use the head before we lift off." Steven rose from his seat and stepped into the isle. "Oh, Major, a minor point ... I never did ask you where this plane is going."

"Geneva, doctor, we're going to Geneva in preparation for the G-7 talks. Sorry to put you through this but there was no time. It was the only way to get you and the Chief together."

"Well, Jerry, I trust you'll explain this to my wife. She's always wanted to go to Switzerland."

Major Barnes laughed, "We'll make it up to her somehow."

Steven left for the back of the plane and Major Barnes reclined in his seat with a stack of confidential memos destined for the Chief of Staff.

Steven was latching the door to the rear lavatory when the shock wave from the blast flattened him painfully against the compartment wall. He was falling, everything was falling.

The intact tail section of the huge jet collided with unforgiving cement. He felt pain, all over ... then blackness.

***

"Steven, wake up ... come on, Steven," Megan cried, seeing he was coming around. "Please, Steven!"

With his eyes still tightly shut, Steven was moving his head slowly from side to side on the pillow.

"Steven! Wake up!."

Both eyes blinked open half way.

"Where ... am I?" Steven asked with a banging headache.

"Oh, Steven, you're back."

"How long have I been out, Meg?" His eyes began moving around the hospital room.

"Two and a half days, Steven. You've had a concussion."

"You're telling me."

He was trying to move his head back and forth. "A concussion, huh? Doesn't feel like all I've had."

"The doctor says you have badly bruised ribs, in fact ...."

"Give it to me straight, Meg," Steven said groggily.

Megan's face glowed. She was so happy she could burst. "Well, the doctor says just about everything you have is badly bruised, but the good news is, nothing is broken. Oh, Steven, God was protecting you."

"How do you figure, Meg?"

The smile vanished from Megan's face.

"All the others ...."

"The others?" Steven asked. "What happened? All I remember was a blast."

Megan pulled a chair next to the hospital bed and fell into it with a heavy sigh. She covered her face with her hands. Without looking up she said quietly, "The entire plane exploded, Steven. Everyone was killed, everyone, except you. Oh, Steven, you're alive."

"Everyone, Meg?"

"They're saying someone, some terrorist organization, planted a bomb. Only a few of the bodies could even be identified."

"You mean the Chief, the Chairman, Major Barnes ... but Jerry Barnes was only a few feet from me."

"Everyone."

"It's ... it's beyond belief," Steven said.

"Everyone," Megan said, "when you're up to it I'll show you the newspapers. It's front page all over the world."

"Let's have a look," Steven said reaching out with a sore arm.

Megan instead came out of her chair and climbed onto the bed with him. She lay next to him and rested her head on his aching shoulder.

"Steven, oh Steven, thank God you're alive."

They remained motionless, together, in the small hospital bed, loving one another and giving thanks. Megan Capterville had lost her daughter and just now she had come inches close to losing her precious husband. But Steven was alive, right where she liked him best, right here in her arms.

A short while later the door to the room opened and a rather portly nurse looked in.

"Dr. Capterville, you're awake! Wonderful." The nurse was giggling. "And Mrs. Capterville, you don't waste any time do you?"

"Of course not, Nurse Fix," Megan said proudly.

"Pardon me, Mrs. Capterville ... I don't mean to interrupt, especially at a time like this, but there is a Mr. Elliot Jaynes on the phone for you. He called twice before, but you finally fell asleep and I didn't want to disturb you. It sounds rather urgent. Should I put the call through to your room?

"Yes, nurse," Steven said, struggling to sit up in bed, "we'll take it right here."

"Hello, Elliot, how are you?" Steven said, excited to hear his friend's voice.

"How am *I*?" Elliot said, "good grief, man, how in the heck are *you*?"

Steven glanced at Megan and winked. "It was a rather bumpy flight."

"That's what I hear," Elliot said. "Steven, seriously, is it possible this had anything to do with you and your work?"

"Well, I haven't had much time to think about it."

"Yea, they told me you just woke up. Sorry to barge in like this. Want me to call back?"

"No, no, it's OK. I can't imagine I could be the reason, though. If somebody wanted to bump me off it wouldn't be too difficult. Besides, they want what I know so why would they try to kill me."

"I suppose so," Elliot agreed.

"And," Steven continued, "my being here was a last minute thing. Whoever planned the bombing didn't know I'd be on board."

"Yes, you're right, of course."

Steven noticed after just a few of his friend's words, the odd, troubling tone to Elliot's voice. It appeared something had upset him, something that was difficult for him to discuss.

"What's wrong, Elliot, I can hear it in your voice. Is it Corrie?" Steven asked with concern.

"No, no, I have heard nothing about Corrie," Elliot said.

Squeezing Megan's hand, Steven gave her a look that told her it wasn't about Corrie.

"But I'm afraid I have some bad news, very bad, actually," Elliot said uncomfortably. "Somebody broke into my house this morning and ransacked the place ... tore it apart, even ripped sections of the walls out."

"Oh, no!" was all Steven could get out.

Megan became alarmed. "What, Steven, what?"

"Someone robbed Elliot's house."

Elliot broke in, "No, Steven, not robbed. Nothing was taken, but they were obviously looking for something."

"We're so sorry, Elliot."

"But that's not the worst part, Steven."

"What?"

"Rupert Mitchell from the bank called while I was at the house with the police, asked me to come right down. The firm's ... our safe deposit box at the bank, Steven ... it's empty ... the Russian translations, your patent work." Elliot's voice was cracking, "It's all gone, Steven, I'm so sorry ... I just don't know how ...."

"Taken? From a bank vault, a safe deposit box?"

"None of the other boxes were touched and there wasn't a mark on our box, like someone had a copy of our key ... and free access to the bank vault. Mitchell noticed it on a routine check because the drawer was slightly off. I don't know what to say, Steven, I'm just so sorry."

210

Steven looked at Megan in shock. He lowered the phone from his ear.

"What is it Steven?" Megan asked.

"I can't believe this, Meg."

Steven thought back to the evening Corrie had been taken from their home. Then he put the phone back to his ear and asked, "Elliot, your house, was there red on your walls, like blood, and a really bad smell?"

"Why ... yes, Steven ... how did you know that?"

CHAPTER 24

The founding of Elliot Jaynes' law firm had been a faithful leap of financial and professional courage. His original office had consisted of himself, a full time secretary who had enthusiastically agreed to a part-time salary, and a hand-me-down typewriter whose 'e' key worked only when it chose to.

The four hundred fifty square foot office in a 1920's brick building on Spring Street included one small window looking east, a twenty book law library and a fifteen hundred dollar business loan which years later had mushroomed into so many problems, that company policy came to preclude any form of debt whatsoever.

As the years progressed the typewriter was repaired and, once again, handed down. Elliot Jaynes' first wooden desk, which he had sentimentally taken to his home, had been replaced with a large handsome desk donated to the firm by the family of a railroad baron. The secretary, Alice Beasley, still with the firm, was richly rewarded for her early entrepreneurial spirit. In fact, as Elliot Jaynes' paralegal and assistant she was at the heart and soul of *Jaynes, Cameron and Hale,* one of the most successful and fastest growing law firms in the country.

The firm had recently entered a thirty year sweetheart lease for three complete floors in a modern fifty story office tower, just prior to the building's all cash sale to a British banking concern.

The firm's executive committee, just yesterday, approved the hiring of seven new lawyers, bringing the total to three hundred and five. Of the forty-five partners, ten were senior, and all ten, close friends and associates of Elliot Jaynes, were considered founders.

At the behest of bearded DeWitt Winston Riles, Manager and President of the firm, the ten were ceremoniously assembled in the well used forty-fourth floor conference room.

Elliot Jaynes uncharacteristically sat at the far end of the table, tie askew, one arm thrown over the back of his chair. He was clothed in stress. He looked exhausted.

He had no idea why the meeting had been called. Given the complexities of their calendars unscheduled Senior Partner meetings were rare.

"You called this party, Winston. What's up?" Elliot asked.

"Elliot," Winston began, "we are all of one mind in this. All of us ...."

"In what?" Elliot interrupted, sitting up straight in his chair.

"For the foreseeable future," Winston continued, "for however long it takes ... we, the nine of us, have reassigned our active cases to other partners. Our associates and appropriate staff members have been instructed to coordinate information flow, document preparation, and client contact. They will see to it that our clients receive first rate representation and we will, of course, be available, but only on a very limited basis."

"What are you going on about, Winston?" Elliot asked. He was truly lost.

Richard Cameron, Elliot's oldest professional friend, was sitting next to him, his back to the window. He had been watching Elliot closely for several weeks and had noticed the strain. This had been his idea, one heartily endorsed by the others.

"Are we partners, or are we not, Elliot?" Richard asked.

"Of course we are."

"Did you and Miss Beasley not start this firm?" Richard asked. "And then I joined you, and then Ed, Sandra, Winston, and so on ... and the ten of us built what we have today, and we did it together. Is that not correct, Elliot?"

"Yes, counselor."

"Elliot," Winston said softly, "We are all aware of how hard you have worked on behalf of Dr. Capterville. You've been concerned for some time that you were on to something dangerous, and that has been proven ...."

"And," Richard interrupted, "you must remember, Steven Capterville is not just *your* client. He is *our* client."

"Thanks, Richard," Elliot said, "I guess I lost sight of that. It's all become so frustrating ... and personal. I want to help them so much but every time I think I'm on to something I hit a dead end."

"From now on," Richard said, "think of things this way. An attack on you, or the C0oapotervilles, is an attack upon all of us. As a group we have already been insulted most egregiously, and we are going to do something about it."

Richard Cameron, a large, stocky ex-UCLA linebacker was now a lawyer, a CPA and acting head of the firm's International Law and Banking Departments. He had, as they all had, a love and affection for Elliot Jaynes.

"Elliot, what you need ..." Richard paused, "is a good lawyer."

All ten of them, Elliot included, erupted in laughter.

Elliot said, "Well it seems I just found nine of them all in one room ... and I thank you all very, very much."

Elliot sat erect in his chair and straightened his tie. "What do you suggest? Winston?"

"Number one," Winston said exercising his extraordinary organizational skills, "you need to bring all of us up to speed on the fact patterns with which you have been dealing, and in each case lead us right up to where you got stumped.

"Number two, each one of us will take that information and immediately start digging ... research, business associates, computer searches, whatever it takes. Richard has already initiated contact with bankers and finance types around the globe. Manny is doing the same with the brokerage houses. I have some ideas concerning real estate transactions ...."

"Real estate?" Elliot wondered.

"Right," Winston said, "and Tom is going to run with it. The patent and copyright guys will be up in an hour."

"Here, in an hour? But why?" Elliot asked.

"To meet with Dr. and Mrs. Capterville, of course," Winston said enthusiastically. "To review the doctor's patent papers, and to hear their perception of events."

"Steven, Meg? Here? But his papers, his papers were stolen from our ...."

"Elliot," Winston said with emphasis, "your Dr. Capterville is one smart bird."

"But ...." Elliot began.

"You can ask him yourself when he gets here, but for now, please Elliot, you've got to fill us in."

"But, Winston, I've got to re-schedule my clients, my appointments, and I've got a hearing in an hour and a half."

"Robert Knowles is handling your appearance for you," Winston said, relishing every word, "and Miss Beasley has already taken care of your appointments ...."

"She WHAT?" Elliot shouted.

The years told Elliot that Miss Beasley was bound to have her ear pressed to the conference room door. He hollered, "Alice, come in here this instant!"

Miss Beasley was opening the door before Elliot could finish his sentence.

"I'm terribly sorry, sir, but I was getting so concerned, and all the ...."

Winston politely interceded for her, "That's quite all right, Miss Beasley. You were perfectly correct."

"By golly," Elliot said smiling, "I'm the victim of a bloody conspiracy!"

"Say it any way you like," Richard said, "we're all in this together now."

"Well, it appears I'm outgunned on all sides," Elliot sighed. "Miss Beasley, since you seem to be in total control of my practice, would you be so kind as to bring us a large pot of coffee, and bring me all the Capterville files."

"Refreshment is on the way, sir, and your Capterville files are right behind you against the wall, sir. Oh, and there's a copy of those Capterville patent papers right on top, sir."

Elliot thought back to the day he left Shirali and Steven in the parking lot. He had stopped by his office briefly on his way to the bank.

"Miss Beasley, you copied the patent papers? But ... I was only here a minute that day."

"Yes, sir. Shall I also order in a late lunch, and perhaps dinner for everyone?"

"Yes," Winston said, "a capital idea, Miss Beasley. I'm sure we'll be here most of the night. Now then, ladies and gentlemen, shall we roll up our sleeves and get to work? We'll stay put until Mr. Jaynes has thoroughly informed us as to facts and events ... and his interpretation of them.

"Three days hence, same time, we shall reconvene and correlate what we have independently uncovered. It is evident, at least from what we know so far, that everything, including the break-ins and the kidnapping, is leading back to motives in the securities, finance and banking arena.

216

"For that reason, Richard and Sandra will coordinate all information and documentation and we will begin building our case against the responsible parties. If you come across anything critical, please contact me or Richard immediately."

"Why do I have the feeling," Elliot asked, "that I have been re-assigned to less critical responsibilities?"

"We cannot do this without you," Winston said, "but part of the reason for this approach, Elliot, is to take pressure off of you ... and put some color back in your cheeks."

"I agree, I agree and once again, thank you all," Elliot said, overwhelmed by the support. These are not just bright lawyers, he thought, they are wonderful, compassionate people and I am very, very fortunate.

"Once we have heard from Elliot, and Dr. and Mrs. Capterville, we can begin our work," Winston said, still directing the meeting. "Elliot, the floor is yours."

Elliot Jaynes reached behind him and grasped one of many red-brown Capterville file folders. He placed it on the desk before him, untied the cloth binding strings and revealed the file title, *RAM PHARMACEUTICALS - PERSONAL NOTES*.

* * *

Three days later the ten partners were again assembled, only this time Elliot Jaynes had taken his usual seat by the door. It was a habit from the three room law office days, a product of having ready access to Miss Beasley during meetings and document executions. Elliot had been a Public Notary then, but was unable to notarize his own signature ...

so it had become necessary for Alice Beasley to put on yet another of her many helpful hats.

In the intervening three days the conference room had come to look more like a war room. Much to Winston's delight, the group had not departed and reconvened as he had proposed. Rather, the ten of them and their staffs had worked around the clock and the forty-fourth floor was transformed from law office to investigative beehive.

Winston once again chaired the meeting and, looking up from his notes and beyond his bifocals, he sounded solemn. "We can prove that RAM is making an enormous profit that is not being reported to its shareholders. Those who control RAM are diverting the monies to RAM subsidiaries that are within their control, and also, to RAM's parent holding company ... which, in turn, appears to be a joint venture between a German chartered universal banking concern, a Soviet aerospace company, and lesser participations by twenty some-odd industrial groups that are highly rated.

"One of the subsidiaries referred to, is, of course, Preferred Financial, Inc.. You will recall that PFI was the company that started Elliot down this path in the first place. PFI's scheme is quite ingenious. It is a far more sophisticated version of some of the laundering done by Savings and Loan owners in the 1980s. The plan was designed to quietly amass cash while the participants remained obscure and anonymous. And they have succeeded on all counts to date ... except for Mr. Jaynes."

Elliot said pensively, "And we wouldn't know about any of it were it not for little Corrie."

"Quite right," Winston went on, "But my point is this ... we have, at least preliminarily, examined the other RAM subsidiaries expecting to find the same methods of transfer. But in each case the laundering procedures proved to be very different and extremely complex. They were implemented over a long period of time by people who must be creative and quite inventive.

"Keep this in mind as you do your research, because Richard and I have come to believe that the interlocking nature of the companies that we do know about, may well extend to organizations about which we presently know nothing.

"In sum, I am sorry to report that we really have not been able to determine anything of substance beyond that which Elliot has already told us. Each lead, by design we are certain, can only be traced so far, at least with the approach we have been taking.

"Richard, Sandra, I believe this is an appropriate time for you to take over."

Sandra Hale, a brilliant, energetic hummingbird of a woman always demonstrated intense loyalty to Elliot Jaynes and to the firm that she helped to create. A top-notch securities lawyer and certified tax specialist, she and Richard Cameron frequently teamed up on more difficult matters.

"We must," Sandra said, looking from partner to partner, "continue to follow our information lines from the ground up. But last night, at a virtual dead end with everything we were pursuing, Richard and I began discussing a different approach. Taking into account Elliot's discoveries, the postcard and certain similarities in the behavior at both the Capterville house and Elliot's home, we can conclude there is a definite connection between the technology, the kefir, and Corrie, on the one hand, and the RAM family of finances on the other.

"And we have agreed upon two things. First, exposing what we know at this time accomplishes nothing for our clients. In fact, such a move could produce severe consequences. Secondly, as Elliot sensed at the outset, this entire fact pattern smells of collusion and conspiracy that somehow goes beyond RAM Pharmaceuticals.

"Since we find ourselves at an impasse with our RAM leads, Richard and I have been asking ourselves if this whole thing might not go all the way to the top."

"The top of what?" Winston wondered out loud.

Richard responded, "Good question. We are curious ourselves. Our present recommendation is that we all concentrate our efforts and our searches at the international level. We should be investigating possible connections between RAM's activities and world organizations ... global trade pacts, administrative bodies, and so forth."

"You think it could go that high," Winston asked.

"My guess is that if it does," Richard said, "there are probably a number of surreptitious layers between RAM and whatever it is we are dealing with."

"Richard," Winston said, "you've had more international policy experience than all of us combined. Given the marketplace, world events and all, would you define your recommendation as something more than our only alternative ... something more than a shot in the dark?"

"Indeed I would," said Richard. "There has not been a time since America's Great Depression that global financial markets have been so susceptible to organized manipulation."

"How do you mean?" Elliot asked, having many of his suspicions confirmed.

"This may sound trite, Elliot, but it's an exciting financial time in which we live. I can't remember anything like it this century. The financial structure of every industrial power has been forced into profound change. Nations are not only endeavoring to solve their own problems, they are now compelled more than ever to address the impact of proposed

220

solutions upon their worldly neighbors ... an exciting time, one replete with opportunity ... and especially fertile for those willing to ignore the rules. We had a taste of it here in America in the early eighties with deregulation of the S&L industry. A legitimate attempt to aid an ailing segment of the U.S. economy was not sufficiently protected from those desiring to abuse the law."

"But," proffered Winston, "that was then."

"No, Winston, we're doing the same thing right now in banking. Five hundred U.S. banks are in the process of failing and our elected representatives are going to reform the industry by giving bank owners more power."

"More power?"

"New holding companies," Richard continued, "will be able to own banks and securities firms."

"Both?" Winston asked.

"Since 1933, federal law has prohibited this. Holding companies presently owning U.S. banking subsidiaries in different states will be able to immediately engage in interstate banking."

"Is that so bad?"

"It's not inherently bad, Winston. Anytime we can rid private enterprise of undue government interference it's bound to have a positive influence on our businesses and our lives. But if the private sector is to accept deregulation it must become a committed guardian against the tempting abuses that are sure to be present."

"Which is one good reason we're all here, isn't that true Richard?" Winston's bifocals slipped lower on his nose.

"Yes, Winston," Richard continued, "all around the world, nations and international bodies are presently restructuring financial services systems. When this happens, when you make adjustments in financial markets, you can dramatically effect the allocation of credit and capital worldwide. This is why I say it's an exciting time, and a time in which we should be wary. Should any one group develop the ability to redirect the flow of industrial investment ...."

"Look at Japan for example," Sandra said. "Since World War II the giant industrial groups, the *keiretsu*, have for all intents and purposes controlled the availability of capital in Japan. And at the heart of each amalgam one is bound to find a securities house, or a bank, or both.

"But now, even Japan's sacred markets are in turmoil. The stock manipulation and customer reimbursements disclosed by the international press have forced a governmental review of Japan's entire financial services sector."

"And speaking of turmoil," Elliot said, "let's not forget events in Europe and the eastern republics ... Soviet Georgia, for instance."

"Quite right, Elliot, and as Richard said, it is an exciting window in time in which a foundation can be laid for the support and stimulation of economic growth, and a time ripe for those intent upon fraud."

"And your next step, Sandra?" Elliot asked.

"As you requested we are just completing our investigation of Battengill Securities, Ltd., what they've been recommending to their clients, with whom they are trading, who's running the show and from where, etc.. Battengill is one of the major trading groups authorized to bid at U.S. Treasury note auctions, and we already know of certain irregularities."

Miss Beasley quietly opened the door, waited for a pause in the discussion and said, "Excuse me Mr. Jaynes, but you wanted me to let you know when the President's press conference was starting ... shall I turn on the television?"

"Yes, thank you, Miss Beasley."

Miss Beasley switched on the small black and white television that sat in the near corner next to the coffee pot. She dimmed the lights and left the room.

After a lengthy introduction by the White House Press Secretary, the President of the United States glanced at his notes and began speaking:

"Ladies and gentlemen, proper protocol dictates that I make the announcements of my two selections at respectfully different times, but under these extraordinary circumstances I have felt it absolutely critical to immediately fill these positions.

"The loss of my Chief of Staff, especially at a time when world events are moving so rapidly, has been most disheartening. And I don't need to tell you how sorely the Chairman has been missed in debate and negotiations at both the domestic and international levels.

"I intend to keep my comments brief because I know you will have many questions for these two remarkable individuals.

"The gentleman I have chosen as my new Chief of Staff we have all known for many years. His reputation and his record are beyond reproach. I should like to introduce to you, Mr. Lucius Otterstein ....

"And I take great pride in announcing our selection for the next Chairman ... excuse me ... the next Chairwoman of the Federal Reserve Board, Dr. Edith Wolman. Dr. Wolman has impeccable credentials and, of course, will play a key role in the shaping of monetary policy both at home and abroad ...."

Sandra Hale rose from her chair, walked to the television and aggressively snapped it off.

"What's wrong, Sandra?" Elliot asked. "You look like you've seen a ghost."

"Worse than that, Elliot," Sandra said with a pale, concerned expression. "Lucius Otterstein runs trading and arbitrage at Battengill Securities."

"Oh, brother!" Winston exclaimed.

Sandra placed the back of her hand on her forehead. She paced, slowly, thinking quickly.

Elliot had seen this expression periodically over the years. "It appears there is more?" he asked.

"Edith Wolman ... I have known from business school days. She's brilliant, made all the right career moves, well respected, influential in international finance circles."

"And ..." Elliot pursued.

"I've always wondered," Sandra said, still in thought, "whether it was my personal reaction to another woman in the same business, or ... whether it was something else"

"And it was something else," Elliot prodded.

"Yes, it appears so. I always had a feeling, I had this feeling that she would ...."

"Do anything to get ahead," Elliot said trying to be helpful.

"Not quite. More than that, Elliot. It was as if she wanted to take what she knew, which was considerable even back in B-school and, well, go beyond what she knew to be permissible, go beyond what she knew to be inherently fair."

Elliot decided to push her a little further. He asked quietly, "Why do you think that is, Sandra?"

Sandra finally exploded. "Because she's a lying, cheating bitch that'd do anything to get power," she howled.

224

There was a brief silence.

"Well ... I'm glad we finally got that out," Elliot grinned.

There was another brief pause and then all of them, including Sandra, laughed for several minutes.

Smiling, Sandra wiped away tears. She said, "You should have been a shrink, Elliot."

"As of late, Sandra, I would have been my own best patient," Elliot replied, still chuckling.

"Well, Sandra, it seems your classmate got what she went after," Richard suggested.

"No, I don't think so," said Sandra, "at least not yet."

"How do you mean?"

"Edith was never interested in titles and positions unless they provided her a means to her objectives. And I think our discussion today has shed some light on what those objectives might be."

"The possibilities are really quite frightening, are they not?" proffered Winston.

The door opened a crack and Miss Beasley said, "Pardon me, sir, but Dr. Capterville just called. He was in a hurry ... was on a pay phone somewhere. He sounded rather upset."

"Doesn't surprise me," Elliot said thoughtfully. "He probably heard the president's speech on the radio."

"He said to remind you about the postcard ... said perhaps the Chief wasn't an Indian after all."

"I expect Dr. Capterville is quite right. Thank you, Miss Beasley."

CHAPTER 25

"This was a great idea, Steven. It's a wonderful day," Megan said, breathing in the fresh pine-scented air. "I just love the mountains, especially when it's cold like this."

"I guess we both needed a break more than we realized," Steven said with a sigh. "Thanksgiving without Corrie was downright depressing."

"Woody, Topper! Stop that barking!" Megan hollered, "and sit down ... RIGHT NOW!"

"Come on, Meg, there's a female spaniel back there with her tail in the air, give 'em a break."

At six thousand feet in the mountains, east of Los Angeles, Steven and Megan wound their way on forested back roads familiar to both of them, from Crestline to deep blue Lake Arrowhead.

"Uh oh, here comes another one," Steven said looking in the rear view mirror.

"Now-a-days, everyone up here tailgates," Megan said. There was a red Toyota pickup following them. It was towing a smoking tar trailer and it was glued to their bumper. Megan sighed, "I guess mountain folks are importing city habits."

"One habit best left below," Steven complained as he moved to the side of the road. "Let's pull over here and let him pass ... I'll bet he has a bumper sticker that says,

**IF YOU CAN'T READ THIS,
YOU'RE NOT CLOSE ENOUGH**

The truck and smoking trailer flew past them. Steven shook his fist at the driver, but he was laughing uncontrollably. Megan opened the sliding window that looked back into the bed of the truck, and yelled through the wind, "Hey dogs, your father's gettin' crazy again!" and she thought to herself how good he sounded ... it had been months.

They took the winding two lane road past Arrowhead Village and turned right at the ice skating rink onto North Bay Road. At the far end of the lake, at the bottom of an incline that was treacherous in winter, Steven turned left onto the state highway ... not right toward the lake. The simple green and white road sign with three rusting bullet holes read, **CALIFORNIA 173**.

Megan, who knew the roads well, looked at Steven accusingly, "I had a feeling when we left this morning that this was more than a Sunday outing. You had this planned all along, didn't you?"

"Meg ... ahh ... gosh" Steven mumbled, "it really didn't hit me until I saw that state highway sign. **173** is one of the roads I was on when I was searching for Corrie way down below. And I've been thinking. The funny old guy who runs the gas pump and market, the one who said he saw a little girl playing games in some boulders ... even if he's part crazy, or all crazy, maybe he really did see our Corrie. Maybe I just didn't ask him the right questions. Maybe there's something important I overlooked."

"Oh, Steven, we've been over this a thousand times," Megan complained.

"I know, I know, but it wouldn't hurt to check," Steven said, "as long as we're already up here. Besides, Woody and Topper will love a good run in the desert. You know how much they love it."

"And who's going to spend the hours picking cactus needles out of their paws?" Megan groaned. "They're hunting dogs for Heaven's sake! Remember the last time we let them loose in the desert?"

"But this is high desert ...."

"So is El Paso, Steven, and the hills outside Reno, and the saguaros in Arizona. Remember? ... where the three of you, barking and laughing and howling, chased anything that would move."

"Including you," Steven said grinning.

"There can't be a rabbit left in the entire state of Arizona."

"If there is, the mutts'll find him ... if you ever let us go back."

"I repeat, who is it that always pulls the needles?"

"But, Meg," Steven pleaded, "if there's a chance he's seen Corrie ...."

Megan looked straight ahead and said nothing. She was furious. Instead of arguing, she grasped the side of her seat and squeezed as hard as she could. As the truck began its descent out of the mountains, the paved road abruptly turned to dirt ... dusty, hard to breath, hair-pin-turned, pot-holed dirt.

"At least the view's spectacular, isn't it Meg?" Steven said with false cheer.

There was no response.

"I sure hope that old fellow is there today. You'll get a kick out of him, Meg."

Megan looked out her window, refusing to speak.

With one passenger, arms folded in frosty silence, and two happily barking bird dogs, the Capterville pickup truck left mountains covered with sugar pines and killer cone spruce, made a winding descent through rocky hills matted with brush and California black oak and, ten degrees warmer, rolled into the upper Mojave desert.

***

Tinyon's Gas n' Go, for sixty years, had been called, simply, Tinyon's Market. The fact that Ed Tinyon and his late wife, Marie, had a bright green gas pump and the desert's finest soda fountain, well, that was just something that folks knew from birth, and word of mouth. But since there was no longer much of a market, except for canned foods and such, and since their best attraction, Marie, was gone, Ed had decided some years back to go modern and call his place a Gas n' Go. It didn't do much for business, but it did a lot for Ed.

Steven pulled off the road, passed the faded green pump, and parked in partial shade along side Tinyon's north wall. Megan removed her jacket and filled the dogs' water dish.

Steven and Megan, still not speaking, marched across the sand-covered pavement, swung open Tinyon's squealing screen door ... and stepped back in time.

What they noticed first was the smell, the wonderful scent of an old country store. They looked at each other and smiled, remembering their childhoods, their parents, their grandparents and all the memories, all brought back by this ... scent.

"If we could bottle a country store fragrance, Steven, we'd be rich."

"What is it about this scent, Meg?" Steven asked under his breath, "is it coming off of the old wooden shelves, the counters, between the planks in the floor? Where do you think it's from?"

"I think it's decades of cookies and candies, vegetables, and fresh baked loaves of bread, Steven ... and the joy of all the kids and moms and dads that came in to buy them."

"Howdy folks," Ed said, "be right there. Marie's stepped out fur a bit, but I'm next best."

Ed put down his broom and came around a counter polished by time. He looked at Megan, and then at Steven, and said, "Say, don't I know you? Never furget a face. See here, lookit this. Carson came through here with Fremont, traded me this here skinnin' knife for three cans of peas. Say! Don't I know you?"

"You have a good memory, Mr. Tinyon. I was in a while back, looking for my ...."

"That's it, that's it," Ed said all excited, "yu're trying to find yur daughter." Then glancing at Megan he said, "y'see, young lady, never furget a face. Well, Mr. ...?"

"Steven, Mr. Tinyon, call me Steven."

"Well, Steven, I'm glad y' found yur daughter. She's a good'n, she is. Now then, is there anything y' be need'n ... soda pop, maybe ... or some candy?"

Megan was giggling, already fond of the old man.

Steven said with a smile, "This is not my daughter, Mr. Tinyon, this is my wife Meg."

"Oh my, you are a looker, aren't you, Meg?" Ed said without hesitation. Ed Tinyon always had a way with the ladies.

"But that means," Ed asked with concern, "that yur still need'n t' find yur daughter?"

"Yes," Megan said. "You said you may have seen her ... in ... some boulders?"

Ed took Megan by the hand and said, "Come on over here, Meg."

He led her through the screen door and on to the far side of the wooden porch. "See over there," Ed said, pointing with his bony left hand, "look past the mail box, the one way over there by the edge of town ... in them big boulders, see the three biggest ones. I think I seen a little girl playin' hide-n-seek, least it looked like she was hidin'."

"You *think* you saw?" Steven asked.

"Well, Steven," Ed said, "out here, since Marie got on, I'm alone a lot, and you'd be shocked if'n I told you some of the things I think I've seen. A little girl playin' in the rocks'd be a tame'n. Plus, I don't quite see the way I used to."

"I understand," Steven said.

"R'member that ol' horror movie, Steven? Black 'n white, the one with the huge ants, big as houses, they were. Attack'n everythin' in sight?"

"Sure, I think so."

"Well, one night I thought I seen 'em ... heard 'em too, right out there by the mail box. Went out blazin' with my shotgun ... got every one of 'em, dead as coal."

"You did?"

"Yep. Next mornin' I seen 'em. I'd shot up three cactus real bad ... the mail box too. They had to put a new one in."

Megan and Steven looked at one another and smiled.

"Anyways, like I said, I ain't seein' like I used to."

Megan bought two cold sodas and several other items from Tinyon's Gas n' Go while Steven filled the pickup with gas. Steven started the engine as Megan checked on the dogs. With everyone loaded, Steven pulled up in front of the old screen door and, leaning out the window, he yelled, "Thanks for your help, Mr. Tinyon."

231

"Call me Ed, young fella, and by the way, you take care of that Meg. She's a real looker, she is ... reminds me of my Marie."

"I'll do just that, Ed."

Steven drove past the mail box and headed straight for the boulders. They searched the area for almost an hour.

Wiping his forehead in the shade of a huge boulder, Steven finally said, "If someone has been here, Meg, the tracks have been well covered. I can't find a thing."

"I can't find anything either, Steven, but Corrie has definitely been here."

"What?" Steven was surprised. "Are you sure? How can you tell?"

"Nothing I can see ... nothing I can explain, really," Megan said mysteriously.

"Megan ...?"

"Call it a mother-daughter thing, Steven, call it what you like, but Corrie was here ... right here."

Megan and Steven Capterville sat with their backs to the same weathered boulder that Corrie had rested against months before.

"It's so beautiful here," Megan said, "I just wish ...."

"I know, Meg, I know."

The sun of late fall was touching the distant western hills. Arms of evening shadows reached eastward across the land. A small gray lizard scurried across the sand in front of them in search of shelter. The dogs were barking restlessly back at the truck.

"Say! I have an idea," Steven said. "Do you have anything, anything with us, that belongs to Corrie?"

"We've got her old socks, the ones the dogs play with," Megan said.

"Perfect," Steven said jumping up, "We've got two trained hunting dogs ... it's about time they started hunting."

"Steven! We should have thought of that hours ago."

Megan and Steven took the collars off the dogs, made them sit and gave them a good sniff of Corrie's sock. On the command to fetch, the English Springer Spaniels tore around the boulders, white tails whirling. There was no doubt. Like Megan they recognized a Corrie who was no longer there. On command, they began running crossing patterns out from the boulders.

When Woody reached the mailbox he went on point, frozen in position with his right paw raised. Megan and Steven ran, the exact same dash that Corrie had made.

"Look," Megan said in the growing dark.

"What is it, Meg?"

"It's one of those colored shoelaces, the kind the kids wear. Why didn't I see this before? Oh, Steven, I knew it! It's Corrie's!"

"Are you sure?"

"You bet! I'm positive," Megan said with excitement. "She begged me to get them for her the last time we were shopping. See all the pink little hearts."

"Sure! I remember now."

"Oh, Steven, this is wonderful!"

"Ok, let's get the dogs in the truck," Steven said. He whistled three times. "If Corrie was here, there must be footprints, or some sort of clue. We can spend the night at a motel and come back first thing in the morning."

Last light from the sun disappeared behind distant volcanic ridges as the pickup truck roared back toward civilization.

Ed Tinyon quietly closed his store-front window and latched it shut. He pulled together the red checkered curtains. With a curious smile, he crossed the room and went behind his counter. He returned his binoculars to their leather case, and hung them on one of the many wrought-iron hooks protruding from Marie's favorite antique baking rack. He tilted his head back and took a deep breath. Then he bent down below the counter and grabbed a dusty bottle of prized cognac that he saved for very special occasions. He poured an ounce or so into a small glass, stared at it for a moment and then raised it into the air.

"To you, Marie. I wish you could be here to see this."

* * *

At first light the Captervilles were back at the boulders and the dogs were working every square inch of ground.

"Steven, if Corrie had gone toward town she would have called us, or been seen by somebody. And since she seems to have made it to the mail box, it makes sense she would have gone into Ed Tinyon's place."

Steven was watching the dogs closely.

"That's what I've been thinking, Meg. If she didn't reach the mailbox from the town, she must have come from this direction ... from the south, out of the mountains."

"That must be it," Megan said looking up to the hills.

"And look at the dogs, Meg, they're definitely favoring the hills. I'll get the pack. Keep your eyes peeled."

For four hours they steadily climbed and searched. They crossed a dirt road at one point but found no evidence of Corrie, or any other human being. Then they unexpectedly emerged from the rocks and brush. They beheld a beautiful little valley dotted with pinion and ponderosa pines, and enormous old growth oak trees. Red headed woodpeckers were noisily hammering acorns into the trunks of trees and it seemed there was a squirrel or two in every tree. Here and there lay rounded granite shapes rising like gray whales from the meadow floor.

"Steven, look at the holes on the top of those rocks."

"Well, I'll be. They're the size of grapefruit! The Serranos must have ...."

"The what?" Megan asked.

"The Serranos, Meg, *The People of the Mountains.* That's what the early Spanish explorers called the native Indians. They're a tribal group of the Shoshone, I believe ... they traded with the coastal Indians, and the Mojaves along the Colorado River."

Megan said, "You and your history, Steven, I do declare." But she was really thinking, "This man is always surprising me, and I love him so."

"The Indians would winter below, and summer up here ... hunting, fishing, gathering ... and they'd grind up the acorns in these stone holes for food. Meg, do you realize?"

"What, Steven?"

"We must have stumbled onto one of the secret Indian encampments. I've never heard of one in this area. There's a good sized one off **173**, near the Pinnacles ...."

"If nobody knows about it," Megan interrupted, "then we ought to be able to find Corrie's footprints. Let's start looking."

"You're right. Woody! Topper! Go!"

Steven was correct about the presence of the Indians, and the natural isolation of the vale. But there were no footprints or signs of recent human life in the valley ... and Megan was heartbroken. Holding hands, they pressed through a thicket of tall Manzanita trees. They sat, all four of them, on a rock outcropping that overlooked Southern California's high desert. It was ten in the morning and in the distance, far across the desert, the sun was lighting the sharpened peaks of the Sierra Nevada mountain range.

Deep in thought Megan looked down at the granite beneath her knees. Her long blond hair fell across her beautiful country western face, a work-tanned face delicately chiseled with the character of her ranching forefathers. Even laden with grief, as she was now, Steven thought her the most exquisite woman he had ever seen.

Megan asked pensively, "What do you think has happened to the kefir from Bukol, Steven? Why has God allowed it to pass into evil hands?"

Steven put his arm around her. "I wish I knew, Meg. Whoever they are, they've got the kefir and the ancient translations that teach how to grow it. But then, Corrie has said we must believe in things when our own logic tells us otherwise. Right?"

Steven paused, and frowned. "Logic tells me RAM Pharmaceuticals is growing the kefir right now. They're analyzing priceless manuscripts from Abkhazia to make a fortune for themselves. Why would God want something so wonderful in the hands of those people?"

Megan scratched the granite below her with a crooked twig. "Corrie would say He was up to something. She'd tell us the same thing Shirali said. Have faith, and be patient."

"Not too easy when your little girl's been stolen."

"Steven?"

"What is it, Meg?"

"Corrie is somewhere near. I can feel her."

"I've had the ...."

"Steven! Did you hear that?"

"Only us Indians," Steven said.

"I'm serious, Steven ... listen, listen," Megan whispered.

"I hear it now! ... sounds like a car," Steven said with a puzzled look on his face. "A car? Up here?"

"Some secret valley, Steven!"

They watched a black, dust covered GMC truck appear and disappear as it snaked through the trees and up the mountain.

"Can you see the road, Steven?"

"Yes, but only in places," Steven said with irritation. "I never would have noticed without hearing the truck. Good grief, Meg, it's coming right for us."

"Steven, we've been all over this valley. There are no roads up here."

The black truck, spewing dirt, was less than one hundred feet below them and approaching fast. They held the dogs and ducked behind the rocks, listening.

"It's gone!" Megan said in a loud whisper, "no sound, no dust ... it just disappeared! Look over the rocks, Steven. See if you can see it."

"Well, how about that!" Steven said, scratching his head. "There's no trace of it."

Megan leaned back against her rock and said to herself, "OK, now let's think about this from the beginning ...." It was an old Capterville trait.

Thinking aloud, she said, "We get a postcard from someone with Corrie's handwriting, and it's postmarked *Apple Valley*, which is right down there ..." she pointed with a stiff arm. "We talk to a nice old man who saw a girl playing in the boulders. Woody goes on point and we find Corrie's shoelace by the mail box. And now, a big black truck disappears into a mountain before our very eyes. Steven, am I exaggerating?"

"I'd say you're right on, Meg. Now, aren't you glad I turned left yesterday ... instead of right?"

237

"Is this an *I told you so*, Steven?"

"Of the highest magnitude, my dearest Megan. Let's go, we've got to find where the truck ...."

"In a minute, Steven ... wait." A wave of emotion swept through Megan. She grabbed Steven's arm, and made him sit down against her rock.

"What's wrong, Meg?"

"I can't help it, Steven. I'm just ... the trees, the mountains, Corrie. It reminds me of Corrie ... her favorite song ...."

"Her favorite song? Meg, you're talking crazy. Let's go, we don't want to lose the truck."

Megan Capterville knew the black truck had something to do with her daughter, but she could not force herself to move. "But, Corrie's song, Steven ... I know she's near. We should sing it for her."

"Do you want to sing songs or find Corrie? Now, let's go!"

"All right, all right."

They ordered the dogs silent and scrambled down through the rocks. Megan spotted the seldom used dirt road first.

"Can you believe this, Steven, a road right under our noses."

"Must be an old logging road, or mining. Look at the ruts and brush. They could be hunters or four wheelers, or maybe a utility crew ...."

"Or kidnappers," Megan broke in, "and I'd like to get my hands on them."

"So would I. We'd better leash the dogs and stay off the road until we know what we're dealing with. Let's see, we were sitting right up there ... when the truck was about here."

"Then it vanished," Megan said.

"So it's got to be close. Let's cut through the trees and have a look over there."

They hiked over a carpet of fallen yellow oak leaves that rustled noisily with every step, and then through another thicket of brown Manzanita bushes. Sticky Manzanita blooms stuck stubbornly to their clothes. Massive oaks and huge pines towered above them and they could tell they were once again coming close to the cliff wall.

"The road can't be more than a few feet away," Megan whispered, "but how do we get through this?"

They were stopped by a ten foot barrier of tangled brush and thorn bushes.

"Over here!" Steven motioned to a spot with open sunlight.

Gripping a long crooked pine bough Steven forced back the thorny branches so he and Megan could see. They saw the road clearly. It dead-ended at the cliff and there was just enough room for a car to turn around.

Two small orange butterflies chased one another among the plants growing from the cliff face. Blue jays chirped and squawked to one another ... as though there had never been a black truck.

"That truck is here somewhere, Steven."

"Shhhh ...."

"But it never left," Megan whispered, "We would have seen it or heard it."

Steven stood on his toes to get a better view.

"Look! Meg ... can you see them?"

"What?"

"The tire tracks. They're hard to see with the sun over-head ... see, right in the middle of the road."

"No, I don't ... Oh, yes ... there! ... Oh, my gosh, Steven, they go straight into the cliff!"

CHAPTER 26

As the camouflaged rock and steel door closed behind them, Giancarlo Panatta jumped from the black truck and hit the light switch. The huge concrete and granite chamber glowed with eerie orange light that flickered from old-fashioned light bulbs. Marlin Moss swung the truck around, backed up to a loading dock and opened the tail gate.

Panatta ran up a steel staircase two steps at a time and slid back a panel in the hidden observation window. He had a clear view of the road below and the descending countryside beyond. He saw no one.

"Think we should cover the tracks?" he yelled to Moss.

"We won't be here that long. Come on, let's get going."

Panatta and Moss pushed aside a heavy steel door and moved swiftly through a long man-made tunnel.

The labyrinth of passageways had been picked, shoveled and blasted at the turn of the century by an enterprising group of people who realized that the sale of water to the arid plains to the south could be quite profitable. With much expense and anguish the Valley of the Little Bear was dammed, and it rapidly filled with water. The result was twelve miles of beautiful pine-studded shoreline which was coronated, Lake Arrowhead.

But the energetic entrepreneurs had not appreciated the fact that the mountains' natural watershed flowed north to the high desert, while their customer base lay up and over the peaks to the south. The logical solution, they calculated, was to engineer and dig tunnels through the mountains that would carry the water down the hill in the right direction ... to the south.

However, difficult engineering and successful water rights law suits brought by the thirsty folks to the north, effectively shut the spirited project down.

It was through one of these abandoned and forgotten tunnels that the two members of the Committee of Six now ran. And it was through one of these tunnels that Slavic and Bob had dragged poor little Corrie.

"How did you ever find this place, Marlin?" Giancarlo asked gasping for breath.

"A long story," Marlin said. "A friend of my father's in the Army Corps of Engineers told me about it ... turned out to be the perfect spot for our western hemisphere data base."

"And it has proven most convenient concerning the girl," Giancarlo added.

The two men stopped suddenly and opened a massive iron door that led into a large concrete bunker. Panatta turned on the lights and reached for a heavy metal dolly. Marlin Moss headed for his computers.

The room was full, row upon row, with the world's most sophisticated computer equipment. This was one of three global sites from which Edith Wolman, Lucius Otterstein and the others routinely entered and extracted the information that was crucial to their objectives.

"The four boxes in the corner are loaded with the disks we'll need to take," Marlin said pointing to the stacked file cartons. "Go ahead and plant the explosives. Just to be certain, I'm going to make sure our master files are erased."

Panatta placed the G-4 plastic explosives in locations certain to destroy the entire room. He wheeled the dolly with the four boxes out into the tunnel and returned in time to see Marlin delete the last of the files.

"That won't be necessary, Marlin. There's enough fire power in here to melt a hundred times this much."

"I know," Marlin said. "Just like to cover things more than once."

"That's what makes me wonder ..." Panatta's voice trailed off.

"Wonder what, Giancarlo?"

"You are so cautious, how ... how could you be in favor of the two additional projects?" Panatta asked guardedly. He knew he was out of his area of expertise.

"And you are speaking of ...?"

"The space station, Big Freedom, and the new mainland China airport."

"Giancarlo, my friend, I have always loved you for your candor," Marlin said. "The truth is, I have reservations myself about pursuing these two, at least at this time. But I have complete confidence in Lucius and Edith in these matters."

"So do I, but as long as we are speaking candidly I'd like to tell you what I think. And I intend to bring it up at the next meeting."

"What is that, Giancarlo?"

"I don't think Lucius and Edith want to take them on either, but they are being pressured to do so by the other two."

Marlin studied Giancarlo closely. Giancarlo spoke sparingly. He was blunt and often crude, but his Spartan insights were worthy of serious consideration. He may not know finance and policy-making, but Giancarlo knew people.

"An interesting observation, Giancarlo, one that had not occurred to me. And you could be quite right. The other two have been most insistent."

"I don't know all they're planning," Giancarlo said, "and I'm confident they're implementing the standard safeguards and precautions. It just seems that three sister airports in the

U.S., Britain and China, all linked to a new orbiting space station is, well, it's ...."

"Too visible," Marlin volunteered.

"Exactly."

"You're right, Giancarlo. At the upcoming meeting we will both ... Hey! How much time have we got?"

Looking at his watch Giancarlo said, "Twenty one minutes and change."

"Let's move it!"

Marlin Moss put a blue, three and one half inch computer disk into his pocket and ran out of the bunker into the tunnel. Giancarlo was hurriedly pushing the dolly in front of him. They loaded the boxes into the truck and, standing on the dock, Marlin asked, "What about the girl? Need we do anything?"

"No," Panatta answered, "Slavic was given instructions to terminate her. We tried every method ... for months. The girl knew nothing."

"Sorry it came to that."

"I suggest we move fast or we'll be buried with her," Panatta said leaping into the truck.

"But shouldn't we check the window first?"

"No time ... step on it!" Panatta growled.

He pressed the remote control and the outside door rolled slowly upward. Bright light of the mid-day sun poured in upon them and the truck moved out the opening. Thirty yards down the dirt road Marlin Moss stopped the truck and Panatta leapt out. He ran back to the entrance and with a long leafy branch smoothed over all traces of their presence. Back in the truck they watched the cliff door lower to the ground. Seconds later Panatta and Moss were bouncing and winding down the mountain with years of secret data in their possession.

Two small orange butterflies chased one another among the plants growing from the cliff face. Blue jays chirped and squawked to one another ... as though there had never been a black truck.

CHAPTER 27

Once they spotted the tire tracks, Megan and Steven and Woody and Topper convened a quick and quiet family conference behind the thorny hedge. It was decided that an assault upon the cliff, or whatever was inside, would be foolish.

While Panatta and Moss were secretly inside the mountain, the four searchers had scrambled down the mountain as fast as their twelve feet would carry them, staying out of sight as much as possible and keeping an eye out for the lower end of the road. Leading the way, Steven was now following a steep, dry creek bed whose tumbled white rocks provided an irregular staircase that stepped them out of the hills.

Hopping from rock to rock, Steven could hear Megan's footsteps behind him. She was taking deep breaths and singing Corrie's song.

> *Love, and joy will flow into you*
> *Like sunshine into trees;*
> *Share, and your cares will fall off*
> *As autumn leaves;*
> *Give, and God will breath into you*
> *The freshness of a thousand winds.*

"Watch this one, Meg, it's slippery."
"OK."
"We've got to find her, Meg."
"I know, Steven, I know."
"Watch this one!"

"I see it ... I still have this feeling Corrie's nearby, like we've just missed her, or something."

Megan kept singing Corrie's song as she stepped from rock to rock. It made her feel better. As long as she sang, she felt Corrie was with her.

For you shall go out with joy
And be led forth with peace;
The mountains and the hills
Shall break forth before you into singing,
And all the trees of the field will clap.

The four of them landed on the road at once ... not the main road but the secretive dirt road that had wound unexpectedly below them.

"Meg, look!" Steven huffed, "the little white bridge! Remember the postcard ... see, crossing the creek! ... yellow and black warning signs on both sides."

"Whoever sent the postcard must have been here, Steven. But why, and was Corrie here too?"

The little bridge completed the tip of a tight hair-pin turn. The surrounding hills were covered in low silver brush with occasional outcroppings of grotesque granite shapes. But the crossing, where the ancient stream bed rolled beneath the old wooden bridge, was packed with berry vines and red Indian paint brush. Three towering sycamore trees with large five-fingered leaves shaded the lower side of the freshly painted bridge.

"Come on, Meg, we've got to get back to our truck."

"But shouldn't we look for clues? There might be ...."

"Not now. There's a black truck around here somewhere. Let's go."

They stayed off the road and followed the creek bed. At the last available sighting through dense mesquite they guessed the dirt road would join the main road about a mile from where they had parked the pickup.

***

Megan drove the pickup along the shoulder of the highway while Steven and the dogs stood in the back searching for the dirt road. There was no sign of any kind of intersection so Megan doubled back and they looked again.

Steven spotted a small corner of the dirt road where it made its last turn coming out of the hills. He banged on the cab for Megan to stop.

"I'm going to slide under the barbed wire and get past these tumbleweeds. I'll run along the fence line ... see what I can see."

"OK, but be careful, Steven," Megan yelled over the sound of the engine.

After fifty yards Steven ran back to the fence and hollered, "This is it!"

He climbed into the truck on the driver's side and Megan slid over. "Let's turn around. We can park, let's see, back at that bend in the road, in the brush alongside the boulders."

"But I don't see a road."

"See the latches on that post?" Steven said wheeling the truck around onto the pavement. "It's a wire gate ... and the tumbleweeds have been cut and placed out there."

"We'll attract little attention parked here by the boulders," Steven said. "We can wait in the shade, up there in the rocks. We'll have a good view and be ready to leave quickly."

Just then the pickup shook noticeably.

"Steven, an earthquake!"

Then a second or so later, a dull boom echoed from the direction of the mountain.

"Must have set off a landslide," Steven said.

"I'm not sitting up in those rocks, Steven."

He didn't answer right away, watching ....

"You won't have to, Meg. We have company. Look over there."

The black truck, moving fast with swirling sand rising behind it, approached the barbed wire fence. It plowed over the tumbleweeds and came to a sliding halt at the fence posts. A man jumped out, drew back the wire gate, and the truck moved onto the highway. The man latched the wires back to the post, kicked away the tire tracks with his shoes and leaped back into the moving truck.

The truck came straight for the Capterville pickup.

Behind the steering wheel Steven fumbled with the small disposable camera he kept in the glove compartment. He wound it to the next frame, and as the black truck came at them he put his arm casually around Megan and rested the camera against the side window. As the truck sped by, he pointed the camera, guessing, and snapped the picture. When the truck disappeared in the rear view mirror Steven turned on the motor and, wheels screaming, swerved onto the pavement in quest of the mysterious black truck.

"Steven! What are you doing? Are you crazy?"

"Those could be the men who took Corrie."

Megan scowled.

"Let them stay way ahead then," Megan pleaded. "I don't like this at all ...."

"At this rate we'll be back at Tinyon's in no time," Steven said.

But well before Tinyon's Gas 'n Go the truck turned right at a nondescript intersection onto a road paved in timeworn asphalt. It led both trucks, now curving, now straight, into the vast rolling expanse of the high desert.

"Let's pull over, Steven, I'm getting nervous. What if they stop? What could we do out here?"

"OK, we'll go to the top of this next dune and pull over ... man, those guys are really moving! We've been going ninety."

Steven stopped on the shoulder about fifty feet from the top of the rise, and he and Megan walked the rest of the way.

"Look, Steven!" Megan cried as she reached the crest, "it's a jet!"

They overlooked an oval section of desert enclosed by low, randomly arranged hills. In the center of the valley was a small wooden building. It was surrounded by two long runways laid out in the shape of an **X**. At the end of the far runway sat a medium sized jet. It was prepared for take-off.

At high speed the black truck turned onto a road that led straight to the runways.

"Come on!" Steven shouted, running for their pickup.

Megan stood firm and yelled, "You've got to be kidding! You're going to get us both killed!"

"Come on!" Steven shouted, "come on!"

Megan and Steven roared over the crest of the dune with the dogs barking in the back.

"Steven ...?" Megan said gripping her seat.

"I just want to get close enough for a picture, Meg ... besides, those people are in such a rush they're paying no attention to us."

The black truck skidded to a stop on the runway and the front doors flew open beside the awaiting jet. Burdened with boxes, Panatta and Moss rushed up the stairs and into the jet. The engines were at full throttle and the aircraft was moving as the side door was being closed.

The Capterville pickup, also at full throttle, turned onto the airport road and was headed for the jet.

"Hold on, Meg!" Steven shouted as he slammed on the brakes. He sprang from the pickup, steadied his hands and took a second picture. In a few seconds the jet was airborne.

"I understand now, Steven. That was smart, very smart. Who would have thought ... a United States Air Force jet."

"Thanks, Meg. A shot with the black truck and the jet together. If the pictures come out, it could be interesting. Who knows what we'll find?"

"I'll bet Corrie knows."

"NOW THEN!" Steven shouted with a gleam in his eye, "what say we have a look at the inside of that black truck."

Megan rolled her eyes and held onto the seat with both hands. "I married a quiet biochemist ... and now I've got a commando."

The old shack at the center of the airfield, long since abandoned and in disrepair, had little left of its original roof. Its four square windows had long ago been shot out during youthful target practice, and anyone looking might wonder how the little building still stood. As the Capterville pickup truck headed back to the main road, a thin, boney hand pulled shut the off-center, creaking cedar door. There was a latching sound, then silence.

Excepting the whine of the departing Capterville truck, an occasional far-away bark and the distant roar of a high flying jet, all was quiet in the high desert.

***

Giancarlo Panatta was looking out the window of the ascending jet as it made its first low altitude bank to the east, and for the first time in his life he felt an uncontrollable, terrifying fear ... a fear of failure, and of having made a fatal mistake.

"Marlin, the pickup truck down there. It's the one we passed at the fence, the one with the ... dogs."

"Take it easy, Panatta, you're gettin' too jumpy," Marlin cracked as he sipped a fresh martini. Marlin gazed out the window past a thin layer of clouds and, below, scanned a vanishing painted desert.

"Can't a guy take his dogs huntin' now and then?"

CHAPTER 28

Commander Capterville was sweating profusely inside his space suit. He was nervous, very nervous, and he was kicking himself for not beginning sooner. He had been seduced by the incredible beauty of the primordial planet he was leaving below, and he had taken too much comfort in the Lander's programmed flight.

Jake was enraged. He was furious ... with himself.

"I should have checked the trajectory first thing. Inexcusable, Capterville!"

Jake's fingers feverishly worked the computer's keyboard. "That's one stupid mistake that could cost you your life."

Behind him revolved rust-red Mars. Ahead lay a blanket of brilliant stars imbedded in deep black, and the mother ship, Little Freedom.

Four hundred yards and closing ... the Lander containing Jake Capterville, following its present course, would slowly, silently move past its mate into the far reaches of the universe.

"Blast!" Jake screamed into his fogging mask. He was trying to concentrate. He must re-load the data, or die.

He was keenly aware of his status. If he could not regain control of his craft it would pass Little Freedom at its docking speed of less than one quarter of a mile per hour ... at a distance of three feet. For a few moments in time Jake would be able to look, window to window, into the lifeless eyes of his best of friends, Orville and Jim.

As Little Freedom's orbit began its decay, Jake would be moving through space in the opposite direction, and he would be out of air. As Little Freedom was plunging helplessly to the planet surface, Jake would be flying to where he had always dreamed of going, to the outer limits of the Solar System and beyond. But he would not be alive.

"Hold on, Jake. Keep at it," he told himself, "there must be no distraction now."

One hundred yards and closing ....

Jake Capterville was unaware of just how proficient he had become under stress. Training, testing and education aside, the project leaders at NASA had noticed this quality in him early on. It was something that could not be taught and it was the real reason, ·the unspoken reason, that he was the Commander.

Stress to Jake was an evil to be avoided through proper planning. But there could never be blueprints complete enough to account for the risks he would always take, and Jake knew this better than anyone. He did not like pressure, but in it he was the best.

Jake had reviewed and dismissed all options but one.

"NASA is going to hear about this too," he thought without interrupting his calculations. "Two tin cans in space and my only control is through this blasted keyboard. We're all too computer-reliant."

Little Freedom was suspended like a Christmas tree ornament fifty yards in front of him.

"If I'd been born in another century I'd throw out a grappling hook, swing aboard and pop the hatch ... or at least navigate manually."

Program planners, of course, had counted on Orville Bittain to captain Little Freedom and, if necessary, to override the Lander's control instructions with commands from the orbiting mother ship. And in defense of those with responsibility for anticipating all possible contingencies, no one could have expected that the lone survivor of three astronauts would attempt a solitary Martian descent.

Little Freedom was now ten yards from the leading edge of the Lander. The Lander, still several feet off course was barely moving, in anticipation of an imminent coupling.

"Well, this is it. Last two entries. We'll enter speed, **.35 knots**, here ... distance, **7.4 feet**, here ... last key, **ENTER**."

There was an almost imperceptible hiss of a starboard thruster, then another. The Lander moved sideways a precious few feet. There was a stabilizing hiss from the port side. Forward motion remained unchanged. Jake shut his eyes and prayed.

He felt a slight jolt and heard the familiar locking sound.

"Bingo!"

CHAPTER 29

The Polo Lounge at the Beverly Hills Hotel remains unchanged. The cuisine is delightfully continental, the outside garden patio wonderfully charming and the inside booths and tables are filled with those wishing to be seen and those hoping to see. Hollywood movie deals are still hammered out over California salads, and unimportant people become even more so by having themselves paged.

Seated in a private alcove at the far end of the old flagstone patio were Steven and Megan, Elliot Jaynes, Richard Cameron and Sandra Hale. It was two o'clock in the afternoon and low December sunlight filtered through leafless wisteria vines. The air was chill. The conversation was not.

"But Mr. Cameron, what about Corrie!" Megan demanded with an uncomfortable strain to her voice.

"Meg, please ..." Steven said putting his arm around her.

"But Corrie is still missing and all this talk sounds like complicated intellectual ... nonsense." Megan's voice cracked and large tears began cascading down her flushed cheeks.

The waiter placed a hot pot of tea water in front of her and carefully arranged thin lemon wedges on a small side saucer. Megan buried her head in her hands and began to sob. The waiter was understandably concerned. In all his years of sterling service his lemon slices had never had this effect.

"Is anything ... wrong?" he asked looking from setting to setting, surveying his province.

"The service is excellent. Thank you," Steven replied.

"Very well," the waiter said with a condescending tone. He left them, moving smoothly in and around his other tables,

255

periodically glancing at the Capterville table with an expression that said, "I thought I'd seen it all."

After an uncomfortable silence Megan recovered in honorable fashion, delicately blew her nose, and said, "Please excuse me. I really am sorry."

"Everyone is here to help, Meg," Steven said.

"I know. I didn't mean a word I said. Please go on. Richard, you were discussing the banks."

Gathering his thoughts Richard placed his elbows on the table and with a long clear straw randomly moved the ice cubes in his water glass to more strategic locations.

"Richard," Sandra said quietly, "perhaps it would be helpful if I summarized things for Meg and Steven, and then we can discuss all the possible alternatives. It's really no wonder Meg's confused. We dove right into the middle of things before we even sat down."

"Good idea," Richard said reaching for his briefcase. "But first I want Steven to see this."

Richard produced a beautiful, royal-blue glossy folder, trimmed with an intricate gold foil border. Embossed in the upper center was a burgundy red dragon crest. Below the crest were black and gold letters,

MARKETFORCE, INC.
"Your Journey to a New Way of Life"

Richard handed it to Steven. Steven looked at the cover and without hesitation said, "This is Tom's company ... Tom Gulling. I've designed a complete line of health care products for MarketForce. I just talked with Tom this morning. His contract is on my desk. That's what we're doing tomorrow."

"I doubt your contract will ever be signed," Richard said sternly. "If it is, it will never be honored."

"What?"

"Look inside."

Steven folded back the impressive cover. The two inside leaves were artistically cut with pockets containing eye-catching informational sheets. An array of products was presented ... microclustered water products, products containing Russian kefir.

"Wow! Tom never told me he was this far along with his art work and printing."

"Your buddy Tom never told you a lot of things," Richard said dryly.

Steven reviewed the folder. His puzzled expression became even more so with each page.

"Take a look at the bottom of each product flier," Richard said, "and the company description. The manufacturer is not your company, Pacific Rim, Inc.."

"No!"

"Well, look," Richard insisted.

"This can't be ...."

The foot of each informational sheet read,

Manufactured by
MARKET RESOURCES INTERNATIONAL, INC.
Salt Lake City, Utah, USA

"But ..." Steven was speechless.

"Market Resources, MRI, is a wholly owned subsidiary of Pen Products, Inc., also of Salt Lake."

"And?" Steven asked, becoming angry.

"Pen Products," Richard continued, "is a wholly owned subsidiary of ... RAM Pharmaceuticals."

"Oh, no," Megan moaned as she squeezed Steven's arm.

Sandra leaned across the table and held Megan's hand. "But, Meg, this is a positive development, especially for Corrie. It's another link."

"That's true, Meg," Richard said. "Sandra, go ahead, explain how things are beginning to fit together."

"Wait a second," Steven said, "I've been working on this distribution deal for six months and I'm the only one who knows how to make the products. How does RAM Pharmaceuticals or anyone else figure they can manufacture my products?"

"Evidently they believe they'll be able to very soon," Richard said.

258

"But it's impossible for them to do so," Steven said. His face was turning red. "In the patent papers they stole, I intentionally omitted several key steps. They can duplicate absolutely nothing I've done."

"Obviously they don't know that, Steven. They've probably got top scientists working on it around the clock. It's the future, and they know it."

Richard hesitated, contemplating his ice water. "And don't forget," he continued, "they have the parent sample of the kefir and the Abkhazian writings from Bukol to instruct them in its growth. This brochure certainly indicates they believe they're ready to distribute, and do it big, with a full discussion of microcluster technology and the Russia story."

"But how, Richard?" Megan asked.

"Take a look at the brochure. It's all laid out right there."

Megan fumbled through the pages feeling betrayed.

"But it's more than that, Meg. The couple that brought me the MarketForce brochure are clients of mine, friends actually. They wanted my legal opinion on the marketing format. The two of them have earned over thirty thousand dollars a *month* for several years in network marketing, and before they change companies they want to make certain this company is properly formed."

"Is it?" Megan asked.

"With the exception of the RAM issue, it's first rate," Richard said. "Multilevel marketing companies frequently don't make it because they don't adequately plan for the growth they experience, or because the authorities shut them down for illegal marketing practices. In this case your friend Tom has written the Attorney General in every state and submitted the MarketForce business plan ... very smart."

"I know," Steven said, beginning to fume, "that was my idea. I wasn't about to go to all this work only to see my distributor shut down."

"What's interesting," continued Richard, "is that they already have over three hundred top distributors and motivational speakers under contract."

"What?" Steven shouted, "With RAM as the manufacturer?"

"Right, or at least RAM's subsidiary, this MarketForce. My clients just attended one of their meetings. They said it's the best they've ever been to. It must have been, for them to give up thirty grand a month. It rather looks like your friend Tom has been using you, Steven, or at least he thinks he has ... for information, and marketing sizzle."

The waiter was delicately hovering and refilling as Steven left the table to telephone Tom Gulling. For the first time since Steven had been introduced to him, Tom was unavailable. Nor did Tom respond to the pager that had become a permanent part of his person.

"No luck, I'll wager," Richard said as Steven returned and sat down.

"He wouldn't take my call."

Megan squeezed Steven's hand again.

"I just don't understand any of this," Steven said with unexpected calm. "The kefir has full patent protection under the new biotechnology laws. Shirali's company owns the patent."

Steven waived the blue folder in front of him, "And we control the processes by which all these products are made. So what in the world can all this mean?"

Sandra Hale smiled discretely. She leaned forward looking intently at Steven and Megan. "It means," Sandra said lowering her voice, "whoever is controlling RAM and the other companies is planning a key move very soon."

"Other companies?" Megan asked.

"Yes, Meg, this is what I wanted to explain. We have to look at Steven's achievements, and the kefir, in the context of a bigger picture."

"Please go on." Megan said with interest.

A solitary breeze blew in a gust through the patio. The warming rays of the sun were rapidly vanishing from the table when the waiter patiently brought a fresh hot pot of coffee. An assistant replaced their coffee cups with clean pre-warmed cups, and with a silver blade he removed bread crumbs from the white linen tablecloth. Sandra pulled a thick wool sweater over her shoulders and began speaking with the excitement of someone who has uncovered something important.

"We believe **The Big Six** referred to on the postcard is a group or a committee of six people. Thanks to Elliot's digging and Steven's heroics we have identified four of these people.

"Lucius Otterstein, past Director of Battengill Securities, Ltd., is now Chief of Staff to the President of the United States. We have confirmed through our sources that he remains active in controlling the trading at Battengill.

"Doctor Edith Wolman, now Chairwoman of the United States Federal Reserve Board has, through her connections to several international finance bodies, greatly expanded the traditional duties of a Fed Chairman. Our friends tell us the World Bank and related policy-making tribunals are rapidly falling under her thumb."

"Dr. Wolman is an old school chum of Sandra's," Elliot said, winking at Richard.

Sandra pulled her sweater closer and ignored the comment. "Another two we have been able to trace because of Steven's famous one-handed, perfectly timed photograph."

Elliot beamed, "I have yet to congratulate you, Steven. A marvelous piece of detective work ... Bravo!"

All of them, including a reluctant Megan, applauded and raised their glasses.

Steven grinned, "Thank you, thank you, thank you. Perhaps I'm in the wrong profession. What do you think, Meg?"

"I'm never really sure *what* profession you're in."

Sandra drew out of her valise an eight by ten inch blow up of the photograph Steven had taken. She placed it before Megan and Steven. "This man here, Giancarlo Panatta, we know little about ... very mysterious fellow. There are reports linking him to terrorist groups in Europe, but we can find nothing substantive.

"The other gentleman is Marlin Moss. The folks at the U.S. Treasury know him well ... a brilliant mind, but insiders say they can never be sure which side he's on. Just the kind of guy we need programming our nation's central computer network."

Steven and Megan looked at one another. "Marlin Moss was in that truck?" Steven bellowed.

."Goodness!" Megan exclaimed, "who would have thought ... all this time. You never did trust him, Steven, even back in Bukol. Remember when he left the mountain without saying a word?"

"I've always wondered what became of him," Steven growled. He squeezed Megan's hand.

Sandra continued, "We have no clue as to who the other two might be. We are hoping that as this intricate web of business relationships unfolds, we might discover who they are."

"Perhaps we should send Steven after them," Elliot quipped.

"I'm ready," Steven said quickly.

"Stop it, you two!" Megan said. She was intrigued with Sandra's thinking. "What business relationships are you talking about, Sandra?"

"The first thing we noticed in our securities search was a group of highly rated companies, thirty of them, that increased sharply in value late last summer."

"That doesn't sound so unusual," Steven remarked.

"Let her finish, Steven."

"It may not seem unusual at first glance, Steven, but all thirty had little or no economic reason for such a move. Their price/earnings ratios remained stable and there was nothing startling or new about any of their business plans ... no major contracts signed, no new product lines unveiled."

"That *is* odd," Steven said. "What have you found out, Sandra?"

"Battengill Securities ramped the stock," Sandra said flatly.

"Ramped?" Megan asked.

"Lucius Otterstein has an impressive network of relationships at securities firms around the world. After he achieved voting control, or its equivalent, in these thirty companies he put the word out to all the major houses that these stocks should be aggressively promoted. As a consequence, the value of Mr. Otterstein's holdings increased by many billions literally overnight."

"How can one man do that?" Megan asked.

"One man didn't. The Committee of Six did," answered Sandra.

"But how, Sandra?"

"We still haven't put all the pieces together, Meg, but this is how it looks now. Let's take RAM Pharmaceuticals which is, of course, one of the thirty companies. Someone controlling RAM finance systems has diverted money illegally in two different ways, at least that we know of so far.

"First, it has grossly inflated its payments to Preferred Financial, Inc.. Money the stockholders think is going to the Internal Revenue Service is passing instead to a holding company account at the Los Angeles branch of Prime Bank.

"Secondly, RAM has also inflated its costs of production. For every dollar of *actual* cost, RAM instead reports three dollars of cost to its shareholders, and transfers the other two dollars from retail profit to ...."

"... to Prime Bank," Steven volunteered.

"No, Steven, to a different holding company with an account at another institution," Sandra said. "But you're on the right track, because both holding companies are wholly owned by a private European trust, which we expect to find is controlled by this committee of six people."

Elliot Jaynes had been listening intently, and proudly, to his partner. He knew precisely where she was heading and what she was thinking. "And, Sandra, you believe each of these thirty corporations is in some way directed by a holding company that is, in turn, controlled by one of these private trusts?"

"That is correct, Elliot."

"But how have these trusts amassed the kind of assets necessary to take these enormous stock positions?"

"That's the part that's fascinating to me, Elliot. There are banks, insurance companies and savings and loan associations being shut down by regulators all over the world. Officers and securities dealers are going to jail right and left. Yet the regulators and the world press ... all of them, are missing the boat."

"How so?"

"Nobody is tracking where the money actually went. Since the S&L industry was deregulated in the early eighties, billions of dollars have gone into real estate, junk bonds and a multitude of exotic financial instruments that have long since proven worthless. But where did the money go?"

"I'm not sure I'm following you," Megan said with a frown.

"Well, let's take a single example," Sandra said. "A real estate developer utilizing a shell corporation goes to an S&L with elaborate plans to build a luxury resort hotel and conference center for, say, fifty million dollars. The S&L appraises the raw land, agrees with the projected profits and makes the loan, not based on performance, but in rapid advances before construction even begins."

"But why before ..." Megan began to ask.

"For points, fees and interest payments on the loan, Meg. They show a healthy profit as a company, generate more deposits, and carry the project on their books for a value well in excess of the loan. Stockholders and regulators alike are happy. But rarely is the transaction at arms length."

"At arms length?" Megan asked.

"There is an unhealthy relationship between the lending institution and the borrower, Meg. The borrower has a dishonest relationship with someone at the bank. Sometimes they're the same person."

"Goodness."

"After five years of covering up and adjusted entries, regulators take over the institution. Since the project never got off the ground, they are forced to sell the undeveloped land for two or three million dollars, if they can sell it at all.

"Taxpayers everywhere make up the forty-eight million dollar difference ... for those depositors who had their money in federally insured accounts. Those who didn't lost their money, all of it."

"That's unbelievable," Megan said.

"It's just one example, Meg, an example of what some will do to profit at the expense of others. Unfortunately, similar lawlessness is prevalent in other investment arenas ... stocks, bonds and other financial instruments. But, Meg, the point is this. Where did the money actually go?

"We believe," Sandra continued, "that a portion of it, not all of it of course, was systematically funneled into these private trusts. It's ingenious, really. People all over the world work, pay taxes and save their hard earned money in a supposedly rock solid financial institution, and after their money is stolen they have to replace it themselves by paying higher taxes, because their federal government has guaranteed the losses ... and they earn their money and pay their taxes by working for companies that are controlled by the very people that stole from them."

"Goodness!" Megan exclaimed again.

"What's incredible, and terribly impressive," Sandra said, "is that the whole operation, as far as the Big Six is concerned, is almost untraceable. It's as if this was their Phase One, planned many years ago, and now it's cleaned up as though it never happened. I've never seen anything like it."

The Maitre d', dressed in a starched black and white tuxedo, approached Elliot Jaynes and discreetly said, "Excuse me, Mr. Jaynes, but you wanted me to let you know if your office called."

"Oh, yes, thank you."

Standing up, Elliot said to the table, "Please go on, I won't be long."

266

"You may take your call in the foyer, sir. Please, follow me."

Richard's eyes were flashing. "Go ahead, Sandra, finish it off," he said.

"There's more?" Steven asked.

"What I am about to tell you is entirely speculation ... on my part," Sandra said guardedly.

"Yet an idea we think eminently plausible, given the facts," Richard said supportively.

"Our sources tell us," Sandra stated quietly, "that the Federal Reserve and the Finance Ministers for the other six GATT nations, in conjunction with the new republics, are about to reveal plans for the establishment of a new bank. In fact, we understand it is already partially capitalized. What will be especially interesting to you, Steven, is that the president of the newly proclaimed Georgian Republic has close ties to the people chartering the new bank."

"Not the World Bank?" Steven asked.

"No, although it will unavoidably have dealings with the World Bank and the International Monetary Fund. This bank is to have it's own autonomy. It is to be called **Universal MasterBank**. How's that for a dose of ego?"

"Really," Steven agreed.

Sandra made no attempt to hide the anger in her voice, "We believe that this MasterBank has been created, capitalized and manned, unbeknownst to the other participants, as part of the overall conspiracy being perpetrated by the Committee of Six."

"No!" Steven said.

"Does this Prime Bank I keep hearing about have anything to do with this?" Megan asked.

Richard answered, "We're not certain exactly how much, Meg. We know there is a connection with RAM ... and we

267

know Dr. Wolman has had many dealings with Prime Bank Paris, particularly with a man named Karl Bulow."

"I'm afraid we'll learn nothing from Mr. Bulow," Sandra said with a touch of sarcasm.

"Why's that?" Megan asked.

"The Air Force seating charts for the GATT flight Steven was on, the one that exploded, show Karl Bulow was sitting three seats in front of Steven."

"Heavens!"

Megan and Steven watched Elliot run in full stride onto the patio. In the midst of tables full of patrons and hovering waiters, the usually proper and always conservative Elliot Jaynes yelled across the flagstones, "Steven! When was the last time you had good news?"

"I can't remember that far back," Steven said.

Elliot crashed into his seat, "That was Miss Beasley. NASA's been trying to reach you two all day. They received a transmission from Jake! He's alive!"

Megan and Steven embraced. Megan whispered into his ear, "Corrie was right!"

"What did they say, Elliot ... how ...?"

"Jake actually landed on Mars! By himself! Can you believe it?"

"Jake would be incapable of any other decision," Steven grinned. ·

"Miss Beasley said Captain Siever kept apologizing. She said he was actually crying over the phone. He kept repeating himself ... said he should have figured it out weeks ago."

"What, Elliot, what?" Megan asked excitedly.

"Siever has been pouring over transmissions, background noise, studying everything possible from the mission. This morning he replayed what they originally thought was interference ... turns out it was Morse Code from the surface of Mars."

Meg was so excited she could barely stay in her seat. "So how'd they know it was Jake?" she asked.

"Because, Meg ... you're going to love this! The letters spelled out ... " and Elliot pronounced each letter slowly,

C . O . R . R . I . E .

"Oh, my word!" Megan said. She was beside herself.

Steven said with a giant grin, "Boy, does that sound just like Jake."

"But that's not all," Elliot said. "As soon as Siever realized what it meant, he started calling you."

"And we've been with you all day."

"Right. So he finally called Miss Beasley. But in the meantime they actually got a live transmission from Jake ... just an hour ago. He was horsing around as usual ... threatened to sue NASA and all."

"That's Jake all right!" Steven hollered.

"So there!" Elliot thundered, pounding his fist on the table, *"Hurray for Jake Capterville! He's on his way back!"*

CHAPTER 30

As early morning sunlight crept into the serene sleeping city of Rome, the cold stone figures crowning St. Peter's Square began to glow in a living, moving pink. Giant marbled faces stretched and yawned in the warming new light and golden rays, almost imperceptible, touched the capitals of the enormous stone columns that define the symmetry of the Square. Hewn and polished by man, weathered by the centuries, solid marble came alive in the arms of the waking city.

Far above, high enough to view the entire city, two angels spoke to one another in silken voices.

"It is not difficult to see why Michelangelo preferred marble to paint."

"Yes, but the ceiling of the Chapel. Think of it! Magnificent!"

"He never desired to paint it, you know. He didn't like painting."

"Surely he did."

"No ... his passion for marble work consumed his life."

"But he must have liked to paint."

"No."

"Then, why?"

"A Pope insisted."

"Ahh, yes, I think I remember now."

"Shh! Look, down here ...."

The comprehensive all-night conference of the Committee of Six had concluded shortly before dawn. Lucius Otterstein

270

and Edith Wolman strolled alone through the still silent Square that for most would elicit an array of wonderful emotions. Yet the quiet joy, the rapture or whatever feeling this place might possibly avail to them would, by their own choosing, be left to the senses of others.

"It is saddening, is it not," one angel asked, *"how often the brilliance of human creation and the lessons of destruction from one millennia ... are lost upon the people of another?"*

"It is, indeed."

"One would think that people could learn from the past."

The angels surveyed the dawning Roman city below them, but their innermost thoughts were elsewhere.

"It would seem the young couple is beginning to understand."

"Yes."

"Do you think ...?"

"Wait! We must listen!"

Below, with no regard for their magnificent surroundings, Lucius and Edith walked and talked in the sinister world that had become their artistic passion.

"The mistakes have been most costly ... inexcusable," Lucius said with disgust.

Edith stared down at the stone terrace upon which they stepped. She had warned Lucius. She had warned all of them.

"I've repeatedly given my opinion concerning terrorist activities. Necessary perhaps, but messy, very messy. It could be our undoing if ...."

"It will not be our undoing," Lucius growled, "but you are right. We must control that aspect of our operations much more closely."

"Yesss ..." Edith hissed with satisfaction. She had her vindication.

"One damned computer chip the size of a pinhead has cost us billions," Lucius fumed.

"In the long run, certainly."

"Panatta and Moss were to take out all communications and life support on that damned space craft," Lucius went on, "and now all our aerospace holdings are in jeopardy, not to mention China and the new Freedom station."

"Perhaps he will not make it back," Edith offered.

"Jake Capterville should be dead with the others! Those systems failures would have buried the companies that built them, and made our holdings valuable beyond belief."

"Perhaps, still ...."

Lucius Otterstein was livid. "All the years of positioning, the contract work, insuring that our companies would lose the initial bidding so that we could gain control for next to nothing ... making sure they were next in line ... and now this."

Edith said without emotion, "Giancarlo and Marlin are responsible."

"Jake Capterville should be dead. If he makes it back, the computer defect will eventually be traced to our sabotage."

"But you have said many times there is no way of tracing it to any of us," Edith said with concern.

Lucius snapped, "No, but the manufacturers will be absolved, and a large portion of our portfolio will lay dormant."

"If I know you, Lucius, you are already devising creative ways to ...."

"Capterville! I am sick to death of hearing the name Capterville. We should have shot the whole damn family right off ... DAMNATION! ... the entire world is now focused on Jake Capterville. He's a bloody hero ... thanks to Panatta and Moss!"

"Now, Lucius, you know the value of the Captervilles."

"Hah!"

Edith voiced genuine pleasure when she said, "At least the Capterville girl is dead."

"Yes, and Slavic buried along with her!" Lucius raged, "a top operative ... dumb, but reliable. Another bungled job by our two friends."

"At least there is no trace of our western operation ... or the girl," Edith said with encouragement.

Lucius remained quiet for several minutes. Looking down with a frown he walked steadily forward with Edith hugging his side step for step. When he finally spoke, his countenance had changed.

"This has all been verified? The girl, the data base, the transfer of files?" he asked.

"Yes. Bob has given a full report."

"OK then," Lucius said almost cheerfully, "let's concentrate our energies upon the agenda we covered in our meeting."

"That's the Lucius I know and love."

"We'll take events as they come ... and be creative."

"I don't like the sound of this," one angel said.
"This is no surprise. Hush, pay attention."

Since assuming their positions at the White House and the Federal Reserve their ability to meet in person had become more restrictive. This opportunity, following a scheduled

International Monetary Fund meeting had been a perfect opportunity for the Committee of Six to inconspicuously gather.

Chief Otterstein and Dr. Wolman approached a line of waiting automobiles and anxious Secret Service agents. They stopped between two black limousines and were immediately surrounded by the protective agents. They made a point of discussing matters germane to the IMF conference, they shook hands formally and then left for their respective vehicles.

As the car door slammed behind Chief Otterstein he could still be heard muttering epithets about something called a Capterville.

Two groups of important vehicles drove off in different directions through the empty streets of Rome, weaving silently and unenlightened through ages of art and culture. For the Chief and the Chairman, unhappily, it would all remain uninstructive.

Michelangelo Buonarroti had the ability to see below the surface of his raw marble blocks, a capacity for feeling movement within the marble itself and a genius for unleashing ultimate expression from an eternal stone prison. His creativity and the ingenious life efforts of many others now looked down upon the speeding vehicles ... and wondered how such intellect had come to this.

"It is truly a shame, is it not?" one angel reflected.
"Indeed. It's enough to make one cry."

CHAPTER 31

High in the Italian Alps on a winding road between Bolzano and Innsbruck a white special edition Ferrari was executing perfect four wheel drifts around turn after turn. Belted firmly into the passenger seat Marlin Moss held tight, stoically enduring the ride. Giancarlo Panatta had always loved racing cars, on track and off, and Moss was aware of his proficiency. He was also aware of Giancarlo's tendency to push everything to the limit when he was upset, and Giancarlo was upset, very upset.

Gliding perfectly from a sharp turn with the accelerator almost to the floor, Giancarlo's growling voice was octaves lower than the engine's cry.

"I should've strangled that fat bitch while I had the chance."

Marlin stared out his side window at the peaks beyond the Monte Giovo pass. He said nothing in response.

"How could that damned chip have failed?" Panatta asked, needing desperately to talk.

"You tell me," Marlin said still looking out the window, "you had it installed."

Panatta glanced at Moss as he blasted them out of another hairpin turn. "But you had the damn thing built," Panatta snapped.

Marlin Moss continued to glare out the window and watch the mountain peaks come and go.

Panatta persisted with his questions, "Didn't you compare the diagrams, before and after?"

Marlin finally spoke with resignation. "Yes," he said. "I spent days with our people at the RAM laboratory. We double checked everything ... even did transparent overlays to compare circuitry on the micro-chip. There is no way possible a life support system could remain functional."

"Tell that to Jake Capterville," Panatta quipped.

"We even coupled the life systems failure with communication shutdown. I just can't understand it," Marlin said.

"It didn't take Capterville long to restore communications," Panatta said.

"No, and at some point they're going to realize it was more than a NASA screw-up."

"Maybe, but they'll never trace it."

"That's of no consolation to Lucius," Marlin said.

"He's acting like the world's coming apart, and that toad Wolman is prodding him on ... makes me sick," Panatta growled.

Marlin looked out the window again and rested his chin on his right fist. He muttered into the glass, "I can see how he feels. All that work, all the years, and the aerospace category is falling apart. The closer Jake Capterville gets to earth the sicker Lucius becomes."

"Actually, I thought he took it rather well under the circumstances," Panatta said. "You've got to admit, he's a team player. He's stood behind us all the way."

"Yes," Marlin said, "and I'd like to have the confidence that our female member would be as loyal in times of crisis."

They came out of a turn and before them lay a long straight stretch of road. Panatta pressed the accelerator to the floor.

"You know, Marlin, in a way, Lucius and Edith got what they asked for. If they hadn't been so secretive about all their fancy financial plans maybe we could've been more effective."

"Yea, maybe. Right now, let's just get to Munich and arrange the shipments. We've got to be ready for the next Geneva meeting, and this time there can be no mistakes, or we're history."

The gleaming white Ferrari was back in the steep mountain curves for which it yearned. Its fresh black tires held the exotic race car tightly to the narrow road.

One hundred yards above, hidden in rocks and snow, crouched a man ... waiting. Through an enormous pair of binoculars he followed the speeding car up the mountain.

Returning the binoculars carefully to a green camouflaged case, he locked and loaded a solitary round in the high powered rifle that was cradled in his arms. Through the rifle's long scope he tracked the Ferrari. Then he lifted the large gun and trained the scope on the tight bend in the road that was directly below him.

"Perfect!" he thought.

He waited.

To his right and below he heard the roaring purr of the engine. He moved the rifle to the car and kept the hairs of the scope crossed over the Ferrari's left front wheel. He knew precisely when he would fire.

As the car passed below and entered the turn, Panatta gave the engine a bit more fuel. All four tires, clawing at the road, began the subtle drift that is a racer's dream.

Panatta was smiling, feeling the turn.

The rifleman fired.

The Ferrari's tire exploded and the car slid uncontrollably sideways. At high speed the car hit the rocks that served as a guardrail, flipped in the air spinning like an awkward top and plunged over the cliff.

277

As the rifleman shouldered his gun, he heard the car smash once against the side of the cliff and then a split second later the loud thud of heavy metal impacting with rock and ice ... no explosion, no fire, just a simple bass sound that echoed briefly through the valley.

The man disappeared. He was moving fast, somewhere behind the gigantic rock blocks that nature had strewn randomly along the side of the alp.

Badly smashed, the Ferrari had landed right side up. Marlin's lifeless body, belted to the seat, had been crushed from the chest down. His eyes still gazed out the side window, unable to appreciate the beautiful alpine valley in which he had perished.

In excruciating pain Panatta's arms and legs were pinned under what remained of the dashboard. Still in a sitting position he was alive and conscious.

The wetness and odor of gasoline permeated the compartment.

He repeatedly tried to free himself, enduring the pain. But it was no use. He was trapped. He looked over at Moss's crumpled body and groaned.

Panatta felt the pain gradually ease, and he knew that to be a bad sign. The chill mountain air was draining his body of precious warmth. He felt the cold move to his insides.

"How could this have happened? I made no mistakes. I was in complete control." He thought to himself how everything he had done, everything he had planned had been thoroughly, meticulously checked and re-checked. Yet the results, the important, critical results had back-fired on him, and on the Committee of Six.

"How, Giancarlo, how?"

It could not be the fact that all his plans had been laid to foster pernicious ends. This had never entered Panatta's reasoning as a factor in the important decisions he had made, even now, when he believed he was to die. When evil achieves its success, it is invariably due to deceit, diversity and disguise. For Giancarlo Panatta the sinister character of his behavior could not be a factor in his failure, because the very nature of evil itself would not allow it to be.

To his left and up the slope Panatta heard footsteps and falling rock.

"Damn! I'm going to make it! Someone's coming."

Resignation instantly became hope. Panatta slowly and painfully swiveled his head to see out the windowless door.

Only inches away, a huge head peered in at him.

"BOB! What the hell are you doing here? Get me out of here, quick. I'm trapped."

Bob's ugly face broke into an enormous grin. He looked past Panatta and saw Moss. He stood up and examined the car, then scanned the road above and the surrounding terrain. Bob bent back down, his hands on his knees. He stared coldly at Panatta.

"I been wait'n on this a long time, Panatta."

Bob swung the rifle from his shoulder, loaded another round, released the safety and slammed the bolt forward. He placed the muzzle between Panatta's lips and moved his finger to the trigger.

"Stop screwin' around," Panatta said jerking his head, "you're not funny, Bob."

Bob reset the safety and shouldered the rifle.

"OK. Now, get me out of here. It hurts like hell."

Bob stood calmly in place keeping an eye on the road above. He took a pack of cigarettes from his shirt pocket, and then a book of matches. A cruel smile came to his pockmarked face. He thought not of these mountains, but of those in far away California. With the same sweeping motion he had repeatedly used in the small dark room with Corrie Capterville, Bob struck a match and lit the cigarette.

"What are you doing, you idiot, I'm covered with gasoline!"

Bob deeply inhaled the hot smoke. He bent over, moving his large lips to Panatta's face and blew the smoke into Panatta's eyes.

"No! ... Don't! ...."

Bob flipped the match onto Panatta's lap and with an immense tooth-filled grin, rested his chin on the window sill.

"Bob! ... DAMN YOU! ...."

Panatta twisted and twitched torturously trying to free himself.

Bob watched sadistically while flames licked Panatta's shirt and leaped for his anguished face. Without moving, Bob looked and listened. Only inches away, he delighted in Panatta's horrible screams. Like frying bacon, Panatta's skin began to crackle and spit.

Bob relished his torture as long as he dared, but he knew the car was about to explode. He began to rise.

High above, from the rocks in which Bob had hidden, came another loud report from a high powered rifle.

Before Bob could hear the sound, a large bullet sped through his neck, passed through the lifeless Marlin Moss and lodged with a forceful clack in the far door. With a stunned expression Bob slumped forward through the window and settled head first against Giancarlo's blazing chest.

All three distorted faces were on fire. The compartment ignited and the Ferrari exploded in flames.

Far up the mountain a lone figure climbed into an older gray car of German design.

Black smoke curled in an ominous column up the center of the peaceful valley, winding in random spirals, carried by gentle wind.

*＊＊

Minutes later a modern tour bus stopped on the side of the road just before the fatal curve. The experienced driver opened the door and looked carefully over the edge. He examined the rock retaining wall, stepped back onto the bus and radioed the home office.

"We have a car over the side," he reported casually.

Through the static he heard, "Are there any survivors?"

"Not a chance," he replied.

"What kind of vehicle? Can you tell who it is?"

"No way ... probably some rich kid takin' daddy's car for a spin. You know, the usual."

"OK. We'll alert the police."

As the driver pulled his bus onto the road an old gray car came slowly around the corner and passed the bus going in the opposite direction. The bus driver watched in his rear view mirror as the car inched its way down the alp.

"Now that's the way a person should drive."

CHAPTER 32

"Hi, Steven, it's Elliot."

"Hi, Elliot. I was just about to call you. What's up."

"I'm at the office. I need your permission to open something."

"What is it?"

"It's a small flat package wrapped in brown paper, tied with a string. It's addressed to you. You want to come down and open it? I thought to save time ...."

"By all means, open it. Who's it from?"

"Doesn't say, but it's the same funny block printing that was on the postcard."

"Well, open it, quick."

"OK. Miss Beasley already had security check it to make sure it wasn't a bomb."

"Good idea," Steven said. "I've had enough of that in my life."

"It's a ... well, I'll be ...."

"What, Elliot?"

"It's a three and a half inch computer disk ... blue ... says 'Master' something on it."

"Put it in your computer, Elliot. Have a look."

"Interesting. My gosh ...."

"What's on the screen, Elliot?"

"Whoever our friend is ... has just opened the door for us to the Committee of Six. Steven! This is unbelievable! The title is,

6 MASTERFILE

Below it there are a series of file headings. I won't read them all ... don't understand them all. I'll read the ones I recognize."

"OK."

"The first is **UNIVERSAL MASTERBANK** ... then there are sub-categories **Currency**, **Account Numbers** and **Corresponding Banks**."

"You think those are on other discs?"

"Probably, but just for kicks let's see if we can access the **Currency** file ... there ... all it gives is a coded file number for a Disc 25."

"Try **Account Numbers**."

"All right ... this should ... Wow!"

"What?"

"Steven, there must be hundreds of them! They're all listed under bank names, and there must be fifty banks ... full account numbers."

"Incredible. Any balances?"

"No, but a subpoena will take care of that. This is fantastic. Steven, I think we've finally got them."

"What else?"

"Under ... **Corresponding Banks** ... there's a heading called **Merged Banks**, and below that numbers one and two are titled, **Under 6 Control** and, **Targeted**.

"Interesting. Skip that for now and go on."

"Let's see ... the next heading is **PORTFOLIO 30** ... and ... yes, here's the list of companies ... Wow! It's the same as

Sandra's list! There's a notation to see Disc 26 for complete data."

"No doubt RAM and PFI lead the parade," Steven said caustically.

"Yes, and here's a heading called **NEW ADDITIONS-LINKAGE** ... and underneath ... **China Airport** ... then ... **Space Stations**."

"Stations?" Steven asked.

"Yep. Plural. Below that it says,

Father Freedom Station - Contractors,

and then,

Big Freedom Station - Defense Co's."

Steven thought out loud, "Jake's due to dock at Father Freedom for decontamination. But what in the world is Big Freedom?"

"Got me," Elliot said, intently scrolling the file. "Now there are pages of file names that mean nothing to me, at least not yet ... Uh oh! ...."

"What now?"

"Hold on to your hat, Steven. Here's a category entitled **CAPTERVILLE**."

"Made it to the big time, have I?"

"Yea, but you're not first on the list."

"Huh?"

"The first line under Capterville reads,

J, terminal."

"Wonder what that means? The **J** is Jake, but why **terminal**."

"The second line reads, **S**, and under the **S** are the headings **Patents**, **Kefir** and **Suit**.

"The third line reads, **C** ... oh ... no!"

"What's wrong, Elliot?"

Elliot didn't answer.

284

"Elliot?"

"The **C** is followed by the word ... **TERMINATED**.

There was a long silence. Corrie had been terminated.

Elliot finally said, "This proves nothing Steven. Let me get this to Richard and Sandra. We have all we need ...."

"To what?" Steven snapped.

"The plan is to prepare a civil suit against these people, including the White House Chief of Staff and the Chairwoman of the Federal Reserve Board. We will also ready all the information that the Justice Department will need to seek criminal indictments. We will simultaneously hold a press conference in Washington DC. and demand a comprehensive Congressional investigation. However, Steven, before we release anything, we will privately contact Otterstein and Wolman to demand Corrie's return."

"Well, all right," Steven said with a defeated sigh, "call me when you think it's time."

"Oh, and Steven, don't tell Megan about this yet. Please."

"I have to, Elliot. That's the way we are. But thanks for the concern."

"But, Steven, Christmas is next week. Can't you wait until after ...?"

"No, I'll have to tell Meg."

In the background Elliot heard Megan say, "Tell me what, honey?"

"I'll call you later, Steven. Remember, it might not mean a thing."

"Uh huh."

They both hung up.

Elbows on his knees Elliot leaned forward, buried his face in his hands and sobbed so heavily his entire body convulsed.

After several minutes, he wiped the tears from his eyes, dried his face and slammed his fist to the desk.

"Alice! Get in here."

Miss Beasley peeked through a crack in the door. She'd heard this tone before.

"Yes, sir?"

"Assemble the troops. We have work to do."

CHAPTER 33

With Little Freedom still on the drawing board the world press had instantly and affectionately referred to earth's orbiting Freedom space station as 'Father Freedom'.

Little Freedom, Commander Capterville and his two silent friends were moving at a speed of approximately seventy-five thousand miles per hour toward a point in space that in short order would place them in orbit around the revolving planet earth, and inside the trusted docking bay of an expectant Father Freedom.

From a side viewing port Jake could see both the earth and its attendant moon. The earth was a blue and white dime fixed to his thick window, the moon a small silver dot.

"NASA. This is Jake. Come in."

"We are sorry, Mr. Jake, but we have no Commanders by that name."

"Real funny, guys. Have you any readings on the white light. Can you see it yet?"

"Negative, Commander."

"Hard to believe ... it's growing."

"We're continuing our searches. We will keep you advised. Have you isolated the Life Supports problem yet?"

"Yes, and Orville and Jim would not be pleased. Routing Chip 8666bi19-ls was designed to cut oxygen at Transmission Stage 5. They never had a chance ... even before earth lift-off."

After a long pause a garbled, barely audible transmission came back to the Commander.

"Impossible!"

Jake responded, "Take a look at the diagrams for the 86 chip. Looks obvious to me, but I had to backtrack with Matilda. You folks have the originals. Check it out."

There was a radio silence of some twenty minutes.

The sprawling Moonbase Kepler was snuggled like a sleeping octopus into a boulder-strewn interior shelf in the crater Eratosthenes. Kepler's personnel, as well as the people manning Father Freedom were glued to their receivers. All work had stopped. They had been following the communications between earth and Commander Capterville for several days and with the exception of sustaining life they had little interest in anything else.

Unbeknownst to Jake, he had, with the exception of an evil few, become envied and loved by every man, woman and child on and from his home planet. While many heroes are fabricated to achieve the ulterior ends of others, Jake had without design proven himself genuine. He had taken action and there was now proof of it ... a steady stream of transmission from the planet Mars. Seismic activated as soon as the long Martian storm had passed.

Yet it would be more than brazen action that would intrigue the human race. Boot Hill is crowded with courageous and long-forgotten residents who were unable or unwilling to bestow the value of their experience upon others. Jake Capterville was now imparting the benefit of his unique encounters honestly and with an insight all his own, and he was doing so now through the spoken word.

Every comment he made, every postulation, was influenced by a perspective to which he alone was privy. And there could be no doubt for those who listened. Conclusion was open for debate, but Jake's words were honest and from the heart. They were faithfully true and intellectually elevating. In a tender but forceful manner they challenged the minds of men in an unfamiliar way.

At the present, his voice, along with reams of data, were traveling through space between speeding Little Freedom and the two planets he had made his home.

While the live discussions were delayed for most earthlings, the people on the moon and Father Freedom were eagerly listening. For the past few hours, given the position of both the moon and the earth-orbiting Freedom station, they had been receiving Jake before anyone else. They were captivated. They devoured every extraterrestrial sentence.

Able to be heard by five planetary bodies, Jake spoke with gentle intimacy of matters difficult for the human soul ... the moral and ethical distinctions guiding discretions for Orville and Jim, life and death decisions under other-worldly pressures, colorful and sometimes unbelievable descriptions of the cosmos, the probable presence of novel life forms.

To his listeners it sounded as though something more than good-natured Jake was speaking. His transmissions communicated more than the words contained within them. They issued individual, personal challenges to those who listened. With this new knowledge what will you create? When it becomes your time will you be prepared? To whom will you commit your soul?

"Jake. Come in."

"I'm still out here."

"We can find nothing wrong with the 86 chip."

"When was the last detailed circuit check?" Jake asked.

"Over a two week period. Completion ten days before lift-off. Software, right up to countdown."

"Ten days, huh? I'm telling you, NASA, it's the chip. Matilda's checked it twice."

"Who the hell's Matilda?"

"Don't cuss, NASA. She's sensitive, and she's doing your job."

"Jake, our psychiatrist wants to know how long you've been romancing your computer."

"The good doctor is jealous. He's been after her for years ... I've loaded the chip data. You can do an overlay and see for yourself. Got your high priced machines turned on?"

"Fire away."

"It's off."

"Oh, Jake?"

"Yea?"

"Assuming you're right about the life support chip, how do you figure you made it ... and Jim and Orville didn't?"

There was a brief pause filled with intermittent static. "Because," Jake said matter-of-factly, "whoever sabotaged that chip placed my circuitry so close to the master line it shorted out ... kept my system open ... might explain why I felt so bad when I woke up. It could have been going on and off for days."

The people at Moonbase Kepler looked at one another with incredulous expressions. Sabotage?

Seconds later, the scientists on Father Freedom did the same.

Seconds later, all of NASA was in shock.

Another pause, then Jake issued his challenge, "I hope for his sake you people find him before I do."

"Jake, if this was anyone but you ..."

"Just check Matilda's blueprints. You'll see."

"Alright, it's coming in now."

"Hey, NASA, talk with my friends at Kepler, will you? Find out if they can see this light. It's getting brighter and whiter. I can hardly see the stars anymore."

"What do you see up there, Jake?"

"I'm picking up traces of it on the heat sensors now. It's a spherical shell of light ... started out surrounding the entire Solar System, like we're all inside a hollow ball of light and it's contracting, getting closer, brighter, all around us."

"You sure, Jake?"

"Don't you read it?"

"Negative, Jake, but we're searching."

"Ask Kepler."

"We'll call the Moonbase. Promise. How do you feel? Our monitors show you're healthy as a horse."

"Feel like a young stallion. Someone needs to explain this white beard though."

"Look like Moses do you?"

"If only I had the wisdom."

"OK, Father Time ... signing off for now. Keep us posted."

"Roger."

Seismic continued to transmit from Mars. A final diagram of the 86 microchip flowed from Little Freedom. Other than these communication waves, mixed with ever-present interstellar signals, there was silence in space. Then, after a few minutes,

"Hey, guys ...."

"Yes, Jake? We thought you were asleep."

"Merry Christmas!"

"Merry Christmas, Jake."

"What's my earth ETA?"

"We should have you back by Christmas Eve."
"You got that right. I have big plans. Over and out."

***

"Father Freedom, this is NASA. Go to coded channel
five-one-zero."
"Roger. Go ahead NASA."
"Put on Dr. Tyrone."
"OK, NASA. Here he is."
"Doctor, our Commander Capterville has ... some form of
space sickness. Please prepare the strictest Decon protocols.
We may have to isolate him for a time. Be ready to ...."
Dr. Tyrone interrupted, "I have listened to all of the
Commander's transmissions. We are well prepared for Jake's,
Commander Capterville's arrival."
"Very well, doctor, but please make certain you conduct
appropriate psychological ...."
"Excuse the interruption, NASA, but I must tell you, I by
no means concur with your assessment of Jake's condition."
"What?"
"There is nothing wrong with Jake. Besides, up here ...
we can all see a faint glow in the heavens. Better check with
Kepler, like Jake said."
"What the ...?"
"And, NASA?"
"Yes, doctor?"
"Merry Christmas!"

At Houston control, Captain Robert E. Siever turned to
the Air Force general standing next to him.
"Is everyone up there going mad?"

CHAPTER 34

Steven and Megan were sitting in the empty conference room at *Jaynes, Cameron and Hale*. Megan was reading and Steven was fumbling through small bottles and rumpled, dog-eared papers in the depths of his ever present briefcase. Behind them the door opened quietly. Elliot Jaynes entered the room concentrating on the several legal size sheets he was clutching with both hands.

"Steven, Meg, hello. Alice didn't tell me you had arrived."

"Hi, Elliot," Steven said. "Got here early. Thought we'd get some work done."

Without looking up Megan said, "Steven's been creating at a fever pitch, Elliot. Better watch out."

Keeping his papers pressed securely between his fingers Elliot asked, "What's the latest in the world of water?"

"Well, let's see, we've imprinted an immune system drug into a solution with the kefir. We've had ten final-stage AIDS patients drinking the water for a little over four weeks."

"No drugs?" asked Elliot.

"Right, and we made certain diet and daily routine remained the same."

"You used a control group?"

"Very good, Elliot, yes, a double blind protocol," Steven answered.

"And?"

"Every patient drinking the kefir solution has stabilized. Blood chemistries have almost returned to normal."

"Steven! You've found a cure for AIDS?"

"No, no, Elliot, not yet. But we're on the right track. Chemicals and vaccines, of course, will never cure the disease. The virus is too adaptable. With more testing, though, and the right equipment we could zero in on the ideal clustered water formulation that will kill the virus."

"Really?"

"If we can't kill it, my guess is we'll be able to strengthen the immune system to the point where the body will defeat the virus by itself."

"So," Elliot thought aloud, "if you had charge of the RAM Laboratory, you could ... I mean, if you had the facility, and those clowns were behind bars ...."

Megan said, "Stop it, Elliot."

"But ...."

"Steven has been dreaming of just such a laboratory for twenty years. Don't get his hopes up again."

"All right, Meg. I understand. But now it may be possible, with what we know ...."

"Elliot!"

"OK, OK. Say, Steven, if the kefir was stolen, how are you still making kefir solutions."

"I had a small sample in the refrigerator at my office, but it wasn't the parent, Elliot. I used the last of it making the solution for the AIDS study."

"And what's going to happen to the AIDS patients when the water runs out?"

"We don't know, Elliot. They could remain stable, or revert back to ...."

Megan interrupted them, "Let's change the subject. There's still a bunch I don't understand about all this banking stuff, and what it means to Corrie."

Steven welcomed the change of subject. "I'm with Meg, Elliot. It's pretty confusing. You say it's an exciting time, but we'd all better be careful, and all that business on the computer disk about Universal MasterBank."

"Capterville, are you fishing for free legal advice?"

"Not me. But we do have a few minutes before the others are due."

"Ha!"

Megan had that broad country smile on her face. "Really, Elliot, you shouldn't be so mercenary. Steven's just trying to help you sort out your thoughts. In the long run it will be most beneficial for your firm."

"I know when I've been had," Elliot laughed. "What is it you two pirates would like to know?"

Megan rested her chin on her folded hands and looked sweetly at Elliot. "How about starting from the beginning."

Elliot glanced at his watch and grumbled.

"Come on, Elliot," Steven prodded.

"All right, but just for a few minutes. There is a lot you both need to decide, and the others will be in shortly."

"We've already decided, Elliot," Megan said casually.

Elliot studied them both. He had been so involved with the many tactical moves necessary to launch the legal assault upon the Six that he had not realized how cut and dried things had become for Steven and Megan. Corrie was by all accounts dead, but their faith would not allow them to believe it. If she was somehow still alive, should they allow Elliot to press ahead, and risk Corrie's death?

Elliot finally said, "Very well, then." He paused and thought a bit. "Meg, when you're grandfather built your home he probably borrowed a portion of the money."

"Yes. And part of it was used for irrigation and the planting of trees."

"And your dad, did he refinance the property at any point?"

"It was kind of complicated, with the sale of some of the acreage and all, but he did decide to leave a mortgage on the house since we lived there, because the interest is deductible ... right?"

"Right. Do you still have the same loan?"

"Yes, we do."

"What's the interest rate?"

"Four percent. Why?"

"For many years a Savings and Loan could not make that kind of a loan. It would've gone broke, which is what many of them have done."

"I guess that's what we don't understand," Steven said.

"OK, real quick, here's what happened. Your dad and grandfather would sell their crops and put the profits in a savings account. The S&L would lend the money back out in secure long-term mortgages and charge a slightly higher interest rate. Your family's savings account increased with the compound interest, and the S&L made a profit with its loans."

"So what happened?" Steven asked.

"For more than thirty years after World War II banks, S&Ls and stock brokerage firms ... all of American financial services were controlled by federal regulations. It was an industry closely watched by Uncle Sam. The fee for a stock trade or the interest on a savings account was set by law."

Steven said, "Doesn't sound like something you'd be a fan of, Elliot."

"I'm not, but hear me out. Remember in the late seventies ... how interest rates went through the roof?"

"Sure."

"Your dad and thousands like him took their money out of S&L passbook accounts and invested in higher interest money-market accounts. So the S&Ls started paying higher rates just to keep customers like your dad. But they were paying out more in interest than they were taking in from their mortgage portfolios. So, guess what? Almost overnight, they're insolvent."

"How'd they make it another ten years?" Megan asked.

"That's the tragedy, Meg. Today, there are thousands of insurance companies, hundreds of regional brokerage houses and well over twelve thousand banks. A great majority of them are undercapitalized and by and large unfit to compete in a world which has technologically passed them by."

"I didn't know it was that bad," Megan said.

"As a consequence you will be seeing mergers, acquisitions, consolidations and billion dollar capital infusions throughout these industries. There will be hundreds of thousands of people laid off, and unfortunately a lot of pain in most financial sectors. But in the long run the companies that survive will be lean and healthy and able to compete in ever changing world markets."

"And the tragedy?" Steven asked.

"You are right in that I do not believe in excessive government regulation, Steven. Free enterprise should be just that. Controls are most effective when they are administered at the lowest possible level by the people who are the closest."

"Hear, hear!" Steven agreed.

"It is fashionable today," Elliot said, "to blame the savings and loan crisis strictly on the absence of regulation. But there is more to it than that."

"Really?" Megan wondered.

"The tragedy, Meg, is that financial services did not take its licks and adapt in the early eighties. Instead, the ailing industry began aggressively lobbying Congress."

"So they eased the rules?"

"Yes and no, Steven. Congress served their electorate by slapping a few bandaids on the problem. They changed accounting and reporting rules. The result was that the health of the institutions could effectively be disguised. That's why they made it another ten years. As long as real estate and bond portfolios kept increasing in value, their books retained a solid appearance. You've seen what's happened since. They also increased depositor insurance, assuring that all of us taxpayers would cover the losses."

"But a lot of the bad guys have been caught," Steven said.

"Yes, they have. A lot of the bad guys have marched off to jail. But what I'm upset about is what I believe is happening in the midst of all the restructuring. As I've said, we've got to guard against the abuses, like this Committee of Six business, what it's done to you and our Corrie."

The fact that Elliot had said *our* Corrie had not passed Megan unnoticed. Elliot had come to consider Corrie his own, and Megan was very, very pleased.

The conference room door opened and Winston, Sandra and Richard entered and took their seats.

"Oh, Good!" Elliot exclaimed, "I was about to wage World War III upon the Committee of Six right here in front of the Captervilles. You've saved Meg from one of my tirades."

Sandra slammed her stack of files to the table. "Quite the contrary, Elliot, we've come to help you wage the war!"

Miss Beasley pushed the door ajar and said, "Excuse me, sir, but before you begin ...."

"Yes?"

"I have the Washington office on the line. Should I have them alert the press? We have arranged a room at the Capitol for this afternoon at four, Washington time."

"Not just yet, Miss Beasley, but thank you. Tell Herb I'll call him within the hour." Elliot looked at Megan, then Steven. "This is a decision for our clients to make."

298

Miss Beasley looked discretely at Megan. Moisture filled Miss Beasley's eyes. She knew what they would be discussing. She had typed every word. She closed the door softly, saying, "Yes sir, I'll let him know."

"The stack of documents," Elliot began, "that Sandra has so delicately placed upon the table before us, is bound for the Justice Department. There is no question in any of our minds that there is enough verifiable and admissible evidence to put Mr. Otterstein and Miss Edith behind bars for the rest of their lives regardless of the positions they now hold."

"The plan," Sandra said sternly, "with your approval, Meg, is to ...."

"What about me?" Steven interrupted.

"Guess we know what Sandra thinks of you," Elliot winked.

"You two be quiet," Megan said, "let Sandra finish."

"As I was saying," Sandra continued, "the plan is to hand deliver these to Justice. Herb Wyman has a complete set as of an hour ago. Criminal indictments for Marlin Moss and Giancarlo Panatta will undoubtedly follow. As we press the cases, we should uncover leads to the other two."

"Cases?" Megan asked.

"Right. We will simultaneously file a civil complaint in Federal Court. The complaint has already been prepared and is ready for filing today. It has been meticulously tailored to parallel the information we are supplying to Justice. All it requires are your signatures."

"Good show," Steven said aggressively. "Sounds like they're done for."

Winston, who had supervised the complex effort from the beginning, looked tired but pleased. He spoke with an even tone, "With your permission, Dr. and Mrs. Capterville, we intend to hold a press conference ...."

Elliot held up his hand. "Winston, excuse me. I've given this a lot of thought ...."

"I knew it!" Sandra exclaimed.

"What?" Winston asked. "What?"

Sandra smiled an odd smile. "Elliot's been racking his brain about something for several days. Haven't you recognized it Winston? Richard, surely you have."

"Why, yes, now that you mention it."

"We've all seen it before," Sandra said excitedly. "You know, the slumped shoulders, the furrows in his brow shaped like the Grand Canyon. Remember the GM case?"

"Yes," Richard said, "we all thought we were done for."

"So," Sandra said, "what have you got up your sleeve this time, Elliot?"

"You mean," Winston said, pointing to the foot high stack in front of him, "we're not going to use this?"

"Yes, of course we are," Elliot said, "assuming the Capvervilles wish it. I just thought we might use it in a slightly different way." Elliot picked up the phone, "Miss Beasley, would you come in please?"

"What sort of way?" Winston asked.

Miss Beasley entered the room, "Yes, sir?"

Elliot held up the several papers that had not left his fingers since entering the room, "Would you make five copies of this, please."

"I already have, sir. Here they are ... unless ... have you made any changes during your meeting, sir?"

"No Miss Beasley, thank you. As usual, you're way ahead of me. Oh, and call Herb, will you. Tell him there will be no press conference, but to clear the decks and stand ready."

Miss Beasley left the conference room with a smile she was certain nobody saw.

"No press conference?" Winston asked. "But that's a key part of the strategy."

Elliot said, "I know, Winston, but there are two things that trouble me. The first is Corrie. We must make the assumption she is still alive. While we have evidence sufficient to establish the elements of a number of crimes against these people, the same cannot be said of first degree murder. If we make a public statement, there is no incentive for the Committee to keep Corrie alive. To the contrary, it would serve their purposes if Corrie disappeared."

"You're right, of course," Winston said.

Richard asked, "What else bothers you, Elliot?"

"America."

"America?"

"If we hold a press conference and expose what we know," Elliot said, "it will have devastating effects upon our country. The President has already lost his Chief of Staff, and the U.S. has lost its Fed Chairman, both in a terrorist bombing. One can only imagine the consequences, what could happen to the stability of our government, especially if investigations reveal a connection between the bombing and the Committee of Six."

"But," Megan said suddenly, "these people must be brought to justice. We can't allow them to stay where they are."

Steven looked at Megan approvingly.

Elliot said, "Precisely."

"So what do you propose, Elliot?" Steven asked.

Elliot handed them each a copy of the papers he had prepared. "I would ask that you carefully read this draft, and feel free to make any suggestions you like. I have absolutely

301

no pride of authorship. I propose we make any changes you deem necessary, and that we fax it out immediately to the appropriate parties."

The room went silent as they read:

DRAFT   File: Com6Ltr1
JCH

Mr. Lucius Otterstein   December 22
(address - White House)   ab change
Chairwoman Edith Wolman
(address - FRB)
Mr. Giancarlo Panatta
(address - unknown)
Mr. Marlin Moss
(address - last known, US Treasury Dept.)

Re: The Committee of Six, Criminal Indictments,
**   Civil Pleadings, Miss Corrie Capterville.**

Gentlemen and Madame,

You are about to be sued in United States Federal Court as well as in related international tribunals. Simultaneously, documentation detailing your activities shall be presented to the United States Department of Justice.

The purpose of this communication is to demand the following:

1. The immediate release of Miss Capterville to her parents. You are to leave her at the nearest metropolitan hospital, and you are to confirm before departure that she has in fact contacted her parents.

2. Your formal public resignations by December 31 of this year, from any governmental office or appointment now held by any of you. Said demand includes, but is not limited to, any decision making position whether domestic or foreign.

3. The personal identification and location of the remaining two Committee of Six members.

4. The immediate transfer of all cash and securities accounts within your control world-wide. Said transfer is to include, but is not limited to, all accounts delineated on your 6 MASTERFILE disk.

Transfers will be effected pursuant to the bank routing instructions set forth in Schedule A herein. All transfers shall be COMPLETED by December 31 of this year.

5. The immediate transfer of all real estate, other tangible and intangible assets, and all contractual rights of any kind within your control, of either present or future value.

Whether by assignment or other legal instrument, this law firm shall prepare or review all documentation.

All transfers shall be recorded and final by March 1 of next year. All assets shall be identified and in process by December 31 of this year.

6. The immediate return of the kefir, also known as Culture, Abkhazian Culture, Russian Culture and Critters. This includes the immediate return of all writings and translations, in Abkhazian and English, relevant thereto.

7. Your first transfer shall be the seven hundred million dollars U.S. you hold in your accounts at Prime Bank Amsterdam. You are to utilize the routing instructions on Schedule A, and you are hereby directed to finalize said transfer by 12 P.M. tomorrow, Pacific Standard Time.

The transfer pursuant to this Paragraph 7, and the release of Miss Capterville, must be accomplished by noon tomorrow PST or it is our intention, at that same time, to hold a press conference in Washington, D.C. for the sole purpose of exposing your activities. We shall, at that same time, file suit. We shall also submit all relevant documentation to the Justice Department, as well as all forums with which you are involved.

To facilitate your decision making process we include herewith the following:

A. Records of cash accounts, securities accounts. (first twenty-five of each listed on Schedule B herein).

B. Title searches for real estate acquisitions, other assets of record. (first twenty listed on Schedule C herein - legal descriptions on file).

C. Reconstructed paper trails showing methods of accumulation, and the companies and banking institutions that were utilized. (first ten listed on Schedule D herein).

D. Photographic corroboration of Mr. Moss and Mr. Panatta copied on Schedule E herein. Also included are relevant Air Force flight records.

E. This law firm's written legal opinion concerning the legality of your actions. Of the three hundred fifty three pages, only the Summary is included herewith on Schedule F. The entire document is to be forwarded to Justice along with our recommendations concerning your prosecution.

You should note we have recommended that all six of you be prosecuted for First Degree Murder in a jurisdiction that calls for the death penalty. Given the extent of your business dealings, it is our opinion that we shall have unrestricted choice of venue.

Understand that this is extremely serious. It is not a joke, nor a bluff, nor will there be any negotiation whatsoever.

Should you wish to contact me prior to the times stated above, you may reach me at the above telephone number or via fax around the clock.

Elliot Jaynes
Jaynes, Cameron & Hale

6File/comltr1/ab

Megan was the last to finish reading. When she looked up everyone was staring at her.

"Goodness, I hope I didn't take too long, but it's so interesting. You all have really done a lot of work. It's all so, well ... legal."

Winston and Richard were smiling. They both returned to their copies and began making notes.

Sandra was grinning ear to ear, "Elliot, it's a masterpiece. Forget their doodling," she said as she pointed at Winston and Richard. "I say we send it right now just the way it is ... word for word."

Sandra looked at Steven and Megan. "What do the Captervilles think?" she asked.

"A smart piece of work, Elliot," Steven said.

"And sensitive too, Elliot ... for Corrie," Megan said. "Thanks. I can't think of a better way to get her back. I vote yes. Let's send it."

"I agree whole-heartedly," Steven said.

"Very well," Elliot said, "but let's make certain we haven't overlooked anything. Richard, Winston? What do you recommend?"

"My notes," Winston said, "consist of several *Bravos* and *Go For Its* in the margins."

"Same here," said Richard.

"OK, then, it's a go," Elliot said. He pressed the intercom, "Miss Beasley, get me the White House. I wish to speak to Mr. Lucius Otterstein. Also, please word process the Com 6 draft letter to final with today's date."

"The original and five copies are on your desk, sir ... oh, sir?"

"Yes, Alice?"

"With all due respect, sir, what makes you think Mr. Otterstein will want to speak with you ... I mean, how can I hope to get him on the line?"

"You are to tell him, Miss Beasley, that I am calling about the Committee of Six, Portfolio 30 and Corrie Capterville, that I am sending a fax to him at the White House and that if I don't hear from him within thirty minutes he could become most embarrassed."

"Yes, sir." Miss Beasley disconnected her line to the conference room ... rather, she thought she had. Heard quite clearly through the speaker in the conference room was Miss Beasley muttering, "That ought to get the bastard's attention!"

"Everyone laughed heartily. Elliot spoke into the intercom, "I've always cherished your opinion, Alice."

Miss Beasley turned a glowing red that matched her new designer lipstick. "Oh, dear," was all she could manage.

In the background Miss Beasley heard Megan say, "Don't worry, Alice, I'm with *you!*"

A few minutes later a re-composed Miss Beasley rang the conference room.

"Mr. Jaynes, Mr. Otterstein has taken your call."

"Excellent, Miss Beasley, put the bastard on."

"That's not a very nice way to treat an old lady like me, sir."

"If I thought you were an old lady, Alice, I wouldn't be teasing you."

"But I am an old lady, Mr. Jaynes."

Megan interrupted, "Who's getting the best of whom here?"

"Thank you, Mrs. Capterville ... are you forgetting the White House, sir? The gentleman's on line three."

Elliot picked up the telephone and hit line three. "This is Elliot Jaynes."

"That was a very strange message your secretary delivered, Mr. Jaynes, but I am afraid I ...."

Elliot sounded professional and firm. "Mr. Otterstein, I have not called to have a discussion with you."

"Then why have you called?" Lucius had been shocked at the message, and was having terrifying thoughts about what might come next. This was impossible. Only the Six know of such matters. Giancarlo, Marlin and Bob have been eliminated, and Slavic and the girl are dead. So who is this Los Angeles lawyer and what can he want?

"This is a courtesy call. I am calling to advise you to stand by your fax machine," Elliot said calmly.

"Say, what is this, some kind of ...."

"This is no joke, Mr. Otterstein. The communication I am sending ... well, let's just say you would prefer that it be seen by your eyes only. We are sending now."

"Listen, Jaynes ...."

"I am assuming you will pass this along to Edith and the others. I have nothing further to say to you, Mr. Otterstein."

Elliot disconnected and rang Miss Beasley.

"OK, Alice, send it!"

"It's going out now, sir. Anything else?"

"Say a prayer, Miss Beasley, say a prayer."

CHAPTER 35

Following Elliot's brief telephone conversation with Mr. Otterstein, the meeting in the forty-fourth floor conference room had broken up and the participants were now standing and chatting. Elliot and Megan stood together, talking quietly, looking through the large window that ran the length of the room. The unhealthful, orange-brown haze outside prevented them from seeing the ocean, the buildings in Century City or even the low hills that loomed nearby.

Megan pressed her nose against the window. "I can barely see the ground."

"It's pretty bad today," Elliot agreed.

Megan sighed, "It seems that everything in the world today is so depressing, Elliot. All the people we know are having such horrible experiences. When is it all going to stop?"

Before Elliot could answer, Megan said, "Shirali says to have faith, but when things are terrible for so long, I just don't know. What is going to happen to America, Elliot? What is going to happen to Abkhazia, to all the other countries, to us? ... oh, dear."

Elliot thought a moment and then, trying to be helpful, said, "All around the world we are seeing people fighting for their freedom. And many are winning, Meg. Totalitarian regimes are falling, communism has been dealt a severe blow in what used to be the Soviet Union, and the European community is in transition. These are wonderful, exciting events, Meg."

"What you and Sandra have explained lately doesn't sound wonderful and exciting to me."

"Well, perhaps we've spent too much time talking about all the problems. There really is a lot to be encouraged about."

Elliot realized he was speaking to a woman who had lost her child and many of her friends in the east. Her house had been ransacked and her husband almost killed in a terrorist bombing. "And here I am," Elliot thought, "trying to cheer her up with politics, of all things. But I really don't know what else to say."

"There's so much fighting and killing ... and kidnapping," Megan sighed.

Elliot had his arms folded across his chest and was gazing straight ahead, out the window. He spoke aloud as he thought. "It is a thing of beauty to fight for and to implement democratic reforms. But giving birth to a democracy is a terribly painful event and those involved must realize that it is just the beginning, that there is new responsibility, a new life to care for and nurture."

"What's that, Elliot?"

"Oh ... sorry, Meg. I was just thinking out loud."

"You're trying to cheer me up, aren't you?"

"Los Angeles used to be a sleepy rancho. Today it is a force in world markets and politics. It was not built by politicians alone. It was built by men and women of great courage, people who had vision and were willing to step out and take risks when it counted. Your grandfather, your father, you, Steven, Jake, Shirali ... are all like that."

"And Corrie," Megan said wistfully.

"Of course," Elliot agreed.

"I wish I shared your enthusiasm, Elliot."

"The Pueblo of Los Angeles used to be a hot, dusty, flea infested collection of wooden shacks. It was transformed by hard working railroad men, farmers and builders of many things. And every step of the way they had to fight dishonesty and fraud. They had to contend with the evil in the world, just like you are having to do, Meg."

Then Elliot looked down at Megan and said with complete conviction, "You will win, Meg. I know it."

Megan smiled and looked back at him, "You sound just like Corrie."

"Well, she was right about Jake, wasn't she, when everyone else thought he was dead?"

Megan said softly, "You're a good friend, Elliot. I'm starting to understand your feelings about Steven, his work ... and the Big Six."

"I intend to put the Big Six behind bars."

"You're really very passionate about this aren't you, Elliot? That's why you want Steven to have his laboratory so badly, why you and all your lawyers put everything aside to fight those people."

Elliot frowned. "There are emerging democracies all around the world, Meg. But a democracy, particularly in its infancy, is a breeding ground for evil. Its continued health depends entirely upon the resolve of its participants, its citizens. Steven has told me of your friend, Khimbei. I would like to meet the man. He is willing fight for what he believes in."

"He certainly is," Megan said.

"One man's freedom, Meg, is another man's opportunity to deceive. Your husband's technology will one day clean our air. Some day, God willing, it will revolutionize medicine. But it must remain in responsible hands."

Just then Miss Beasley flung open the conference room door. It crashed against the wall so hard the half full coffee pot fell off its stand and shattered on the table. Miss Beasley

311

staggered into the room, her mouth wide open, looking as white as a ghost.

Elliot ran to her. "Good heavens, Alice! What has happened?"

"There's a ... oh, dear! ... I'm sorry ...."

"What is it, Alice?"

"There's a ... a girl on the phone. She insists her name is ... oh, my! ... she says she's Corrie Capterville."

"WHAT?" Megan screamed, "Put her on the speaker, Alice!"

"OK ... I just wasn't sure ...."

"Go ahead," Elliot said, "come back and listen when you've switched it over."

"Hello? Hello? ... Mommy? Daddy?"

"IT'S CORRIE!" Steven hollered. "We're here, honey, we're here! HOW ARE YOU? WHERE ARE YOU?"

"I'm just fine, Daddy. How are you?"

Megan could barely contain herself, "Corrie, Honey, we're just fine too ... Corrie, listen to me. Where are you?"

"I'm washing the dishes, Mommy."

"You're what? ... Corrie, where are you?"

"I'm in the kitchen, Mommy. How come you left the dishes? That's not like you."

Steven and Megan stared at each other. They were thrilled, they were filled with joy.

"YOU'RE HOME??" they both shouted at once.

"Sure. I just got here. I used the secret key in the bird house."

"Corrie, don't go anywhere. We'll be home soon. We're at Mr. Jayne's office downtown. Stay there, OK?"

"OK."

"Promise, Honey?"

"Yes ... but you don't need to worry. Everything's OK now."

Steven couldn't resist, "Corrie, we're on our way home ... but tell us ... where in the world have you been?"

"It's a long story, Daddy. I got out of the mountain two days ago. I walked out. There was nobody there ... just like Paul and Silas."

The four lawyers looked at one another. Two days ago? The fax to Chief Otterstein had nothing to do with Corrie's release.

"It took me a long time to get down the mountain this time. It was cold. Then I met this nice man. Mr. Tinyon is his name. He gave me a ride all the way home. He said he knew you. He wanted to stay and see you again, but he had to go back. He said his wife Marie would be worried about him. She must be a really neat lady. He talked about her all the way. He says she looks just like you, Mommy ... oh, Mommy?"

"Yes, dear?"

"I found my colored shoelace on a road, by a little white bridge. I know it's mine ... I wonder how it got there."

"We'll have plenty of time to talk about it, dear. We're going to leave now so we can get there as fast as we can. We love you, Corrie."

"I love you too, Mommy ... Mommy?"

"Yes, dear?"

"How is Uncle Jake?"

"He's fine, dear. He's back from Mars. He's in Houston now and he'll be home with us tomorrow ... just in time for Christmas. Isn't that wonderful?"

Meg collapsed into her chair and began to cry.

"Daddy, Uncle Jake's not fooling again is he?"

"He'll be there, Corrie. I promise."

"Oh, good!" Corrie said. "I have lots to tell him."

The Cappervilles left for home to see, squeeze and hug their precious Corrie. Miss Beasley, muttering to herself incessantly had just finished mopping up coffee and broken glass. Elliot and Sandra had remained in the conference room discussing alternative tactical moves, trying to guess what the Big Six would do next.

Over the intercom Miss Beasley's excited voice said, "Mr. Jaynes, there's a fax coming in. I think it's from ... yes ... it's from Mr. Otterstein."

"Bring it in when its finished. Oh, and you'd better alert Winston and Richard."

"It's already in, sir. It's only a page. I'll bring it in now."

"Well, Sandra, this is it. You ready?"

"Ready as I'll ever be."

Elliot pressed the single white page to the table and he and Sandra nervously read the message. Not surprisingly, it was not on White House stationary.

Mr. Jaynes,
  All terms will be complied with. However, the following will be impossible:
  - Corrie Capperville cannot be returned. She is dead.
  - The Russian Culture cannot be returned. It is dead. The translations will be mailed over night to you.
  - The last two members cannot be revealed. The consequences for all, including you, would be far more grave than your threatened actions.
  All other demands will be complied with.

L.O.

Just outside the open conference room door Miss Beasley hung up the telephone from yet another call.

She exclaimed, "My goodness! Mr. Jaynes!"

"What is it, Miss Beasley? You sound like Megan Capterville."

"That new trust account you had me set up ... the one for the new non-profit corporation?"

"Yes, Alice."

"Our banker, Mr. Mitchell, just called. The sum of ... let me see ... seven hundred twenty four million, eight hundred ninety-five thousand, three hundred fifty-two dollars and ... twenty-seven cents ... has been deposited into our account. He says he has been alerted that there is much more on the way."

"Thank you, Miss Beasley. Please inform the other partners of this astounding news."

"Yes, sir."

"Oh, and Alice?"

"Yes?"

"This does not mean you get another raise, so don't even ask."

"You're a cruel man, sir."

Alice Beasley went back to her telephone. Elliot Jaynes and Sandra Hale, with enormous grins, reached across the table and shook hands.

CHAPTER 36

"Hello, this is Elliot Jaynes."

"Hi, Uncle Elliot. This is Corrie."

"Well ... hello, Corrie."

"Mommy said it would be OK to call you *Uncle* Elliot ... since you did so much, and since you're so nice. Is that all right?"

"Of course it is, Corrie. I'm honored. I love your parents very much."

"Mommy wants me to make sure you're coming tomorrow ... for Christmas Eve. You will come, won't you Uncle Elliot?"

"I'll be there with bells on, Corrie."

"Oh good, and come early. I have lots to tell you, and you have to see Uncle Jake. He just got back from Mars. He's going to tell us all about it ... and Shirali's going to bake neat things from Bukol."

"I can't wait."

"OK, good. Bye!"

"Good-bye for now Corrie."

"Alice!"

"Yes, sir?"

"Get me a box of Kleenex."

CHAPTER 37

It was mid-afternoon on Christmas Eve day. The air was crystal clear and cool. Christmas carols from Corrie's pink plastic radio wove among the rafters of the old Capterville farmhouse, then drifted out through row after row of sleeping orange trees. A beautiful pine tree had been trimmed in the living room and the outside gables were strung with waiting lights.

Corrie was setting tables for dinner. Megan and Shirali were busy in the kitchen. The smell of baking cookies and cakes mingled with the unforgettable aroma of roasting turkey.

"Shirali, put the cookies down for a minute and come over here."

Shirali set a metal baking sheet filled with hot cookies on top of the stove. As she crossed the kitchen Megan wrapped her arms around her and gave her a big hug.

"What's that for?" Shirali asked with surprise.

"Shirali ... are you happy?"

"What in the world do you mean, Meg?"

"Well, I'm so happy and proud I could burst. Corrie is home, Jake's back, it's Christmas, those horrible people have been found out, Steven is ... well, I'm so much in love."

"But that's wonderful, Meg. What are you going on about?"

"It seems so unfair. Your family, your village ... gone. The terrible civil war in Georgia and Abkhazia. And the kefir, dead in the hands of those evil people."

"But I *am* happy, Meg, and I have a new family now. The unpredictable, wonderful Captervilles!"

"Of course you do, forever. But it must be so ...."

"God has a way of doing things in His own way, in His own time, and it is always for the best. As for my parents and my people, well, I think of it this way, Meg ... they have all been promoted in Heaven ahead of us."

Megan broke into one of her famous countrified smiles. "You're a remarkable woman, Shirali Lasuria. What incredible faith."

"As for the kefir, God created it once ... He can do it again. So don't be concerned about me, Megan Capterville. As long as I know I am in God's will and doing His work, I'm the happiest woman in the world. Besides, I have my eye on someone very special ...."

"*You do?* Shirali Lasuria, shame on you! You've been holding out on me. Who is he? What's his name? How old is ... oh, dear, I ...."

Shirali giggled, "Perhaps you are wondering how I could find a companion in my age bracket who is not on life support."

Megan also giggled. "Shirali, stop it. Now tell me who he is."

"There doesn't seem to be anybody alive who is old enough for me so I had to find someone younger who is very understanding and, well, special."

"Shirali, you look and act thirty years old. Who cares? So tell me, who is he?"

"I can't tell you. I'm too embarrassed."

"Shirali!"

"I said I had my eyes on him, but I'm not sure he has his eyes on me. He is so much younger, and knows nothing of my country."

"Because he's never been to Abkhazia! I knew it! I knew it! I knew it! I told Steven weeks ago you two would get together. Steven didn't believe me. Oh, Shirali, I'm so excited ... I knew it!"

"Please don't say anything, Meg, I don't want to look like an old fool."

"I won't say a peep. I promise."

"Now ... perhaps we should get back to these cookies," Shirali said. She was completely flustered. "We don't want our guests to starve."

Megan leaned over the sink and looked out the window. "Speaking of guests, I think I hear a car." She looked back at Shirali with a giant grin on her face. "Oh, I knew it, I knew it, I knew it! Now everything's perfect!"

Steven opened the wooden front door, swung open the screen door, and walked onto the porch.

"Merry Christmas, Elliot, come on up."

Elliot and Steven sat on the porch in two of the large wicker chairs. Megan and Corrie brought out dishes of cakes and five different kinds of fresh baked cookies. Shirali carried a silver tray with a tea pot and cups and saucers. She placed it carefully on the glass-topped wicker table that was centered between the chairs.

"Boy, this is the way to enjoy the holidays," Elliot said, leaning back in his chair. "Corrie, come on over and sit on my lap ... you can help me pick out cookies. Look at this one, a Christmas stocking ... and a Santa Claus, and heart shapes. I like those."

As Corrie climbed into his lap, Elliot unfolded a newspaper. "I thought you all might like to see this."

"What is it, Uncle Elliot, what is it?"

"It's the late edition of the Times. Take a look."

Steven came out of his chair, and the others leaned forward. The front page headline spread the width of the page.

WHITE HOUSE CHIEF OF STAFF RESIGNS
Cites Health and Personal Reasons

Lucius Otterstein's name was printed under his full-color picture.

"Wow," Steven said, "Looks like they've taken you seriously, Elliot."

"They really had no choice. Feels good to be on the winning side for a change, doesn't it?"

Corrie was fidgeting in Elliot's lap. "Uncle Elliot?"

"Yes, Corrie?"

"There was a mean man inside the mountain ... that's him! He was asking me questions, but I didn't tell him anything."

Uncle Elliot gave Corrie a squeeze, "Good for you, Corrie. Before I leave I want to hear the whole story, right from the beginning, OK?"

"OK."

Steven asked, "What do you think Edith Wolman will do, Elliot?"

Corrie sat straight up in Elliot's lap. "Wolman?" she asked. "Daddy, I remember, I told myself to remember. She was in the mountain too! She was really, *really* mean. But I didn't tell her anything either."

"Excellent, Corrie, I'm proud of you." Steven paused, and looked at Elliot, "Do you think she'll resign?"

"Absolutely. Sometime next week. It would seem mighty peculiar if they both quit the same day. She'll be gone by our deadline."

"It still gets me," Megan said, "that those people aren't behind bars."

"But their punishment will be worse than any jail term, Meg."

"What do you mean?"

"I'd be surprised if they're alive six months from now. The other two, whoever they are, have too much at stake, and any way you cut it, Lucius and Edith know too much. My guess is, after they've been out of the headlines for a time, they'll quietly be eliminated. In the meanwhile, their lives are bound to be quite miserable."

"Goodness," Megan said, "eliminated!"

Changing the subject Steven asked, "So what's the current total?"

"Many billions, Steven, in cash, securities, real estate, gold, silver ... everything imaginable. It's growing by the minute."

Shirali had calmed her nervous hands. She poured them all a cup of tea and settled back into her chair. She looked at Elliot and asked, "What do you plan to do with it all?"

Elliot smiled, "That's an excellent question, Shirali. Winston, Sandra, Richard and the whole gang are still at the office trying to sort out what can and should be done. None of us have experienced anything like it. There are a myriad of tax and securities issues that need to be answered, and in many instances we're on new legal ground."

"Well," Shirali said, "we know it's all in good hands."

"Hear, hear!" said Megan, raising her cup.

"Hear, hear!" Corrie repeated, raising her cookie.

Corrie examined the plate full of cookies, carefully selected a heart shaped one for Elliot and handed it to him.

"Thank you, Corrie."

Elliot took a bite and wiped the crumbs from his mouth. "Just to give you an idea of how complicated it all is," he said, "listen to this. You've all seen the building my office is in?"

"Sure," Corrie said, "it's a skyscraper. It's ten miles high."

"Now, Corrie, don't exaggerate," Megan said.

"Guess who owns it," Elliot asked.

"Not the Big Six!" Shirali exclaimed.

"You got it, Shirali. Our office building is owned by a private British trust controlled by the Six. As part of one of her intricate trades with Karl Bulow at Prime Bank Paris, Edith Wolman negotiated a secured interest in the property. She foreclosed when her second lien defaulted. She paid off the first deed of trust at a substantial discount and took title to the building in the name of the trust. She and Lucius Otterstein are trustees of the trust. Pretty shrewd stuff. She's done the same thing with countless other real estate holdings."

"Then that means," Steven said, "your firm has been paying rent to the Big Six! I'll bet Sandra's blood is boiling."

"Let's just say I've never seen her so excited," Elliot said. "She's on Edith's trail like a bloodhound. This morning Sandra received the deed to the building, transferring title to the non-profit corporation we established. The deed was signed by Ms. Wolman herself. Sandra was having it recorded as I left this afternoon."

"But, Elliot," Steven said, "it's Christmas Eve!"

"You don't know Sandra. She tracked down the president of the title insurance company on his ski vacation. They're insuring title immediately and doing a special recording as we speak."

"How wonderful!" Shirali said impulsively. She had no idea what a special recording was, but it sounded just grand.

322

Elliot finished his heart shaped cookie. He looked at Megan and said, "Meg, you remember when I was trying to cheer you up ... with politics, of all things?"

"I'll never forget it, Elliot. That was really special. It was a difficult time for all of us."

"Remember PFI? The company RAM used to launder money?"

"Of course," Megan said.

"It turns out that over a million dollars *a year* was donated by PFI to members of the United States Congress."

"No!" Steven sat up straight in his seat.

"That's right, Steven. They profited using your technology and they've been buying votes in the finance and tax committees for years. Richard is investigating the political expenditures, and the results are most disturbing."

"The Republicans or Democrats?" Steven wanted to know.

"Both," Elliot replied.

"Both?"

"During an election, PFI donates equal amounts to each candidate ... until there is an apparent winner. Then it contributes heavily to the winner."

"But, why?" Megan asked.

"Influence within the government, Meg. It's a sickness within our political system. Lobbyists, corporate contacts, private campaign contributions set America's agenda and enact her laws. We citizens have little voice, Republican or Democrat, when huge sums of money are made available to those who will vote the *right* way. When RAM Pharmaceuticals needed Congress to approve an international import duty waiver for components it needed ... to save RAM, at the expense of us taxpayers, several million dollars a year ... the appropriate committees approved the waiver. The key votes came from senators and representatives who would never have voted for such a waiver. But they received from RAM money sufficient to assure their re-election."

"That is positively sick," Steven said.

"Abraham Lincoln would turn in his grave," Megan said with disgust.

"What makes it worse," Elliot continued, "is that all of the companies within control of the Six have done the same thing. And what's even worse ...."

"Worse?"

"Many of the largest corporations in America are doing the same thing. It's all public record."

"Good grief!" Steven said. "You mean it's legal?"

"The Supreme Court of the United States has ruled that the contribution of money, in the case of political candidates, is protected free speech. Is it legal? Arguably. Is it right, the way it's being done? No."

"That doesn't seem ...."

"The good part is, Richard's hot on it. He's preparing all the corporate political contribution statistics and coordinating everything with Sandra. The goal is to let America see who and what we've been voting for."

"And," Megan said excitedly, "we wouldn't know about any of this if someone hadn't sent that computer disk. I wonder who it could have been."

"Good question," Elliot said. Changing the subject, he turned to Steven and said proudly, "I think it's only fitting and proper that you take over the helm of RAM Pharmaceuticals and become its president. Thanks to the nefarious doings of the Big Six we now control the company."

"Thanks for the confidence, Elliot, but that isn't what I'm interested in doing. I'd never have time for what I really love to do."

"That's what I thought you'd say. Corrie, would you run out to my car and get a stack of papers for me?"

"Sure, Uncle Elliot," and Corrie took off running.

"They're on the front seat."

"OK."

Megan smiled. "You certainly have a big fan, Uncle Elliot. Corrie won't sit in just any body's lap."

"Must be the cookies ... works every time with the ladies."

Shirali shifted in her wicker chair and she and Megan looked at each other. Corrie ran back onto the porch with the papers.

Elliot pointed to Steven and said, "Let your father have them, Corrie."

"What's this?" Steven asked.

"The resumes, employment contracts and consulting contracts of all the top scientists at the RAM Laboratory. We stockholders just put you in charge. You have an unlimited budget and can concentrate on anything you choose. Go through those and keep the people you want ... can the rest. Fire them all if you like."

Steven was groping for words. "But ... is that ... financially responsible?"

"Steven, you could throw wild parties at the lab all day long, and the stockholders would be better off than they are now. By the time we stop the monkey business with PFI ... and don't forget the product markups ... we'll increase cash flow by thirty percent. Then, with your permission, we'll begin to introduce an entire line of microclustered products. You can tinker and create in the lab all day and all night if you like."

"Not all night!" Megan demanded.

"Financial responsibility? Steven, the stockholders will be kissing you! And say, I almost forgot, remember your buddy, Tom Gulling?"

"Yes," Steven said, "at MarketForce. He never did call me back."

Elliot winked at Megan. "Well, Steven, you're his boss now. I'd recommend firing him before you have me sue him."

"I have no intention of suing anybody," Steven said cheerfully.

"OK by me," Elliot said, "but if you need him, you'll probably find him in the county jail."

"Goodness," Megan said.

"In any event, it seems we have at our disposal an international distribution network with hundreds of top sales people already educated about cluster technology."

"How wonderful!" Shirali chimed.

Corrie was back on Elliot's lap and was looking up at him with her wisdomful eyes, "You sure get excited, Uncle Elliot. You remind me of Uncle Jake, only he's like that all the time."

"I'm looking forward to seeing Uncle Jake. He's quite a fellow."

"He is, he is!" Corrie exclaimed.

"Corrie, do you know who sent the postcard to us?" Elliot asked, "and the computer disc?"

"No." Corrie thought a while. "I tried to once, when I escaped. I got all the way to the mail box, but they caught me. They hit me, and put me back into the room ... Bob and Slavic."

Elliot gave Corrie another squeeze, "That's alright, Corrie, you don't have to talk about it anymore. You're back safe, that's the important thing. And those people will never bother you again. "

"It's OK, Uncle Elliot, I don't mind. Everything's OK now."

A pumpkin sun began lowering itself behind the first row of chilling orange trees. Its final rays lit a solitary cloud that slowly changed colors from yellows and reds to purples and blues. A few of the brighter stars began appearing in the pale sky.

"We'd best move inside," Megan said, "it's getting cold."

Corrie was holding Shirali's hand. They were standing on the steps leading up to the porch. Corrie pointed up to the sky and said, "Look, Shirali! See the bright one up there? The one that's not twinkling. Planets don't twinkle, Uncle Jake says, because it's reflected light. See it, isn't it pretty?"

"Why, yes dear ... I see it."

"It's Mars, Shirali, it's Mars! That's where Uncle Jake was!"

As they were moving into the house, Megan suddenly stopped. She said, "Wait! ... Hush! ... do you hear it?"

They all froze in place.

"I hear it," Corrie said, "Shhh ...."

An old out-of-tune Volkswagen bus backfired its way up the Capterville driveway, slammed on its brakes, and slid to a stop with a rattle and a gasping chug.

"YAHOO!" Corrie cried, "It's Uncle Jake!"

CHAPTER 38

Steven threw his arms around his brother and squeezed hard and long. When he finally let go, Jake said, "Big brother, its easier surviving a trip to outer space than one of your bear hugs."

Steven placed a hand on each of Jake's shoulders and looked at him, up and down. Everyone else stood back and listened ... except for Corrie. She had already clamped all four of her limbs securely around her uncle's right leg and was not about to let go.

"My gosh, Jake, your hair's as white as snow! Siever was right, you look like Moses. You feel all right?"

"I feel great. My physicals actually show I'm healthier than when I left, and there's no question I'm stronger. My eyesight's even better ... figure that one out. Why my hair turned white, nobody knows."

Jake threw an arm around Steven's shoulder, the other around Megan, and with Corrie in tow they all headed for the house.

Jake said, "NASA can't figure it out ... something to do with space and time, so I told 'em I had a brother who knows everything."

As they reached the porch steps, Steven looked across to Megan and said, "He hasn't been back five minutes and he's got me in trouble with the Feds!"

"Guess everything's back to normal," Megan beamed. "Come on in everyone!"

Steven lit the dry pine logs in the old river-rock fireplace and in a few minutes they were crackling and laughing and lighting up the room. Corrie turned off the house lights and stood on a chair next to the Christmas tree.

"OK, everybody! Uncle Jake! It's your turn this year."

Jake crossed the room and grabbed the plug. "Everyone ready?"

"Wait," Megan said, "Where's Elliot ... and Shirali?"

"We're over here, Megan, behind the punch bowl."

"OK, Jake, light the tree!"

Jake put the plug in the wall and the tree lit up in every imaginable color. Uncountable kinds of light reflected off Christmas tree ornaments, new and old. Strands of glistening silver tinsel dangled from branches sending out cheer. Little glass tubes, filled with colored water and shining with colored light, began bubbling from bottom to top.

"These are my favorite," Corrie said pointing to a bubbling green one.

There were presents, packages and boxes of all sorts and sizes stuffed under the tree. Woody and Topper were running about, sniffing for candy and nuts. At the very top of the tree, arms outstretched and standing tall, were two joyous glass angels, praying for all.

Jake stood by the Christmas tree for the longest time. Steven and Megan were watching him closely. His eyes became wet and a strange expression transformed his face.

Corrie began leading Uncle Elliot, Shirali and Woody and Topper in Christmas carols.

Steven gently put his hand on Jake's shoulder. "Is anything wrong, Jake?"

Jake took a deep breath and looked at his brother, making no effort to wipe the streaming tears from his face. "We have a lot to talk about, Steve. This tree, this light, this love. I saw it on another planet. It's hard to explain, but I know for certain it has something to do with you ... and your water."

Megan gave Jake her handkerchief.

"I had to dump all the recording equipment and cameras before take off, so I have no proof. NASA thinks I'm wacko, of course, and I guess I can't blame 'em ... white hair and wild stories."

Megan winked at Steven, "But, Jake, you were like that before you left."

"Siever thinks I've got deep psychological Martian phobias, or something worse. If it wasn't for politics, my pals at Kepler and Markhti Tarba, I'd probably be in a top secret holding tank somewhere."

"Dr. Tarba!" Megan exclaimed, "How is he?"

"He's just fine, Meg. He stuck up for me when I got back. I'm not sure I would have been released by now if it weren't for Markhti. But he was crushed when I told him I had to jettison all the Martian rock samples seconds before lift off."

"You did?" Steven said with disappointment.

"Either that or I would have spent the rest of my brief life on Mars. If *you're* disappointed, you should have seen Markhti. He was balling like a baby. He'd brought all his rock samples from Canada and the Antarctic to compare with the ones from Mars."

"What did you see on ...?"

Shirali was yelling over the singing, "Jake, Oh Jake! Telephone ... it's a Captain Siever."

"Thanks, Shirali. Would you tell him it's Christmas Eve ... and that I'm off duty."

Shirali smiled, "Whatever you say, Commander."

Jake said, "I like that woman. Is she available?"

Megan and Steven laughed.

"What's up, you two?"

"There's a lot you need to learn about Miss Lasuria, Jake."

Shirali was waving from across the room. "Jake! He says it's important. He's very persistent ... something about getting life readings from one of the Units."

"Shirali, please tell him that I already explained that to him. Tell him it's *Unit Seven.*"

"Yes sir, Commander." Shirali disappeared into the kitchen once again.

"Yes, indeed ... I like that woman." Jake yelled into the kitchen, "Hey, Shirali! Got a date for New Years Eve?"

Elliot hollered from the piano, "I already asked her, Capterville. Get your own girl ... besides, she's much too mature for you."

Jake put an arm around Megan's waist and another around Steven's neck. "... and I think I might like him too, even if he didn't go to Bukol with us."

"You should like him, Jake," Megan said, "he sounds just like you."

"He says what he thinks," Jake said, "I like that."

"You have no idea how much," Megan said. "While you were away, Jake, Elliot saved us all from certain disaster."

"So I hear. I can't wait to hear all the details. Markhti says you all have turned the world upside down. Evil plots in high places, and all that. Anyway, Elliot Jaynes says what he thinks. I like that."

Steven laughed, "Judge Eve Richardson might not concur with you, Jake."

"Judge who ...?"

Shirali, phone in one hand, was waving with the other, "Jake, Jake! This man's going crazy on the phone ... wants to know how you knew it was Unit Seven ... says it's life or death."

"He's got that right," Jake declared. "Shirali, tell him the Martians will still be there tomorrow. I'll call him in a couple of days ... and tell him, Merry Christmas."

"OK. Consider it done."

"Life readings from Mars?" Steven asked, "from one of the LDCUs?"

"Yep. I told 'em it would happen, right about Christmas."

"But how did you know which one, Jake? There were ten of them weren't there?"

"Yea, except two got smashed when I fell through a rock wall."

"What?" Steven exclaimed.

"It gets better, believe me."

"But how did you know it would be Unit Seven?"

"Because that's the Unit with your water in it."

"Well, I'll be!" Steven said with a broad smile.

"Yea," Jake said, "the one in the colored cavern with the carpet of light, and the tiny glowing crystals that turn to gas in the presence of light ...."

"Whoa, Jake, whoa ... slow down," Steven said.

Jake slapped his brother on the back, "I told you we have a lot to talk about."

CHAPTER 39

Amid the singing, the barking and stories of a long Martian day, there came a soft knocking on the Capterville front door.

Megan excused herself, crossed the room and opened the door. Before her stood a giant of a man with a huge head and broad strong shoulders. His large features were interesting but by no means handsome. Megan looked up at him. His eyes were red and damp. It appeared he had been crying.

"Pardon me, Ma'm, don't like to bother you on such a night 'n all."

"Yes?"

"Are you Mrs. Capterville?"

"Yes, I am."

With that the man's eyes wrinkled up and his face contorted terribly. He folded his big ham-like hands together in front of him and fell heavily to his knees before Megan. He began crying, his barrel-like chest heaving in and out. He pressed his open hands to his face and between his palms he sobbed, "I am so, so sorry, Mrs. Capterville ... please, furgive me ... please, find it in yur heart to furgive me ...."

The man sat further down onto his heels, sobbing convulsively, "*I am so ... sorry.*"

Steven had come to the door and was standing behind Megan. "Who is it?" Steven whispered.

"I don't know, Steven. What should we do?"

The man looked up at them, completely spent. "My name is Saul Slavic. I'm the one who stole yur daughter ... me n' Bob. We burned her ... and ... ohh, God save me, I'm so sorry ..." and Slavic once again buried his face in his hands and cried uncontrollably.

Anger, hate and protection of family welled inside Steven. In front of him was the very man who had tortured his little Corrie and caused them all so much pain. He fought the age-old feeling that enters the hearts of men at such a time. There was nothing, absolutely nothing that could prevent his revenge. It was the familiar spirit that justified the wars within the hearts of men. It was the deception that placed forgiveness beyond reason. Nothing could stop Steven now.

Still on his knees, Slavic straightened himself. He looked past Megan and Steven, through the door. He saw the Christmas tree, the lights, the fire, the love, all the things he had never known. If he saw nothing else in his life, this was enough. He saw other people, staring out at him. Then he saw ... CORRIE! ... she was running, in slow motion ... for him ... *MY LITTLE CORRIE IS COMING!*

Corrie ran to the front door. Steven reached for her to stop her, but he missed. Slavic opened his long arms and held them out. Corrie flew past her mother's dress and into Slavic's waiting arms. She wrapped herself around his thick neck.

"Slavic, Oh, Slavic ... you're alive!

"But, Corrie ..." Steven stammered.

"It's OK, Daddy, really. Slavic, I mean Paul ... he was mean at first, but he saved me from Bob and the others."

"But ...."

"It's OK, really ... Paul's changed."

"Paul?" Megan asked, "I thought you said your name was Saul."

"Mrs. Capterville, yur daughter has changed my life ... and my name."

Megan looked at Steven wide-eyed. Steven looked back, perplexed, sorting out his thoughts ... avoiding the intellectual and spiritual tanning he felt might be due him.

"Well," Megan said, "it seems there's a lot we still have to learn. Let's not stand out here and freeze to death. Mr. Slavic, Paul, you are welcome in our home. Please come in and meet the others."

"But, are you sure, Mrs. Cap ...?"

"Absolutely." Megan gave Steven a sharp look. "Isn't that right, Steven?"

Steven looked at Corrie clinging to the man's neck. She was overjoyed. The man was obviously her friend. "Ah, yes. Yes, of course. Please come in Paul, and Merry Christmas."

Paul Slavic stood up, unwinding to his full height with Corrie still clinging to his neck. He gently put her down and she took him by the hand and led him into her house.

"Uncle Jake! Uncle Elliot! Shirali! This is my friend Paul. I want you all to meet him, but first I want to get him some punch and cookies."

Corrie pulled Paul by the hand but he could not move. He slumped into a chair and clamped his hands over his face. He cried and cried, but for the first time in his life they were tears of joy.

"He'll be OK, everybody ... he's been through a lot."

* * *

The tales told around the Capterville fire this Christmas evening would come to be told by generations of Capstervilles, Jaynes, Lasurias, Ladariyas, Slavics and many others. Woody was curled up on the couch with his head resting on Jake's right leg. Topper was on the other side of Jake, running in place, mid-dream.

There was a break in the story-telling as Megan went to the kitchen. The fire continued to speak to the room with crackling sound and light. Shirali put her tea cup down with the same rattle that had been her father's. She looked across the coffee table at a calm and happy Paul Slavic. She said to him, "I am interested, Paul, in why you say your life has changed."

"Hard to put into words, Ma'm, but Corrie here done it."

"How is that, Paul?"

"I've always been a mean person, Ma'm. But it's like I never knew I was bad, it was just the way to be ... like I'd been fooled or somethin'. But Corrie here, she showed me the light. Me n' Bob, we worked for the Six group. They wanted to know things from Corrie. Things about her dad n' stuff. But she wouldn't tell 'em, no matter what. Then one day me n' Bob was told to do her real bad ... make her talk ... and she up n' started givin' the devil orders like he was some fool kid ... she was shoutin' and claimin' things in the name of her Jesus. Me n' Bob was shocked. Bob ran clear out of the room ... never did come 'round Corrie again. He was downright scared of her. He kept tellin' the Six we was doin' her bad, though, 'cuz he was scared a' them too."

"Bob sounds like quite a fellow," Shirali said.

"So anyways, I figure, here's this little pea-bucket girl, if you'll pardon the expression, Ma'm ... and she's readin' the riot act to me n' Bob and the Big Six, and then she goes n' takes on the devil his'self. Right then n' there I figure I'm on the wrong side, and sure enough I start feelin' things I never feeled before ... like I'm finally doin' the right thing n' all. Then Corrie explains it to me real simple. Turns out she's got more punch in her little self than all the fists in the world. Like I said, Ma'm, it ain't easy to put n' words."

"I'd say you've done a wonderful job of explaining, Paul." Shirali got up from her chair and walked over to Paul. She gave him a kiss on the cheek. "Would anyone like more tea?"

Shirali was on her way to the kitchen when the telephone began ringing. "I'll get it."

She remained in the kitchen for quite a while. Then, phone pressed to her side, she leaned through the door and said, "Elliot, I tried to explain, but this man won't get off the phone. What is it with you and Jake and Christmas Eve phone calls, anyway?"

"Who is it, Shirali?"

"He's calling from New York. He says his name is Marcus Baranoff. He's a lawyer and he says it's very important. He says he thinks he knows the truth about RAM Pharmaceuticals. He says he's quite embarrassed professionally."

Elliot and Jake nodded to one another. At the same instant they broke into the most mischievous of smiles. Then they began to laugh with a recognition allowed only to uncles who from separate experience had become allied and resolute.

"Shirali, would you please give Mr. Baranoff my regards," Elliot said, "and tell him I have family commitments, and that I'll have to call him later."

"Whatever you say."

"Oh, Shirali!"

"Yes, Elliot?"

"He's bound to be upset. After he's calmed down, tell him the Martians will still be there tomorrow. And be sure to tell him Merry Christmas!

Shirali rolled her eyes, went to the kitchen, and ended her conversation with Mr. Baranoff.

* * *

There was quiet in the house once again. Colored lights blinked on the Christmas tree. Colored bubbles bubbled. Occasionally, two ornaments would kiss and there would be a tinkle. The dry pine firelight sent shadows dancing cheerfully around the walls and the two shining angels atop the tree surveyed and protected all.

Paul Slavic was staring at the timeless, warming fire. Without taking his eyes from the fire, he said in a gentle voice, "I hope you got the postcard."

Elliot had been absorbed in thoughts of Christmas and a colorful cavern on Mars. Then it registered.

"YOU!!!" Elliot came clear out of his seat. "My gosh, Paul, do you realize you've changed the world!"

Shirali sat back in her chair, chuckling merrily. She winked at Corrie who was sitting in her father's lap.

"I don't write too good, and I didn't have no time. Bob was always with me ... watchin' like a hawk."

"And the computer disk," Elliot said, "you sent that too, didn't you?"

"Yea. That was kind 'a scary. Moss n' Panatta ... you heard of 'em?"

"Have we ever!" Elliot said.

"They're dead."

"Really?" Steven asked.

"Yea. The Six sent Bob after 'em. Bob's dead too. The Six did a contract on 'im too. They really clean things up."

338

"Not any more," Megan said.

"Anyway, Moss n' Panatta come back to the mountain to get all their fancy computer stuff n' I watched 'em ... listened to 'em. I'm not too smart but I knew what they were doin'."

"Yes you are smart," Corrie said. "You stop talking like that."

"Like mother, like daughter," Steven smiled.

"OK, Corrie, I'll try. So when Panatta goes over to talk to Moss, I took the number one blue disc from the top box ... it said 'Master' somethin' on it so I knew it was a good one. I hope it helped."

They all grinned, one to another. Steven stood up and raised his glass, "I should like to propose a toast ... to Mr. Paul Slavic ... for heroic efforts above and beyond the call of duty. Paul, welcome to the Capterville family! You are one of us now."

Paul's face became a giant smile and before Steven could finish, Paul said, "Do I really have to?"

There were cheers and laughter all around.

Jake hollered, "Nice going, Paul, you really nailed ol' Steve that time."

"I told you he was smart," Corrie said.

As the laughter subsided, the smile left Paul's face and he looked down at the floor, remembering the past. "After I grabbed the disc I ran as fast as I could through the tunnels, to beat the explosion ... back to Corrie's new room."

"We fixed it up real nice," Corrie interrupted, "with the things Paul brought back. They ordered Paul to kill me, so he told them he would. It was our secret."

"Explosion?" Megan asked.

"Yea," Paul said, "They planted plastic explosives to blow the place up ... to make it look like they hadn't been there."

Megan said to Steven. "I wonder if that's the earthquake we felt down by the fence, and the rumble. Remember, Steven? No earthquake was reported."

"As I got back to the room," Paul continued, "somethin' hit me ... everythin' went black."

"Oooh, it was terrible," Corrie said, covering her head with her arms. "The ceiling fell in ... you should have seen it, Mommy."

"I had a feeling you were somewhere close by, dear."

"It knocked me out, Mommy ... I don't know how long. When I woke up Paul and tons of rock had fallen on me. He saved my life. Half the mountain was on top of him. I thought you were dead, Paul. I shouldn't have left, but you were ...."

Paul said quickly, "You did the right thing, Corrie. There was nothing you could do. Besides, you told me all along we'd get out some day."

Jake rolled the dogs off his lap and stood up to stretch.

He looked at Corrie and winked. He placed his hand on Paul's shoulder and said, "All this time, I thought *I* was having a big adventure. It's you two that should be in the headlines, not me."

"Aw, come on, Uncle Jake."

"I'm going to take the dogs for a quick walk," Jake said, "be right back."

"Try not to get into any trouble," Steven said.

"You should talk, brother dear, you should talk."

CHAPTER 40

In a vast shifting cavern many miles below the surface of the earth, molten rock pulled and stretched against semi-solid walls. Rivers of glowing liquid stone lit the hot underground chamber with grim colors, and knifelike formations cast ghostly shadows from one to another. Shut off physically from the outside world the continually adjusting airless space was filled with a repulsive sulfurous stench.

Deep in a dark rocky recess the devil's messenger pressed *its* hideous body farther and farther back into the crevasse. *Its* sharpened senses held *it* firmly in place, locked in fearful blackness.

It was terrified. *It* knew.

There would be no mercy.

Satan was approaching. Satan was near. The fallen angel, master of the earth, was coming for his favorite demon son, as he had come for so many others.

The creature's only salvation lay in prayer to a deity *it* would reject not out of ignorance but out of misguided commitment. The one power infinitely greater than *its* master, *it* would disavow with vehemence ... even in the throws of spectral death.

The essence of evil, the presence of Satan moved through the core of the earth. Without physical shape, without audible words, Satan's terror ripped into the creature's soul.

"You have failed me!"

"No ... it ... it was not my fault."

"My evil grows like cancer across the face of my earth, yet you ... you have cost us more than a thousand years."

"No ...."

"My subjects must ... we must control the Heavenly gifts. We must have them, *YOU HEAR!*"

"Yes, yes," *it* whimpered.

"The kefir is mine! The minds of men belong to me!"

"Yes, my Lord, of course, yes."

"You fool! We were so close. Corruption, war, famine, disease, greed in the highest places ... it is so beautifully planned, and you have failed where it has hurt us the most."

"But the girl. I had no choice. She said it, the horrible little girl. She said it in the name of her ...."

"DON'T EVER! ... use that name."

All the painful power of Satan bore into the once regal demon. *It* screamed and clawed for a mercy that did not exist. The rock surrounding the agonizing creature became a fiery liquid red and *its* horrid body hissed as *it* melted and merged with the molten stone. The hellish anguish in Michelangelo's painted tormented souls would not equal the creature's pain. The spirit that once was the demon melded with the millions of helpless kin that contort through eternity, in the abode of the damned.

*   *   *

The abhorrent master withdrew shadow-like from the dark chamber to attend to more important madnesses.

Making the same critical mistake he had made at the crucifixion, Satan looked only to the body ... and believed command was his once again. Had his preoccupation with his fearful earthly plans not been so all-consuming, he may have felt the movement sooner, but it was not until this very moment that he recognized the ancient preordained trap.

342

He looked upward ... searching. He felt the presence, and then he saw it. White light! It was growing, becoming brighter. The white light that meant salvation and eternal bliss for some, would bring spiritual death and fearful existence to the many souls that were, for whatever reason, adhered to this most traitorous of commanders.

"It cannot be so soon! ... *NO!* ... it is not possible." In his innermost being dwelt the terror he had not suffered for thousands of years.

"No! This cannot be. It is not time!"

CHAPTER 41

"NASA, come in! This is Little Freedom. Come in, NASA! Come on, you guys ... it's Jake."

Commander Capterville switched channels.

"Father Freedom, come in. Can you hear me? It's Jake. Kepler, can you hear me? Can anyone out there hear me ... emergency ... can you see the white light? It's closing ...."

Commander Jake Capterville had passed the moon and was using its gravity to slow Little Freedom's velocity. The earth now appeared the size of a large apple in the viewing port. He could see it clearly, his first and favorite home. Beneath swirling layers of pure white clouds, brown continental land masses rose proudly from vast blue seas.

The Commander pondered its beauty and its fragility for only a moment. The white light had been closing on earth and Little Freedom for over a week, and Jake still did not know what to make of it. He had no radio contact with anyone. The sky had grown so bright he could see no stars.

"Maybe the guys on Kepler can see this now."

Jake released himself from his seat and floated past Orville and Jim to the aft viewing port.

"Oh, no!"

The moon could not be seen. Only a white, full-color light. The compressing light had enveloped the moon and passed it. Inside the orbit of the moon the brilliance was contracting around the earth, and Jake knew it must pass him to do so.

"NASA, this is Jake, come in ...."

Jake was unable to continue. Full spectrum light and sound flooded the little cabin. It was not light that would shine on matter, nor sound that would cause vibration. It illuminated everything, inside and out. It suffused all matter. For one glorious moment in time Jake could see with other eyes, could move by merely thinking, could communicate instantaneously. He heard music beyond earthly scales and felt the joy, the unbridled joyous feeling of all things made new.

The light drained from the cabin and Jake slowly opened his eyes. In the direction of the earth he could see only light. Behind him, where the moon had been, there was blackness. No moon, no stars ... more than blackness, there was emptiness.

The lights on all instrument panels were out. All systems were completely shut down, including life support.

"But I'm alive. I know I'm alive. I'll just check the air lines."

Jake released himself from his seat and swiveled in place.

"But ... how ...?"

The bodies of his two friends, Orville and Jim had disappeared. Their crumpled space suits floated empty above the two unoccupied seats.

All systems came on suddenly. Jake checked communications. There was intermittent static. He looked out his port window. The light had encircled the earth and was contracting, becoming brighter. Everywhere else there was total blackness. No stars, no planets, no warming sun.

From habit and training, Jake double-checked his instruments and made certain that all systems were 'go' for docking with a space station that no longer existed. He looked out the window. He rubbed his eyes. He rubbed them again in disbelief. He studied the earth ... concentrating.

The earth was clearly visible, yet encircled with a crystalline shell of light. At equal distances, surrounding the earth were seven pure-white angels holding gleaming trumpets at their sides.

Jake began hearing sounds, beautiful but fearsome sounds, like the shouting of a huge crowd, like the waves of a hundred oceans beating the shore, like the mighty rolling of great thunder. Then began the singing ... the singing of millions.

The seven angels raised their trumpets to their lips and together blew loud, fearful blasts that filled the void and pierced the earth.

A violent earthquake shook the trembling planet. Oceans parted around the world and a great chasm wrenched open upon its face. Dragged screaming and twisting by an unseen force, a giant red dragon was pulled against its will from the bowels of the earth. It had seven heads and ten horns, and a crown upon each head. Its long red tail thrashed and whipped as it was made to leave the earth. Clinging to the tail like a terrified animal was a strange creature with bear's paws and a lion's mouth.

The two were ripped screaming in agony from the bottomless pit and away from the earth. They were followed by a stream of fallen angels who were bound by law to millions of suffering souls, all committed to frightful existence with their master of deception.

The red dragon, trailing a long winding line of helpless adherents, began an involuntary spiral into its appointed hole in space. Satan's ultimate master had come unexpectedly like a thief. With a grimace of resignation the dragon and its entire line were swallowed forever by the imprisoning black hole.

The seven angels sounded their trumpets once again. The sun and moon and stars returned in even greater splendor. A great voice boomed from the Heavens.

346

Jake heard, and he was terrified. Little Freedom shook violently.

"Uncle Jake! Uncle Jake! ... Wake up, Wake up!"

Corrie was shaking Jake's arm, trying to wake him. He was lying flat on his back with his legs crossed, on the lawn in the back yard. Woody and Topper were draped over his legs watching vigilantly for whatever it is dogs watch for on clear winter nights.

Jake stirred.

"Uncle Jake, come on, wake up."

"Oooh ... Corrie?"

"You were dreaming."

"Was I ever. How long ... how long was I out?"

"About an hour."

"Good Grief, your mother will be upset."

"No. I told her you were asleep."

"You did? How long have you been here?"

"About ten minutes. You were saying some really neat things in your sleep."

"Like what?"

"You kept repeating something. I think it's from the Bible."

"What?"

"Let's see, it was ... *'Let the heavens be glad, and let the earth rejoice.'* You said it several times."

"No kidding. I said that? I don't remember hearing it before."

"Well, you did. I was sitting right here. Woody and Topper heard you too."

"Anything else?"

"Oh, yes. I got worried. You started shaking. You said, in a real deep voice ... it didn't sound like you ... you said, *'I am the Beginning and the End.'* You said it three times. *'I am the Beginning and the End.'* Then you started shaking again, so I woke you up."

Jake stood up slowly and steadied himself. Corrie stood next to him and held him by the hand. A dog heeled on either side of them. All four looked to the star filled sky.

"I'm real proud of you, Uncle Jake."

"Thanks, Corrie, that means a lot. I'm proud of you too."

"I knew you'd come back."

"You know, Corrie, I kind of thought I would too. You told me I would, remember?"

Corrie squeezed Jake's hand.

"Uncle Jake?"

"Yes, Corrie?"

"You said something else."

"What?"

"You said, let's see ... I have to get it right ... it was hard to remember. Oh, yes, you said, *'I will give to the thirsty the springs of the Water of Life, freely, as a gift!'* What does it mean, Uncle Jake?"

"I guess it means that God is here for everyone, no strings attached ... of course, I expect a preacher could say it better."

"I don't think so, Uncle Jake." Corrie thought a while, then asked, "What is the Water of Life?"

"His word, Corrie, His promises."

"Does it have anything to do with Daddy's water?"

"We don't know, Corrie. It's been a burden for your father ... a big responsibility."

"But *you* think it has a lot to do with Daddy's water, don't you, Uncle Jake?"

Jake said nothing, but he looked down at Corrie with one of those giant Uncle Jake grins. Corrie squeezed his hand again and they looked back to the night-time sky.

348

"I showed Shirali which one is Mars."

"Yep," Jake said, "there it is ... right there," and Jake stretched out his long arm and pointed with his finger to his home away from home.

"Corrie?"

"Yes, Uncle Jake?"

Jake remained silent.

Corrie looked at him. "What is it Uncle Jake? You can tell me."

"I don't think anyone but you would understand ...."

Corrie said nothing. She waited.

Jake looked down at her. "I think I almost got into Heaven ... up there somewhere."

"YOU DID?"

Jake fell silent again, but Corrie was not about to let him stop now.

"What happened, Uncle Jake? What do you mean *almost*."

"Orville and Jim were dead, and I didn't know if I was going to live or die. The sky was turning white with light. Then I saw it in the distance, and it got bigger and bigger as I got nearer. It was an enormous wall."

"Like the Great Wall in China?" Corrie asked. She remembered the picture from her history book.

"Sort of, Corrie, only much, much bigger. It was made of solid white marble and it was huge. I came up to a tremendous gate. There was a tall pointed tower, a gate tower, on the left of the gate. It was solid gold. Then the gatekeeper appeared in the tower."

Corrie was so excited she could barely speak. "What did he look like, Uncle Jake? What did he look like?"

"I don't know exactly, he was so far up. But I know he was there. I could see him moving."

"Wow! Then what?"

"He yelled down at me in a booming voice, *'Why are you here? What do you want?'*"

"What did you say, Uncle Jake?"

"All my life I've never been certain that what I was doing was, well, what I was supposed to be doing. Do you know what I mean, Corrie?"

"Yea, I think so. Lots of times I'm not sure what to do ... like whether to run for the mailbox. But I knew *you'd* do it, Uncle Jake, so I did it too."

Jake smiled, "I hear you got caught."

"Yea, but ..."

"Don't say 'yea', Corrie."

"OK. But if I hadn't got caught, maybe Paul wouldn't have sent the postcard. Do you know what *I* mean, Uncle Jake?"

"I think I know just what you mean, Corrie."

"What did you tell the gatekeeper? What did you tell him, Uncle Jake?"

"I felt so lost, so uncertain, like I didn't know which direction to go in. One way I'd die, another way, maybe I wouldn't, but ... even that didn't seem to matter. I felt so unimportant."

"You, Uncle Jake?"

"Yea ...."

"Don't say 'yea', Uncle Jake. So what did you say to him?"

"I asked him to give me a bright light, Corrie, my own light, so that I could move safely ahead into the unknown. I've always made decisions, Corrie, and somehow most of them have turned out OK. But I wanted to be able to see ahead and make the right decisions."

"Me too. What did he do?"

350

"He said, *'There is no such light.'*"

"Oh, dear!" Corrie said, sounding like her mother.

"Then the gatekeeper said, *'Go out into the darkness ... and put your hand into the hand of God.'*"

"Wow!"

"The gatekeeper shut the door to the tower. Then everything disappeared and I was sitting in Little Freedom. I remember feeling wonderful ... but I was real disappointed too."

"Why, Uncle Jake?"

"I was really hoping he'd open the gate so I could go in, Corrie."

Corrie thought a while. "You know ... he's right, Uncle Jake, about what you should do. Shirali had to do it when she left Bukol."

"And you did it, Corrie, in that little dark room."

Jake and Corrie and Woody and Topper stood on the grass silently for the longest time, gazing and thinking. Jake finally said, "I just wish I could have done more."

Corrie said, "I wish I could have done more too, Uncle Jake."

An inch or so behind Jake's right heel a tiny sparkling particle split into three, and then seven.

"We'd better go back in, Uncle Jake. We don't want to miss anything."

"You're right, Corrie ... gosh, all of a sudden I'm starved. I can smell the turkey from here, can't you?"

"You're imagining things, Uncle Jake."

"I've had to imagine one of your mother's home cooked meals for a million miles. Come on, let's get going!"

"Oh, Uncle Jake, you're exaggerating."

"I used to, Corrie, but not any more."

With Mars watching from above, Jake took Corrie's hand and they walked together across the lawn. Woody and Topper joined them as they stepped onto the porch and went through the backdoor. The seven glistening crystals momentarily became a tiny hovering cloud of gas and then, for an instant, blanketed the lawn with light.

As the backdoor slammed shut the light subsided and the seven little particles sat together, waiting ... sparkling beneath the stars.

CHAPTER 42

After dinner the men and the dogs were talking by the fire. Megan turned out the lights in the kitchen and joined them. Shirali and Corrie were warming up the piano and flipping through sheet music, selecting songs.

There was a loud knock on the front door.

Megan looked at Steven, "What a busy Christmas Eve!"

KNOCK, KNOCK, KNOCK.

It was even louder the second time.

"I'll get it," Megan said. "We wouldn't want you men to strain anything."

Megan opened the door and a boy stood in front of her with his fist raised, ready to knock again. He appeared to Megan to be seventeen or eighteen years old. His dirty baseball cap sat off-center on his head. Printed in red soiled letters over a leaping rainbow trout, the cap announced **BIG BEAR LAKE, California**. Underneath the trout was stitched the slogan, *"The Seasons are the Reason"*. One plaid shirt tail was out. An old model compact car idled behind him in the driveway. He seemed to be in a hurry.

"You're Mrs. Capterville aren't you?"

"Yes, I am."

"I'm Jimmy. I work in the mail room down at the post office. Your mailman, Fred ... Fred Rutherford ...."

"Yes," Megan said, "he came yesterday."

"Yea, well, he didn't deliver this because he couldn't read the address. See, it's all smudged up."

Jimmy handed a crumpled and dirty letter to Megan.

"You can't see the address ... can hardly see the letters in the name," Jimmy said, "but Mr. Rutherford said it might be for the lady who's staying with you. He asked me to bring it out this morning, but I forgot. I'm really sorry."

"Well, thank you, Jimmy. It was nice of you to bring it out so late on Christmas. Would you like to come in for some ...."

"Oh, no, thank you, Ma'm. I've got to get home. My folks'll be worried ... but thanks anyway."

Jimmy ran off the porch and before he got into his car he yelled toward the house, "Oh, Mrs. Capterville? Merry Christmas!"

"Merry Christmas, Jimmy."

Megan shut the door and sat down at the little drawing desk by the door. She turned on her grandmother's Tiffany lamp and looked at the letter. There was no return address, but it was postmarked.

"Shirali! It's from Russia."

Megan studied the yellowed paper.

"Shirali, it's for you! I can make out the first part of your last name. Here ... look!"

Megan got out of the chair and Shirali took her place. Corrie had her chin pressed to the desk-top and Megan looked over Shirali's shoulder.

"Open it," Corrie said, "open it, Shirali."

Shirali placed the letter directly under the colored glass lamp, and carefully peeled back the flap with her finger tips. She pulled the letter slowly from its envelope. With several crinkles, two old sheets of paper unfolded in her hands.

"Wow," Corrie said, "I can't read that."

Megan said, "That's because it's written in ... what, Shirali? Abkhazian? Russian?"

"Read it, Shirali, read it," Corrie implored.

"Corrie, this is a private letter to Shirali. We don't ...."

"No, Meg," Shirali said, "it's all right. We're all family.
Let's see ... it starts out,

> **Our Dearest Shirali,**
>   **Your father and I are alive and well, although it took
> us forever to get down the mountain ....**

Tears streamed down Shirali's cheeks and splashed on the
desk. "Ohh ... Meg, Corrie, my parents are alive! They're
really alive!"

"Oh, how wonderful! Steven! Tarkil and Khfaf are
alive!"

Corrie said, "Read some more, Shirali."

"No, Corrie. Let Shirali finish the letter by herself."

"OK, OK."

Megan tried to keep a conversation going around the fire
to give Shirali some privacy, but it wasn't easy. After a few
minutes Shirali rose from her seat. She moved across the
room and sat on the couch next to the fire. Corrie
immediately crawled into her lap.

"What's the matter, Shirali?" Corrie asked, "you look so
sad."

"I am elated, Corrie, to know that my parents are alive.
They sound happier than ever ... arguing as always, about me.
They have made a new home part of the way down the
mountain, and it turns out that not all of our people were in
the village that night. The kefir is gone, however, so they
have other matters about which they differ."

"Like what?" Corrie asked.

"Mother likes her new home and her new friends. Father is determined to move back to the old house."

"The one on the cliff?" Corrie asked with surprise.

"Yes." Shirali paused and thought for a minute. "But I'll bet you anything Father's just saying that to get Mother to thinking. It would be like him."

"But, you sound so sad, Shirali."

"It's ... it's because of the kefir, Corrie. It was entrusted to me."

Steven hung his head.

Corrie asked, "Did your mother mention it in the letter?"

"No, Corrie ... Father did."

"But ...."

"When my parents write a letter they take turns writing. It's a custom of our people, a family tradition. There are parts of the sentences that are too torn to read, but I will read what I can see. Father ends the letter saying,

... in the days after the earthquake your Mother came to realize that it was all in God's plan that you take the kefir from our village. Bukol was not a safe place for it ... and this horrible war within Georgia ... it is what we thought, Shirali, you and I. After seeing things more clearly, she began talking of you with great respect, especially to our friends. She has always loved you, of course, but now she knows there could be no one better to care for the kefir ... God trusts in you, Shirali, and so do we.

We Send All Our Love and Pray This finds You Well,

Your Adoring Parents

Corrie crinkled up her nose. She had a curious expression on her face. She looked at Shirali and said, "Everyone keeps talking about the kefir. Daddy and Paul and Bob and those people in the mountain ... and now you, Shirali. What is it, anyway?"

Megan said, "You know, Corrie ... the Critters."

"You mean the Critters are the kefir, Mommy?"

"Yes, Corrie. Your father and Shirali and I discussed it and decided it would be safer for you not to know exactly what it was."

"Guess you got that wrong," Corrie proclaimed.

Jake howled with laughter. He threw his head back and laughed and laughed.

"Jake, be quiet," Megan said, "this is serious. Shirali, all of us ... we feel responsible."

"But why, Mommy?" Corrie asked.

Shirali answered Corrie. "Because the kefir, was very important, dear. It was helping so many people." Shirali was close to tears. "And now, thanks to me, it's gone ...."

"No it isn't," Corrie said.

"Honey, don't be funny," Megan said.

"Really, Mommy. The Critters are in the pantry."

"What?"

"Sure. Don't you remember? When you were talking to Captain Siever that day, you told me to put the Critters in a cool place ... so I put them in the basement, way back in the dark."

"But they took the Critters, Corrie," Megan said.

"No they didn't," Corrie insisted.

Megan looked straight at Paul.

"We found some," Paul said uncomfortably, "but it was in the study."

"My sample," Steven said. "It wasn't the parent culture, though ... must be why the RAM boys couldn't keep it alive."

"But, Corrie, are you sure?"

"Sure I'm sure. It's the first thing we did after Mr. Tinyon dropped me off."

"We?" Steven asked.

"After I called you at Uncle Elliot's, Woody and Topper and I washed out the Critters. I washed them out again this morning. I put them back in the pantry ... want me to get them?"

"The pantry?" Shirali cried, "I've been in and out of there all day long!"

"They're in the glass pickle jar on the third shelf," Corrie said casually. "I'll go get them."

Shirali sat with her mouth open, unable to speak. Corrie ran to the kitchen, but stopped at the door.

"You're going to be surprised, Shirali."

Shirali still couldn't talk.

"They've tripled in size ... and they're moving around a lot more. That's why I had to put them in the pickle jar."

"But," Megan said, "... but why didn't you say something, dear?"

"Why didn't *I* say something ... Boy, you guys should talk!" and Corrie disappeared into the kitchen.

Jake Capterville leaned back in his chair and howled with laughter. "Merry Christmas, Shirali!" and he howled some more.

Corrie ran through the kitchen and into the pantry. But she didn't stop there. While the others were talking with much animation, Corrie went quietly out the side door and ran around back. She walked across the lawn to where she and Jake had been standing. Corrie looked up to the sky, and with a knowing look she gave an extra special wink. "Thanks for all the neat things you did, God. You sure fooled everybody."

She glanced quickly at the rooftop of the house. She squinted, straining to see. Then she bent over and pinched the seven little sparkling grains between her thumb and forefinger.

Corrie ran to the porch and without making a noise, went in the back door and down the hall to her father's study. She went in, closed the door and turned the light on. Behind the large and very busy desk, Corrie looked up, and up.

"There it is ... Daddy's latest one."

Corrie stood on three thick books and barely reached it. The small clear glass bottle had a piece of tape across it. It read,

BURGESS SHALE / KEFIR SOLUTION
Template #1

Corrie carefully unscrewed the cap and dropped the little crystals into the bottle. She twisted the cap back on securely and shook the bottle as hard as she could. It glowed brightly for an instant and then went out.

"There!"

Corrie took a black pen from her father's desk and scratched out, # 1. In its place she wrote, # 2.

She placed it back on the shelf in the same spot, and for a few seconds she stared at it. "Merry Christmas, Daddy ... you're going to love this one."

Corrie turned the lights off and left the room, quietly shutting the door behind her.

Megan was calling from the living room, "Corrie, where are you, dear?"

"Right here, Mommy." Corrie ran through the pantry and grabbed the pickle jar. "Here are the Critters, Shirali. See ... how much bigger they are! And look at the clear part, right in the middle. It's like they're making something special, a medicine or something."

Shirali turned the jar in her hands. The jar was full with white milk, top and bottom, but in the center was a band of perfectly clear fluid. "How odd," Shirali said, "I've never see the kefir do this before."

"We've always washed the Critters every day," Corrie said matter-of-factly. "They just needed more time together, by themselves."

Shirali raised her eyebrows. She looked down at little Corrie and then over to Megan. Shirali was stunned. The precious kefir had left Bukol for reasons even she could not comprehend. And little Corrie! Such insight could only ....

"Corrie, would you mind bringing me the cookies?"

Corrie climbed down from the couch and ran to the piano to get the cookie dish for Shirali.

"Meg," Shirali said with her eyebrows still in the air, "we have to talk."

***

With Shirali and Corrie both playing the piano, the entire family began to sing. The old Capterville farmhouse was filled with joyous sound.

Woody and Topper, however, were not in the room. They both had their noses wedged firmly under the door to the study. Something was glowing inside, and the light was shining, flickering under the door ... like someone had left a television on.

"What do you think it is?" Topper asked.

"Don't know," Woody said, "but I'd sure like to get in there. I have a feeling we could really score. You saw Corrie go out back, didn't you? She's up to something again."

"Yea, this is gonna be a doosie ... we'll have to keep an eye on her."

The glow became brighter suddenly, then the room went dark.

"Boy," Woody said, "this is somethin' else."

Woody and Topper heard Corrie talking in the other room, "OK, everybody, it's time for Uncle Jake's favorite ... Say! Where are Woody and Topper? Where'd those two get off to?"

"Uh, oh. We'd better scram, Topper."

"Sure don't like to leave this what-ever-it-is," Topper said.

"Yea," Woody said, "but you know somebody's bound to drop a cookie or two while they're singing."

"Good thought."

"Besides, I have a feeling that whatever this is ... is going to be around for a long, long time."

"I know what you mean. You're right," Topper said, "let's go. I'll race you to the piano. Ready, set ...."

"Wait a minute, Top, not so fast!"

"OK, OK," Topper said, "English rules?"

"Now you're talking! First one gets his pick, and the peanut butter cookie's all mine. On the count of three. Ready, one, two, three ... GO!"

Forty claws clawed, eight legs spun. Tails flashing, they were off like a shot.

"Well, it's about time," Corrie said, "where have you two been?"

The dogs took their positions on either side of the piano bench.

"OK, everybody," Corrie said, "let's ...."

KNOCK! KNOCK! KNOCK! There was another loud pounding on the front door. Megan looked at Steven with an expression of total surprise.

"My Heavens, Steven, this is ... who could be out at this hour?"

KNOCK! KNOCK! KNOCK!

Megan opened the door. "Mr. Rutherford! What in the world, you should be home ...."

"I know I should, Mrs. Capterville, but it's been a real rush at the post office. Right after I asked Jimmy to bring that letter out to you ... say, was it for Ms. Lasuria?"

"It certainly was, Fred, and we all thank you very much. Would you like to come in?"

"Thanks, but no. My wife is already wondering why I'm not home. Anyway, after Jimmy left, this Army sergeant came into the post office with a diplomatic pouch. He'd driven by your place on the main road but couldn't find your house in the dark. He wanted to get home to his family, so I told him I'd bring this out."

Mr. Rutherford handed Megan a package the size of a thick telephone book.

"You and Jimmy have been very kind, Fred. Thank you."

Fred Rutherford yelled, "Merry Christmas!" as he ran to his car.

"Steven, it's addressed to you," Megan said. "Its got foreign postage on it."

Steven sat on the couch by the fire, and Corrie snuggled in next to him. He placed the package on his lap and peeled off the outer brown wrapping paper to reveal a brown cardboard box. The box was filled with shredded packing paper which Steven handed to Corrie.

"We can save this to wrap our presents, Mommy."

Inside was a dark red box with ornate gold printing that Steven could not understand. Steven lifted it up.

Megan said, "Oh, how beautiful!"

Elliot admired the box, then glanced at Shirali. He noticed the smile come to her face, and he thought, "Shirali knows what this is already."

Steven lifted the red felt top off the box and removed a large round silver can. The metal lid was intricately embossed with a fierce eagle with outstretched wings. Steven could not read the printing below it.

"What in the world is it?" Megan asked.

Steven turned the silver can in his hands and studied the eagle carefully. He smiled. He knew what it was and who had sent it. Steven looked across the room to Shirali.

"That's right, Steven, it's caviar ... caviar from the great Beluga. The eagle on the top is the warrior eagle, the eagle of Abkhazia that saved my people in legend many years ago. The Choir was singing of the eagle that night at the lake. Khimbei knew how much that evening meant to you and Meg. He has said for many years that he wished to send you some."

Shirali began to cry.

Megan began to cry too.

Shirali said, "Oh, dear, I guess I'm just too sentimental."

Corrie began to cry also because she knew all about the lake in the mountains with the big fish, and how her parents were there together. "No you're not, Shirali."

"Excuse me," Elliot said, "but could someone explain to me why everyone is ...."

Shirali blotted the tears from her cheeks and said, "Because, Elliot, Khimbei has respected Steven and Meg very much and he has wanted to do this for them for a long time."

"And ...?" Elliot said curiously.

"This caviar is not Russian or Georgian, Elliot, or Khimbei would never have sent it. It is Abkhazian, from the mountains. Many years ago Khimbei asked my parents, Tarkil and Khfaf, to wait for just the right fish ... a big one. My parents are very particular, and a fish suitable for such an honor ... my Father loves Steven so ... such a fish was never found."

"Wow!" Corrie said.

"Then that means," Elliot said, "the caviar ...."

"Came from the high mountains, after the earthquake," Shirali said, "which means the fish are back, some of my people must be back ... which is undoubtedly why my Father wishes to go back up the mountain, and, yes ... yes, of course, how stupid of me ... Tengiz!"

"Who is Tengiz?" Elliot asked.

"Tengiz is my father's younger brother, Elliot."

"Younger?"

"Never mind, Elliot. Steven, read the letter. I'll bet ...."

"There is no letter, Shirali."

Shirali smiled sweetly. "Open the can, Steven. Corrie, would you be a dear and get us some crackers. Bring different sizes ... oh, and a small knife. I'll show you how to eat caviar."

Corrie was already running for the kitchen.

Steven twisted the top off the can. The can was packed tightly with thousands of tiny glistening black eggs. Corrie

364

returned with a plate full of crackers. She looked into the can and said, "Wow!"

"Steven," Shirali said, "there will be a small black string somewhere along the inside of the can, pointing straight up."

"Why?" Corrie asked.

"It's a family secret," Shirali said.

"So you can tell *us*," Corrie said proudly.

"I'm going to show you, dear."

"I found it, Shirali." Steven pinched it between his fingers.

"Pull it up slowly, Steven ... here, I'll help you. You pull up, and I'll hold the caviar down with the knife."

Slowly, a tightly folded wax paper envelope emerged from the bottom of the container.

"Yuk!" Corrie said.

Steven held the envelope while Shirali cleaned it with the knife.

"But, why?" Megan asked, "what a strange way to send a letter."

"Obviously," Shirali said, "Khimbei wished to say things to you that he could not let fall into enemy hands. We must remember the circumstances at home."

"Hurry, Daddy. Let's see."

"We have to be careful with this, Corrie. It has come a long way, and people have risked their lives to send it."

Steven unfolded the envelope carefully and withdrew three creased sheets of paper. He stood up and crossed the room, followed by everyone else. He placed the pages of the letter on the table, side by side, underneath the Tiffany lamp so everybody could see them. They were typed, and in English;

ABKHAZIAN PEOPLE'S ARMY
Sukumi, Abkhazia

My Dearest Steven and Megan,

Please forgive me for not writing to you sooner, but there has been so much to do. Just as we win a battle, we are beaten back, and we have so little to fight with now. The Georgians still want to assimilate us and obliterate our history. Different segments of the Russian army continue to help us with supplies and arms, but official orders from Moscow continue to favor Georgia. There is talk now of a U.N., C.I.S. and Russian peacekeeping force that will provide security along the Inguri River. Pray with us. This could mean our independence.

Thank God for Tengiz and Tarkil. Tengiz has managed to collect and hide in the mountains all of the Sagas and many of our unpublished works. We are slowly having all the works published outside of the country thanks to the same foreign ambassador who has brought this Beluga to you. Tengiz has secured our defenses in all strategic passes, while Tarkil has organized the Army's resistance throughout the mountains. The people, even down here by the sea, are fond of saying that not a blade of grass grows, nor does a bird fly, without the approval of Tarkil Lasuria.

366

Tarkil and Khfaf have moved higher up the mountain with the few from Bukol who survived. They have been joined by people from other villages that were also destroyed.

There is debate over what to call the new community, but it will not be called Bukol. The feeling now is that there will never again be any place like Bukol. I expect that feeling will change as people get settled, but I understand what they mean.

We send our blessings to you with this Beluga. The small lake is still there, although much changed. For some reason, there are more of the big fish appearing, while reports from the Caspian Sea show fewer. Shirali will know. She knows the big ones better than any of us.

I understand Shirali is in Africa. She reminds me so much of her mother. She is always helping. If you see her, please tell her we desperately need the kefir ... to heal our people. I am sad to report it is needed now, more than ever. Also please tell her that she was right to take a parent from Bukol. Had she not, a wonderful gift would not now exist. Please tell her we all know how difficult it has been for her.

I must conclude my letter to you soon, so please excuse me if I must end abruptly. I am expecting Tengiz at any moment. It is late, after mid-night, and we must once again move our headquarters camp.

I cannot tell you how much your brief visit, so many years ago, has meant to my people. You were giving, and did your best to understand us. You will be pleased to hear that the Nartaa Choir, though smaller, still sings. It could be my imagination at times, but each night, even way down here, I believe I hear the singing flowing out of the mountain valleys.

They have written a beautiful new song ... a long rhythmic ballad that is the favorite of everyone. It is about a man from the west who cures a little boy, and the gift of a timeless timepiece that brings endless laughter to the mountains ... then there are earthquakes, a solitary house sits high in the sky ... laughter fades, and there are the drums of war, wars within countries, wars within families, wars within the earth ... the eagle of Abkhazia soars into the sky, and many die ... finally, heroically there is peace ... quietly, slowly, drumbeats are replaced with strings ... love and laughter return ... Abkhazia, land of the soul, never gave up.

It is a wonderful and beautiful song we will sing always. And I, for one, will never give up. It was a promise I made to Vasha-Tamava.

God Bless You,

Khimbei

Shirali went back to the fire and sank into the couch. She covered her face with her hands and wept. Paul Slavic sat down next to her and wrapped his long arm around her. He understood little, but he knew it was his time to comfort. Soon, without knowing why, he too was crying.

Elliot was speechless. He sat in a chair opposite Shirali and Paul. He was staring at the fire. Real people, real emotions, real feelings had in one letter been imparted to all of them. He wished he had met this man, Khimbei.

Megan and Steven, Corrie and Jake stood in a small circle, embracing.

With Paul's huge arm still around her, Shirali straightened and wiped away tears with one of her mother's lace handkerchiefs. She looked across at Elliot.

"I will begin packing in the morning. I must go back," she said.

Elliot looked down to the floor, then back up. "The legal matters ... the Six ... are in good hands. Perhaps it is my turn for an expedition to Abkhazia."

***

Late in the evening, well past Corrie's normal bedtime, Elliot, Jake and Steven were standing by the Christmas tree. They were facing it, enjoying it, and talking among themselves.

Elliot said, "You two have had quite a year."

Jake replied, "I'd like to thank you for everything you've done, Elliot. You've been a real friend."

369

"I am no longer a friend, Jake. Corrie has elevated me to family member."

"Of course she has, and I agree completely. And I never should have given you such a bad time about the Abkhazia trip."

"If you ever stop, I'll know there's something wrong with one of us. All I ask is that you keep telling your stories from Mars. You've seen things the rest of us can only dream about. That incredible cavern ...."

"I'm still waiting for big brother, here, to arrive at some important conclusions," Jake said.

Steven was staring straight ahead at Corrie's favorite green bubbler.

"Hello, Steven? Earth calling Steven."

"Oh, sorry, Jake ... yes, I heard you. I'm afraid I'm a long way from any conclusions."

"Watch out, Elliot. Anytime Steven says that, he's ready to pop out with something dangerous." Jake tapped on Steven's head with his knuckles. "So out with it, Steven ... there's more in there than Christmas tree lights."

"Actually," Steven said, "that's just what I was thinking about. This whole tree is lit up because it has a current running through it."

"And?"

"When you plugged it in, Jake, it came to life all at once ... or at least it appeared to. A signal went from bulb to bulb until they were all lit. But it happened very fast."

"And?"

"Our water is clustered. It puts out a signal."

"Like the water in our cells," Elliot said proudly.

"Right. Take the PS-51 solution for example. A drop of the water on the skin sends a signal to those cells, then the cells amplify the signal and send it to other cells that, in turn, talk to other cells. In a split second the information from the water is communicated to the entire system ... like when Jake plugged in the tree."

"Yes?" Jake prodded, still watching the tree.

"Daddy, come on! Let's sing."
"In a minute, honey."

"The cells, Jake, are passing information ... talking to one another, in a way."
"So?"

"Well, I'm wondering if the same principle isn't applicable to your little friends on Mars. Might explain why the clustered water in Unit Seven is activated."

Jake's eyes got wider and wider. "Ah, hah! See, Elliot, I was right. I told NASA and Kepler my brother had the answers to anything and everything. But ... wait a minute. Steven, where does the energy originate? What's the power source?"

Steven crossed his arms over his chest, threw his head back and laughed a laugh reminiscent of his wilder younger brother. "You'll have to consult with Corrie on that one, Jake."

"OK, OK, and I'll ask my pals on Father Freedom too. At least they saw the white light."

Steven looked at Jake with an understanding smile. "Meg and I knew there was something else. Perhaps ... whenever you're ready?"

"OK, but it'll be hard to believe."
"We're becoming experts in that department, Jake."
"But, you're not going to ...."
"No 'buts', Jake."

371

Jake's eyes lit up. "Say, Steven! How would you and Elliot like to help me explain the Christmas tree theory to the folks at NASA?"

"Be happy to," Steven said. "If they try to interpret the incoming data by traditional means, they won't understand a thing.

"Or worse," Elliot concluded, "they'll come to the wrong conclusions."

"What do you think, Elliot?" Jake asked.

Elliot thought a while, trying to comprehend law, water, Christmas trees and science. "Let's meet at my office at nine, Monday morning. I'll be loaded for bear."

Steven thought a moment, stroking his chin with his thumb and forefinger. "Let's make it noon, Elliot. Jake and I need to stop at Caltech and the Jet Propulsion Lab on the way in."

"We do?"

"Sure do. Like you said, Jake, we have a lot to talk about. Did you know that when you freeze water, the molecules form into squares and cubes?"

"No, I didn't."

"Have a guess at the molecular shape *our* water takes when it's frozen," Steven challenged.

"What?"

"A Christmas tree!"

"No!"

"That's affirmative, Commander. We're doing X-ray defraction on the ice crystals at JPL right now and I thought you might like to take a look at the results. The test was run on the same water that's in Unit Seven."

"No kidding!"

"The guys at Caltech are going positively nuts. They proved to themselves that it's pure water, and now they're trying to figure out all the crazy things they're seeing. They can't explain it so they're blaming it on their equipment."

"A Christmas tree. That's wild."

"Anyway, Jake, the drive in will give you plenty of time to tell me about the mysterious white light ... won't it?"

"OK, OK."

Corrie had been watching the three men from across the room while she rubbed Topper's tummy. "Boy, they sure are having a big-time talk." She giggled. "Just wait!"

Corrie got up and stood on the piano bench.

"Come on, everybody, let's sing! Come on, everybody, get closer ... OK, Uncle Jake, you start us off."

"Me? Corrie, you know I can't sing a note."

"Well, try! You have to ... it's your favorite."

"All right, all right. Shirali, play extra loud, will you?"

Shirali volunteered, "I'll even start it off with you, Jake."

They lifted their voices in Christmas song,

"Joy to the world, the Lord has come
Let earth receive her King ...."

CHAPTER 43

Upon the uppermost gable of the Capterville rooftop, precisely where the dark creature had perched, stood two observant angels. Unbeknownst to and unseen by the good people they were assigned to protect, they watched and listened. At their feet blinked a long string of colored outdoor Christmas lights.

Both angels were very tall and fierce of countenance. One was sobbing softly. The other felt the same, but was maintaining his composure.

"It is just so wonderful," the sobbing angel said.

"It is indeed, it is indeed."

They stood on the rooftop, listening and watching and enjoying.

"This is my favorite part."

"I know it is. It always feels like the very first time."

The sobbing angel tilted his head, listening to the singing and the laughing. He didn't want to leave.

"You know?" he asked.

"Yes?"

"I'm positive Michelangelo loved to paint."

"No, he did not."

"How can you be so sure?"

"Because I was there ... long before you were born. Now let's be off. We have work to do."

"Not just yet ... you know this is the part I like the best."

Music and love were pouring from the house.

"Do you think she saw us?"

"Don't be silly, you know people can't see angels."

"Yes, but little Corrie ... she's, well, I wonder about her sometimes. You saw her looking up here when she went back to get them."

The music stopped for a few seconds, then,

"Listen! Do you hear that? They're starting a new song. Listen ...."

"I hear it. I hear it."

*"It's **Hark, The Herald Angels Sing**! That's us! We've just got to stay a while."*

"We can't. You know we have other places to ...."

"That Jake's right. He can't sing a note. Maybe I could fix that for him."

"Don't meddle. And don't think you're fooling me ... you're stalling. We've got to leave. And stop all that sniffling!"

"I still think Michelangelo liked to paint."

"No, he did not. Now, let us go."

In an instant, the two angels were stopped at exactly three thousand feet ... directly above the Capterville home.

Below them, the darkened land lay flushed by the light of the stars. Miles of silent orange trees inhaled the late night air. The tiny home shined like a brilliant diamond set against black felt.

Speaking forcefully to a world made new, love and music and joy and light continued to flood from the little old house.

"We must leave, now!"

There was more sobbing.

"NOW!"

There was one more sniffle ... and they were gone.

The End

EPILOGUE

In April, 1991, Zviad Gamsakhurdia declared the independence of his country, Georgia, from the Soviet Union. The next month, in the country's first democratic election in history, he was elected president. In less than a year he was overthrown by a military junta and replaced by Eduard A. Shevardnadze, former Soviet Foreign Minister who is credited with helping to end the Cold War.

In July of 1992, Abkhazia, a small autonomous republic within Georgia, revived its 1925 constitution and declared independence from Georgia. Georgian President Shevardnadze then waged war upon Abkhazia, as well as upon his overthrown predecessor, Zviad Gamsakhurdia, presumably to maintain Georgia's control over port cities on the Black Sea, and to consolidate Georgian territory.

On September 27, 1993, after twelve days of fierce fighting, Abkhazian forces re-captured their capital sea coast city of Sukhumi, and dealt President Shevardnadze a humiliating military and political defeat.

On December 31, 1993, Georgia's first elected president, Zviad Gamsakhurdia, shot himself to death when his stronghold was ambushed by Georgian troops.

On February 3, 1994, two weeks after THE WARS WITHIN was first printed, the presidents of Russia and Georgia met in Tbilisi, Georgia to sign twenty-six agreements of military and economic cooperation that, among other things, would allow Russian military bases within Georgia. Two hundred dilapidated buses and hundreds of Georgian police officers blocked Tbilisi roads to provide security.

As Boris Yeltsin and Eduard Shevardnadze were signing the agreements, a powerful, remote-controlled bomb exploded, less than a mile away, killing Georgia's deputy defense minister and his mistress. Georgian Defense Minister Georgy Karkarashvili was caught in a second terrorist explosion and received a concussion. A Georgian Defense Ministry statement said the professionally executed bombings were "one more link in a chain of terrorist murders, none of which have been solved."

Sources suggested a number of explanations, but the attacks were suspected to have something to do with elements within the Russian Army who were providing arms, intelligence and volunteers to the Abkhazians who were fighting to preserve their independence.

According to correspondents reporting from Tbilisi and Moscow, the Protocol signed by the two presidents provided for Russian military bases in Batumi on the Turkish border, in Akalkalakhi near the Armenian border, and in Tbilisi. The agreements envision deployment of Russian border guards on the frontiers of the former Soviet republic, Russian arms sales to Georgia, and a Russian pledge to help establish a Georgian National Army.

On May 20, 1994, Associated Press from Tbilisi reported Georgian troops battling Abkhazian separatists along the Inguri River after a week-old truce. More than 3,000 people have been killed and tens of thousands of refugees remain homeless since mid-1992 when Georgian President Shevardnadze sent troops into Abkhazia. Abkhazia, once known for palm-lined beaches, tangerine groves and elegant resorts, has become one of the hottest flash points in the former Soviet Union.

Early July, 1994. Under the auspices of the Commonwealth of Independent States, and with tacit United Nations approval, 3,000 Russian troops are deployed as a peacekeeping force along the Inguri River within Abkhazia. Russian news agency Itar-Tass reports the 97th Parachute Regiment, traveling in light-armored vehicles, came under fire on its way from Sukhumi. Sukhumi-based Abkhazian leader, Vladislav Ardzinba, refuses to allow the return of Georgian enemies. Georgian and western diplomats speculate that Russia is reinforcing Abkhazia's de facto independence.

It is apparent Khimbei Ladariya never gave up.

WFS
July 21, 1994